A New Life

A New Life

Randi Triant

SAPPHIRE BOOKS PUBLISHING
SALINAS, CA.

A New Life
Copyright © 2021 by Randi Triant.
All rights reserved.

ISBN - 978-1-952270-28-4

This is a work of fiction - names, characters, places, and incidents are the product of the author's imagination or are used fictitiously. Any resemblance to actual persons living or dead, business, events or locales is entirely coincidental.

Editor - Heather Flournoy
Book Design - LJ Reynolds
Cover Design - Fineline Cover Design

Sapphire Books Publishing, LLC
P.O. Box 8142
Salinas, CA 93912
www.sapphirebooks.com

Printed in the United States of America
First Edition – 2021

This and other Sapphire Books titles can be found at
www.sapphirebooks.com

Dedication

For my brothers

Acknowledgements

I'm so very thankful to Christine Svendsen and Sapphire Books for once again believing in me and this story. Also, to be paired again with the inimitable editor, Heather Flournoy, was a dream come true.

Thank you to Fiona Sinclair, Richard Triant, Maria Flook, Christine Destrempes, Jessica Warley, Sarah Anne Johnson, Nicola Sinclair, Valerie Sinclair, and Laura Murphy for reading and giving invaluable feedback on the initial drafts. Whenever the story lost its way, you all steered it (and me) back on course.

Thank you to Chris Teubner for opening my eyes to the plight of right whales and for being a steadfast friend. During the course of my research for this book, I was fortunate to live in the same town as the nonprofit Center for Coastal Studies. Over the past 30 years, CCS has been dedicated to whale rescue and their researchers also have worked to learn more about right whales, their use of Cape Cod Bay, and their habitat requirements. Their current research includes aerial surveillance, habitat and food resource monitoring, and investigation into the acoustic behavior of right whales.

To learn more about or donate to CCS please visit: https://coastalstudies.org.

Finally, without the bedrock of my family, both past and present, I could not have started nor finished this story. I'm deeply grateful to my wife, Fiona, and the wondrous Triant family: my parents, who faithfully showed me the magic of words and story; and especially my beloved brothers, Philip and Richard, who taught me what a shattering loss is, but also how love ultimately does endure and live forever.

PROLOGUE

She is drugged and fast asleep when the whale hits. *Stillwater* is big enough to be considered a yacht, yet small enough with its automated mechanics to be handled by one man with no crew. Moments before, four passengers on deck lost sight of the whale that they'd been pursuing heedlessly. It'd been straight ahead, breaching in a tremendous arc just three hundred feet away, a performance worthy of SeaWorld. Then, it disappeared. The boat's bow null effect continued to muffle any sound from the engine as they, unknowingly, drew closer and closer. Then, without warning, the whale ascended for another breach, striking the bow's fiberglass hull on the port side, immediately rupturing it, the impact shattering part of his jawbone and tilting the eighty-thousand-pound boat too far over to the right.

Inside, everything is tossed to the starboard side, straining *Stillwater*'s ability to stay upright. The galley cabinets and dishwasher pop open, spilling and smashing glasses and dishes. In the salon, finger bowls of pimento-stuffed olives and peanuts, and martini and champagne glasses slide across the bar, crashing onto the floor where olives race to the dipping side. All the salon furniture—the L-shaped banquette, the teak coffee table, the bar stools—remain bolted to the floor, but the staterooms are a different matter as beds and tables and luggage collide. A monstrous groaning, an awful rumble begins as the boat's keel strains against water pressure and a lopsided load. The boat lists farther, its right side dangerously submerging into the freezing ocean, the damaged left side following closely behind, its gaping wound shipping water fast.

Stillwater's owner is catapulted from the flybridge into the ice-cold Atlantic. Three other passengers are heaved from the upper deck as if the boat coughed them up, and they land in a maelstrom of teak lounge chairs, cushions, tables, and champagne bottles.

In a cabin below deck, she is flung over with her small bed. Another twin bed, a nightstand, a foldup stool, and the desk that is the size of a tiny vanity crash about in a tornado of confusion and chaos and noise. What was once floor soon becomes ceiling. She falls so hard the wind is knocked out of her. Her wrist snaps.

Upside down, the boat quickly fills with salty water. The six bilge pumps can't keep up. They, along with the engine, shut down in despair. The ocean rushes through the overturned deck, the salon and galley, picking up velocity and volume especially down the submerged side she's in. The water hurtles through the gash in the hull and along the passageway toward the staterooms as if hunting for *her*. By the time it pounds against her door, starts to slip through the gaps in the doorjamb, she's barely regained consciousness, struggling to understand what's happening, where she even is. Something is chaining her to a dreamworld, reluctant to let her go. Her eyelids flutter open. It's dark in the room. She can hardly see. Pain in her wrist, her drugged sleep still tugging, almost makes her black out.

She crawls, drags herself to one of the beds and, grabbing its upturned leg, pushes herself to her knees. She stumbles to the door, over furniture and luggage, holding her wrist against her chest. She continues as best as she can, floundering, terrified she'll fall down. *Wake up,* she thinks. *Wake up!* There is the door. But it's upside down. Her fingers tremble as they touch it. Her pajamas by her knees are wet, the floor around her sopping. Groggy, she can't make sense of it. Then, she does. Water. The room is filling with water. Did a pipe burst? *Get out!* she thinks, but when she turns the doorknob, the door won't budge. Someone's locked her in.

Then, a foggy memory surfaces. A key unlocks the door from the outside, but she can also unlock it from the inside. She fumbles for the twist mechanism in the knob's center. Her inept fingers slide away again and again. The water is rising. With a click, the door unlocks. She opens it, then realizes too late it's the wrong thing to do. The restrained ocean breaks free, barreling into her tiny cabin and knocking her off her feet. On her way down, her temple smashes into a bed's metal leg. Her scream is swallowed whole underneath the numbing water. And then…darkness.

Chapter One

The last time I saw my sister she was waving at me through a glass wall at Logan Airport. Paper cutouts of Halloween pumpkins stretched across the lower half of the glass. Actually, Sandy gave me more of a jaunty salute than a wave. I thought it was her wacky way of somehow keeping with the sailor motif. She was headed for a weekend boat trip with work people around Cape Cod. "Please kill me," I'd told her when she'd asked if I wanted to join in the fun.

Maybe that salute was a last dig at me. Growing up, although Sandy was two years older, I'd tried my best to order her around, with little result. "You're not the boss of me, *Isabel*," she'd say. She and our mother called me Isabel, my real name, when they were annoyed or angry with me instead of my pet name, Tibbie. So, maybe she was saluting me in the airport because I'd been ordering her around too much the night before. She'd come to Boston to stay with me overnight before leaving in the morning for Provincetown. We'd argued. She wanted her ex-girlfriend to move back into their Brooklyn apartment. They'd been separated for a few months after the ex, Hayden, had had a one-night stand with some trashy bartender.

"I can't talk about this. It's a soap opera," I

snapped at Sandy. I wasn't only upset that she'd decided to forgive Hayden. That there *was* a Hayden at all was the problem.

"You know," said my sister. "They say whoever protests the loudest has the most to hide."

"Other than Shakespeare, no one says that," I said sharply.

Sandy tapped her bangs then, as if she were straightening them, a habit she fell back on whenever she was anxious or nervous. For all her bluster about me being a little dictator, my sister was what I'd call outwardly confident, inwardly a cream puff. Me, on the other hand, well, there's no guesswork between outside and inside: I'm who you want to be next to if the bomb goes off. Trust me.

But maybe Sandy had some premonition that day at the airport. Maybe the salute was simply a final see ya of sorts. A fatal sayonara. A signing off.

Whatever the salute's meaning, my sister turned away from me, handed the Cape Air agent her ticket, and that was that. Fifteen minutes later, I found my car in the parking lot, slipped into the driver's seat, and sped home. End of story.

Wait, that's a lie. I promised I'd be truthful, and if I'm going to do this, I'm going to do it right, damn it. So, the truth? Before I slid my Saab into first gear, I exhaled loudly. A huge sigh of relief. It's one of the hundred things I regret.

By nightfall, my sister was dead at the age of forty-five.

The thing is, Sandy was a kickass swimmer. She was the only one, male or female, I knew who'd ever swam the length and back again of Abenaki Pond in the New Hampshire town where we'd grown up.

Yet she was the only one who drowned on that boat carrying four other people. I found that out when Captain Eldridge from the Provincetown Coast Guard station called me that night. Between what Eldridge told me and what I knew already from Sandy, I quickly pieced together some of what had happened. The boat, called *Stillwater*, was owned by Lucas Blackmore, my sister's boss at *Freedom Press*, the boutique New York City publishing company where she worked as an editor. On board were Lucas—whom my sister had always referred to as Luke—and his daughter, Penelope Blackmore. They were joined by Hayden Pierce, Sandy's ex-girlfriend, and Myles Small, *Freedom Press*'s graphic designer. And, of course, my sister, Sandra Dyer. At six o'clock in the evening on October 16, 2018, *Stillwater* set out from the harbor at Provincetown, Massachusetts. At approximately 9:00 p.m., the Provincetown Coast Guard received a distress call that *Stillwater* reported, "Mayday, mayday. We've been hit by a whale." At nine thirty-two, the Coast Guard found *Stillwater* "badly damaged and sinking with its passengers holding on to the hull." Except for one passenger. My sister.

I wrote down all of these details as soon as I hung up the phone from Captain Eldridge. You might think I should've been too distraught to even *think* to record what he told me. Maybe you think I didn't love my sister. But you'd be wrong. Writing down "the facts" is second nature to me. Like breathing or making sure my nightly Scotch has one and only one ice cube in its short glass. I've spent the last twenty years as a journalist at a Boston newspaper. A pad of paper and a pen are always rubber banded to my cell phone, so it's not strange that I immediately scribbled down everything Eldridge was telling me. In the face of something so unthinkable and painful, the journalist in me came to the rescue, shutting every other emotion down.

Jotting down the details of her death was one thing, but if I were writing "the story" of my sister and me, of how much I loved her, I would tell it differently. I might start with the night when I was six and she was eight, and we were lying in our twin beds in Bellport, New Hampshire, waiting for sleep to overtake us when a full moon suddenly slid into the middle spot of our window like it was a parking space.

"Lookit," I whispered to her. I was used to seeing lots of moons in that window, but this one seemed unusually large, as if it were a giant hot air balloon just waiting for us to climb aboard and fly away to parts unknown.

"I hung it for you," Sandy said. "It's a present."

"When?" I asked, doubting yet wanting to believe her.

"You were helping Mom with the dishes. I ducked out. You didn't see me."

"I want to do it," I whined.

In the moonlight, I saw her shake her blond head. "Too young. I'll teach you when you're older. And it's our secret. If you tell Mom, I won't be able to do it again. They won't let me."

"Who's they?" I asked, sitting up. We didn't have two parents. We only had our mother. Our father had died right after I was born. There wasn't a "they" as far as I knew.

Sandy shook her head again. "One day I'll tell you. Now go to sleep."

From then on, whenever a full moon was about

to appear, Sandy made a great show at the dinner table
of chowing down as fast as she could. Then, after lying
to our mother that she'd forgotten a book or a toy or
her mittens in the car, she'd disappear into the night
for a few minutes. Not long enough to worry our
mother, but certainly long enough, I believed, to grab
the moon from its secret hiding place—which she also
swore she'd tell me about someday—and to hang it up
in the sky. Every month it was in a different location.

"Do you keep it in a freezer or something? Is
that why the moon's white, cause it's frozen?"

"Shut up and just look at it, will you? I worked
hard on this one."

This went on every month for a whole year
until I turned seven and we learned all about the
moon in third grade: its phases, the fact that it's the
only permanent satellite around the Earth. How Neil
Armstrong was the first person to set foot on it in 1969.
How our tides are a result of the moon's gravitational
pull. Nowhere in my science textbook was there a
mention of Sandy Dyer being responsible for hanging
the moon every night as easily as when she slipped her
coat on a hanger in the hall closet. When I confronted
her with my newfound knowledge, she shrugged
and said, "But I *wanted* to give it to you, Tibbie, and
isn't that more important than some stupid facts in a
book?"

"You lied." I felt my lip start to quiver, which
only made me madder and her sweeter.

"Look." She reached out to pull me into a hug.
"I'll tell the stories and you tell the truth. We need
both."

So, yes, I might've become estranged from my
sister, but I loved her. I loved her for the imaginary

worlds she created for me, for us, and for the unbreakable thread of decency and care that she flooded our days and nights with. I loved her for the stories.

Now that three months have passed since she died, however, I'm not so sure that's the whole story of what happened on that fateful day in October. I've begun to question whether Captain Eldridge really knew everything there was to tell me. I'm pretty sure, though, of two things: my sister was the best swimmer I've ever known, and I'm going to find out why she was the only one who died on *Stillwater*.

Okay, I admit it. I lied. Ever since Sandy died, I've found it easier to fudge the facts than tell the truth. Where did telling the truth ever get me?

"Where did telling stories ever get *me*?" I hear Sandy say. Sandy talks to me daily now, something she didn't even do when she was alive.

"I guess either way the ending is the same, isn't it?" I say out loud, not really expecting an answer. Either way, my sister is dead. Maybe, though, it's not an either/or situation. Maybe the strongest way to get through life is a fifty-fifty deal: half lies and half truths.

I wasn't completely honest, though, when I said I only want to find out why she alone died that day. There is something else I want to know: How are those four survivors living with themselves now? I leave tomorrow to find out. Failing that, I hope to make their lives as miserable as they have made mine. You see, I'm the only one left to tell the stories *and* the truth.

I wonder how many private investigators the Internet has put out of business. It takes me less than an hour to find addresses and contact information, even their ages, for all four of the people who were on *Stillwater*. I'm surprised to find out that Luke, my sister's boss, is the only one still living in Manhattan, where *Freedom Press* has its office. It's only been a few months since the accident, a word that sticks in my craw. Why not call it what it was: a *murder*?

It's odder still that Luke's daughter, Penelope, and Sandy's ex-girlfriend, Hayden, are living together in a tiny town in upstate New York. Penelope was the vice president and director of marketing for *Freedom Press*, so why would she leave what she stood to inherit? Myles Small has also apparently left his graphic design position there and has relocated to, of all places, the scene of the crime: Provincetown. *Freedom Press*'s website only has a photo and brag sheet about Luke now. Gone is any mention of my sister or Penelope, both of whom used to fill out the past triumvirate that made up the "Our Team" page, now called simply "About Us." Only there is no "Us," just Luke and his head that reminds me of a high school wrestler's: blocky and wide, dark in complexion, almost dwarf-like.

Originally, I thought that I'd begin with Hayden on my search-and-destroy mission. She'd been my sister's girlfriend, after all; wouldn't she be the most truthful? But my relationship with Hayden isn't exactly cordial. And it worries me that she's now living with the daughter of her ex-boss and *Stillwater*'s owner. As soon as I saw that Myles had actually moved to Provincetown, I switched up the plan. Years of interviewing people, of getting them to tell me what they really don't want to admit, has taught me how to suss out a story. Who moves to the very town where a tragedy happened that they were personally involved in? Only someone who is guilty of something. Someone who needs a penance of sorts, a constant reminder of what they have done. A visual flagellation.

"That's not the only story it could be," I hear my sister's voice say.

I shake my head, baffled. "Okay, smarty pants, what then?"

"Love," Sandy replies. "It could be for love. Like when a couple divorce and the one who didn't want the divorce still goes to the same diner every Saturday morning that they used to go to together."

Yeah, yeah, I think, dismissing her as I grab my beat-up leather rucksack from the closet in my Boston apartment. I stuff it full of T-shirts, a thermal sweatshirt, another pair of jeans. As a second thought, I open up my nightstand's drawer and find Sandy's cell phone and charger, throwing them in as well. They were both found dry in her waterproof knapsack that was floating among the debris. I don't know why I pack them now. All I know is I'm headed to Provincetown. Whatever the truth is, either way I have a feeling that out of all of them Myles will spill the beans first. Guilt *and* love can do that to you.

I'm familiar with what the locals call P-Town, although I've only been there once, three months ago, the morning after Captain Eldridge called me. From the moment I saw that arm of land curling like a headlock into the ocean from a small oval airplane

window, I couldn't wait to leave. I met with Eldridge
and a town cop, Paul Brant, in Eldridge's Coast Guard
office, which had a government-issued wooden desk
and chair facing two fake leather chairs, and several
large framed maps on the walls. The only thing going
for it was its view over the ocean.

In addition to what I'd already been told over
the phone, Eldridge explained that the boat had been
struck by not just any whale, but "a juvenile right
whale."

"What?" I wrote down *juvenile right whale* on
my notepad.

"It's a kind of a whale we see a lot up here," Officer Brant filled in, as if we were all the way up in
some northern territory in Alaska or Greenland, not
on Cape Cod. "Not very many of them left."

Eldridge shot him a hard look and then looked
back at me. "We're very sorry for *your* loss," he said
kindly. He waited a moment and then went on. "With
young whales, which is what this one was, they're like
teenage drivers. They have trouble judging things. The
one that hit your sister's boat breached at the wrong
time." He said it like the whale had driven through a
stop sign.

"It wasn't her boat," I mumbled, looking down
at my notepad as I circled the word *right*. I glanced up.
"So, I guess he wasn't so right after all?"

Both of the men didn't know what to say to
that. Was I being funny? Or just perverse? I often
say something ridiculous when I'm either nervous or
frightened.

"Do you know a good B and B I can stay at for a
couple of days?" I hurriedly asked, despite my being
already booked into the Deep End Inn, a posh ram-

bling hotel perched atop a cliff with the ocean down below. It was an extravagance, given what I earn at the newspaper is about as much as someone wearing a paper hat at Taco Bell, but I figured it was going to be hard enough as it was. I might as well stay someplace where I didn't have to add bedbugs or bad coffee in the morning to it. There was no way I was going to change that reservation, but I simply find the easiest way to sidetrack people is to ask them a question, usually one that you already know the answer to.

Eldridge suggested a few local places and then we all stood up together, like they'd been interviewing me for a job. He pumped my hand, told me that Brant would be accompanying me to the morgue, and if I needed anything to give him a call.

In the reception area, Brant touched the sleeve of my parka to stop me.

"Sorry about what I said before," he said. He looked agitated by something more than that, though. "Look..." he began. He rubbed his cheek the way that men do when they don't want to tell you something: they've broken your favorite lamp inherited from your Aunt Mimi, or they've been having an affair for two years. He went on. "I wouldn't mention to anyone in town that you are who you are. You know, about your sister."

I stared at him for a beat to avoid snapping at him that this was hardly going to be a community potluck dinner visit for me. Instead, I said, "And that would be because..."

He glanced over at the receptionist and then at me. Lowering his voice, he said, "Well, some of the townspeople are upset about what happened."

Staring over his left shoulder at a nondescript

ocean landscape on the wall, I shifted my feet. Why would I care whether people who didn't even know my sister were upset? Didn't he realize it was me who had lost something?

"Not in the way you might think." Brant moved his hand up off his cheek, rubbing back and forth over his buzz cut now. If we didn't stop the conversation soon, he might give his entire body a massage before we were through. "Some people are really upset about another whale being killed," he said. He held up a hand. "I know, I know. Your loss is so much bigger, right? I agree. But they're really worried about them becoming extinct, and—"

"Wait," I interrupted. "Didn't Eldridge say it breached at the wrong time?" I could feel my jaw tightening.

Brant fingered the brim of his police hat in his hands. "That's what we were told. Some people don't believe that's what happened."

"What?" I felt my heart start to race. With anger? Frustration? I didn't know.

Brant slipped his cop hat on. He adjusted the brim and at the same time planted his stance a bit wider. "Look, we can only go by what the survivors told us. They've no reason to lie. Especially right after it happened. We interviewed each of them separately and they all told the same story. They were each a mess. People don't lie then." For some reason, his "they all told the same story" pitched my stomach. Before I could ask him about that, however, he said, "I'm just saying be careful who you tell what to in town. There are a lot of whale huggers living here." I opened my mouth to jump all over that. Whale huggers? How exactly does one hug a whale? It was so ridiculous I started to sputter. But, then, like a tour guide moving a crowd along, Brant interrupted my stammer in a tone that clearly indicated he wouldn't be taking any further questions. "We should get going. We need to get to the morgue."

In his police cruiser, Brant tried a few times to engage me in conversation, but when my answers were monosyllabic we rode the rest of the way with only the female voice on his police radio breaking the silence, announcing a few suspected disorderly conducts and break-ins. Brant turned down the volume so low it was almost meditative. That was good because the longer we were in the car, the more nervous and nauseous I was becoming. By the time we parked and I was opening my door, I felt faint, as if I'd swallowed something utterly undigestible and poisonous, a jungle frog whole or a fistful of rancid beef. I have no recollection of what the building looked like other than a rather long hallway with many closed doors, the kind you'd race down in a very bad dream. I do remember it being very cold even with my parka and hat on. A medical assistant finally showed us into the room where the gurney with my sister was, her body covered by a sheet folded down by her shoulders. Sandy could've been a patient heading into surgery: her skin bleached out like a piece of driftwood, her golden hair stiff and unkempt as an unused wig, a gash at her temple that peeked through studiously applied concealer. I noted all of that down in detail on my pad just as I would've if I'd been assigned a crime story at the newspaper. Any emotion was again stymied by my journalistic instincts, which thankfully had kicked in as soon as I'd walked into the room. Although, my hand holding the pen trembled so badly that, months later when I tried to read my notes, the words were barely decipherable as if they'd been written by someone elderly on their deathbed. The trip to the morgue to identify my sister was followed by waiting a few never-ending days at the Deep End Inn—unfortunately decorated with dead things: ghouls and ghosts and skeletons for the upcoming Halloween festivities—and finally retrieving Sandy's ashes, with all the ease of picking up a package at the post office. Sign and date here, please, and then, I was back on Cape Air, my sister cradled in my lap, or at least a small cardboard box bearing what remained of her. I was the only one left to do it; our mother had died five years before, hit by a drunken driver on his way home from his company's Christmas party. Coupled with my sister's sudden death, I now expect nothing and everything from life.

If there's no traffic, Boston is only two hours away from Provincetown by car. The ferry doesn't run in the winter, and although the last gasp of a late December nor'easter is still blustering its way out to sea, the roads are surprisingly clear. By eight thirty in the evening I'm rapping on Myles's front screen door, the metallic rat-a-tat-tat sounding both lonesome and confident at the same time in the surrounding darkness and trees, made all the more desolate because our Myles lives in a damn train. Actually, it's one of four abandoned boxcars that are scattered about like some kid threw a tantrum and tossed his Lionels. They peek out through the scrubby pine trees, the beeches, the oaks.

It's clear there's been some effort expended to make the four buildings—and I use that word loosely—seem artistic or funky. One train car is almost invisible in the darkness painted coal black as it is, windows unlit. Another boxcar is brilliant silver, like those 1950 Airstream trailers your nana and pawpaw dragged around exploring Yellowstone or the Adirondacks. There are dim lights glowing in its jalousie windows. Smoke rises from a metal wood stove pipe jerry-rigged out of its roof. Can that even be legal? Its two windows have blinking Christmas lights framing them, although they're almost hidden now by ivy that has grown up the siding over the years. The third car is a stone's throw from where Myles lives. It has a wide deck attached to its front where snow is piling up and blocking the front door. The windows are boarded over with plywood. Its owner is clearly away for the winter. He's no fool. Myles's pick of the litter is the runt: the original red color now faded to a rosé, one lone double-wide window located off-center and crooked as if it were an afterthought by some guy who, sick of all the hectoring and nagging by his wife clamoring for *a view*, jigsawed a hole through the metal side and chucked the blasted thing up willy-nilly. A guy with no use for a level. There's foot-wide silver flashing wrapped around the window's circumference instead of a wooden frame.

Curtains are drawn over that window. They're a bright, lime-green, shimmery material, a color that calls to mind a kids' television program in which a wacky science experiment goes awry and ends with sickly goo all over everyone's face. A ray of soft light steals through the gap where two curtain panels strain to meet.

When Myles opens the door, he's backlit, which seems to emphasize the look of utter surprise on his face after I introduce myself. With the snow blowing around me, I must look like an apparition. He's so startled I step past him and scoot inside before he can say what he wants to say: *Stop!*

By the time he can come to his senses and object, I'm quickly sitting down at his junky Formica table in his junky one-room home. The boxcar is maybe forty feet long and ten feet wide. Every steel wall is covered inside with Tyvek wrap as a way to insulate the place. Forget about painted walls; there's no drywall, period. The Formica table is the only place where two people can sit together, other than a very lonely looking futon at the farthest end of the space, on the other side of the kitchen area. This droopy bed sits on two rows of wood pallets, the kind you usually see discarded in a factory parking lot.

Looking around the train car, I know at once that although Myles has fallen, he isn't trying to even make the best of what he has: every piece of furniture looks like he found it on the side of the road before the weekly garbage pickup. There's a La-Z-Boy in a corner opposite the front door, which is the same lime green as the curtains, only covered in what has to be the biggest human mistake in textile history: Naugahyde. Next to the La-Z-Boy, there's a large wooden spool once used for cable wire, with a thin propane lamp you'd take camping. It would seem coolly retro if it didn't resemble a truncheon that a murderer could bludgeon someone with. On the floor halfway between the La-Z-Boy and the Formica table, an electric heater is blasting out heat. It's the type with coils that glow red. You could mistake it for one of those grocery rotisseries that chicken rotate on, their sizzling fat dripping to the bottom.

I start to unbundle myself from my parka. Miracle of miracles, Myles joins me at the table. I unravel an oversized scarf from my throat.

"Christ!" I think he says. It could've been that or "Christmas!" Or "Cannoli!" I'm not sure. My hand automatically cups the typewriter tattoo on the side of my neck as if I'm catching a butterfly there. My face blushes despite my cheeks still being ice cold from outside. Myles is so agitated he stands up from the table.

A tattoo of a typewriter the size of a salad plate is inked into the right side of my neck. It's no fifties-bland IBM Selectric, either. It's a steely black Remington 5, and let me tell you every single one of those round keys practically killed me. I regretted it before the inker at Gothic Goat Tattoos had even finished the letter *A*. She'd insisted on going alphabetically, which basically meant the pain hopscotched all over the place because the keyboard, as any writer or typist knows, follows the QWERTY layout. No sooner was the *A* done on the mid-left side of my neck that the *B* was being inked and pain was radiating one row lower, center.

Besides saddling me with a daily reminder of just how impulsive I can be, my tattoo scares the shit out of some people. Such as anyone between the ages of one and one hundred who doesn't have a tattoo themselves. Some see it as an instrument of torment; all of those metal keys that you stab and the platen, the rolling pin that stretches paper to your will and whimsy, are like a medieval torture rack.

"A pencil would've been easier. Did that hurt?" is something I get a lot when someone sees it for the first, or even the fifth, time. Or, "That *must* have hurt."

Once, at a dinner party, a poet that I'd counted as

one of my friends turned to me and, after swallowing a forkful of swordfish and capers, pointed that very same fishy fork at my throat and said, "Does it mean you're gagging on your words?" I wanted to wrench her wrist backward and, using that fork, poke out her eyes.

So, there's Myles trying to get a grip on the situation of having a stranger in his home whose throat seems to portend bad things to come and who's the sister of the woman he saw drown, which he might've had a hand in.

"D...d...*do* you," he starts and then clears his throat. "Want some i-i-iced *tea?*"

Shit, he's one of those. "No thanks. Anything stronger?" I was hoping Myles was by now, three months into his penance, a full-blown alcoholic. Someone who'd look at me as his savior. Then I watch as he takes a gallon jug of iced tea from the fridge and pours a canning jar full for himself, dumping sugar straight from a five-pound bag into the glass. It looks like a snow squall from outside the boxcar has somehow gotten into his jar. He gulps it down. Our Myles has a bit of a sweet tooth. A bit of a hidden drug habit. Methinks our Myles has fallen to bits and pieces. Tsk, tsk.

Chapter Two

M yles Small could kiss his phone when it rings because the Provincetown Rescue Squad number pops up. For the first time since he's been working for them he feels as if *he* is the one who is being rescued. Not the poor overweight slob who has had a surf and turf in town and finally, fatally, suffered the heart attack that's been hiding out, like some kind of assassin, in an artery. When Myles and his partner, Patty, arrive on the scene at the Claw Trap Restaurant, he almost kisses the prone man, who, despite their trying three times to put the paddles to him, never revives. Usually, Myles would've been upset about that. Usually, he'd have ended up in his rusted-out home for at least a week, snorting perfect white lines. Usually, he can't abide losing anyone. He didn't join up for *that*. "Rescue" was the key word. This should set him back, should end with him obsessively turning over, like some tilled field, what happened back in October. Afterward, back at his home, he should put his personal defibrillator to his own scarred chest, struggling for some kind of reenactment of what he wants to happen with this man on the floor in front of him. *Punding* is what Ronald ("Please call me Ronnie"), his drug counselor at the clinic in town, had called it.

"Persistent non-goal directed repetitive behavior," Ronnie informed him.

"It's g...*got* a goal," Myles muttered.

Too loudly, it seemed, because Ronnie immediately responded, "You're alive. You don't need to do that."

But he does. When someone dies on him it's as if he can't forgive the person. "Goddamn it, put a little effort into it, would you?" he wants to mutter under his breath as he listens for a heartbeat, a breath, getting ready to zap the victim one more time.

His own chest scarring is from the couple of times when, high as a Sherpa on Kilimanjaro, he'd zapped himself too much. Two small constellations of permanent pinkness can be found above his right nipple and on his left ribs. He'd thought about getting tattoos to cover each but decided that would only bring more attention to them if he ever had sex again. Which he doubted he ever would. Besides, he didn't see the scars as a sign of weakness to hide. Rather, they were signs of strength.

He can't remember exactly when the last time he was naked with somebody anyway. In his first three years at Cornell, he'd slept with a few other students, but his attraction to anyone else petered out in his senior year after he met Penelope.

He scoffs at the bumper stickers sold in town that spout messages like *What would Buddha say?* or the more commanding one saying *Let go of that shit.* He can't seem to set that as his daily goal over coffee every morning. Ronnie encouraged him to fix such goals as he might adjust a clock after a power outage. Ronnie is big on goals. "Without them the day is rudderless," he told Myles. Myles thought it was a poor choice of words considering the past event that landed him in front of Ronnie.

Let go of that shit. But how to do that?

"You drink until you can't drink anymore," Patty, his EMS co-worker, told him once. "That's what I do when someone kicks the bucket." Patty always talks in clichés for death. Kick the bucket. Cash in one's chips. Beyond the veil. Bite the big one. Count worms. Myles's favorite is "dead as a dodo."

He's told Patty that drinking doesn't help. There's not enough booze in the world to give him the blackout he craves. The loss of memory. Sometimes snorting coke does it. Patty alone knows about his little secret, but nowhere near the extent of it. The need for it. She believes Myles only dabbles on special occasions: birthdays, a lone Friday night, that sort of thing. In reality, Myles is swept away on the current of white hyperdrive on a daily basis, but alas for just an hour or two, only to find himself crashing. It reminds him of when he sailed off the barn roof as a kid on his skis. He'd thought at twelve years old it'd be just like the Olympic jumps he saw on TV that winter from Norway. Then, it's back up on those skis, with all the hope and excitement that this time it will last.

Isn't that how life truly is? A study in crash and burn? Before *the accident* he'd thought life was about controlling your choices. Choose Option A and you'll end up in the hospital with two broken legs, spending the rest of sixth grade being homeschooled. Choose Option B and you finish the winter skiing at the local kiddie mountain. He'd made the wrong choice at twelve, that's all. But after the accident on *Stillwater,* he struggles to remain in control. Things happen according to some wild spin of the wheel of fortune. Things happen because they are ordained. Things just fucking *happen.* Why can't he find a bumper sticker espousing the philosophy of say, Heraclitus? His gem that strife and change are the mutual conditions of the universe? Myles would gladly paper the outside of his truck with that bumper sticker.

∿∿∿∿∿

Looking down at the dead man in the Claw Trap, Myles is grateful to this stranger. Grateful that the restaurant's 911 phone call enabled him to shut down Sandy's sister at his boxcar's beaten-up table.

"Sorry, I-I-I *have* to go," he had told her as he hung up his cell phone. He should've ended it there. But, stupidly, he added, "I'm on call. There's an er... er...emer*gen*cy." What's worse, when her face showed confusion, he tacked on, "I work for the re...re... *res*cue squad."

That's when her face changed. For a second, Myles saw Sandy's face again, the look he knew so well: a warm mix of sympathy and concern. But then Sandy's face quickly morphed into this stranger's, which he could swear showed fleeting anger before artfully disappearing into a blank face that showed nothing.

When he'd first opened his door to her knock, she'd introduced herself. "I'm Tibbie. Sandy's sister?" Her inflection sounded like she even doubted it herself. He'd almost fainted. In the swirling snow, he couldn't really see her standing on the makeshift steps. As soon as she'd scooted past him inside, Tibbie threw off her black parka and scarf still lightly covered in snow. At the table she slipped into a chair as if she'd been a regular visitor. She did and didn't look like Sandy. More attractive than beautiful. In place of Sandy's long blond hair, Tibbie wore a saggy knit hat pulled down that tried to corral all of the stray blue and black strands poking out. Still, the resemblance was there, in the mouth and especially in the eyes. Those strange eyes that in dim light or the dark looked yellow, like a panther or hawk. Myles turned up the Coleman lantern on the table. Her eyes immediately softened to a hazel with flecks of green. Just like Sandy's.

As soon as he said where he worked, Tibbie's face became that phizzog of scornful disbelief and, worse, anger. Something Sandy never would've shown, yet alone felt. *Why didn't you rescue my sister then?* this stranger's face said loud and clear. *Why is she dead?* Myles was so caught off guard he'd started to stammer an answer even though she hadn't actually said a word.

"I-I just star-star*ted* lair-lair-lair-*last* month. I took a course after..." Why was he telling her this? *Shut up*, he thought.

But the phone call and the dead man saved him. Death means procedures to follow. Paperwork. Delay. It takes hours for the dead man to be ambulanced by Myles and Patty to the closest morgue in Barnstable and all the paperwork finished. By then, Myles is itching for another line. His self-imposed rules won't permit any until his on-call is finished for the night. Now that it is, there's no stopping him from speeding for home as fast as he can through the snowdrifts left by the nor'easter. Nothing except Tibbie. As he hurtles his rickety 1975 F-150 truck up the long, wooded path home, he breathes a sigh of relief. Her car is no longer there. He'd left so quickly she was just getting into her car by the time he drove away. Part of him wondered if she'd sat in her car the whole time waiting for his return.

Maybe she realized he isn't going to tell her any-thing. Maybe she headed to town to find a place to stay. There aren't many B&Bs still open. After Christ-mas, most close down and the owners slip out of town as fast as they can for a few months away on some hot Caribbean island. Maybe Terrible Tibbie has gone back to Boston. He silently laughs at his naming her.

Just imagining her on his doorstep, however, and his hands have started to tremble again. He drops the key to the front door in a snowdrift, and for the next fifteen minutes he's out there in the cold on his knees, pawing through the drift until he sees the dirty brass key already settling into the ice pack below. Myles has a brief urge to lie there with it.

Ronnie has told him that while the U.S. doesn't have it as a formal classification, he's got all the symp-toms of a neurasthenic. Physical and mental exhaus-tion, headaches, insomnia, irritability, anxiety, heart palpitations, hands trembling, depression.

"They call it PTSD now, but it's the same thing," the therapist said and shrugged as if it didn't matter to him what they called it. Ronnie is entertained by the history of things. His wingtips and wide-lapeled suits, his pocket watch on the long fob that rests against his vest, his greying handlebar mustache vouch for that.

Poser, Myles thought during that first session.

Ronnie also is fond of the phrase "Right as rain," as in, "We'll get you right as rain, you'll see." Or, "You'll be right as rain on this medication." This troubles Myles no end. Rain isn't right, is it? Who likes rain? Farmers, maybe, although too much of it and your spinach crop turns to a fungus mush. Lovers? Not so much after a few days of a downpour. Then, it's a steady stream of bitter remarks under breaths, a relentless stabbing of each other with a couple of toothpicks. Myles knows he's not now, nor will he ever be again, right as rain. It's not going to happen.

He's back in the boxcar, shaking from the cold and his nerves and his craving that is easily rectified by snorting four and only four lines of coke. Two in each nostril. If he misses one, disaster. The whole experience is off-kilter. Asymmetrical. He is, after all, a man who is governed by nothing but rules now. It's the only way to survive in this freefall called life.

Tibbie showing up on his doorstep has brought it all back. Not that *it* is very far from his thoughts. The memory is somewhere loitering in the background, like when a painter includes a specific object or memento in a corner of every artwork he paints, and suddenly that object takes center stage. Isn't that why he moved here in the first place? To give *it*, the horrible accident and the even more horrible death of Sandy, a backdrop of sorts to his life? In one of his undergraduate art classes the instructor told them about the mind's "top-down psychological processing" when it comes to art. It's a phenomenon that happens if you stare long enough at an object: the object ceases to be the object itself but takes on other characteristics that you superimpose on it from your own experiences. That's what he'd hoped to do with the ocean surrounding P-Town. He'd stare at it long enough so that it would no longer be the place where Sandy's life, *his* life, failed. He'd transform it into something else.

If he could just have his four lines now, he might be able to stop the memory from rushing in again. But it's too late for that. The memory starts to unspool, and he's lost.

The storm was two miles away, headed toward them from Boston. Everyone was oblivious except for Myles, who'd been nervously following the weather reports on his cell. It was early evening. Their first night together. They were moored off Long Point, watching the sun slowly set over the water. It was the time when most boats were headed into the Provincetown piers, their owners ready for a quick shower, then a night out eating lobster and clam chowder, and getting stinking drunk. Luke Blackmore, the boat's owner and Myles's boss, was confident that the rain would never reach them. That it would take a left turn somewhere off Boston's bay and sweep up north, not toward the south.

"Look at that sky," Luke shouted above them all from the boat's pilothouse, one hand on the steering wheel, the other sweeping, like he was goddamn Hemingway, across to the west where the setting sun was bright and orange and yellow. "Come help me with dinner, P," he called down to his daughter. He cut the engines, set the automatic lowering of the anchor, and descended the steps to the main deck.

Penelope Blackmore was lounging at the front of the boat, her legs dangling over the bow. Sandy was next to her, lying down, with her feet hanging off the side too. Myles and Hayden Pierce perched stiffly on the banquette of cushioned seating in the stern as far back as possible. Both of them were nervous, Myles knew, but for entirely different reasons. He'd be spending the whole weekend with Penelope. Yes, the others would be there, but in his mind, he believed the weekend would change everything between him and Penelope.

Hayden, on the other hand, Myles was sure, didn't like being on the boat, period. When they'd all come aboard at MacMillan Pier there'd been a cross breeze, and as Hayden boarded, the boat had shimmied a fraction of an inch before the mooring line had held it fast to the dock.

"Mind the gap, there's quite a fetch today," Luke had said. *What a wanker,* Myles had thought. He hated when Luke dropped such idiotic phrases into the conversation. *You're not from London, you wanker,* he'd wanted to shout at him in the office, and now on this boat. Then, he realized how ironic that was given that "wanker" was British slang.

"Oh!" Hayden called out, alarmed, and grabbed the nearest thing she could find, which happened to be Myles's arm. She quickly dropped her hand, saying a terse "Sorry!" Myles had laughed at her. He's ashamed to think of this now, knowing what he knows: Hayden could barely swim.

After Luke dropped anchor and asked his daughter to come below and help with the cooking of the lobsters, husking the corn on the cob, and mixing the red potato salad, Penelope called back, "Be there in a minute, *Dad.*"

From the stern's built-in sitting area, Myles watched as Penelope tightened the topknot holding her brown hair tucked on top of her head. He smiled. He knew that Penelope stressed that one syllable—*Dad*—to indicate she was really thinking that Luke was a nuisance, a gnat to be swatted away. At the *Freedom Press* office, she routinely called him "Lucas" as if they weren't related, or if she was really irritated with some cockamamie policy he instituted, "Master Blackmore." Myles alone picked up on her subtleties, the way she used her inflections to show disdain or happiness, or sometimes, when he was lucky, her desires. Everyone else missed them, too smitten by her runway-model beauty or because she was the boss's daughter. He alone knew the real Penelope.

Myles watched as she said something in a low voice to Sandy and Sandy laughed.

Penelope didn't get up. Instead, it was Hayden who rose from the banquette next to Myles and started to follow Luke down below. "I'm getting my camera. Need anything?" Hayden absently asked Myles over her shoulder, but she didn't wait for his reply before disappearing.

In the glare of the setting sun, Myles could just make out the two women ahead. Sandy was laughing about something else now and so was Penelope. Then, Penelope leaned over and kissed Sandy on the mouth. Just as quickly she sat up and stared out toward the sea. For a moment, Myles thought the sun had played a trick on him. That nothing had happened. Then, Penelope bent over again, only this time Sandy's hand came up, stopping Penelope at her shoulder. Sandy said something that Myles couldn't hear. Penelope laughed, then stood. She strode toward Myles, who had the good sense to close his eyes and pretend he was sleeping, even though he was sitting up. He heard her clamber down the steps below.

"You need to be less obvious," Myles heard Sandy's voice say softly. He opened his eyes. She was right in front of him. "The more you stalk her, the more she'll avoid you. She has to do the chasing."

To be on even ground with her, Myles stood. They were so close they could've kissed. He immediately felt his face flush. He was ashamed. He hated that

Sandy was treating him as some kind of schoolboy. She always acted as if she had all the answers. Truth was, she did. But you didn't have to be a show-off about it, did you?

"I bet Lu-Lu-*Luke* won't like what's go-*go*ing on b-b-be*tween* you two," he said.

Sandy laughed good-naturedly. "Trust me. There's *nothing* going on." She paused. "She told me about your bird book. It sounds...well, interesting. I doubt Luke will be interested, but let me see it. I might be able to help. Did you know Hayden..." She pointed to the steps. "She photographs birds? You should talk to her. You have a lot in common. You'd like her."

At first, Myles was hurt. How could Penelope have told her about *their* secret? She'd been the only one he'd told about the book and now Sandy knew as well. Then he got angry. *Interesting*? Sandy called his work, the thing he cared most about other than Penelope, *interesting*? Everyone knew it was a veiled word for anything but. And then she'd just cavalierly swept it all aside. How did she know whether Luke would want to publish it or not? She hadn't even seen one page of it. Why had Penelope kissed *her*?

Sandy touched his arm. "Myles, I didn't mean—"

Before he could stop himself, he shoved her hand away, harder than he meant to, and she lost her balance and fell against the back of the seating. There was a cracking sound.

"Shit!" Sandy said. She rubbed the back of her head. "Christ, I'm only trying to help you."

Myles started to say he was sorry, but Sandy brushed it off as she got up and went past him, still massaging the back of her head. "I'm fine. We should join the others," she said quietly.

Now, at his boxcar's kitchen table, Myles runs his fingers through his hair. He looks at his hand. He's sure that Sandy's head wasn't bleeding when he watched her go below. It wasn't, right? Was it? He stares at his own hand as if it's Sandy's, studying his fingers for signs of distress. His fingers shake more. His heart has started to race in some kind of Morse code: *It was. It was. You know it was.*

Maybe he's just shivering from being outside. He's lost so much weight he's always cold, even at home despite wearing long johns and jeans under a Carhartt jumpsuit, an earflap hat, a too-long, red knitted scarf that doesn't suit him. It makes him look too effeminate. He wears it every day anyway, ever since he'd found it in the back of the ambulance, left by a diabetic woman he saved. To get a better grip on himself at the table, he averts his eyes from his hands and focuses on the one window in the boxcar over the small sink area. His orchids are there, perched on a rough, wide plank he nailed to the thin windowsill. Orchids were Sandy's favorite flowers. Or at least that's what she always grew in her *Freedom Press* office. Hers were all white while his are a mix of grocery store salvaging and mail-ordered exotic, discontinued specials, the colors of sunsets and deep red rashes on white. One flown in all the way from Japan is his pride and joy: *Dracula simia luer.* The palest of pinks, its petals form a center imprint with the face of a sad monkey. Some nights, high, he imagines showing Sandy the blushing, quivering petals that whisper sex and beauty and death to him. He used to think he was in love with Penelope, but now he knows he was wrong. It was always Sandy. Which makes him plummet more. If he loved her so much, why did he shove her so hard?

Chapter Three

After leaving Myles, I waited at the only straight bar open in town, the Schooner Tap, nursing a Scotch and fending off dumb overtures from a smattering of townies. "You could use a friend," bellowed one, holding out his arms while wearing a T-shirt with "Free Hugs" written across the chest. It was almost midnight before I returned to Myles's home. If you can call it that.

For the second time tonight, I park my Saab next to his truck. Grabbing my leather rucksack from the passenger seat, I follow the tamped-down-by-footsteps-path from Myles's truck and up two rows of stacked cement blocks to his front door. A shovel is stuck like a scarecrow into a mound of snow.

I'm betting again on the element of surprise and the snow to be the pass cards to get me into Chez Myles for at least tonight. *Keep your friends close, your enemies closer,* my boss at the newspaper carps whenever I balk at interviewing some scumbag. Although, I've often wondered if he tells me that because of some deeper meaning behind it. We've been sleeping together ever since I passed the human resources probationary period of three months. Which means, for ten years. He's married, of course. Saying that "of course" somehow justifies my having twice-a-week sex for the last decade with a man older than my father would've been. As if being married makes it all acceptable. My sister would have none of it.

"Please don't tell me I have an Oedipus complex or some psychobabble like that," I told Sandy on the phone when I finally came clean to her about a year after it had started.

She snorted. "*Dad* was nothing like your Mister X." She'd nicknamed him that after I refused to tell her what his name was. If she wanted to know so badly, I reasoned, she could look it up herself on the newspaper's website.

"He's not *my* Mister X. And anyway, how do you know? You've never met him."

"Dad had morals. He knew right from wrong."

"Oh yeah," I scoffed. "Right." I didn't have to say anything more. She knew what I was getting at. Our father's suicide couldn't be deemed "moral" in anyone's book.

Whether Myles is actually my enemy to keep close, I have the made-up excuse that I've tried every B&B in town and came up with nada. I actually shout that to Myles as I'm standing on his jerry-rigged front steps and the wind howls around us for the second time tonight.

"That means 'nothing' in Spanish, which is what I'll be if I stand here freezing my nuts off in this cold any longer." I like using that kind of locker room talk with guys. Coming from a *girl*, it throws them every time. They can't decide if it's raunchy in a good or a bad way. If they like it or they don't. I tell Myles this as I'm doing a sort of two-step shuffle on the balls of my feet just to drive home the point that it's fucking cold, dude, let me the hell in.

Finally, he does.

I drop my rucksack as soon as I get through the door and head for the Formica table again. Myles quickly shuts the door behind me against the wind and snow. Even so, a dusting of snow immediately laces the linoleum floor by the entrance.

He slumps down across from me at the table. Before he's sitting two minutes, however, he jumps up and fiddles with his beast of a heater's temperature dial.

The kitchen area, which includes the table and two metal fold-up chairs, also houses a small sink in a slab counter supported by cement blocks. One plate, one bowl, one mug, and one set of eating utensils are on a towel on the counter. The sole window in the entire boxcar is over the sink with a rough wood shelf jammed with orchids. They're the only things alive and beautiful in the whole place. Were they a memorial of some sort to Sandy? I file that away.

The place smells of cooked bacon, or maybe it's that electric heater on the floor. There's an overtone of incense too. Not the cloying, too-sweet kind. Earthier than that. Comforting. The kind that reminds you of spring soil, the family dog, brownies.

I take in all this in seconds and then turn in my folding chair to look at him. Now, he's busy making tea, this time hot, filling and then placing a dented metal teakettle on a metal hotplate. The kettle's spout lid is permanently twisted open. Something about that is unsettling. I imagine Myles throwing a temper tantrum, so sick of the kettle's high-pitched screaming that he wrenched the lid as hard as he could. Somehow the plastic hinge wouldn't break, though, and Myles... what? Hurled the whole kit and caboodle across the room, where it smacked into the kitchen table's metal edge? The water within boils contentedly on the hot plate. *Focus*, I think, forcing myself to stop this wild, violent imagining and concentrate on him.

When I showed up the first time this evening, I'd been so set on dashing in before he could stop me, so bewildered by his "home," and then so rushed out the door after he hung up his *emergency* call, that I hadn't really had the time to examine him. Now I do. Myles is skinnier than I thought the first time. He's still wearing the one-piece stiff canvas suit you see construction men in, but now that he's standing in front of me it's obvious from the folds of it that he's way underweight. He's wearing clothes underneath it: the cuffs of a flannel shirt and a sweatshirt stick out from his sleeves; jeans peek out at his ankles, which bunch up the legs. The whole appearance is of a kid who hasn't grown into his clothes yet. His work boots are utterly worn out; there's a gash in the top of one which looks like it stopped a falling ax. During my first visit, he was wearing a hat with flaps and a ridiculous red scarf. The hat has since been discarded, leaving his sweaty, wavy, longish brown hair crumpled. The scarf is still on. Although he's tall, a little over six feet, the scarf practically drags on the dirty plywood flooring. Even so, he's handsome, the natural kind, not studied. His face has that lean, Scandinavian appeal that might've been foxy were it not for the slight beard growth that softens it. I'm guessing the downy hair is more a result of his lazily shaving every few days rather than it being intentional. In essence, he needs saving.

After he pours water into the one mug with a Lipton tea bag string looped over the side like an anchor, he slides it in front of me. He fidgets with the electric heater's dial again and then steps back a bit to look more intently at the coils. He bends over and tweaks the dial.

"Aren't you having any?" I ask, knowing fully well he only has the one mug that's chipped and has a worn decal of Tweety Bird.

From the table, he lifts his canning jar of iced tea that was left over from my previous visit, immediately lowers it without taking a drink, then sits down with a thin smile on his face. The kind of smile that reminds me instantly of a skeleton. It's a painful grimace. His skin is taught over his cheekbones. He rubs his face with both hands.

"What d-d-*do* you want?" he asks wearily, as if even he is tired from his constant stammering.

A memory jolts of my sister laughing and telling me on the phone one night how she'd nicknamed Myles in her head as Billy Budd. Budd was the stuttering sailor in Herman Melville's novella of the same name. Sandy knew that I'd instantly understand the reference; she'd read the book to me at night when we were kids. I was partial to escapist tales of sailors and pirates. People who knew how to get shit done. Who took prisoners when they had to.

"You're going to burn in hell for that," I told her, laughing.

"Probably," Sandy replied.

"You publishing types are a vicious lot. Sitting around making fun of the junior staff."

I was only kidding, but I could hear her gasp over the phone. "No one else knows this! Only you would understand. He doesn't do it all the time anyway. It's an emotional thing, I guess. Some people only stutter when they're angry or frustrated or upset."

"Which is all the time. Maybe you should ask him to sing a country western song, like Mel Tillis."

"Very funny. It's more than just the stutter. He is Billy Budd, Tibbie. You know, innocent. I swear every decision he makes is the wrong one. Remember I told you about Penelope? Luke's daughter? She's a horrible tease. Anyway, she's who Billy Budd—Myles—is fixated on. He's a graphic designer and yes, he's talented and handsome, but he's thirty-six and still reads comic books on his lunch break. I only know this because he eats at his desk every single day, waiting for Penelope to cross by his cubicle on the way out to lunch. You should see his face. He actually blushes as she walks out the door. It's so sad."

"Marilyn Monroe stuttered, you know. She did that breathy thing to compensate. Maybe he should sing happy birthday to Penelope."

"I'm hanging up, Tibbie," Sandy said, but as she did, I could still hear her laughing.

Now, Myles sighs, leans back in his chair at the table, and says, "I don't know w...*why* you're here."

I have the urge to lie and say, "Nei-nei-neither do I," but instead I take a sip of my tea, which burns my mouth. My eyes tear from the burn, which is, I hope, the only sign that I was just in excruciating pain. I don't want him feeling sorry for me. Not yet, at least.

"Nice flavor," I say, tapping the mug and yawning to cover my watery eyes.

"Tibbie, right?" he says. His hand trembles slightly on his own glass. He clears his throat. Sniffs loudly. Looks over my shoulder in the direction of the orchids. They must be his salvation. That and whatever he's snorting, along with his EMT stints. Orchids need special care. Not how most people think, either. The best thing you can do for them is leave them alone. My sister taught me that. Give them a spot in indirect light. Water once a week. Run a steam bath every few days, if you remember. Most of us set them in windows that get direct east or southern sunshine. We hover over them, plucking out anything that seems a little brownish. And we drown the poor things with too much water. They're tropical, we tell ourselves. Sun, heat, and water are essential. But we'd be wrong. Most of us are orchid murderers. My sister wasn't. Myles isn't. Myles's orchids are not your grocery store variety either. Looking at them, even I can see they're specimens of beauty.

Raising my mug again, I blow on the tea and eye him over the rim. "Sandy loved orchids too." I know he already knows that—after all, his cubicle was outside her office where she kept hers—but if I didn't, his face offering that skeleton smile again would've told me so in a heartbeat.

"Yes, I-I-I *know*," he says. His face colors. "They're n-n-*not*, not *hers*." He sits up straighter in his chair.

I shake my head. "I didn't think they were." I don't tell him that I have those orchids now. I took them in, like an abandoned family pet, right after Sandy drowned and I found them practically keeled over on their plant stands in her office. The *Freedom Press* staff was still recovering from the accident; no one was in the office. Luke had made a special arrangement with the building's doorman to let me in so that I could corral the orchids before they were completely dead and became horrible reminders of Sandy's same fate. Amazingly, although they were a bit droopy, their white flowers were still in bloom.

One night, after I'd drunk too much Scotch, I got very angry that she'd left me with nothing but orchids, that she hadn't tried harder to survive. Everyone else did. "Why not you?" I demanded out loud in my Boston living room. Then, I jumped up from the old couch we'd grown up with and that I'd taken after our mother died, grabbed scissors, and proceeded to lop off every single petal. They fell to the floor. Immediately, I burst into tears, knowing I'd made a huge mistake. If only I'd ended my tantrum there. Instead, I ran into the bathroom. I snipped angrily at my own hair, a form of some kind of crazy penance, I guess, for what I'd just done, cutting my blond hair so haphazardly I ended up with a hairdo that a punk rock star would envy. Even that wasn't enough. That was the night I also made a midnight visit to the twenty-four seven CVS to buy Manic Panic's After Midnight and another dye called Bad Boy Blue. *There*, I thought two hours later, looking at my finished makeover in the bathroom mirror. *Now, I don't look a thing like you. I don't deserve to.*

What a fool I was. For one thing, the orchids rebloomed months later. But deeper than that, sometimes now when I see my reflection in the mirror I feel only regret and a deep longing to see my sister again, if only in a facsimile on my face. By altering my appearance, I took away the one chance of ever catching a fleeting glimpse of my sister in mirrors, or in the daytime reflection of windows.

I could tell Myles this as we both look over at his orchids, but I don't want him to think he and I have anything in common. I don't want to bond with him over anything, yet alone orchids. But, maybe they're the means through which I can get more information.

"Did you always like orchids? I mean, was that something you shared with her?" I say to keep him off-center. I say it in the same fake-concern voice that cops ask a victim if there is anyone they can call.

Myles coughs and sniffs loudly again. Just when I think he's going to say something, he lifts his glass and drinks one, two, three gulps' worth. By the time the glass slides back atop the table, he's composed himself. *Shit.* At this rate, I'll be here till next Christmas.

"Listen, can I ask a favor?" I pause when he looks at me with interest. "I need to stay here. Just for one night," I add hurriedly when I see his face has gone from imposed placidity to...what? Irritation? Disappointment? Fear? I plunge on, repeating what I said when I knocked on his door. "I checked in town, honest, but everything is either closed for the season or booked." I clasp my hands in one of those hipster Buddhist prayer gestures. "Please? You did like my sister, right? She liked *you*. I always thought she had a bit of a thing for you, actually," I throw in for good measure, although it's completely ridiculous.

Again, he stares past my shoulder at the orchids.

I angle my head so his line of vision to them is blocked. "I'll sleep in the La-Z-Boy. Well, really, I hardly sleep these days. Not since, well, you know." I stop there for effect. "I promise I'll be gone in the morning."

He looks down at his hand. His right middle finger is doing this weird stroking, dactylic rhythm on top of its neighboring index finger. It's almost insectile. Some kind of mating ritual of a praying mantis that you'd see on the Nature Channel. Right before she bites the fucking head of her mate off. One long caress followed by two quick taps. Myles seems equally distracted and fascinated by it. I know I am.

Finally, he glances up at me and says, "No, you can have the fu-fu-*futon*." He blushes again. He cups one hand on top of the other to quiet the rubbing and leans forward. "But you have to tell me w-w-*why* you're here."

I mold my face into a mask of utter astonishment. "This is where she died, isn't it? Where the boat went down? Where the *accident* happened? Why wouldn't I come here?" I pause deliberately. "If she were your sister, wouldn't you?"

He raises a hand. "S-s-s-*sorry*." His face almost matches his scarf now. Suddenly, he pushes back from the table. He rubs his face and stands. "I'm just tired."

"Of course. You must be exhausted from saving that guy earlier," I murmur as I get up.

He immediately looks as if I've just snipped off every one of his orchid blooms.

"Oh, sorry," I say, covering my mouth with one hand. "Did he die?"

"I-I-I *got*ta get my s-s-s-*sleep*ing bag," he says. He charges by me to a cupboard by the futon and, pulling out a sleeping bag, strides past me on the way to the La-Z-Boy. He makes a show of rolling out the bag on the chair. "Good night," he says, sitting on top of the bag, although the chair is still upright. Then, he reaches over and switches off the propane lamp perched on the cable spool.

I can't decide if he's rude or shy or hasn't the foggiest idea how to deal with me. *What difference does that make?* I reprimand myself. *You're not here to sing kumbaya.* But, just as soon as I'm thinking that, I hear Sandy's voice, "He's living like the Unabomber, for Pete's sakes, Tibbie. He's scared." *Good*, I think.

He should be.

There's another camping lamp burning over by the futon on an orange crate. At least we'll be even in the weapons category if it comes to that. Grabbing my rucksack, I stroll over to the futon. Up close, I can see that there's a small stack of Edward Gorey books next to the lamp. I appreciate Gorey. He's just the right blend of macabre and whimsy for my tastes. Anyone who has written an entire book—*Gashlycrumb Tinies*—in which every child from A to Z is killed off by some unfortunate event has my vote. *A is for Amy who fell down the stairs. B is for Basil assaulted by bears...*and so on. My personal favorite? *O is for Olive run through with an awl.* Didn't Sandy say something about some bird book Myles was illustrating? I can't quite remember what she told me, but something about it had been off. I wonder if he drew his birds with crosshatching or if they looked like Gorey's platypus-like creature in high-top sneakers and a scarf.

Across the room, I hear Myles unzipping his sleeping bag and then he crawls in. He pulls the chair lever, which jettisons him backward into a lying position so fast he grunts in surprise, as if I've stabbed him in the gut with my lamp.

"Well, goodnight, and thanks a lot for this," I call over as I rummage through my rucksack for my toothpaste, toothbrush, and a towel I stole from a hotel during my first out-of-town assignments. I've taken that towel as my lucky charm whenever I travel.

"O-kay." Myles's voice is small in the corner darkness. It doesn't sound like his voice at all. Not that I'd known him that long, but while before he'd barged his way through all his stumbling and grasping for words with a can-do attitude, now he sounds like a kid forced outside for recess by a well-meaning teacher who doesn't have a clue that the class bully is lurking on the playground with his bastard pals, just waiting for this particular kid to give him his daily thumping. *Do I have to?* this voice suggests, knowing fully well the answer. It's not a weary voice. It's a resigned, beaten-down one. One without hope of a better tomorrow.

I find the bathroom, which is really a closet with one of those cheap acrylic sand-colored shower stalls the width of your hips and prone to mold, a toilet, and a sink the size and shape of a football set into a tiny cabinet. There's a triangle-shaped shard of glass the length of my forearm glued at eye level over the sink. At least it's not an outhouse. On the back shelf of the toilet is another Gorey: *The Doubtful Guest.* I'll have to ask him why the only books I see in his home are by an eccentric gay harbinger of disaster and mayhem.

Toothbrush in hand, I duck my head out the door. I don't want Myles to sink into a deep sleep yet. "Hey, are you hooked up to a town sewer?" Emerging from the bathroom, I walk into the center of the room where I start to brush my teeth.

"What?" His body is turned away from me, mummified in the sleeping bag. He struggles to raise his head while turning to look over his shoulder at me. "No. Septic. We share s-s-*sep*tics."

"That's neighborly." Three steps and I'm back in the bathroom, spitting out the toothpaste. I don't close the door. I run the water for a bit. Drink some water right from the tap, pretend to gargle, and spit that out into the sink. I stick my toothbrush in the tiny plastic cup that holds Myles's toothbrush and spoon my travel-size toothpaste next to his *Thirty Percent*

More! Crest tube perched on a rough wood shelf. My towel piggybacks his on the one hook in the room. In two seconds, I've transformed the bathroom into a "his and hers." *That'll do it.* I snap off the bathroom light and head to the futon.

"We can talk in the morning," I say cheerfully, slipping my unhooked bra through my sweater sleeves but crawling fully dressed under the covers because it's so cold in the boxcar. I turn off the lamp. I'm pretty sure I hear a gasp, or a catch of breath, a kind of strangled noise coming from his corner. But maybe I just imagine that. The duvet's organic cotton is so stiff it makes a rasping noise every time I move. Given the rest of the décor, the duvet and its inner down comforter are surprisingly good quality. I've seen the duvet for sale at one of the chichi organic cotton and linen shops near where I live in the South End of Boston. I wonder if Myles's mother bought it for him when she visited him after the accident. At his mother's request, he'd first been medevacked to Boston's Massachusetts General Hospital and then, when he'd recovered from his near drowning, they'd shipped him over for a ten-day stint at McLean's, a mental health facility that was known back in the day for its treatment of the rich and famous poets Robert Lowell and Sylvia Plath. Susanna Kaysen made it even more infamous with her memoir and the subsequent film, *Girl, Interrupted.* Let me tell you, even Angelina Jolie's Oscar performance couldn't get me to stay there. I found out all this by getting Myles's medical records at both hospitals through an old friend who worked in IT at the central office. That's the problem with these conglomerates that rule the medical industry in Boston, or any other big city. In the interest of efficiency, all the patient records are swooped into one big mixing data bowl. You have one person who owes another person a solid, and before you can say "Check me in" you have access to everything and anything from wart removal to electric shock treatments. Myles has none of the titillating cachet that those famous people had, though. He's just a boy who was on a boat that killed a whale and my sister.

I'm sure that he sleeps about as much as I do, which is zilch. When someone turns over in a sleeping bag it's never pretty, yet alone on a La-Z-Boy. It sounds like he's battling a straitjacket on a cot at McLean's. There's a lot of body tussling and material thrashing sounds with some groans and moans thrown in for good measure. I'm glad. I don't want him to sleep. I want him haggard in the morning, nerves frayed, headache pounding, nauseous. Nothing will stop me then from getting some answers. Stutter or not. *Don't even say it*, I warn my sister. *I know what I'm doing.*

Still, a few minutes later I hear her voice: *I thought I did too.*

❧ ❧ ❧ ❧ ❧

I hear him getting up as the morning light starts to seep like an evil stain through that crack in the curtains. The bathroom door closes. He runs the water to disguise whatever he's doing in there. Coughs a few times as if he's unsettled by the thought of silence in the main room. Well, Sandy said he was shy. The toilet flushes. He's brushing his teeth now. I get up, slip my bra back on under my T-shirt and sweater, and am filling the teakettle when Myles joins me. He has the look of someone who's been on a weekend bender: his long bangs wet and plastered to his forehead under the flap hat I saw him in the first time I arrived, his overalls rumpled, stubbled patches on his pale cheeks and chin. He's startled that I'm in his kitchen, taking control of the kettle, but he hides it by making a beeline for the heater, where he once again crouches and screws around with the knob.

"It's not cold," I lie and chuckle. "Don't worry about me. I'll get by," I say with the thinnest veneer of snideness. I click on the hot plate.

"The orchids need it." He blows his nose in a handkerchief. It's a big honking blowout. The kind that someone with a nasty cold makes or an old man whose hearing is shot. "S-s-*sorry*. I think I'm coming down with the bug."

The bug. It's something a kid would say. As if there is only one illness in the world at this moment and Myles has it. He scratches his forehead, which sets the flap hat slightly askew on the top of his head, but he doesn't fix it. Immediately, I see him as he must've looked when he was five years old and sick: clothes disheveled, nose red and dripping, eyes pinkish. He walks over to the table. The lace on his right work boot is untied. As he scuffs across the plywood floor, it makes the tiny slapping sound of a plea for help: tie me, tie me, tie me. Is it untied due to negligence or affect? Part of me wants to get on my knees and tie it for him and another part wants to strangle him every second I hear that slapping sound.

He slumps down at the table and his fingers start to play out their insectile dance again. Is it to a beat of some sorts? A lullaby that only Myles can hear that calms his nerves? *I need to get to the bottom of that*, I'm thinking.

"You need to be in bed, mister," I tell him in a calm yet commanding mother's voice. It's everything I can do to keep the excitement out of it. This is more than I could've hoped for. Me, Nurse Ratched, taking care of Billy Budd over the next few days. Him, weak, unable to hide anything. Defenseless. Dependent. I'll feed him canned chicken soup, Saltines, and toast. Mop his brow with a cool washcloth. Dose him— not too much, just enough—with cold medicine and maybe tea laced with hot rum. I glance over to his kitchen counter where there's only a half-empty bottle of wine. No matter, I'll drive into town for supplies.

"I'm all ri...*right*," he says, forcefully. "Wa-wa-*ter's* ready."

Before he can stand, I'm pouring the water into the Tweety mug, the tea bag bobbing. I imagine Myles, then my sister, floating in the ocean. In the last few months, anything remotely moving in a liquid reminds me of Sandy. There must be a psychological reason for that. I wonder if there's been a study of family members of drowning victims, what they visualize, their triggers in the months afterward. The night before I left it was an ice cube nodding sleepily in my glass of Scotch.

"Here, you need this more than me." I slide into the seat across from him, passing him the tea, and smile. Usually men like it when I smile. I have a killer smile. Or so I've been told. In photos of Sandy and me, you'd be hard-pressed to identify my smile from my sister's. And that's undoubtedly who Myles is thinking of now because he winces. He hasn't drunk any of the hot tea, so it's definitely my smiling.

"I know," I say, jumping on the opportunity. "I know. How do you think I feel? I have to look in the mirror every day."

He stares at me. Murmurs, "You should b-be glad. It's a g-g-*gift*." He blushes.

Then, unexpectedly, awkwardness floats into the room between us. Is he flirting with me? *Shit, no, no.* My stomach lurches. What the hell am I doing here? He's a mess. I shouldn't be here. Sandy would be so pissed. I can almost hear her say, "Pick on someone your own size, Tibbie." The thing is, Myles needs protecting, not someone taking advantage of him. He's the dweeb in the back of the class, drawing comic book heroes on the textbook fly leaf. Dressed in too-small or too-big, never-quite-right clothes. Not the cool straight outta Compton kid. More like the straight outta Appalachia. The kind who wore glasses from the time he was eight, constantly pushing them up on the bridge of his nose as he bent over his illustration, the bitten-up Bic inking feverishly, trying to get down lickety-split the creative thoughts that no other kid in the class has.

"But she was blond," he says quietly. It disrupts my imagining him thirty years younger.

"What? Oh, yeah." Automatically, I touch my bangs under my hat. Like my sister would have. Then, I stand. "Listen, you look like you have a fever. You should be in bed. I'm going into town and getting us lunch and some medicine for you. I'll be back in an hour."

"Wait, no—"

Before he can spit another word out, I'm snatching my parka off the futon and striding for the front door.

"W-w-*wait*—"

I don't. After I slam the front door, I sprint for

my car. I don't turn around either when I hear the door open behind me. And although I see him through the front windshield, waving his arms at me from the front steps, I start the engine and speed away as fast as I can.

He'll have to let me back in, I reason. I'll have groceries for him. Besides, I left behind my rucksack and all my things. I've left behind our "his and hers" bathroom. I've left behind my *presence.*

Chapter Four

As soon as Tibbie's car skids away, Myles grabs his mug and, dropping heavily into the La-Z-Boy, pulls the sleeping bag on top of him. His nerves jangle, he feels sick, but also relieved that she has gone. Maybe she won't come back, although he knows that's a lie. Of course she's coming back. More than anything what he wants right now is another line. That would make him feel better. But if he has the one now, which nostril should he use? It's all off-kilter with an odd number. Maybe two, then. But that'll mean he only has two left for the day, and four…four is the exact amount needed to set things totally straight. It's only eight thirty in the morning. He's fallen into what his therapist called punding, again. He can hear Ronnie's weaselly voice telling him, "Persistent non-directed repetitive behavior. Avoid it, and you'll be right as rain." *Shut up, shut up.* He massages his forehead. He can already feel the headache coming on. If he does four now, that's it. The day will stretch out to infinity. There'll be nothing at the end of the rainbow. No pot of gold. Just this day followed by endless night. The headache will morph into a migraine. He sips his tea, which is bitter; Tibbie didn't put any sugar in it. *Four is what I need*, he thinks again. To get himself on what his father used to call "an even keel." His father would say it as a toast as he lifted his whiskey glass every night at another silent-as-death dinner with Myles and his mother, after another volcanic day at his start-up, praying that he'd finish developing the software before anyone else did across the country in Silicon Valley. "Here's to an even keel." The memory jars, however, as Myles remembers that a keel is the bottom part of a boat that supports the whole shitty framework. How didn't he make *that* fucked-up association before now?

He leaps up. Practically runs for the tackle box, not so hidden under the kitchen sink in between his defibrillator in its bright red warning case and the cement blocks holding up the sink. He purchased what he calls "the zapper" online. He couldn't afford it, of course. He'd had to ask his mother for the money, telling her that he needed it for his new job.

"They don't have one in the ambulance?" she'd asked, baffled.

"I want a b...b...*back*up," he'd lied. "S-s-s-*some*-one's life may be at *stake*."

Now, hands shaking, heartbeat scampering like a bat evading a broom, Myles hauls out the tackle box to the Formica table. Flips open the lid. Reaches in underneath the fishing lures, the bobbers, the split shots, and fishes out the vintage orange-and-brown striped tin box: *Peek Frean's Biscuits* in raised lettering next to an impressive coat of armor. Inside the tin box is a diminutive silver spoon and several small packets with labels he printed, saying, "**Hope**" in bold, sans serif font—the typeface that's all business. Once a graphic designer, always a graphic designer. He quickly fills the spoon with the pure whiteness. He doesn't have time to etch out four straight lines on the Formica. Suddenly, he's anxious that Tibbie may come back at any minute…though, what? She's only been gone ten minutes, at the most fifteen, and she has to drive into town and shop and then drive all the way back here. The spoon is quicker, used when he cannot wait another second. Not even the short time it would take to roll a dollar bill. Once upon a time the spoon had been his grandmother's and it was paired with a small Dutch white-and-blue salt cellar. The spoon and the word **Hope** simultaneously connect him to the past and the future. Connect also to his wretched present. He sniffs one, two, three, four spoonfuls, and quickly packs everything up, just so. He slides the tackle box into place. Races to the La-Z-Boy as if he doesn't want to be caught snooping around, his fingers in the cookie jar, and yanks on the lever with everything he's got, like he wants to eject himself into outer space, breathing hard.

Oh, that's better, he thinks. He feels better lying back already. He wasn't sick. Not at all. Shit, his heart is beating like a trapped bird. He counts his breaths, willing his heartbeat to slow like he's some kind of goddamn yogi. *It's okay. Breathe, breathe.* He remembers there are only two and a half packets remaining now. Normally, this would be easily rectified by a phone call to Jacko, his thirty-something, gay supplier who actually makes house calls during the winter when his usual gay clientele has left for Key West or St. Bart's. Jacko knows how to keep his year-round, largely straight customers coming back for more. But Myles hesitates to make the call. What if Tibbie suddenly comes back when Jacko is here? Better to wait.

Twenty minutes later, he can feel himself already coming down, his head starting to throb. *Shit. Lines would've been better. There's more in a line. The spoon*

is a bust. That's funny. Open up. Police. This is a bust.
He jumps up, does the whole thing all over, except this
time he does the bloody line. In fact, four. Fat. Ones.
He's gone over his quota. *Special circumstances,* he
thinks. His wet finger scrapes up the residue to slide
onto his gum next to his cheek—Hi neighbor!—like a
pinch of chewing tobacco.
Immediately, he feels guilty. He's broken his
golden rule. The rule that he believed kept him from
becoming a gutter addict. *Dammit. Are those tires
spinning out in the snow?* He races to the La-Z-Boy.
Hurry, hurry. He's almost crying. *Shit, get yourself
together.*
He waits and waits, but there's no other sound.
Was it her? Is she sitting in her car outside? Is she
spying through the window? Waiting for him to make
a wrong move? *Fuck.* He has to get a grip on himself.
He untangles himself from the twisted sleeping bag and
lunges out of the La-Z-Boy. He tiptoes to the window
as if Tibbie is in the house somewhere and can hear
his every move. As if he wouldn't see her in this one
shitty room he calls home. Outside, only his truck is
parked, the drifts of snow glistening in the sunshine.
So pretty. Maybe he should drive away. Leave before
she gets back. Force *her* to leave. She promised it was
only for one night. If he's not here there'd only be one
thing she could do. He's buoyed by this idea. He could
go into town. No, not town. She might find him there.
Track him down like some kind of criminal. He's not
a criminal. He did everything he could. He walks back
to the La-Z-Boy, thinks better of it, and returns to
the window. Lifts the curtain a smidge. Paces back to
the La-Z-Boy. To the window. To the La-Z-Boy. On
and on he marches, striding across the ten feet as if

it's a prison cell, his shoelace slapping at the floor. *I didn't. I did. I tried. Not hard enough*, he thinks. Not hard *enough*. Then, there really is the sound of a car careering, its wheels straining to gain traction on the mounds of snow leading up the hill to the train cars. She's here. He practically throws himself onto the La-Z-Boy, is jolted backward as he flails, wrestling to lie down under the sleeping bag. *Fuck, fuck, fuck.*

Heavy footsteps on the outside steps, the front door crashing open with the wind, and suddenly there's Tibbie, bringing in the cold, her arms hugging bags of groceries. The groceries are plopped onto the table, Tibbie yammering the entire time, but Myles can't decipher the words. It's like they're swimming underwater and they're trying to say something to each other and those fantastic bubbles are popping from their mouths. A memory about that dislodges from behind a boulder, but before Myles can grab it, Tibbie is shaking him. "Hey! Hey!" she's saying. "You okay?"

"Wh-*what*?" he yells, jerking the La-Z-Boy up-right.

"Christ!" Tibbie takes a step back while yanking off her hat. "I thought you had a stroke or something. Are you all right?" She seems genuinely concerned, Myles can see that. She's kneading her slouchy hat in her fists. He notices all of her black-and-blue hair with its jagged, poorly cut pieces. He wonders if she cut it herself with blunt scissors. Still, her facial resemblance to Sandy is startling. It's Sandy wearing a punkish wig. A Halloween Sandy. Or a Sandy who has had cancer, post chemo, and has donned this wig in defiance. Sandy and not Sandy. Sandy by way of Sid Vicious.

Myles clears his throat. "N-n-*no*. I'm fine." He gives her a strained smile. "I w-w-*was* sleeping."

Tibbie shakes her head. "Your eyes were wide open."

Myles forces himself to stand, although his legs feel weak and jittery. Maybe he *is* sick. "I was...I was slee-*slee*-sleepwalking." *Damn it.* He has to stop stuttering. He sounds like an idiot.

"You weren't walking." Tibbie tilts her head. Myles knows she doesn't believe anything he's telling her. Suddenly, he wants to tell her everything. Everything that happened. Everything good and bad. About that day. About the day leading up to that day. About the day leading up to the day leading up to that day. To come clean. Admit everything. Confess.

"I think I s-s-s-should—"

Tibbie interrupts him. "You should go straight to bed is what you should do, mister." She points to the futon. "Go. I'll make you some soup and toast." And before he can object, she is at the table and starts to sort out the groceries. "You have any music?" she asks as she glances over. When he doesn't answer right away, she raises her hand and tells him, "Don't worry about it. I'll use my phone." She switches on some kind of electronica with a male falsetto voice singing in a different language. It's the type of music you hear, Myles suspects, at a rave in Iceland or Yugoslavia: repetitive and full of angst. Not what he expected from her. On second thought, maybe not a rave. More of an ancient funeral ritual involving large stones, a forest, people dressed in monks' robes, a sacrifice.

"Go," Tibbie says, motioning to the futon again. "Before you collapse and I have to call your co-workers to haul you away to a hospital."

Suddenly, he is exhausted. How can that be, after all that coke? Not being able to give it a voice, the weight of his stifled confession sinks into his bones, takes up its familiar residence in his skeleton, *his* keel. *My keel runneth ove*r, he thinks and almost laughs, shuffling over to the futon. After kicking off his boots, he crawls fully dressed under the covers and closes his eyes. Despite his exhaustion he knows he won't be able to sleep, not with all that coke still skipping around somewhere in his system. Usually by now he'd have popped one of his Xanax stash to take the edge off, to slowly slip him off into sleep, but he can't do that now. Not with her here. He must stay vigilant. He doesn't know what she'll do. Not that there's anything for her to find. Other than the coke or the zapper. Yet another thing to worry about.

Tibbie rattles around in the kitchen. He smells the bread in the toaster. Hears something being poured into a glass. Hears her say, "Sit up." Inching her way toward him, she's precariously balancing a plate with a bowl of soup and toast in her hands. As soon as he takes it from her, she returns to the kitchen table where she grabs the jar he'd been using for iced tea, only now it's filled with orange juice. This she places on the end table next to the futon. Then, she sits down by his feet, curling her legs underneath on the bed like a religious devotee or a college ingénue. Except, Myles notes, she still has on her black Doc Marten boots. *At least they're not the steel-toe ones*, he thinks, gingerly shifting his body on the pillows so his head is raised and his knees slowly come up under the duvet without upsetting the bowl of soup on the plate on his stomach. He's created a wall, a dam of sorts between them. All he can see is her head above his knees.

"Eat," Tibbie says. "You'll feel better." Leaning in, she reaches around his knees, retrieves a spoon from the plate, and hands it to him. Then, her chin perches on one of his knees. Just like that.

"I slaved over that, you know," she says, pointing down at the food. She smiles Sandy's smile. That's what Myles has labeled it now: Sandy's smile. He's so stunned by the fact that Tibbie's chin is on top of his knee, it's so intimate and yet childish, so like they're brother and sister, that he can't seem to say anything. He can't even manage a stutter. He's mute. All he can do is what she's commanding him to do.

He doesn't want to eat anything, yet he does what she says, lifts a spoonful to his mouth and swallows, tasting nothing but some kind of salty liquid. "What is th-this?" he says, coughing, and looks down into the bowl.

Grinning, Tibbie lifts her head. Myles is surprised by how absent the air feels on his knees now. He wonders if parts of the body—knees, for example—can feel grief after losing a touch. Does the shoulder grieve the loss of a squeezing hand? The heart can feel a loss, the ultimate abyss after the death of someone you love. Of that he's sure.

"Hey, hey…earth to Myles," Tibbie says, snapping him out of his philosophical journey, his Jim-Morrison-wandering-in-the-desert thoughts.

Myles swallows another spoonful. "What is this?" he asks again.

"Miso," she says. "You're a meat-head right? I seem to remember Sandy saying you even ate antelope once. Sorry, I know bone broth is all the rage with you hipsters, but I don't eat or buy anything that walks or swims."

Immediately, he flushes. Turns his face toward the orchids across the room. He wants to correct her: it was wild boar, not antelope. And it was in Zimbabwe. It wasn't exactly his choice, either. A trip that Charlotte, his mother, dragged him on after his father died. She said it would bring them closer to nature after experiencing such a sudden death, but the only thing they did was go on an extended safari with a group of hunters keen on killing as many animals as they could. Myles can't believe it, though. *Sandy talked about me.* He thinks he's only thought this, but then Tibbie says, "Of course she talked about you. You were her favorite. You knew that. I told you that, didn't I?" Tibbie bangs her forehead with the heel of her hand. "What a moron! I'm sorry." She touches both of his knees with her hands. Well, actually, holds them. No, *cups* them is more accurate. She cups his knees, her hands lingering there, her head resting now on top of her knuckles. How long has it been since he was held or touched? Three months, five hours, twenty-odd minutes. Not since the accident...*no, don't think of that.* He places the spoon on the plate where the toast remains uneaten, the cold butter still in lumps, refusing to bend to the waning heat of the bread.

"She really liked you, Myles," Tibbie goes on. "I had to see you first because of that. You were her friend, right? Her bosom buddy?" She sways his knees from side to side.

Despite his being diverted, his eyes following his swaying knees as if he's watching a tennis match, despite his fever which seems to be peaking once again, one word surfaces, bubbles, stumbles and then, catching, propels out of Myles's mouth. "Fir-fir-*first*?"

❧❧❧❧

She tells him about her plan. About visiting each
of the survivors. How she has a *need* to know. "You
know I'm a journalist, right?" At this, horror streams
across his face. "No, no," she says hurriedly. "I'm not
writing the damn story. God, no. I just need to know
what happened that night. The police have told me
next to nothing. How can I live not knowing?" she
adds, matter-of-factly. She releases her grasp on his
knees then, and swinging her own legs out, pushes
herself off the futon to stand. She casts a glance around
the room as if appraising its value, and then back at
him in a nothing-to-see-here-folks-keep-moving
dismissive look. "Could you live with that? If it was
your sister?" She pauses, runs her hands through her
spiky hair. "I don't even know if you have a sister. Do
you?" Now, her eyes are a gleaming yellow in the dim
light that the train window affords. She doesn't wait
for an answer. "I can't not know. Do you understand?
I mean, she was a really strong swimmer, for god's
sake. Did you know that?" Again, she doesn't wait for
him to answer. Instead, she rubs her neck tattoo. "I
just want your side of it," she says wearily, and drops
her hand to her side. "That's all."

For something to grab on to, some sort of ballast,
Myles stares down into the bowl of uneaten soup,
watches the seaweed flakes sift on the surface. But, he's
immediately reminded of the ocean. It's everything he
can do to continue gripping the bowl and not to chuck
it across the room. His heart is pounding. His whole
body shakes. He's sure he's about to break into pieces.

Scatter across the floor like a game of pickup sticks, only no one will pick his sorry ass up. *Tell her, tell her.*

"I-I-I," he starts and sputters out.

She looks at him. "Yes?" she says, softly.

"I'll t-t-*tell* you." He's struggling, god he hates himself when he can't speak. He feels exhausted and energized at the same time. Over caffeinated. Past his nap time. On the brink of a consuming self-inflicted rage or a complete meltdown. "I'll..." He pauses. Breathes in. Touches the rim of the bowl. It's better if you can focus on one object, his speech therapist told him when he was seven. She handed him a beautiful purple marble, told him to keep it in his pocket and rub it whenever he stuttered. He still carries the marble, but it's no use now under the covers and inside his Carhartt suit, stowed away in his jeans pocket. He forces himself to stare at Tibbie right in the eye.

"I'll tell you everything, if you ta-ta-ta-*take* me wi-wi-*with* you."

At first, she tells him oh, no-no-no, as if she's the one with the speech problem. Her tone is dismissive, scornful even.

"I fly solo," she says. "Always have, always will." She retrieves her rucksack from the floor. It swings easily to her back.

He almost replies, "Then why are you here?"

It doesn't matter. Tibbie continues talking. "See this?" She twists the rucksack around to her front. "It's an exact replica of Martha Gellhorn's." He must've shown his confusion then because she immediately adds, "The greatest war journalist that ever lived?" She shakes her head. "Sandy knew she was my idol. She tracked it down—I don't know where, eBay or someplace. It doesn't matter," she says and waves her other hand at him. *"The point is,* Sandy, when she gave it to me, told me, no she insisted, 'Tell the truth, Tibbie. Tell only the truth.'" Tibbie lets out a huffing noise. "So, that's what I have to do. I intend to know the truth, Myles."

"Who...*whose* truth? Yours? Or what really happened?" Somehow, he's pushed the words out so quickly they're flawless. A miracle.

Tibbie stares at him. She waits before answering. Under her gaze, Myles's face feels like it's about to separate at the bone. He feels undone.

Finally, she says, "Look, how 'bout this? You tell me what you know now, and I'll come back after I see all the others. No, I promise," she says quickly to stop him from saying anything, raising her fingers in a fake scout salute. "I promise I will. I'll come back and tell you everything I find out."

The lack of logic in this isn't lost on Myles despite his still feeling feverish and being slightly messed up from the coke. What could they tell her that he doesn't already know? That's not why he wants to go with her.

"I remember what *happened,*" he says, peeved.

Tibbie's mouth tightens. He can tell she's either trying to muffle a smile or maybe even, god forbid... wait...is she laughing at him? He abruptly slides the plate with the uneaten food on the floor and, throwing aside the comforter, rises from the bed.

"Wait." Tibbie grabs him by the arm before he can walk away.

"I *remember,*" he says again through gritted teeth.

"I know," Tibbie assures him. Her fingers on his arm squeeze slightly. Her voice is smooth, like a mother calming her petulant child down. "You know some things," she tells him. "They'll know others. None of us ever knows the full story. Trust me. This is my business. What I do for a living. The truth is never as easy as it seems." Her voice is wheedling, repugnant to him now.

He wrenches his arm away. "Stop lecturing me. I was there. You—*you* weren't."

At an impasse, they stare at each other. Finally, Tibbie scratches the side of her head. "Look, you're sick. It's clear you're not doing very—"

Myles shakes his head vigorously. He feels his body becoming denser, coming down from the coke, but something else, his stocking feet firmer in their stance, the whole weight of him stabilizing and solidifying. It's the feeling he gets when he zaps himself with the defibrillator, jolting his body out of its numbing sadness into something electric, alive. That split second between utter failure and success. That wondrous leap into invincibility. He's confident she will take him. She'll have to.

"I'm going," he says.

Tibbie throws her rucksack down in frustration, like she's about to throw a temper tantrum.

"I don't get it," she says, exasperated. "If you know what happened, why do you want to come?" she adds, changing tactics. Her voice is less sure of itself, almost whiney.

Myles smiles. It's the first time he's really smiled at her. Unabashedly, he shows her his front tooth with its bottom half chipped off—fallout from the boat's debris that caught him in the mouth when he'd surfaced, causing a bloody mess. The tooth is still ragged on the bottom. His mother begged him to get it fixed. "They're doing amazing things now with implants."

"See this?" Myles says to Tibbie, pointing at the gap where the rest of his tooth should be. He wants to put her off-kilter. Wants her to realize there are so many details she doesn't have a clue about. "Every day, this is what I see." Dropping his hand by his side, he smiles again. "Now I want to see...*them.*"

Chapter Five

We take my car because Myles's truck is almost ready to be put down as part of a mercy killing. He argues the point—amazingly, his stammer has vanished during this heated debate—until I pitch my rucksack into the back seat and, over my car's roof, ask him, "Are you coming or what?" It's so cold outside I'm relieved when he tosses his duffel bag into the back as well.

While at first I'd balked at Myles's suggestion née blackmail that he come with me, once we are in the car I wonder whether it is for the better that he is. *Keep your enemies close* plays again in my head while Myles twists the radio knob from PIXY103, Cape Cod's Rock, which I imagine only potheads listen to while working the register at the head shop in town, to the Cape's only classical station. Immediately, AC/DC collapses into a Bach cello concerto. I switch it back to Cape Cod's Rock.

"My car, my music," I warn him. I notice that the car is already filling with that rich incense smell. It must follow him wherever he goes, like I used to tag after my sister: secretly yet noticeably. I wonder if the dying people he resuscitates are comforted by it. Maybe they think he was baking pies when he got the phone call.

As soon as the Saab slides onto the road at the

end of his *Deliverance* driveway, Myles says, "That story about your bag?" He thumbs toward the back seat. "You made it up right?"

I almost laugh. "No, Gellhorn *is* my hero. My role model. Who's yours?" Stupid geek. Thinks he knows everything, sees everything, like some damn Sophocles. He probably memorized *The Iliad*, in Greek, of course, when he was at school.

"Sophocles didn't write *The Iliad*, Tibbie," Sandy's smooth voice sighs from the back seat.

Myles doesn't answer my question. Instead, he says, dismissively waving his hand, "Not Gellhorn. The part about your sister."

I snort. "What? Are you crazy or something? Sandy gave me the bag. Honestly, you…" the sentence trails off into the gusts of warm air coming toward us from the vents. I feel sandbagged. I can't believe he's actually calling me on my story.

"I'm sure she gave it to you," he says, biting out the words. He pauses. "But what did she *really* say?"

This catches me off guard a second time. First, why is he so sure she gave it to me? Because she didn't. And she didn't say what I'd told him either. I'd made the whole thing up. And I notice he isn't stammering anymore. What does *that* mean?

"Well?" he says, smiling his skeleton smile. *It's more of a sneer*, I think. Cocky bastard now that he's not a bleeding speech pathology poster boy.

In a flash of inspiration, I wrench the steering wheel and propel us at the last minute onto Route 6, away from his miserable life but not in the direction that leaves town.

"Where are we going?" He grabs the dashboard as if he's the Incredible Hulk and will simply stop the car by pushing against its forward velocity.

"You're taking me." I glance over at him and motion my head slightly in the general direction of the ocean.

"N-n-n-*no*."

"Ye-ye-*yes*," I say, mimicking him. Fuck it. I'm the one in charge here, not him. I'm pissed off that he's questioned my sister. Or what I told him Sandy had said. *Twerp*, I think. *Fucking junkie.*

"Just a quick pit stop before we leave," I assure him, although he's not buying it. Who would? "You'll survive," I add sarcastically.

Sandy whispers in my ear, "Play nice, T."

"Nice never pays the bills," I say aloud.

"What?" Myles sits up in his seat, his hand on the door handle. For a second, I wonder if he's going to throw himself out.

"I said, 'nice never pays the bills.' I used to tell Sandy that all the time. She thought if I was nicer to my colleagues, you know at the paper, I'd make more money. Move up and out to a bigger, better, more exposure paper." I let out an exasperated sigh. "My sister was brilliant about some things, but utterly retarded about how the real world works."

I can't believe I'm trashing Sandy this way to him, of all people. What's wrong with me? I'm not mad at *her*. It's him I should be attacking, not her.

The Saab curves around the end of Route 6 to 6A to Province Lands Road, the tires slipping a bit on the less plowed road. The beach dunes are on the right of us now. Just over those hills is the ocean my sister drowned in. It seems like there's a shift in the air. The car feels overwhelmingly hot. Myles reaches over and snaps off the heater. He yanks off his flap hat onto his lap.

"I need air," he says and buzzes down his window a crack.

We're close now. I can see the breakwater, tremendous boulders of stone that form a ribboning walkway that originally kept the town's harbor safe from itsy-bitsy tidal floods in the early nineteen hundreds and now hopes to discourage the coming tsunami aftermath of climate change. Really, it's a dike, but maybe because there are so many lesbians who live in P-Town the tourism industry is reluctant to label it that. Instead, everyone calls it the breakwater. That's at least what Officer Brant informed me as if he was taking me on a tour of the town when he brought me out to the spot where *Stillwater* capsized off of Long Point, a peninsula at the farthest end of the tip of Provincetown. The peninsula curls back on itself, which forms Provincetown Harbor. *Stillwater* went down on the ocean side of Long Point. There are two ways to get to it: walk forty-five minutes over the breakwater boulders or take a boat out there. I have no intention of walking the breakwater today. It's ten degrees out, and more importantly I have no idea when low tide is. You can only walk across during low tide. When the water rises, the rocks in several sections are submerged.

"We had to bail out forty-four tourists last week," Brant told me that October day as he pointed out the breakwater from the safety of a police boat. As soon as he told me that, he must've regretted it. Here I was, the grieving sister, and there he was, complaining about having to send a rescue boat to pick up a bunch of dimwits who didn't have enough sense to check the tidal schedule.

Low tide, high tide…it doesn't matter to me now. I've no intention of actually going out to Long Point again by land or sea. With or without Myles. Once was enough, thank you. I just want to see how he will react. Call me a bitch or whatever you want. But, wouldn't you do the same thing in my shoes? I can't believe I hadn't thought of it before.

"You're pissed he didn't buy the Gellhorn story," Sandy's voice murmurs as I ease into a parking space near where the breakwater begins. The water is a deep slate color. It looks as frigid as it is. "You know, you're not a good liar. 'Tell the truth, Tibbie?' Where'd you get that gem from?" Sandy continues. I glance up at the rearview mirror, half expecting her to be leaning over my bucket seat from the back. She actually laughs. "And when would I ever have bought anything off eBay?"

"You could have."

"What?" Myles voice breaks into my imagining. He looks really scared for the second time since I showed up on his doorstep.

"Nothing." I look past him out across the boulders, the depressing water, toward Long Point's sand dunes, one of the many things keeping me from Sandy.

"Now who's telling stories?" Sandy says, falling back into her seat and folding her arms across her chest.

"High tide." Myles voice is strained with relief. He's barely holding it together, I can see that now, and suddenly I'm disgusted with myself. I wanted to make him uncomfortable. Not fearing for his life. Okay, maybe I was pissed he knows or knew my sister so well he'd know when I was lying.

"Or maybe…you're just a bad liar," Sandy butts in. "You should stick to journalism. To *non*-fiction." "All right, all right," I say under my breath. Sandy clears her throat. "Um, aren't you forgetting something?" In the rearview mirror her eyes cast downward toward my rucksack and then flit back. Shaking my head emphatically, I tell her, "I can't. Not yet."

"What?" Myles says. Leaning over, he fiddles with his heat vent although he'd snapped the heat off already.

"Is that the only word you know? *Nothing.*" I glance furtively in the rearview where the rucksack is nestled against Myles's duffel as if on a honeymoon. Sandy's fingers possessively stroke my bag right on top of where I know a small pewter urn with her ashes sleeps inside.

"'Whatever you're meant to do, do it now. The conditions are always impossible,'" murmurs Sandy. She winks at me in the rearview mirror. "God, don't you just love Doris Lessing?"

Did I tell you that my sister quotes writers now that she's dead? Which you might think is pretty perfect considering she was in the publishing world right up to her death. Still, the Lessing reference throws me. Not for its intent. I'm not about to be pushed into dispersing my sister's bodily remains before I'm ready because some woman I don't know is demanding that I stop dithering about. I don't care if she won the damn Nobel Prize. No, what is really disconcerting, what chills me to the bone, is that Sandy's become someone I don't recognize anymore. I'm not talking about physically. It's not like she looks like something out of *The Walking Dead*, seaweed dripping off plastered hair, a broken tibia sticking through her skin. These days when she does her pop-up visits, she looks the same as she ever did. Soft, shoulder-length blond hair. Hazel eyes. High cheekbones. Beautiful.

So, no, my sister hasn't changed physically. The thing is, though, I remember my sister quoting someone only one time while she was alive and that was when she was trying to teach me a lesson. Sandy was what people would call down to earth. She'd no sooner slide what some brilliant person said into the conversation than name-drop. I fear that my sister, the woman I knew every bit of, has become someone I no longer recognize. Sandy is becoming a stranger. It's what I imagine someone feels when a close family member has their first psychotic break: suddenly your revered uncle begins to laugh uproariously at jokes or connections in the universe only he can see. Jokes and connections that spotlight your foibles, dig fingernails into your weak spots. Hurt. I fear my sister is becoming what people call a loose cannon.

"Leave it alone," I tell her, which makes her fingers instantly lift from the rucksack.

"What? Oh sorry," Myles replies. He sits back against his seat and leaves off fiddling with the heat vent.

⇛⇛⇛⇛

Penelope Blackmore and Hayden Pierce live in a small town called Skyville that is known for only one thing: in the sixties, two hundred acres of it were occupied by a socialist commune. It wasn't Waco or Jonestown. There wasn't a maniacal or charismatic leader. There wasn't sex between anyone or with farm animals on the solstice. There was no Kool-Aid. "We're simply a family of workers, for workers," stated one of the original founders, MayBelle Riveter. She not only assumed that name in honor of Rosie but also looked the same, with her tied babushka kerchief, a grimy apron, and biceps that seemed like she'd been bench-pressing the gigantic looms she stood in front of. I saw her photo and learned all this at the Public Library before I'd left Boston. I'm not a Luddite (although social media is right up there with dusting furniture and watching the Home Shopping Network for time sucks), but for some research there's nothing that beats scouring old newspapers on library databases, especially local newspapers, for a record of what once was.

Once upon a time, like so many upstate New York towns, Skyville had been a thriving stronghold of textile mills. Mills desperately needed water to power their looms and other factory equipment, and Skyville had that in spades with a tributary called the Psatonic, off the Hudson River, that rushed through the town from west to east like a ribbon of commuter traffic. From my first reporting assignment I'd done down in Fall River, I knew how so many of these towns had failed, first after the Industrial Revolution ended and then again after a revival of sorts making military uniforms during both world wars. After the second world war was over, such towns resorted to either knocking down the abandoned mills wholesale for retail malls or tract housing made and sold cheaply, or they tried to give them second lives as artist studios or other industrial offices.

Skyville was different. In 1969, ten people traveling around after Woodstock were struck by the beauty of the abandoned factory buildings and the rumbling Psatonic surrounded by pine forest. They also noticed that most of the town's residents were unemployed, sticking it out from insularity, sheer stubbornness, and a weird loyalty bred from inheriting crappy mill cottages from their ancestors. Besides, they didn't really have the money to move anywhere else.

The ten friends traveling through (and still undoubtedly tripping from Woodstock excess) found out that they could buy the two hundred acres including a mill comprised of three factory buildings for a rock-bottom price. Two of the ten were a husband-and-wife lawyer team, a couple were trust fund babies, and the rest were made up of teachers, post office clerks, and even a pizza deliveryman. Together, they pooled their savings.

They named the working textile commune *The Loom*. Despite its gothic-like, foreboding name, within a year there were thirty families living and working in the buildings. At first, they maintained a somewhat prosperous mail-order catalogue business selling hand-loomed Mexican blankets, ponchos, and even gauchos. When the call for such free-spirited wear dried up in the late seventies, they switched to leather work: wallets and change purses, moccasins and beaded belts like you'd see at 4-H fairs. By the eighties, they were as finished as the town's ancestors. The ten founders sold the buildings to a developer and moved en masse back to New York City and its surrounding suburbs, worried now that time was running out for them to build a retirement fund for the future.

I tell Myles all this on our way to find Penelope and Hayden. At first, I tried to get him to give up some other details about the boat accident, but no matter how I approached it he didn't offer a cracker crumb. From the direct, "So what happened?" to the sideways, hesitantly offered, "They told me that a whale died?" to a bit of levity, "What made you become a railroad man?" In desperation that we'd be driving the entire six hours to Skyville in a deadly silence or, worse, with my sister providing a diatribe on how stupidly misguided the entire trip was or quoting Robert Frost about the road not taken, I resorted to becoming history professor. At least until he'd hold up his hands and, crying "I surrender," spill. Which didn't happen.

By the time I'm wrapping up my Everything You Wanted to Know About Skyville But Were Afraid to Ask lecture, I'm not just speeding along Route 6, I'm practically jet skiing, which isn't the smartest move considering there's black ice in spots, with leftover snowplowed piles every so often poking dangerously out into both lanes. Route 6 is known even in the best of summer weather as "suicide alley" due to its unlit, rather skinny one-lanes going in both directions that are separated by yellow rubber cones that, if hit, snap down and then up again, duckies in a carnival shooting gallery. Given that the snowstorm just ended yesterday, there's no one on the road. Even the bare trees that we whip past are about to say, "Fuck it," yank out their roots, and walk away out of loneliness.

"Sounds awful," Myles says when I run out of steam about the death of Skyville. "I can't b-believe they moved there. It doesn't make sense."

I can hardly keep from laughing in his face. I almost say, "Have you looked at what *you* call home?"

It seems as if every survivor so far has ended up in some shithole, possibly to forget what happened—

we always load on one misery so we can forget about another wretchedness—but I think they're living in cesspools because of something else that is deeply, ineffably wrong. Although, I don't imagine Penelope's father, Lucas, will be living in squalor. Sandy used to describe him as Pompous Pilate. "He'll stab anyone in the back and act like he's doing them a favor and should celebrate it," she told me once.

Although I didn't actually make fun out loud about Myles's living situation, I feel bad for even thinking it. So, I try to ask him nicely, "How did those train cars get there anyway? You know, the one you live in?"

He straightens a little in his seat. "The guy who rented it to me told me that some toy train collector who spent summers here bought them in the sixties when Cape Cod Railroad finally died. He owned the land and I think he had some idea of setting up a train museum here. You could take a train from New York to Boston to Hyannis then. Actually, back in the late eighteen hundreds when it was the Old Colony Railroad it came all the way to P-Town. You can walk the trail off Snail Road where the train used to run."

I notice he hasn't stammered once. Obviously, reciting history has a calming effect on him.

"Wow," I say so unconvincingly that unfortunately I can feel Myles bristle.

"So, you know exactly where Penelope and Hayden live?" Myles abruptly changes the topic as we pass by an almost snow-barricaded exit to Brewster.

I nod. "You don't? Not pen pals then?" I glance sideways at him, but if he's thrown he doesn't show it.

"I had no idea they even lived together. They didn't really know each other," he says matter-of-factly.

This throws *me*. I'd assumed they'd all known each other through Sandy before the accident. I'd thought of the four survivors as a kind of six degrees of separation from Sandra Dyer. Snagged in life, trapped in death. For some reason I thought she'd invited them, that she hadn't been an invitee herself, although I knew fully well the boat wasn't hers. I realize how much I've always imagined Sandy as the sun with all of us, mere planets, circling around her.

Before I can ask him further about Hayden and Penelope, he wrenches the conversation away by asking, "You came before, didn't you?" He pauses. "T-t-to P-Town. For her, I mean."

"Yes..." I reply unwillingly. I don't want to talk about me or the one time I had to go to P-Town to... what's the word Brant used?...*collect* my sister. I want to talk about Myles or any of the others. Anything else, really. Climate control. Was *Streetcar Named Desire* really Tennessee's best play? What are our chances of arriving in Skyville in one piece?

"Why do you think they ended up together then?" I try steering the conversation back to safer ground.

Out of the corner of my eye, I can see his shoulders shrug. That's apparently all he'll say about that because then he says softly, "Was she buried?"

I'm certainly not going to tell him that his duffel bag is almost squashing the urn that my sister is sleeping in. *Two can play at this game*, I think, and I stubbornly revert to Hayden and Penelope again as a topic of great interest.

"That weekend was the first time they spent time together?"

"I guess." He says it in the same tone that a bored teenager would say, "Whatever." Just then a large crow swoops by his window as if it's about to crash through. Myles immediately reacts by rapping the window with his knuckles, which scares off the enormous bird before it hits us and so startles me that I almost slalom the car off into the snowy yellow rubber cones separating us from oncoming traffic.

"Could you s-s-s-*slow* down?" Myles asks, his hand bracing on the dashboard.

Automatically, I ease up on the gas, not because he asked, but because I've even scared myself. The Saab slows to eighty.

"Where'd you st...*stay*?" he asks.

Confused, I say, "When?"

"You know, the first time you came." He's started up his insectile dance on his knee. I'm starting to reconsider what that's all about. Maybe it's not some soothing tic of his. "Why wa-wa-wa-wa*sn't* I graced with your pre...*pres*ence then?" he asks.

I know he's lying. That he wasn't even in P-Town then, so I shrug. "I was busy." My sister makes a soft, clucking noise from the back seat.

His fingers stop moving on the leg of his jumpsuit. "I wasn't there anyway. I was away," he says nonchalantly, and after staring at me for a moment looks out his side window and with his fingernail starts to scrape away some ice particles that are fogging up the inside of the glass. It strikes me that the longer we're in the car, the more Myles is settling in. He made that passing reference to his time at McLean's like it'd been a vacation in the Bahamas. Does he know that I know about his stay? Between the two of us, I've become the more anxious one, driving the car as fast as I can the

closer that we get to Hayden and Penelope. For the
first time, I worry that Myles has been waiting for the
past three months for this very trip to happen.

I didn't really tell him the truth either. I wasn't
that busy. After I identified Sandy at the morgue there
wasn't much else to do except wait around for two
days while the mortuary finished the cremation and
I could pick up Sandy's remains. After Officer Brant
dropped me back at the Deep End Inn, I walked into
town to a liquor store, bought a quart of Scotch, went
straight back to my beautiful room designed like a
Moroccan sheikh's tent, and drank until I passed out.
The next morning, groggy and hung over, I walked to
the breakwater, thinking maybe I'd walk across and
spend more time out on Long Point with the ghost of
Sandy. I honestly didn't know what else to do. But I
only put one foot on the boulders before I immediately
spun around and went straight back to my room where
I crawled under the covers with my clothes and boots
on and stayed until the sun set. I slept fitfully and woke
up in a worse mood. Any shock I'd been lucky to have
numbing me was wearing off. Sandy was gone. For
good. No one was left in our already too-small family
but me. How would I manage? I pulled the pillow over
my head. For a couple of crazy minutes, I imagined
walking out to the breakwater, but instead of climbing
on the rocks, I'd walk *into* the water with that pillow
over my face. And keep walking.

That wouldn't do at all. Finally, I dragged my
ass down to the Barnacle Pub, the liveliest bar and
restaurant in town, at least in October. I wanted to
be with people, but not have to talk to anyone. Unnoticed, but not invisible. I knew if I didn't surround
myself even with strangers, I might just act on that

bad idea I'd had in my room, pillow or no pillow.

The place was cut into thirds: the bar, a middle area of two pool tables, and a dining area where the menu ran more to home cooking than prix fixe. On the bar side, people were gathered around high stool tables playing checkers and chess in the front windows, while others ate platters of barbecued wings and drank pitchers of beer.

The pool table area was crackling with the sound of balls clacking against each other. Some drunk young guys were cheering on one of their own against another player who was backed by a posse of what I assumed were townies. Unlike the drunken tourist gang with their baseball caps turned around backward, the townies wore their baseball caps with the brims pulled low over their eyes, like they were avoiding being captured on security cameras. They didn't look happy. A blues song was playing over speakers—John Lee Hooker, BB King? A baby-done-did-me-wrong song. A band was also setting up in the restaurant area on a small stage at the far end: three black guys in their forties wearing dashikis and one white, stringy-haired woman who was dressed like Janis Joplin with round granny sunglasses from the sixties, a knee-length sheepskin coat, and a pink feather boa coiled around her throat. She kept repeating, "Balls…balls…balls" into the microphone while her bandmates spasmodically tuned their guitars and tapped the snare drum.

Luckily, I found one stool at the far end of the bar despite it being packed. The stool was tucked between the wall and a thick brass railing that was attached underneath the bar and swooped upward in a big loop to be bolted on top of the bar. It cordoned off where the wait staff plopped down their trays and barked out their drink and food orders for customers at tables.

It was muggy inside the bar despite the fall ocean breeze outside. I kept on my leather coat for protection. Imagining what I'd been thinking of doing back in the Deep End's room had unnerved me. I'm not the suicidal type. The road ahead, however, was bleak. Yes, I would soon return to my Boston condo which I'd bought from my inheritance from my mother five years before, but even that, what had been my sanctuary before Sandy died, I now envisioned endless drunken nights in, scared witless by the sense that from now on I'd always be alone, and worse, lonely.

"'The cure for loneliness is solitude,'" Sandy said behind me in the bar. "Marianne Moore."

"How you doin' honey?" A waitress sidled up next to me as she noisily unloaded her tray of grimy beer glasses and an empty pitcher onto the bar. She'd come straight over from the drunken pool table boys.

"Pissants think they can have fresh glasses every round," she said, plopping down the glasses with more force than I thought was necessary. It was hard to tell how old she was. Her hair was shaved on one side and a fairly large nose ring was through her septum. But her face was lined.

"There's a story there," I heard Sandy say, although she'd slipped away from behind me and where she was in the crowd now, I couldn't tell. *Oh great*, I thought. *Now I hear you but can't see you?*

"How are you?" I said, tossing it back to the waitress.

"Me?" The empty glasses clinked against each

other so loudly as she dropped them on the bar that I could hear it above the blues music and all the other noise. "Livin' the dream."

I laughed politely and glanced away toward the bartender. There were two of them. Both men had tattoo sleeves that were showcased by matching tank tops that said OBEY across their chests. They were busy keeping up with the customers pressing toward the bar, pouring two drinks as they took someone else's order. I saw the nearest one jut his chin for a second at the waitress next to me as he held a bottle of gin way above his shoulder and deftly poured a stream into a glass of ice by his hip. The other bartender was doing a marimba dance with two cocktail shakers above his head.

"Better tell me quickly, honey, what you want. It's now or tomorrow," said the waitress. The bartender closest to us was already striding toward her despite everyone on the other side of the bar trying to flag him down.

"Scotch. A double. One rock," I told her.

She smiled, which took five years off. "You've done this before. Jimmy, set me up again for the Hardy Boys." She added my drink and then turned back to me. "Pleasure or business?"

"What?"

"What are you in town for? I know you don't live here. We know everyone who lives here."

"Neither."

"Oh, a mystery woman." She smiled again. I fiddled with a bar coaster. Maybe this wasn't a good idea after all. Two minutes in and already I was being questioned.

"It's okay, honey. We all have a bit of a mystery

here. You're in good company." She patted my arm. By then Jimmy was setting up five new glasses and a pitcher of beer on her tray and a short glass with my Scotch in front of me. "Start a tab for this one," she told Jimmy. "I have a feeling she's going to be here for a while." She patted my arm again and, picking up the tray, made her way back to the pool table.

"She must like you," Jimmy said. "Most people she makes pay in advance."

I did end up staying, just like Rayleen—that turned out to be the waitress's name—said I would. Too long. Despite the acrid farrago of stale beer fermenting under a nightly mopping on the wood floor, and the lingering stink of someone sometime being sick. Around my third Scotch, Rayleen had wheedled it out of me what I was doing in P-Town, about Sandy, about everything.

"Holy shit, your sister was on that boat that killed Woodrow?" she said rather loudly. "Jimmy! Come here," she barked down the bar, flapping her hand at our bartender as if she was in a hurry to get a drink order in.

Then she told him the whole thing too.

"There's some people over there who would love to talk to you," Jimmy shouted, because by now the din in the bar was overwhelming. The band was taking a break. They were, it turned out, a cover band of Joplin hits, which they played at a decibel that sled dogs in Alaska could hear. If they'd been playing straight through, I wouldn't have even tried to utter two words to Rayleen.

"So, now it's the band's fault," Sandy said, who had reappeared next to me.

"Please." I rubbed the bridge of my nose. I was

suddenly exhausted. The drinks, and now my sister, were a one-two punch.

Jimmy and Rayleen both looked at me.

"You all right, honey?" Rayleen asked, genuinely concerned. She touched my arm so briefly I didn't know if she'd done it or not.

Jimmy slid away, ostensibly to fill some more drink orders, but not before I saw him sidle up to a couple of women at the end of the bar closest to the door. Not his territory. Leaning over, he was saying something to them that I couldn't, of course, hear. Then suddenly, the two women were picking up their drinks and weaving their way over to me through the crowd. Other people quickly sat down in their seats, but I saw Jimmy motion for them to get up.

Oh Christ, I thought. *Here it comes.*

"Sorry, honey," Rayleen said in my ear, and left with a bottle of tequila and a stack of shot glasses for the pool table area. The townies had finally gotten tired of letting the Hardy Boys think they were better than they were, and they'd whupped their asses in three straight games. The Hardy Boys were so drunk that Rayleen had them pay unknowingly for the tequila that the townies were going to finish off.

Before I could move, the two women arrived, squishing in next to me in the space that Rayleen had vacated, making me scooch my stool against the wall to create a bit of space between us.

"I think that's the bar back station," I told them, hoping to get them to leave.

One of them laughed. "Rayleen won't mind. We're regulars, sweetheart."

A bolt of recognition hit me. These were the whale huggers that Brant had warned me about. Up close, I could see now that they were both wearing matching *Cape Cod: A Whale of a Good Time* sweatshirts, one in pink and the other blue, like you might see in the sale bins at a Christmas Tree Shop or worn by an octogenarian married couple. They both had their dyed blond hair pulled back into no-nonsense ponytails, although one had hers poking through the back of a golfing visor.

"I'm Linda," said visor girl, although I use the term loosely as she and the other one were in their fifties at least.

The other one held out her hand lickety-split. "Jane."

I shook it. What could I do? Let it hang in the air that was already uncomfortable between us? I figured I should go on the offensive, so I could vacate my seat and run as fast as I could for the safety of the sheikh tent back at the Deep End. "Nice sweatshirts," I said.

They both nodded gravely, missing my sarcasm. Jane looked down into her pint glass of flat beer, but Linda stared me in the eye and said, "Actually, we're whale *warriors*."

I shrugged. "Look, I wasn't there. It was my sister—"

"Sandra." Linda nodded. Turning sideways to face me, she draped a hand over the brass railing barely separating us. Linda looked like she'd have no problem catapulting over the railing to get to me.

It startled me that she knew my sister's name. More than that, only our mother had ever used her full name.

Jane poked her head around Linda's shoulder. "We're sorry for your loss," she said, a bit too mechanically to have any real feeling in it.

"So am I," I replied.

I was, of course, referring to me, but then Linda's face softened just a little. She nodded. She raised her hand from the railing and let it drop there again. "He was such a beautiful whale. You find out anything?" she asked.

It struck me that they knew as much as I did. I was astounded that I hadn't even thought of them as possible people whom I should interview. Brant had told me that the Coastal Studies office in town had been involved, but I'd simply thought that was so they could identify which whale they'd been tracking had died. They kept some sort of registry similar to what hospitals did across the country for blood diseases such as sickle cell or hemophilia. Only the Coastal Studies databank had names of whales that had specific identifying marks, where they migrated, dates they were in the area, how many calves they'd birthed, that sort of thing. So, Linda and Jane were on a fact-finding mission also.

I shook my head. "Just here to pick up her cremains," I said, using the harsher clinical term, the Scotch now in its final stage of worming its well-traveled road into ruthless land. In my experience, this is the time when you get as many digs into the people you're with before ending up passed out on someone's couch.

Even in the bar's dimness I could see that Linda's face blanched. Jane stared down into her beer again. Still, Linda recovered, and when she did, she began what surely was the same spiel that they stopped innocent tourists with on Commercial Street when they were doing their fundraising for their nonprofit. The right whale will be extinct in twenty years. Cape Cod Bay is the primary feeding ground in the country for them. Last year no new calves were born. Seventeen died.

"Entanglement, ship strike, what have you," Linda rattled off. "What have you" sounded funny coming after "ship strike." Linda was a townie through and through. "Born here, and I'll die here too." She said it almost wistfully. I was starting to believe that everyone who lived in this town had some kind of Asperger's around death. Brant. Linda. They blurted anything out that came to mind, forgetting that my sister had just died. Their frontal lobe gatekeeper was asleep at the sympathy wheel.

Jane, shaking her head, downed what was left in her glass and placed it reverently on the bar. "I really miss Woodrow." Like they'd hung out together all the time. Played pool together in the next room.

"Where are you staying?" Linda asked suddenly.

I'd been in a trance during her recitation about right whales, lulled by the dry facts that didn't move me at all. *Who the hell cared about some fish?* I'd been thinking. As far as I was concerned, that fish murdered my sister. Although technically, I suppose, a whale is a mammal. Still, animal, mineral, or vegetable…at the very least it was an accomplice. Had aided and abetted. I wanted to scream at these two that I'd lost my *sister*, but even in my sloppy state I knew that would be a bad move. The trick was to get away from them, escape to the Deep End, retrieve Sandy's ashes in the morning, and skedaddle as fast as I could out of this hellhole.

"Just a B and B," I hesitatingly told her. I stood up.

"I know that." Linda snorted. "Which one?"

"The Swan and Lily," I lied. I'd passed it on Commercial Street on the walk into town. I'd remembered it because it seemed like one of those innocent-sounding English inns you'd see in a British mystery where everyone is murdered in their beds. One year, the year I turned eighteen, my mother took Sandy, who was twenty, and me to London for a weeklong birthday celebration. Sandy and I had spent the entire time trying to one-up each other with fabricated, gruesome names of pubs or inns that would never appear in an Agatha Christie novel: The Gun and The Slug, The Tourniquet and The Gash, or my favorite, which was one of Sandy's creations: The Bludgeon and the Hole in the Head. Anyway, I'd noticed the Swan and Lily, a typical Cape house with weather-beaten grey shingles and an antique wooden swan over the front door.

Jane perked up. "The White Room?"

"Um…"

"You're not in the cottage out back, are you?" Linda snapped, somewhat mysteriously. She paused. "I heard someone got bed bugs there."

"Mystery solved," Sandy whispered in my ear. I hadn't seen her sneak up on me again. "I think it's time we were leaving, don't you?"

"Wait." Linda slid her hand down the brass railing to touch my arm, but unlike Rayleen, she didn't let go. "Let's meet up tomorrow. We can go over everything you know. It's too noisy in here anyway." She acted as if we were on the same team. As if we'd unfortunately chosen the wrong venue for our crime room reconnaissance and I was their informant.

"Hey, maybe you want to go see Woodrow tomorrow?" Jane interjected, once again popping her head around Linda, and shocking me with this bombshell.

"He's still on the beach out there," Linda piped in. "They can't get the heavy equipment they need to bring him back in." Thankfully, she let go of my arm. I felt dizzy suddenly. I shook my head. "I've got to go." I stumbled past them both, only to realize that I was headed to the back of the bar, not out of it. I staggered around several other people, finally heading in the right direction.

"We'll stop by," I heard Linda yell.

By the time I was through the front door I'd already broken into a run as best as I could.

We're barely past the Brewster exit, only thirty-five minutes from P-Town, when Myles says nonchalantly, "Can we stop?" He's staring straight ahead like he hadn't said it.

"What are you, five?" It's not a joke. Mostly, I'm annoyed that he hasn't told me anything new. Added on top of that is the fact that he's already asking for a bathroom.

"Here, this exit!" He says it so authoritatively I swerve the car at the last minute onto the ramp for Exit 8 Yarmouth.

"What the hell!" I shout at him. "Couldn't you wait till we were at the bridge?" There is an easy exit to a McDonald's right after the Sagamore Bridge. The Golden Arches practically hold the bridge up, they're that close.

"Go right," he says, motioning with his hand in that direction.

"Do you know where we're going?" I ask, really irritated.

"It's nearby. Don't wo-wo-worry."

He has me take the next left onto a snowy street that is in the middle of a neighborhood of quaint New England houses.

"Myles…" I say through gritted teeth.

"Here it is, on the right. Pull in here."

When I see where he's taken us, I almost chuck him out of the car into the large snowbank that is surrounding the parking lot he's had me pull into. A white sign, its black letters dusted almost completely with snow, rattles and squeaks as it swings in the breeze in front of a ramshackle elephant-grey Cape Cod house. Still, I can read what it says. *Edward Gorey House.*

Sandy claps her hands in the back seat. "What fun!" she says.

Chapter Six

By the time Tibbie is parking the car, Myles's skin has started to feel like it's been rubbed with ice melt for an hour. He thought he'd jump out of the car ten minutes before. It took all of his willpower to not start screaming at her when she was going on and on about shitty Skyville, "Shut up. Just shut up!" Immediately, he felt awful for even thinking that. At least she was talking, which was more than he was doing. How long would she put up with his silent treatment before leaving him at the side of the road?

Although it's still morning, he needs to do a line or two. Or four. Okay, technically it's morning, but it's eleven o'clock for fuck's sake. Doesn't he deserve…what did they call snack time in *Lord of the Rings*? Elevenses? He blames it on the incessant questioning from Tibbie. A woodpecker hammering away, she will not be diverted. And what was all that crap about Penelope and Hayden? Suddenly she's best friends with them? Sisterhood solidarity? For a brief moment he wonders if this trip is actually a trick: the three of them are in cahoots. Once they get him into an abandoned warehouse, the harpy trio will throw him into a Macbethian kettle and boil him to death. Shit, he really needs to get it under control. *You're all over the place!* the voice in his head shouts. He needs a line.

He's always wanted to go to the Gorey Museum. He's sure they'll have a bathroom. Some place he can quickly snort before taking a leisurely stroll around the museum. Slow things down a bit. That's what he needs to do. See Gorey's books, where he lived. That'll settle him down.

Before Tibbie has turned off the car, he's out of it, practically skipping up the wood stairs onto the porch as if he's going to hug the oversized black-and-white cardboard cutout of one of Gorey's Victorian men standing there. He hears Tibbie snickering in the parking lot as she closes her door. He doesn't care that she thinks he's racing because he has to pee so bad. It doesn't matter. Nothing matters but getting inside and finding a bathroom.

He's stymied, however, as soon as he bursts through the entrance door. He ends up in a small alcove with a store where they sell all objects Gorey. A man, forty-something years old, his face in a book, sits behind a card table with a cash register. An elderly woman stands up from a nearby couch and asks if Myles is there for the store or wants to actually go into the museum.

"Do you want a tour?" she asks.

Myles assures her he wants to see the museum. He explains he needs a bathroom first, however. Behind him, the front door reopens. Tibbie. Without telling her anything, he quickly walks in the direction that the woman is pointing to, barely registering the room he passes through.

The house is old, rickety. His footsteps are overly loud on the wide wooden plank floors. As soon as he closes the bathroom door, he hears the woman asking Tibbie the same questions she'd asked him, and he realizes with horror that probably every sound will echo from the bathroom throughout the house. It looks like none of the bathroom fixtures have been updated since Gorey lived there, almost eighteen years before. Behind a green curtain, the shower stall houses an extra-large teddy bear and a skeleton. Opposite the toilet is a large wood sculpture of a Boston terrier perched atop a white Doric column. Myles coughs to check out the sound buffering. God, his cough sounded loud. He turns on the sink taps. There. That'll do it. Quickly, he takes out the Peek Frean's tin and, uncovering it, scoops out a spoonful. Two. Three. Four, and it's done. He packs it all up, slides it into his jumpsuit's interior breast pocket like a wallet, sniffs hard, flushes the toilet, and turns off the water.

When he comes out, Tibbie is talking amiably with the woman and the man. Turning slightly away from them, she gives him a hard look. Does she know what he really was doing in there? Despite being a dead giveaway, he unconsciously rubs his nose and sniffs again. Stupid.

"All right then?" Tibbie says and shoots him one of her blinding Sandy smiles.

Shit. She knows. Or maybe it's her way of saying, "Okay, you've seen it, now can we get back on the road?"

"Are either of you teachers?" says the man behind the card table. He's lowered his tome, which Myles can see is the recent bestseller biography about Gorey, his eccentricities, and his work.

"What?" Myles says, confused for a moment that they've been mistaken for someone else.

The woman tells them the Museum fee is eight

dollars but five dollars for teachers.

Shaking his head, Myles reaches into his side pocket at the same time that Tibbie, sidling up in back of him, whispers, "Are we staying? We really need—"

"We're not teachers," Myles says quickly as he gives the man a twenty.

"*Myles...*"

"Do you want the tour?" the woman repeats.

Before Tibbie can object any further, Myles is nodding emphatically, and the woman says, "Well, let's start in this first room..."

The tour is fantastic. Myles can see that even Terrible Tibbie is enjoying it despite her urgency to get on the road. Since Gorey was an obsessive in his collections, there are hundreds of objects and posted information to cast your eyes over. One room is filled with glass balls on every surface and in bowls. Another has spindles and wooden potato mashers lined up like sentries. Gorey's stuffed animals lounge on every piece of furniture in a third room. The kitchen, still in its original beige state, centers around a fireplace where empty cat bowls rule next to iron dog andirons. The room farthest from the front entrance is dedicated to the PBS animation Gorey did for *Mystery*. Throughout it all, the tour guide refers to Gorey as Ted, causing Myles to really feel as if he's a friend of the family, not a paying guest, here to take a last look around before they close up the house for winter.

Then, they turn a corner and end up next to a clone-like bodily installation of one of Gorey's fur coats, his Harvard scarf, and white Keds—with holes!—and cases of his occult rings and necklaces.

"Je-*sus*," Tibbie mutters. "The ghost of Ted." He can't tell if she's being facetious or is wonderfully surprised. Myles wants to reach out and touch the fur coat dummy. It'd be like touching the Shroud of Turin.

"After he died, we had to clean up quite a bit." The tour guide pauses effectively. "Especially the cats."

It turns out that she's actually Gorey's very close relative whom he lived with for many years before buying this house. She explains each of the object cases housing the current exhibition, *Murder He Wrote*, in the most perfect way, Myles thinks, with just enough humor to liven up the biographical details but not too much that would devolve into farce, and Myles suddenly wants to find a way to never leave this place where his favorite illustrator once lived. He and the tour guide and, what the hell, even the clerk in the store could live upstairs where the tour is off-limits and they could spend their days talking only of Edward—Ted—Gorey.

Myles insists that they go through the entire tour despite Tibbie's agitation.

"Okay, o*kay*," he hisses at her when he actually feels her pressing on his back, breathing on his neck. Still, he dallies in the store. Although he doesn't have that much extra money to spend—he wonders just how much this trip is going to cost him anyway— he splurges and buys a one-thousand-piece puzzle depicting many of Gorey's illustrated Victorian and 1920s characters; a metal pin of the Doubtful Guest, one of Gorey's most beloved characters; a copy of the biography the clerk was reading ("You won't regret it, I promise," the clerk leans in closer to him to say as if sharing a major secret about Gorey himself); and a teacup and saucer with cats cavorting.

"I'll be waiting in the car," Tibbie tells him in a strained voice, then walks across the house's creaking floorboards and is out the door.

For a moment, Myles worries that she may just leave him there, fed up as she is. *But that would be okay, wouldn't it? Isn't that what I'd just been wishing for?* Part of him—ironically, the sane part of him— knows that he's only fantasizing because of the coke. He laughs out loud. *I snorted in Gorey's bathroom*, he thinks in complete wonderment.

"What's so funny?" the clerk asks as he hands over a bag full of Myles's goodies.

Myles shakes his head. "Just happy we came."

Tibbie has already started the car and backed out of the parking spot. The car is idling, pointed in the direction of a quick getaway. As soon as Myles closes his door, she peels out.

"Are you gay or something?" Tibbie asks him as she turns onto Route 6A.

"What?" Myles says, startled, any good feeling now trampled to death.

"Are you gay? Is that why you wanted to go there?" Tibbie looks disconcerted.

"No, I'm not gay. Jesus. Why would you ask me that?" He sounds more indignant than he wants to. "Are you?"

Tibbie ignores his question and says, "Well, your boy Gorey was, wasn't he? And you *are* living in P-Town."

Myles tries not to rise to the bait, yet he can't help but snap his head in her direction. He needs to ignore her digging around about P-Town. Why he's living there is none of her business, he reminds himself. To tell her it has nothing to do with the town's large gay population will only open him up to other questions. Anyway, he's sure she knows that P-Town is part punishment, part test to see if he can go on living. She's just pushing his buttons to see if he'll break and tell her what she really wants to know. About the accident. Whether he's to blame. He breathes in and out.

"No," he tells her with a forced tone that implies his patience is infinite and she is stupid. "Gorey said in interviews he wasn't one thing or another. And he thought sex was overrated." Myles crosses his arms across his chest as a punctuation point.

Tibbie laughs. "Is that so," she says, glancing at him. "Well, what was the big thing then? Other than you needing a bump or two." She stares straight out the windshield. "I mean, if you're that hard up, man, you could just do it in the car. I'm not a narc."

"What are you t-t-*talk*ing about?"

She glances at him again, then back to the road, and snorts. "Okay, have it your way. And just so you know, I'm not homophobic."

"If you weren't, you wouldn't need to say that."

She gives him a look of surprise. "You know my sister was gay, right?"

"So what? Why are we even talking about this anyway?"

"O-kay...so, tell me why you love Gorey so much."

"Let's not talk, okay?'

"Sandy told me you were doing a book of bird illustrations or something? Are they like his?" When he doesn't say anything, she adds, "Come on. I just brought you there, didn't I? Despite the fact that we have many more hours to go."

In response, he curls his entire body away from her to rest his head on his window, his eyes closed tight.

"Okay, I'm sorry. You don't want to talk about your book, is that is? I get it." Still, he remains stubbornly silent. "Fine," Tibbie adds, peevishly. "I thought you cokeheads love to talk. Have it your way."

Myles keeps his eyes shut tight. He fights the urge to tell her that he's never been a talker. The coke simply lifts the gathering darkness for a spell. Nor would he ever confide in her about the book. The book. The book is so wrapped up in that terrible day on the boat, how can he possibly tell her about it even if he wanted to? Which he doesn't want to. There is Sandy, alive, standing in front of him at the back of the boat, one hand across her sweating forehead, shading her eyes against the setting sun, the last sunset she'll ever see, as she innocently tells him that she knows about the book, will help get it in front of Luke, although she doesn't hold out much hope for its success in that direction. Then, the shove. Down she goes. Her head cracks against the banquette seating. From that moment on, everything was doomed.

Now, he will never finish the book. How could he? The book of birds that once took up all of his non-work hours. All of his thoughts. Sometimes even during work hours. Now, they're cursed forever, his birds of death.

He aches to go back to a time when he loved birds. When he was ten years old, his mother began to keep an entire aviary in an extension off the back of their house in Cambridge. After his father died suddenly of a massive heart attack, his mother had hired the architects and construction firm, built the aviary, and then, precipitously, declined to have very much to do with it, only showing an interest when she had her monthly dinner parties for her philanthropic friends. Charlotte Small had come from an old Cambridge family traced back to poets and statesmen—"Imagination and strength, Myles, you shouldn't have one without the other"—while his father had been "new money," earned from a tech software he patented before the first start-up wave hit. By the second wave, his father was dead. And his mother had fallen back on what she'd done before meeting her husband at a Harvard alumni fundraiser: using her family's philanthropic nonprofit to contribute to the ongoing presence of Harvard's Museum of Natural History, which held a large room of dead birds, as well as to organizations keen on the preservation of live animals, such as the Boston Aquarium, the Franklin Park Zoo, the local animal shelter. When asked what his parents did for a living, Myles had gotten into the habit during his teens of saying, "She keeps dead animals dead and live animals locked up and he was a computer geek who died when he had too much fun one night." That last part was a stretch—his father had actually been at some stupid stamp collectors' convention when he collapsed—but it served its purpose of shutting people up.

Really, the aviary was more of an installation. An enormous room with its Victorian-like iron-and-glass structure. Christ, it even had a glass dome on top. Tropical vines crawled along the interior steel corner beams up to that dome, creeping around life-sized Greek and Roman statues related to people and animals. Artemis with her sheath of arrows slung on her back as she grips the antlers of a rearing up stag.

A spot-on replica of the Vatican's marble of the priest
Laocoon and his sons being killed by serpents. Athena,
in her armor and helmet, an owl clutched in her hand,
its wings and talons outstretched, clearly eager to
chase down its prey. Poseidon, barely holding back
the snarling three-headed hound of the underworld,
Cerberus. None of them peaceful or philosophical to
look at.

"They remind us that animals in real life are neither teddy bears or adorable puppies," his mother had
told him soon after the statues had been delivered and
installed by a couple of beefy men who looked like they
wouldn't know Greek statuary from porn. "It's up to
us to look after them and to control them," Charlotte
said calmly, almost in a bored tone, with one hand
idly petting the top of one of Cerberus's heads.

In addition to the vines, there were large potted
philodendron and monstera plants, fig trees, and
a stand of bamboo. Two daybeds, kept artfully and
yet purposefully apart at either end of the aviary,
surrounded by the indoor forest, beckoned you to lie
down as if you were in an opium den. Other miniature
trees coupled with fake tree branches, which were
cleaned once a month, gave the birds an Eden of
opportunities to perch or to catch mid-flight.

And what birds they were. Canaries, of course,
but even those weren't your pet-store variety. They
were sent over from Great Britain. Yorkshire Fancies
bred in the coal mining towns of northern England.
It was said they were skinny enough to slip through
a wedding ring. The Fife Fancy, larger and a pure
yellow without any markings, which breeders called
"clear yellow." Goldfinches. Waxbills. A pair of zebra
finches whose constant cheeping drove Charlotte

crazy. A pair of virginal white budgies. They resembled parrots to the undiscerning eye. Chatterboxes, they outdid parrots when it came to mimicking sounds and language they heard.

"Aren't they brilliant?" Myles's mother would say to first-time dinner guests. "They're not as loud as parrots. It's the difference between vaudeville and a Shakespeare play. They know how to lower the volume. This one can recite Swinburne."

"Are their eyes *red*?" one guest had asked, peering at the one perched on Charlotte's index finger. "Is he sick or something?"

Charlotte scoffed. "Sick? Nothing a good priest can't fix." When she saw the guest blanch, she added, "It's a joke. They're albinos, dear."

Once, Myles had to remove a mirror from their area because the male kept regurgitating its food thinking it was another bird to feed and ended up dying from starvation. There were disasters too. The time when a pair of peach-faced lovebirds sent over from Africa were not the requested female and male that they could've bred. One night together ended in one being found dead on the aviary floor, pecked and clawed, beaten to death, and the other one dying two days later from his injuries. Myles imagined it was like a Mexican cock fight in some tin building in the middle of nowhere. Not Cambridge, Massachusetts.

"Love is awful, isn't it?" his mother said as Myles laid the first one in a shoebox for burial under the yard's rhododendron bush out back.

"They hated each other. They must've been two *males*!" he told her, simmering with anger.

"Well, how was I to know that?" Charlotte replied as if she were put out, and walked back into the main house.

That wasn't as bad as the peacock, however. The bird was what Myles's mother called her "showstopper." She even named him Houdini, which turned out to be prescient. Somehow, one day, the Indian peafowl squeezed through the metal railings of the yard's iron fence, disappearing in the twilight until a neighbor called three hours later with news of a possible sighting. After that, such sightings were telephoned to the Smalls house almost every day as if they'd set up a 1-800 police tip line for a cocknapping. None of it came to anything. Houdini had simply disappeared into thin air. Myles still wondered if another neighbor, or maybe even the first one who'd called, had captured the bird and was keeping it in a basement somewhere for their own fun and enjoyment.

From then on, Myles vowed to take over the aviary and all the care of the birds. He was twelve years old. Their gardener maintained (rather reluctantly) the aviary's plants and trees, ducking and cringing whenever a bird swooped by. Myles, however, always enjoyed the sudden immersion into the jungle room. It was an escape from Cambridge and his mother. He liked mixing the birds' individual meals, the doling out of them into their tiny bowls and shelves. It was a gift, not a chore at all.

When Myles went away to Cornell University in upstate New York because they had an acclaimed national Lab of Ornithology, he asked his mother to hire an assistant to care for the aviary. He coupled his biology and aviary studies with art courses. At Cornell, he met Penelope Blackmore in a course on print media. By then they were both seniors and had become friends, or at least friend-ly when they saw each other in the class. Whenever Myles saw her outside—on the Commons downtown at one of the shops or cafes or crossing campus—she was always with someone different, like it was a changing of the popularity guard. He was too insecure to go up to her. One day during their five-minute class break she offhandedly asked him what his plans were after graduating. She was using the break time to check her texts on her cell. He shrugged—which she completely missed, focused as she was on her cell's screen—and told her he supposed he'd be going back to Cambridge and would probably end up, despite his "really not wanting to," working for his mother's philanthropic foundation. Sitting at the desk next to his, Penelope murmured something about her father's publishing house looking for another illustrator as her fingers typed a message to someone.

"Really?" Myles said.

Penelope opened her mouth to say something, but then the professor started up the class again and Myles had to sit for another forty minutes squirming in his chair. At the end of the class, somehow, he was able to sputter and ask where he should send his resume. For a moment, she looked at him uncomprehendingly.

"For the job?" he suggested.

"Oh, right." Reaching out, she grabbed his hand and on the back of it wrote with her rollerball her father's name and email. "Just tell him I told you to."

So, upon graduating, he'd followed her to New York. Later, after the accident and his McLean's stay, he'd briefly thought about moving back to Cambridge again where he could immerse himself in the aviary and never see another human being ever again, except his mother occasionally. Charlotte, however, put the kibosh on that when she picked him up from McLean's to bring him home.

"But the birds are long gone, you know that," Charlotte explained in a soft voice that she'd been careful to use with him ever since the accident. "Besides, you'll be bored stiff." She put the directional on and smoothly eased the car onto the ramp leading to Route 2. She told him, "Even your doctors said it'd be best if you got back to your life. Go back to the city. Your job."

"What?" He was incredulous. "When?"

"What? Well, when I met with them…" She paused when she saw his face and realized he'd been referring to the birds, not to his medical prognosis. She waved one hand in the air. "Oh. A while ago. I couldn't…I didn't have the time to take care of them. I told you, I'm sure of it. James offered to take them… oh, I know I told you."

"James! He knows nothing about birds." James was a waste. He'd inherited family money too, although all he seemed to do with it was complain about all the Boards with a capital B that he was forced to sit on. Myles couldn't stand how James always seemed to be cradling his mother's elbow as the guests went into the dining room for dinner, or how he always seemed to laugh too loudly whenever Charlotte made a joke.

"Myles…really. You'd moved to New York. You haven't lived here in so long…it was either that or let them all go. It was really an act of mercy if you think about it. They wouldn't have lasted one day."

Myles didn't last one day either. He told his mother to take him instead to the airport so that he could return immediately to New York City, but once she hugged him at the terminal curb and drove away, he went to the Cape Air check-in and bought a ticket back to Provincetown.

Pretending to be asleep in Tibbie's car now, he thinks of how before the accident he used to love the hours he spent planning which birds he would include in his book and sketching them over and over. God the hours, the days, spent drawing one beak, one skeletal foot, a wingspan, to get it just right. The countless pages he tore out and threw away. Figuring out which birds to focus on alone took almost a year. He didn't want yet another birding book of lovely drawings. Audubon had made that impossible. Neither did he want anything directly connected to an Edgar Allen Poe raven or the Daphne Du Maurier depiction in her story *The Birds*. Hitchcock made that impossible. It must be about the lightness *and* the darkness of birds. Finally, by chance Myles discovered that he should only include birds that were the subject of superstitions— good and bad. It happened one day when he'd decided he'd take a quick walk outside of the *Freedom Press* offices after eating his PB and J sandwich. Usually, he ate his lunch every day at his desk and went right back to work as soon as he swallowed the last crust. It was a beautiful fall day: crisp, blue-skied, the kind of day you'd head up to the Catskills for some apple picking. Two blocks from the office, however, a bird—he never did see what kind it was because there was a swooping flock of them—shat on his right shoulder as it flew past.

"Ugh!" he cried out. He didn't have anything to wipe it with and so he hoofed the two blocks back to the office. Praying that Penelope wouldn't see him, he ducked into the hallway bathroom outside the offices. Unfortunately, before he'd had the chance to clean it off at the sinks, there was his boss and Penelope's father, Lucas Blackmore, coming out of the one stall.

"That's good luck, old bean," Luke told him, laughing as he pointed to Myles's shoulder.

Between the bird shit and Luke using one of his stupid British phrases despite his being one hundred percent American, Myles almost punched him.

Luke held up both hands in surrender. "Honest, mate, it's brilliant. Google it. You might want to buy a lottery ticket on the way home, tickety boo."

Myles hadn't. Nevertheless, he'd looked it up. Luke had been right. Although most of the sites said that the bird shit had to land on your head for it to have any beneficial future attached to it. *Close enough*, Myles thought. From there, it was a matter of minutes before he discovered a slew of bird superstitions, most of them ending in death. Myles had no idea there were so many. Watching an owl in daylight? Sorry, bad luck. Three seagulls flying together, directly overhead? A warning of death soon to come. So is any bird, especially a white one, that flies into your house and dies there. Don't kill a sparrow; they actually carry the souls of the dead. Myles was stunned by the sheer number involving sailors: kill an albatross and you'll get lost at sea. Five crows in your line of vision? Undoubtedly, you or someone close to you will become ill. Six and you die. Magpies? The devil incarnate.

Myles dug deeper and deeper into all kinds of black magic, omens, arcane myths, all involving birds. It wasn't until weeks after the boat accident that he read one night that having a wren can prevent a drowning. Now, he wonders if they'd had such a bird on *Stillwater* whether Sandy would still be alive. And then, there's the dead whale. He obsesses, especially when he can't sleep at night, what superstitions might await him related to *that*.

No, he can't finish the book. At least not now.

Chapter Seven

Well, he certainly had a *horror vacui*," my sister says over my shoulder as we both glance around Gorey's cluttered living room. "What the Greeks called *kenophobia*. Fear of the empty," she explains.

"I didn't know you knew Latin *or* Greek."

"Neither did I," says my sister with a chuckle. "Death is surprising."

"Gorey once said that the Surrealists thought writers believe the most mysterious thing of all is just everyday life," Myles says, startling me as he peers next to my shoulder into another case of mummified creatures. Mice? Lizards? It's hard to tell. He's come up on me silently, like a ghost. I'd lagged behind the tour, hesitating by the case when I saw Sandy examining its contents.

Myles points and reads from a placard on a wall with a quote of Gorey: "'Everyday life is very discomfiting. I guess I'm trying to convey that discomfiting texture in my books.'"

"He's growing on me more and more," says Sandy.

"Gorey?" I ask her. His mournful attitude seems out of keeping with the sunshine and lollipops, positive Sandy I knew. But again—every hour, it seems—she alters my reality of her.

"What?" Myles asks me. "Yes. Who else would've said it? Can't you read?" He points at the placard again.

"No silly," my sister butts in. "*Myles.* I'm so glad we went on this little side trip together. I never saw this, well, darker side to him." Sandy taps her front tooth with her index finger as if she's had a thought, but then quickly shakes her head, dismissing it immediately.

"What is it?" I ask her.

Myles stares at me for a moment. "What's what?"

"Nothing," I say dismissively as my sister strolls away into the next room, still tapping her tooth.

"If you'd like to follow me into the kitchen," interjects the tour guide who's double-backed in search of her lost sheep. "I'll tell you all about how Ted sometimes cooked entire meals that were one color. Blue was a favorite."

⚜ ⚜ ⚜ ⚜

Myles finally talks to me about an hour after we leave the Gorey house. He doesn't really want to either. Basically, I piss him off with the music I slide into the CD player. It's one of Sandy's CDs: the movie soundtrack from *Mama Mia!* His "I'm asleep" act lasts through one rotation, but as soon as I hit Repeat, he opens his eyes and sits up.

"It's one of my sister's favorites," I tell him.

"That's a load of bologna," Sandy says. She's stretched out in the back seat where she's been pretending to be asleep like Myles. For a second, I wonder if her behavior is somehow synchronized with whatever Myles does, a ventriloquist act gone awry.

It *was* one of her favorites. I'm getting a bit fed up with her sudden reversals. I want to yell at her, "Stop with the Dr. Jekyll/Mr. Hyde routine." Instead, I say sweetly to Myles, "Talk to me and you can be D.J. for the rest of the trip." Somehow, I've become the older sister cajoling her pipsqueak brother with promises of ice cream and cake if he'll stop asking, are we there yet?

Myles quickly tries to stab the Eject button, but I grab his hand.

"Uh-uh." I drop his hand back on his thigh and tell him, "Start talking first," like I'm the cop and he's some asshole I collared. On my steering wheel is a very convenient button to increase or decrease the music volume. I tap the up arrow ever so slightly.

Irritated, he rubs his forehead. His flap hat tilts off his head onto the back of his seat. "Fine. What do you want to talk about?" One glance at me and he adds quickly, "Not *that*."

"Fine. Why are you so interested in birds?" I ask him, tiptoeing the line between asking him a seemingly innocent I-want-to-get-to-know-you type of question and outright asking about his book and whether Sandy did or didn't help him get their boss interested in it. It's a topic he's already declared off-limits, but I'm starting to wonder if it would make for a nice motive for murder if she screwed him on that.

He sighs. Hesitates. Then, he begins. He's not even on his third sentence describing his mother's aviary when he ejects the songs of ABBA and turns the radio dial quickly to land on another classical radio station. I'll say this for our Myles: he knows what he wants and, unlike me, he's got laser focus.

By the time we're on the Mass Pike going west

from Boston to Albany, the trees on the turnpike have
changed from the Cape's bare scrub pines to snow-
dusted oaks, maples, and hemlocks. They're pretty
with a faint Christmas card look. Good people live
off these exits, they seem to say. Wholesome people.
People of the earth. That changes after we stop in Albany at the local Mickey Ds where I get in line to order and Myles
ducks into the men's room for what I'm certain is
another white fixer-upper. When he gets back into
the car, where I've been chomping my way through a
cheeseburger over Sandy's warnings about cholester-
ol, heart disease in women, blah blah blah, I hand him
a Happy Meal. It's a joke, which he doesn't find funny
at first until I reach behind his seat and also hand him
a Number Two: Quarter Pounder with cheese, large
fries, and a Coke. When I hand him the drink, I say,
"Sorry, this is definitely not the *real* thing. But I figured you got that covered."

"Very funny." He opens the burger bag, looks
inside, and then closes it up again without removing
anything. After drinking from his soda as if he's going
to drain the entire thing in one breath, he says, "I
thought you were vegan," and points with his straw at
the cheeseburger I'm happily munching away at.

I shrug. "Got ya," I tell him mid-chew and give
him a smile despite the food in my mouth.

He shakes his head, places his soda in one
of the car cups, and rifles through his Happy Meal
box. "Wow, these have definitely gotten better than
when I was a kid," he says, bypassing the food and
unwrapping the toy that comes in every box. "Holy
shit, it's a whisper projector."

He holds what looks like a plastic watch, only

its face is pastel colored, yin and yang swirls with fake hands set at almost three o'clock. There's no band on it. Instead, from the side glance I give it, it seems as if it has an orange plastic key chain hookup. Which doesn't make sense to me, because what kid has a key ring? Which proves what I always suspected: more adult males buy Happy Meals than they're willing to let on, especially ever since Mickey Ds started to collaborate with Japanese toy manufacturers. For a second, I wonder if there might be a story for the paper in that. Then I remember I've taken a leave from my job to do this.

Myles is practically beaming. It's the most alive he's looked since I arrived. Gone is his stutter. What's Sandy making of her dark knight now? But she's disappeared again. *Poof.* Gone.

"I'll show you later. It has to be dark to work," Myles says.

"I thought the bat phone was twenty-four seven."

Myles isn't paying me any attention, however. He's chuckling to himself as he turns over in his hands the...what did he call it? The whisper projector? Do you have to say as quietly as possible, "Next slide," to make it work?

"So, your book?" I ask him, mid-chew on a fry. "I'm sorry, but it doesn't sound too user friendly."

Myles frowns. He slips the toy into his jumpsuit's breast pocket. I hear it clink against something metal. Probably his coke tin.

"Come on," I say, laughing a little. "Okay, so birds are bad luck. Why buy the book?"

"There are g-g-good ones too," he says a bit peevishly, looking out his window as if he's trying to spot one right then and there. He takes a deep breath. "If a blackbird makes a nest by your house, that brings great luck. Seeing a kingfisher, very lucky. A hummingbird buzzes near your head, you can achieve the impossible." Here he raises both hands, reaching to the heavens. Warming to the topic, our Myles has transformed himself into a preacher. "Robins can go either way, though," he adds, pensive for a moment. "Depending on how you treat them. If you're kind to them, you receive good things throughout your life. If not, well, you're doomed...Besides, don't you want to know which ones to avoid?" He asks me this seriously. Nor can I believe that he actually used the word "doomed." I mean, who's used that word since the Dark Ages?

"Wait, you believe all this?" I'm so startled that this grown man actually believes in omens and not just any garden-variety types, such as make sure you toss some spilled salt over your shoulder, although why I'm so thrown is curious given that he's also a grown man who jumps for joy over Japanese anime toys.

Now he looks affronted. "Yes," he says quietly and turns away to his window again. Then, in an even quieter voice he says, "You would too if you'd gone through what I have." His voice is so muffled and low with him talking into his window that I almost think I haven't heard right.

"What?" I say.

In response, his thin body curls stiffly away from me in a half-feminine, quasi-fetal way as he leans his forehead on his cold window and closes his eyes again. I have the strongest urge to say, "No, wait. Please." To reach out and touch his shoulder. To tell him everything is going to be okay, birds or no birds. To take care of him.

"Now you've done it, Tibbie," Sandy says from the back seat.

When I glance in the rearview mirror I half expect to see her grinning, gleeful over my stupid mistake of shutting down Myles once again. Instead, I'm surprised to see she's crying, something I've seen her do only a handful of times when she was alive and those had to do with taking our mother off life support after her car accident, and then, our mother's wake and funeral. Sandy wipes her nose with the back of her hand. Sniffs hard and resettles her shoulders.

"Start the car, Tibbie," she orders, and then... *poof.*

❧ ❧ ❧ ❧

It's on 88 in the middle of New York State that the trees start to look more ominous. The nor'easter hasn't touched New York State. Instead, my headlights show that the sides of the highway are dotted with small mounds that are an ugly mixture of icy, leftover, dirty snow with rocks and stones that the plows drug up on their way to clearing the roads weeks ago. The trees, too, have morphed into a kind of burnt-out landscape of limbed silhouettes: spiny, forlorn, dead. No fire has taken place here. It's just winter in upstate New York.

"You can almost imagine the black riders of the apocalypse riding over that ridge," Sandy murmurs, looking out her side window. I can't tell if she means it as a joke or she's really afraid.

"You're a laugh a minute," I tell her.

Myles picks up his head and, over his shoulder, gives me a questioning look.

"Cliché," Sandy says. "Aren't you a writer? Can't you do better than that?" She taps her front tooth. "God, that food you ate looked good."

My sister, the vegetarian who never put a toxic thing in her body, has become a carnivore. To block out my increasing fear that I'm not so sure I like the new Sandy, that maybe I'm even starting to be afraid of this new erratic version of her, I begin to tell Myles— who has sat up again and, although not looking at me, at least has his eyes open—about growing up in a small town in New Hampshire. About everything that came before.

While we grew up with only one parent, I don't think we ever really thought we were missing out on something because of that. At least, I didn't. I was only a one-year-old. I doubt Sandy did either as she was three when our father died. Whether our mother, Francis Dyer, ever missed him is hard to say. Despite how he died, she kept framed photos of him in the living room on the fireplace mantel and on our night tables in our bedrooms. The ones in the living room showed a black-and-white triptych of him with my mother alone, then with my mother and a swaddled Sandy, fresh from the hospital OB-GYN, and lastly, a snapshot of the four of us sitting on the same couch that was in the house until my mother died. Now it's in my apartment. At least the three of *them* are sitting. I am a baby blanket burrito on Sandy's lap, her hands holding on securely as she smiles broadly at the camera like she's the gleeful mother. Our parents seem to be grinning with joy and expectation in every photograph. Now I know better. It's the same smile I started to use after Sandy died.

The photograph of our father, Bobby Dyer, on my bed table in Boston is more informal. It's a side shot of him sautéing something or another at the wonky industrial stove in my parents' restaurant. He's focused on whatever is sizzling in the large frying pan with his face tilted downward, not even aware that his picture has just been snapped. Everything about him speaks more line cook than chef: the backward Red Sox baseball cap, the black T-shirt and jeans covered partially by a dirty waist apron. No toque blanche, white double-breasted jacket, or houndstooth pants for him. He could be at home in his own kitchen, except for that mega-sized stove.

The Homeport Restaurant featured home cooking before and after his death. Macaroni and cheese made with one cheese, cheddar, not one of those four cheese concoctions you see on menus today. Turkey meatloaf with a ketchup crust, mashed potatoes, peas and carrots. Hanger steak with French fries. Fish was limited to what could be bought cheap in bulk and frozen—cod from Massachusetts or haddock from Maine—and was always served as fish and chips. No panko crust or cream sauces for this crowd. The children's menu had two options: hamburgers or hot dogs. On Sundays there was pot roast, baked potatoes, and a mixed salad with a chunk of iceberg lettuce swimming in ranch dressing in worn, fake teak bowls. If you happened to be from out of town and stupidly asked for a substitution—say, broccoli instead of the peas and carrots—Francis, our mother, or the ancient waitress Marjory, would simply laugh and say, "That's a good one," and walk away after scooping up the plastic menus.

Sandy's framed photograph of our father in contrast to mine was in color and he's laughing uproariously while holding out a tomato that's as big as an apple and that was supposedly grown in the hydroponic DIY greenhouse he'd attached to the garage. Sandy told me once when we were barely teenagers that that's really what Bobby wanted to be: a farmer.

"Maybe everything would've been different then," she said wistfully, staring at the photo in her hands as if willing it to speak, like she was some kind of World War II widow.

"How do you know?" I snapped at her. Back then, well, actually for all our lives, I hated when Sandy would get all pie-eyed and misty.

She started. "Well...people who...who, you know, who...well, they're not very happy, are they? Maybe he would've been happier."

I snorted. "I *meant* how do you know he wanted to be a farmer? Mom told me he hardly grew a thing after he built the greenhouse."

"Tibbie, don't be cruel. And don't lie."

Our mother simply kept a picture of their wedding day on her bed table next to her library stack of art books and a lamp my father had made out of an old ouzo bottle that was a porcelain Greek male dancer figurine. They were married in town hall. It's the only photo of my father in a suit. He looks more at ease than you'd expect, with a wry smile, his tie a bit rakishly loosened, one arm wrapped around Francis's shoulder. Not possessively. More tenderly than anything else. It's just resting there for the moment. My mother has on a simple white A-line dress that shows off how slender she is. She's standing slightly in front of him. Her right hand has reached up and holds my father's fingertips by her shoulder. Her other hand is reaching a bit back, latching on to the hem of his suit jacket. Even then she knew she had to somehow keep him connected to this earth.

Bobby Dyer killed himself. Whether it was because he did want to be a farmer, not a restaurant owner, or was unhappy being a husband or a father, my sister and I never really found out.

"Life was just difficult for him," our mother would say, haltingly, whenever we questioned her for the umpteenth time. "It wasn't me...or you...he loved you both, really he did." Here she'd smile wanly at Sandy and me. "Without the two of you...and me... it would've happened years before. I'm convinced of that."

But that did little to convince me or Sandy. Still, after a while we laid off grilling Francis about it. What was the point? At least he had had enough love or compassion or maybe just respect for our mother to have shot himself at a local park that was deserted at night but was also two blocks from the town police station. Everyone in town knew that any cop on night duty would drive by the park on their route every hour on the hour. When they found him, his body was still warm, I tell Myles, who stares at me from the passenger seat as if one of his budgies is stuck in his throat.

"Stop it," Sandy warns me now from the back seat. "Stop stretching the truth."

"May I continue?" I ask her, and when Myles nods his head, I do.

One thing I knew for certain: our mother had wanted more out of life than what was essentially a

waitress job in a backwoods town. Although she'd
grown up in Queens, she'd gone away to college—
Boston University—to study art history, hoping to
land a job at one of the art museums or galleries in
Boston when she graduated rather than enter the
more competitive Manhattan art environment. Then,
both her parents had gotten cancer, one right after the
other, as if it was some pact of their marriage license.
Five months before Francis would've graduated from
B.U. she was forced to come home, bury both of her
parents, and start looking for a job. Without a degree,
she ended up waitressing at a diner on Staten Island
where our father was a line cook. They started going
out, but before six months had passed his father called
to say that he and Bobby's mother were tired of the
New Hampshire winters, were moving to Florida, and
wanted him to take over the family restaurant, The
Homeport.

"He made it seem so glamorous," my mother
told me one night, late, when I was in my twenties
and visiting for the weekend. "Like we were moving
to Paris and we'd be the owners of this wonderful café
and this great house and I'd be able to curate local
artists' work for shows in the café. I think he even
compared it to the White Horse Tavern in the city. He
remembered that from one time when I was telling
him all about de Kooning and Pollack." Francis didn't
sound angry or even disappointed when she was telling me. More that she was still astonished, twenty
years later, that she'd fallen for it.

She had a lot to contend with raising two kids
under the age of four by herself while keeping the
restaurant afloat. After my father's wake and the
cremation, she quickly promoted the line cook named

Jack but who was called Jacks because his pants pocket always bulged with several marbles that he clacked around whenever he was nervous or just bored. Then, she hired a line cook replacement for Jack's old slot. A week later, The Homeport was open for business again. It remained in business another thirty years, until our mother was driving home one night from work and was hit by a drunk driver four blocks from our house.

"He was still wearing his fake Santa hat from the Christmas party he'd been to," I tell Myles.

"Oh, for Pete's sake, Tibbie," Sandy says, shaking her head but softly laughing despite the lie.

"What happened to *him*?" Myles asks, uneasily.

"Oh him? He died too, thankfully. Two days later. So at least he suffered."

Myles snaps off the radio, whether out of some kind of respect for my mother and her death, or because he's tired of classical music for the time being, I don't know. We fall into a comfortable enough silence after that, although I'm still thinking about The Homeport, my mother and her busted dreams, and of course, my sister.

Sandy and I both worked at the restaurant from the day we were each strong enough to bus tables and carry the trays with dirty dishes and silverware back to the sink. My sister was more sanguine about it, of course.

"Would you rather deliver newspapers?" she asked one day when we were working the same shift, rolling her eyes when I started griping about yet another disgusting tabletop covered with a patina of crumbs and somehow, always, always, poured-out ketchup and salt sludge. "Or maybe you think you'd be happier babysitting? You wouldn't, trust me. Neither would the unfortunate kids."

Sandy always talked as if she were some character in a novel, which irritated me no end.

"*Unfortunate*," I mimicked, trying to piss her off. But she just swatted me with her waitress hand towel and, laughing, started to clean another table.

Despite it being only five o'clock, it's already ten-thousand-leagues-below-the-sea dark by the time Myles and I see a sign saying, *Welcome to Skyville. Where Life Has No Limits.* Even with my high beams on and the GPS on my phone barking out directions, both of us are having trouble figuring out where we should turn. The snow here is so dirty it doesn't reflect the moonlight at all. Streetlights are nonexistent. There's no need for them; residents hunker down at home at night as soon as they return from their jobs two towns over at the Walmart, or from collecting their unemployment or disability checks.

"Jesus," Myles says under his breath. He's leaning forward in his seat, trying to help me navigate what seems like a GPS meltdown as it sends us in one never-ending circle. Getting into town or onto the main street was fairly easy off the highway. But now that we've been welcomed by Skyville, it wants above all else to make us lost idiots. We can see the rows of factory buildings ahead of us where Hayden Pierce and Penelope Blackmore supposedly live, but every time we get close to them, suddenly whatever road we're on jettisons us farther away. After looping around, the GPS re-centers itself, and then the whole stupidity is reenacted. See the factories. Say goodbye to the factories. Do the loop-de-loop. "Recalculating," yaps the GPS and everybody sings the refrain from the Hokey Pokey: And that's what it's all about.

"Call them," Myles says after the third go-around.

I shake my head.

"You don't have their numbers, or you don't want to call?"

"The latter," I say tersely. A lie. I have their address, but their phones aren't listed. "Look! Ask this guy. I'll pull over."

"This guy" is obviously staggering under a cape of blankets around his shoulders and is three sheets to the wind—I hear Sandy shouting "Cliché!"—but he's our only hope of exiting this Dantesque ring of the inferno we've landed in.

I watch as Myles talks to the man in the headlights. Fog breaths gust from both of their mouths, it's so friggin cold. The man points in a wide arc ahead of us, stabbing the air after that. The motion almost throws him down on his ass, but Myles catches him. Then, I see Myles take off his gloves and pass them to the man.

When Myles jumps back into the Saab, a jet stream of deadly cold air sweeps in with him.

"Christ!" he says, clapping his frigid hands and blowing on them clasped together against his lips. For a second, I think he's going to let loose a call to beckon, say, an owl or a moose.

"He's too good for his own good," Sandy says with a sigh. "He needs someone to look after him."

"Well, don't look at me," I snap at her. Myles ignores it, or pretends to, at least. Maybe he's getting used to my non sequiturs, or maybe he thinks I have a form of Tourette's. He'd be the last person to comment on a speech condition.

"Go straight," Myles says, intermittently still blowing on his hands. "Then the first left onto a dirt road. Over the bridge and we're there."

"Did you actually give him your gloves?" I know I should let it drop. What good can possibly come from my pointing out the obvious? But I can't help myself.

When he doesn't answer me, I add, "What are you going to do now, then? There's nowhere to get another pair. Look around you for Christ's sake." I've slipped so easily into that controlling, motherly voice I'd adopted back at his train home. It's sort of like the tone I used to use with my sister. I doubt this is what Sandy had in mind, however, when she said before that he needed someone to take care of him.

"Drive! Straight!" Myles orders, flipping up the car's heater dial and sticking his hands right on top of the dashboard vent.

No matter how drunk our human GPS was, it turns out he actually gave us good directions. Within ten minutes, we arrive at the buildings with a huge sign saying *The Loom*. In the parking lot in front of Building C, I feel my fingers trembling as I shut off the engine. There's only a smattering of cars, mostly American-made SUVs, parked in the lot and those are all, except for one, within the lines facing the first two buildings we passed on the way in that have large A and B letters over their doors. Hayden and Penelope live in C, the last building, which overlooks the Psatonic River. A square-shaped SUV, the type you'd see on an African safari, is parked across two spaces, parallel to the building, making its own rules. I've parked right next to it.

"This doesn't make any sense," Myles says wearily. His head is back against his seat. Then they open. "Never mind. We're here now."

"Wait," I tell him as he reaches for his door handle. "We need to talk about the plan."

Myles barks with laughter. Its honest robustness startles me.

"Wow," says Sandy from the back seat. She giggles in delight. "Didn't know he had *that* in him."

"Plan?" he sputters through laughter. "We're on a crazy roller coaster now. There is no plan." With that, he gets out, slams the door shut, and shouting, "Come on!" into the blowing wind, races for the double-wide wooden entrance door, a superhero on a mission.

"'Life is what happens to you while you're busy making other plans,'" Sandy says from the seat Myles vacated, her cheek now resting on my shoulder. She sighs, lifts her head, and looks at me. "John Lennon."

Chapter Eight

Hayden Pierce knows she won't sleep at all, but she lies and tells Penelope Blackmore she'll go to bed later.

"I just want to finish going over the proof," she says.

Penelope doesn't believe her for a second. Why would she? Hayden's been a chronic insomniac since the accident. Now, with Sandy's sister and Myles sleeping in the loft below them, well...actually, who knows if they're sleeping? Maybe no one will sleep this entire night. On second thought, Penelope will. She has her Ambien, or what she calls, "My sleeping beauties."

As if to prove she's not a liar, Hayden sits down at her desk with the galley of a graphic novel written by a seventeen-year-old runaway who lives somewhere vaguely in Brooklyn. Supposedly seventeen. Supposedly a runaway, Hayden reminds herself. In an unspecified area of Brooklyn. She knows all about the hoaxes involving memoirs and novels purported to be written by young hustlers or juvies that were actually dreamed up by adults living ordinary lives in a small town in Kansas or North Dakota.

"Who cares?" Penelope had said when the manuscript arrived in the mail, unsolicited and unexpected. "As long as it makes us some money. Besides, it's good, isn't it?"

It was; Hayden should give her that. Still. Hayden can't help wondering how a runaway was able to get one of the hottest literary agents in New York to send them the novel. And why Max Feingold is so tight-lipped about his client.

"Again, who cares?" Penelope told her. "We're lucky she did, and he did."

If the author is a she, Hayden thought. Using the pen name "Q" isn't exactly gender specific. Nor is the story that enfolds in its pages. A genderless being, Visc, also the title of the book, mysteriously materializes, crawling out from the ashes and debris left after a multi-storied Manhattan apartment building burns down in a ten-alarm fire. Visc is referred to as *they*, which Hayden, as a gay woman, usually would open her arms to, but Q has insisted on using singular verbs throughout, which Hayden finds terribly confusing as she reads the manuscript.

In it, they is armed with a fire stick, which they uses to incendiary effect on their enemies, namely pimps and johns. Prostitutes are spared going up in flames only if they agree to be chaste for thirty years and join Visc's army of virginal women and men. Otherwise, they're barbecued as well. The army grows and grows, moving through city after city, deftly killing their enemies with the fire stick and leaving in their wake temples "virginized" by the followers.

It's not that Hayden doesn't think its artwork is worthy of publishing. It is. And that's all that she's paid to focus on: artwork, whether it's book covers, illustrations, or graphics. Q clearly knew how to ink each cell with stunning drawings of finely outlined people and objects that are awash in bright colors. Nor is Hayden adverse to Q's basic stealing of the myth of Vesta, the Roman virgin goddess of the hearth. Or naming Visc after the Gallic Celtic word for fire. That did, however, add to Hayden's questioning of the true identity of the author. What runaway would know Gallic, or even know about Vesta, one of the lesser-known goddesses?

"Good," Penelope told her when Hayden raised these objections after they'd skimmed together through the manuscript. "Bad publicity is awesome for sales."

This was Penelope acting the part of a vacuum saleswoman. The truth was, despite Penelope's being the daughter of a publisher and an English Lit major, she hated the classics or, god forbid, experimental fiction. She read airport potboilers. The paperbacks you start on a plane and then stay up all night reading, only to leave them behind in the hotel room. She'd never be a publisher who would someday be viewed as adding to the canon. Never be someone that pushed the envelope but didn't tear it to shreds. Hayden bristled at the bad taste of oily commercialism it left in her mouth. It was yet another instance when she wondered how she was going to continue living in this unbearable situation she'd put herself in. She detests everything Penelope stands for. She suspects she doesn't even care at all for Penelope anymore.

She isn't thinking now, however, of Visc or of their new publishing imprint, despite her staring at the proof on her desk. She's listening for the slightest sound coming from below. She knows this is ridiculous. Each of the three levels in Building C is buffered between the floors and in the walls with thick sound-proofing akin to a bomb shelter or a

CIA interrogation cell. They can't even hear the Psatonic—what the locals call "the Pisser"—rumbling and gushing over its waterfall right below their loft as it crashes on its way to the Hudson. Hayden is thankful for that, at least. After Sandy drowned, any sounds of water, as much as a dripping faucet, can sink Hayden for days into what she calls in her head *the bog*. Once, Penelope made the mistake of buying a machine that played supposedly calming sounds: a rainforest, crashing waves, a waterfall.

"Are you trying to get me committed?" Hayden had asked her, half-jokingly.

The loft below them, where Myles and Sandy's sister are staying, is only one third of the space on that level, tucked in a corner that isn't actually below where Hayden is sitting. Most of Level 2 houses their mailing supplies along with a couple of huge digital printing presses, bought cheap, courtesy of Penelope's father, from an Albany print shop chain that he'd heard was headed toward bankruptcy. Level 1 is a warehouse to store the books once they are up and running. They've already hired some of the Albany chain's staff, moving them lock, stock, and ink into Buildings A and B at *The Loom*.

The publishing imprint was Penelope's idea, of course. The name itself rankled Hayden. Pen & Hay. *I'm forty-five, for god's sake*, Hayden thought. Not a hipster as the name suggests she should be. She'd scoffed when Penelope suggested it.

"What...like all those online shops that use tools or farm animals in their titles?" Hayden told her. "The Hammer and Lamb? The Anvil and Mule? Fine purveyors of the authentic and the artisan. Meanwhile they use words such as 'bespoke' and they sell hockey puck cheese with inedible foraged leaves and one-inch-thick mold and names that you forget as soon as you throw the wrapper out."

Hayden abhors how a new breed of online store owner has replaced the brick-and-mortar stores that made no pretense that they were in business for anything other than to make money. Now, they all pretend to harken back to a simpler, "organic" time. Lookalikes for general store owners during the Gold Rush, with the males sporting buzz cuts and Amish beards and the young women, with their blond plaited hair and sundresses of blue gingham, basking in rays of sunlight in meadows or by beautiful barns, while they were actually raised in homes with Xbox and Beamers and square footage double this warehouse floor. It was true that Hayden, herself, dressed in retro clothes when she was in her twenties. However, that was more because she was poor and the bins at Goodwill provided her wardrobe. Not out of some pretense that she was something she wasn't.

What truly stuck in Hayden's craw about their company name wasn't just the hipster feel of it. It angered her that Penelope wanted to use Pen, the pet name that Hayden had briefly used for her during the initial weeks after the fatal trip on *Stillwater*. "You're the only one who's ever called me that, you know," Penelope had said then. "It's ours and only ours," she'd added.

Hayden had been surprised herself the first time she'd called Penelope by it. Pet names are endearments, signs of intimacy. Yet, they hadn't really known each other when they went on board *Stillwater*. Hayden had seen her at a few publishing parties that Sandy took her to. But she hadn't spoken to her directly other than Sandy introducing them the first time Hayden went to one of *Freedom*'s parties. That, along with the stories Sandy brought home from the office, was what she knew of Penelope. Penelope was a spoiled rich kid handed a plum job in her father's publishing company. A flirt, a tease. Penelope was not to be trusted. It was, therefore, puzzling that they did become friends when Hayden returned to Brooklyn after leaving Cape Cod Hospital alone, grieving, and with ten stitches over her eye.

Penelope initiated everything. A few days after Hayden was back in the city, Penelope unexpectedly called to ask if she could see her. Hayden was still in her pajamas. It was four o'clock in the afternoon. She had yet to leave her studio all week, preferring to open crisp packets of Saltines and warm up cans of soup which she'd end up not eating. She hadn't showered since she'd returned. Mostly, she'd been staying in bed or sitting at a table, sifting through photographs that she'd shot of Sandy during their decades together.

"I have something for you," Penelope purred over the phone when Hayden tried to put her off. "I can easily drop it by. You'll like it, trust me." When Hayden asked her what it was, Penelope said teasingly, "You'll have to wait and see." Immediately, Hayden was tantalized about what the "something" was. Could it be one of Sandy's belongings she'd left in the office? Hayden had hoped to retrieve some— *any*—of Sandy's furniture or books. But that had become impossible when, returning straight from the hospital to Sandy's—what had once been *their*—old flat in Brooklyn, she found that the locks had been changed in the few days she'd been away. She phoned Sandy's sister on her cell straight away, still standing on the brownstone's steps.

"Do you really think you're getting anything?" Tibbie said, shocking her, daring her to answer. "I didn't think so," she continued on. "And before you ask, no, there isn't going to be a funeral or a memorial. Don't call me again." Then, she hung up on Hayden.

Hoping, then, that perhaps she'd get at least one of Sandy's possessions, Hayden gave Penelope her address over the phone.

What the "something" turned out to be was a book.

"It's a first edition. Eighteen eighty-nine," Penelope told her as Hayden read the title. *Birds Through an Opera Glass* by Florence A. Merriam. Hayden didn't remember Sandy ever talking about this book or suggesting that she owned a first edition of it.

"Um..." she said quietly as she rifled through the pages of text. There were only a few black-and-white inked bird illustrations spotted throughout. Hayden was confused. Why would Sandy have owned such a book? She liked birds well enough, but she wasn't as obsessed with them as Hayden was.

"She was one of the first female backyard ornithologists. Don't you like it?" Penelope didn't exactly say it aggressively, more like she was stunned that Hayden didn't.

"It's...great...thank you." Hayden finally looked up at her. "It's just that Sandy never mentioned this book. Did she tell you I photographed birds?"

"Oh, it's not Sandy's. I bought it for you. And no, she didn't tell me. Don't you remember? *You* told me. On the boat, well...you know..."

Now Hayden was really confused. Why had Penelope bought her anything?

"Anyhoo..." Penelope said, and the cutesy word seemed to simultaneously infantilize and middle-age her. She looked around the room. Hayden worried that she'd somehow embarrassed her, but before she could offer something nice about the book, Penelope was making a beeline for the table where several enlarged black-and-white photographs of Sandy were strewn about. She proceeded to pick up one, look at it, and then softly, almost reverently, placing it down again, lifted another. "She was so beautiful, wasn't she," Penelope murmured. It was more of a statement than a question. When Hayden didn't—couldn't—answer because she was suddenly choked up, Penelope added, "Nothing is the same, is it?"

It was that one declaration—"Nothing is the same, is it?"—that led Hayden to believe that she might've misjudged Penelope. That perhaps Penelope was one of the few people who could appreciate and understand how difficult life was now. They were, after all, both survivors of the same tragedy. And tragedies could bring together people who in ordinary circumstances would have nothing to do with each other.

In the days that followed, Hayden realized that they also had Sandy in common. Penelope and Sandy had worked together for years. Who better than her to sympathize, maybe even to empathize with Hayden's grief, her overwhelming sense of loss? Couldn't shared grief make instantaneous friendships, marriages even, between people? Hadn't she read stories of surviving victims of airplane crashes ending up together? Absolute strangers when they boarded the plane, newlyweds two months later. The trick was to figure out if the shared grief was only temporarily shrouding the underlying personality differences that would eventually bubble up, or if it truly was a fated catalyst that bound two complimentary souls together. During those first weeks, Hayden was struck by how considerate Penelope actually could be: phoning every day to make sure Hayden was out of bed, gently reminding her that getting in the shower was half the battle, or bringing over takeout from Dum Dum, Hayden's favorite dumpling restaurant. One Saturday, Penelope showed up with a new Leica M10, a camera that Hayden had coveted for a year but couldn't bring herself to buy given how many cameras she already owned. When Hayden raised an objection, Penelope lightly grabbed her wrist and told her, "Look, right now you and I both need to do anything that makes us happy after what we've been through. Besides, it's time for you to get back into the big, bad world." She said it so tenderly that Hayden found herself hugging Penelope. They ended up walking to Prospect Park and then up and down random streets, Hayden snapping photos for the first time since the accident and with anyone other than Sandy.

Still, when Penelope announced one month after the accident that she needed a change of scenery, a place where she could leave the accident behind and start her own publishing company, and she asked Hayden to be her partner on the visual art side of things, Hayden hesitated.

"Like move in together?" They were having brunch at a café around the corner from Hayden's studio apartment. During those days, Penelope always insisted that they eat only at Hayden's most loved restaurants. Places she felt safe in. Hayden put down the bite of croque madame she was about to eat.

Penelope sipped her orange juice. She lowered the glass. "As partners." When she saw Hayden's startled expression, she hastily added, "Business partners. And roommates." Then she laughed. "Not that I wouldn't consider something more."

For a moment, Hayden felt queasy. This was uncharted territory. There hadn't been the slightest sign from Penelope that she wanted anything more than a friendship. Was she testing the waters? Hayden thought of Sandy then. How the both of them made fun of clichés. And she remembered how Sandy called Penelope an outrageous flirt. She'd even tried to kiss Sandy on the boat. What did that mean? Then, from out of nowhere, a thought tumbled into Hayden's head, startling her. *Say yes.*

"I don't understand," Hayden said, stalling. "Why don't you just do it yourself?"

Penelope smiled warmly. Hayden could see then why so many people might be attracted to her on the surface. She had the appearance of someone that truly cared not just about what she wanted, but also that you approved of it, or, better yet, joined in the fun.

"Well…" Penelope said. "For one thing, I want to get out of here, but I want to at least have one person I know…I *trust*." She paused. "You must think I've got a million friends, but I don't." Hayden didn't think that at all. In fact, she'd often wondered in the last month if Penelope had *any* other friends because her life seemed to revolve around Hayden. She further wondered if the accident had forced Penelope to change in that regard, to reconsider how she'd been living her life.

But Penelope was prattling on. "Okay, honestly, I need someone who can handle all the art direction. I took like one class in college about that. You also know the publishing world…" Here she faltered briefly. "At least through…" It was obvious to Hayden that Penelope was groping for some other word rather than referring to Sandy by name. "…Osmosis," Penelope finally settled on. She sighed as if she was either tired of trying to convince Hayden or was losing interest in it. "Well, what do you say? Don't you want to start over again?"

Maybe it was the idea of doing just that, or maybe it was simply that by then Hayden felt so worn out by her grief and loneliness that she wanted someone else, someone stronger, to decide what she should do next. It would be so much easier. After all, the last major decisions she'd made had ended in disaster, hadn't they? Still, she hesitated again. She looked down at the floor. Under the next table, on the beige linoleum, there was an obvious line where whoever had mopped the floor had stopped abruptly by the iron feet of the table. On one side of the line was clean flooring, on the other, the iron feet surrounded by dust and dirt. It was so easy to cross the line into murkiness. Something snagged at Hayden. Was Penelope really making this decision for her, or was Hayden herself choosing yet again the wrong thing?

Then, there was that voice telling her again, *Say yes.*

And Hayden found herself nodding her head.

"Yes?" Penelope said, smiling more broadly.

"Yes."

Penelope immediately flagged down the waitress and ordered mimosas for the both of them. "I knew this OJ needed perking up." She winked at the waitress as she lifted the delivered drink and clinked Hayden's glass. "To our adventure!" she gleefully toasted.

Now, only two months later, Hayden knows she had been lying to herself that day. Yes, it was true, she needed to leave Brooklyn with its memories of Sandy, but the subconscious bedrock of why she moved with Penelope to Skyville, she's come to realize, was to ultimately keep Penelope close. That's become apparent the longer they've lived together, especially as the grievous cloud, *the bog* dulling Hayden's perceptions, has begun to lift. The weak veneer of their bonding has been scraped away to unveil the fraud it is. Penelope's monthlong sweetness is slowly being eroded by the resurrection of her self-centeredness and the desire to control everything. Sandy had been right when one night she'd suggested to Hayden, "The only thing that drives Penelope is the thrill of the hunt. Once she's tackled her prey, she's bored. She's that awful person at a banquet who loads up her plate, sits down at a table, eyes the heap of food with disgust, and then doesn't eat a bite of it."

With every passing day, Penelope's previous claim that the two of them had embarked on an adventure withers away under her increasing frustration that the daily act of publishing books is actually quite mundane: printing presses must be adjusted and oiled, digital computer programs de-bugged, boxes and labels ordered. Hours must be spent on the phone with agents advocating that theirs is *the* next bestseller, as well as with weary independent bookstore owners.

But Hayden has a bigger problem to contend with than Penelope's narcissism or waning business interest. She must make sure Penelope doesn't suspect her own growing ulterior motive for living together. The voice that ordered Hayden to *say yes* has reappeared lately, demanding something else altogether: *You must find out what actually happened on that boat that ended with Sandy, the strongest swimmer of us all, being drowned.* In the first twenty-four hours that followed the accident, when Hayden was recovering in Cape Cod Hospital, she'd been almost destroyed by guilt. She'd locked Sandy into the cabin they were to share when Sandy had gone to bed early that night. Sandy had been feeling ill. Hayden thought it was the best thing to do. Sandy could also unlock the door from the inside, but it kept anyone else, specifically Luke, from getting into the room while Sandy slept. That was the important thing: to protect Sandy. But what if it hadn't? What if it had put Sandy at risk? Had led to her death? These horrible questions beat and clawed at her, keeping her awake much of that first hospital night despite the sleeping pill the nurse insisted that she swallow.

So, now she must find out what *really* happened. And with that, she has started to question whether Penelope was complicit along with her father in Sandy's death. *It's only a matter of time,* the voice assures her. *The how is why you're here.*

Hayden had tried before to ask Penelope what she remembered of the accident. About a week into the friendship, they were sitting on Hayden's couch and Penelope was cajoling her to eat some of the takeout she'd brought from Dum Dum.

"So, the accident?" Hayden said vaguely as she played with her box of chicken dumplings. She was trying to say it as offhand as she could, but she felt that she was going to throw up.

Penelope's hand poised mid-air as she was

raising a fried spring roll to her mouth. "What do you mean?"

Hayden knew Penelope knew what she meant, but she said more directly, "What do you remember?" Hayden forced herself to take a bite of a dumpling. They tasted good but the dough seemed thicker than usual. She stuck her chopsticks in the white container and slid it back onto the coffee table.

Penelope laughed nervously. "The same thing you do, I expect." She tossed her roll back into its takeout box. "Look. I really don't want to talk about it. Does it seem like this order is unusually greasy or something? I'm going to call them and tell them they have to send us another order." Then, she jumped up to do so.

Hayden doesn't want to harm or even hurt Penelope to get the answers. Penelope is like a prickly teenager, unmoored by whatever self-serving emotion strikes her, without any thought of the consequences. The fact is she had been so kind when Hayden needed it most. Hayden hasn't forgotten that. Yet, she has also begun to grasp that the kindheartedness may have been a strategy or pretense on Penelope's part to see if she could actually manipulate Hayden to give up everything for her. Are her initial benevolent acts then sullied or negated because of that? In a way, Hayden feels sorry for her, not angry. Hayden needed a major change to repair her life, to lift her out of *the bog*, and she wasn't capable of doing that on her own. Penelope gave her that, at least. Hayden got something out of it, whereas Penelope has ended up once again disappointed. Ultimately, Penelope has been left craving her next adventure or conquest. Nonetheless, Hayden realizes that something bigger is at stake now. Bigger than Penelope's adventures. Bigger than herself.

Hayden glances around her loft. It's not truly hers, nor is it technically a loft because it has two enclosed enormous bedrooms on opposite ends of the space, each with its own huge bathroom. Penelope's master bedroom has floor-to-ceiling windows that look out over the Pisser; Hayden's bedroom is an interior room with no windows. The rest of the level's fifteen thousand square feet is wide open. There's a living room area with two L-shaped, snowy-white couches, edging a custom red-and-black rug that sometimes reminds Hayden of a murder scene and on other days an abstract spatter painting you'd see in the Museum of Modern Art. The living room also has matching midcentury, honey-colored maple coffee and end tables, and feeds into a dining area where there is a very long, bleached Danish table and white plastic chairs, which Hayden finds are torture to sit in past thirty minutes. The open kitchen has pickled cabinets, a restaurant-sized chef stove, matching stainless steel refrigerator and separate deep freezer and wine cooler, and a long granite island around which five metal chairs are arranged.

The whole thing is too modern and pristine for Hayden's taste. Sandy once remarked about Penelope to Hayden, "If there's a controlling personality disorder gene, that girl has it in spades." Whenever Sandy related another Penelope meltdown story from the *Freedom Press* office, she'd call her "CPD girl." Sometimes it's hard for Hayden to breathe when she sits on one of the white couches. She certainly never eats in the living room; she's too afraid she'd spill something.

The only part of the loft that Hayden is attached

to is the corner where she's sitting now, the main place where *her* things are: her "study," with its dusty green glass banker's lamp on her roll-top desk, her librarian chair, and a couple of very worn leather chairs that she bought dirt cheap at an estate sale on the Upper East Side. All of it was transported from the studio she'd moved into temporarily in the two months before the accident. A moth-eaten, faded Oriental rug lies on the floor, adding to the whole straight-out-of-bohemia feel.

And now Isabel is one floor below her. Somehow, her pet name, Tibbie, has always seemed too juvenile to Hayden, especially now when she's grown up. As much as Hayden doesn't think Tibbie fits her, she should probably call her that, although she's always called her Isabel. Yet, every time she did, Hayden noticed that she gave her a strange look, which Hayden wasn't sure was from irritation or surprise. Their visit here will be hard enough without Hayden making her even more uncomfortable. But somehow, Hayden can't see her actually forming the pet name in her mouth and saying it aloud. Maybe that name belonged exclusively to Sandy, for her use only.

Hayden hasn't seen Isabel in years. Of course, there's still the startling resemblance to Sandy, but that had always been there. Hayden remembers Sandy bringing her home from college for a weekend to meet Isabel and their mother...what were they? Freshmen? Eighteen? And there was Isabel, all of sixteen, and yet they almost looked like twins. They had the same twins' habit also of finishing each other's sentences despite their being two years apart. Isabel, however, was a bit more hellbent on the straight and narrow. Rules. She didn't have Sandy's imaginative streak. Her joie de vivre. It wasn't really recklessness on Sandy's part. More like a willingness to let go. Yet, they looked so alike that it surprised you when they came across as such polar opposites in some ways.

When Isabel wouldn't let her have any of Sandy's things, Hayden thought that she might be angry that Hayden had survived and her sister hadn't. Wasn't anger the first stage of grieving? Now she wonders if there was more to it than that. Maybe she thought that Hayden had something to do with it. Maybe she was angry that Hayden had moved out on Sandy months before. Hayden felt as if Sandy had been killed twice: once on that boat and then again when everything material that had embodied Sandy's presence, her life, became unavailable and untouchable, vanishing as completely as Sandy had. Before Hayden had even recovered in the hospital, Tibbie had retrieved Sandy's body, leaving Hayden with nothing concretely physical to mourn. In only one way was that palatable: at least now she wouldn't remember Sandy as she looked on a morgue's cold gurney or at a funeral home. All of her imaginings of Sandy were alive. But in other ways it meant she could never fully accept that Sandy was gone. Without the physical evidence, bodily or furniture-wise, it was doubly hard for Hayden to believe she was really gone.

There's no place in the loft to put any of Sandy's things anyway, Hayden sometimes consoles herself. Her own art and graphic design books take up most of the loft study's space. At last count they numbered close to fifteen hundred. The study's bookshelves are old, but came with the purchase of *The Loom*, leftovers from the mill days. They're two wooden planks deep, wide enough to have stored the handcrafted woven blankets and ponchos. Hayden uses the extra depth for her large artist and art history books. Over twenty-feet tall, the bookshelves form a wall that partially blocks off the living and dining areas. Even so, there are ever-growing towers of books and exhibition catalogues and monographs piled against the floor-to-ceiling windows and leaning against her desk. Lately, Penelope has been making snippy remarks about one day the view being blocked entirely and how they'll be showcased on a hoarder TV show.

"Is it my study, or not?" Hayden finally asked her one day after Penelope had again muttered something about hoarding being a condition that is controllable. They were in the kitchen. Penelope was measuring and then cutting up exactly one-inch carrots for a salad. Hayden had meant her question about the study being hers rhetorically, to stake her claim at least in that corner of the loft.

Without looking up from the carrots, Penelope answered, "Actually not. But if you say, 'pretty please,' it might be yours."

Immediately, Hayden remembered the last words Sandy had ever said to her before the boat had been torpedoed by the whale. That was how her memories were triggered: by a word or an object, sometimes directly related, other times not. She'd gone below with Sandy to the galley, their hands full of dirty dishes from dinner, which they'd all eaten at the upper deck's teak table. The others had remained in their chairs. Sandy and Hayden heard Myles's muffled voice whining that they should return to the dock. He'd read on his phone's weather app that a storm was coming. Luke and Penelope were telling him loudly to relax, that undoubtedly the app was delayed due to poor cell service. Besides, wasn't the whole point of the trip to spend the entire weekend on the boat? It was only Friday, their first and what turned out to be their last night together.

"Just look at that sky, old bean," Luke had told him.

"Isn't this exciting?" Penelope added.

Below deck, Sandy began to scrape at the plates despite the lobster shells and corncob carcasses sliding easily into the trash.

"Are you okay?" Hayden asked. She rinsed off forks before sliding them into the small dishwasher corral.

"I can't wait to get off this boat," Sandy told her, running a knife roughshod over the plate in her hand.

Hayden touched Sandy's wrist with her wet hand, stopping the frenzied motion. "What's wrong?" she whispered and checked the stairs for any sign of movement.

Sandy righted herself, the knife and plate still in her hands. She leaned back against the counter. "I just don't feel so good all of a sudden. Like I'm coming down with the flu or something." She touched her forehead with the back of her hand that was holding the knife. "God, I think I have a fever. And did you see Penelope?"

"What about her?"

Sandy shook her head, like she was trying to clear it. "I was lying down up front, she came along and tried to kiss me. Like father, like daughter, I guess. I tried to pass it off as one big joke, but then she tells me I have to say, 'pretty please' to get her to stop..." Sandy paused suddenly. She put her index finger to her mouth. All they could hear was Luke pontificating about how he had his first boat when he was ten years old, which had to be a lie since he grew up in Queens. Sandy tiptoed closer to the stairs and looked up. Then, she came back. Bending over, she popped the knife into the dishwasher.

"Is the boat rocking more?" She felt her forehead again. "I feel dizzy or something. Myles pushed me. He didn't mean it. But I slipped and hit my head." She shook her head as if clearing it again.

"When?" Hayden felt she couldn't keep up. Where had she been when all this was happening? "Myles pushed you?"

"It's fine. He didn't mean it. Can you get me a glass of water?" she asked, gingerly touching the back of her head. "Honest. It doesn't hurt. I think I'm coming down with something."

Hayden lifted a glass from the cupboard over the boat's small sink. She filled it from a bottle of the Italian water that Luke kept on hand. Sandy bolted the entire glass. She rubbed her mouth and motioned for another one. She gulped the second one down too. "I'm so thirsty." She glanced over to the steps again. Leaning closer to Hayden, she spoke low into her ear. "Anyway, then Penelope says, 'Maybe I should tell him you only like girls.' She meant Daddy Warbucks."

Hayden was horrified for her. Although she'd worked for *Freedom Press* for over ten years, Sandy wasn't officially out to her employer. "He'd only see it as a challenge," Sandy had argued after she first was hired. "He'd just say I hadn't met the right man yet." As it was, Sandy would eventually tell Hayden about several instances of Luke standing too close to her or Luke making suggestive remarks. Consequently, she'd only introduce Hayden at *Freedom Press* parties as her oldest friend from college, neglecting to add that they were living together or anything else. Truthfully, Hayden had been glad. She hadn't wanted to deal with Luke cornering her at some get-together, slurping his drink and lewdly joking about some repellant idea of a threesome.

Before Hayden could say anything in the galley to console Sandy about Penelope's threat, to tell her how ironic it was given they'd been separated for the last two months, Penelope came skipping down the steps with a weird smile on her face.

"And what are you two up to?"

Sandy held up the plate, not answering her, and then they continued to do the dishes, ignoring her, until she finally got the hint and went back upstairs. Afterward, Sandy, still feeling ill, went to bed and Hayden went back on deck. Then the storm came, and the boat was struck.

Now, in the loft, Hayden vacillates between being sure it was the right decision to sign on for it all—Pen & Hay, Penelope, their living situation—and hating everything. When she'd been living in Brooklyn all she'd wanted was to live in her studio apartment, do her freelance design projects, and walk around for hours photographing birds on Brooklyn streets who'd mistaken a sunlit window or glass door for a portal into another world and crashed to their deaths. She was discerning in which ones she picked for her subjects, seeking the ones that showed no outward signs of trauma: no blood, no crushed beaks. She especially liked when she captured one with its mouth still slightly open, as if its last breath hadn't yet come, the luster of its eyes fading but not wholly gone. Only Sandy had understood that she'd been trying to capture life, not death.

After Hayden's moving out from their apartment, Sandy and she had forged ahead, forever connected. Was that true? Hayden questions that these days. Honestly, she can't remember what she felt during that time period. Everything she felt not living with Sandy was altered right after she died. Erased, really. How many euphemisms are there for that? *Wiped the slate clean*, of course. Cliché though it is, she actually likes that one. The physical motion of it. There's also *let bygones be bygones*. She misses Sandy again for the umpteenth time today. Sandy would reel off ten of them in the time it took Hayden to utter one. They'd end up doubled over with laughter at the sheer stupidity of them.

Is this what her life will be forever more? Filled with the missing? She feels one of her many moments of doubt. Maybe Penelope isn't fooled at all. Maybe she'll never drop her guard and tell Hayden what she knows about the accident. Maybe all this has been for nothing.

Hayden closes the mock-up cover of *Visc*. There's no sense pretending. Penelope won't come out here and find her dithering anyway. Not after she took her "sleeping beauties" on top of the beers they drank with Isabel and Myles.

It was strange seeing Isabel's blond hair gone now, masked in the jet-black-and-blue streaks of a superhero. Isabel apparently had been doing some slate cleaning too. And that tattoo on her neck. Hayden wonders when she got that.

Hayden admits she doesn't look anything like she used to either before Sandy's death. Her once long and loose auburn up-do has been replaced by an almost shorn head a la Sinead O'Connor during the eighties. Her "Nothing Compares 2 U" years. The new hairdo fails to conceal the still pink foregathered scar above her left eyebrow. Her prior Victorian-like male clothes were boxed up and shoved into the back of her bedroom closet. Now, it's easier to wear all black every day. Less energy is needed in the mornings. Less planning. Getting herself out of bed is enough. Getting herself to spend another minute without Sandy, with Penelope, is killing her.

From the look of it, Myles is struggling too, Hayden thinks. How the hell did they hook up? Hayden isn't buying for a minute Isabel's explanation that out of curiosity she'd looked him up when she was visiting Provincetown. In the years they'd been together, Hayden and Sandy had regularly visited the seaside town during the summer months. Who visits there in the dead of winter? Well, maybe if you're gay and wanting to bring in the new year at a club on the ocean and end up in an hourly rent-a-room with a stranger. But Isabel wasn't gay, was she? And Myles certainly wasn't. Why was he living *there*?

Hayden can't make sense of any of it. She misses Sandy again. Sandy would straighten it all out. She'd be able to think outside of the box. What Sandy called "divergent thinking." Whatever you'd call it, Hayden's head throbs from it all.

There had been a moment, earlier in the evening, when she thought Penelope would rescind her reluctant offer to let them stay overnight. Penelope barely hid her irritation when Isabel complained, "We had no idea there were no hotels here. Don't worry, we'll figure it out, won't we, Myles? We can always sleep in the car." It was so ridiculous that Penelope had to offer the empty loft downstairs. Then, right before they were about to go to bed, Myles carried into the kitchen area the empty box from the pizza that Hayden had phoned in for delivery. Not that Hayden could eat a bite after the shock of finding Isabel and Myles at their door. Isabel, on the other hand, had almost wolfed down the whole pie by herself. Hayden and Penelope followed Myles into the kitchen with the empty beer bottles. They were putting them on the counter when Isabel, leaning against the refrigerator, said nonchalantly, "Thanks so much, Penny. For letting us stay, I mean."

Hayden almost laughed out loud. A heavy silence thudded in the loft. Hayden caught Myles and Penelope stiffening. Penelope hated when anyone called her Penny.

Before Penelope could open her mouth to correct her, Isabel quickly added, "Oh, sorry. You don't like to be called that, do you? Your face." She pointed at Penelope's nose. "Wow. Sorry." Isabel chuckled. Not giggled or laughed. It was so false everyone in the kitchen heard it.

"You know," Isabel went on, undaunted. "We grew up with someone named Penny Nickel. Did Sandy ever tell you that? Stupid, right?" Here, Isabel stuck her tongue out of the corner of her mouth, crossed her eyes, and rotated her index finger in a circle by her ear. Hayden could tell from the baffled faces that no one, including Penelope, knew if Isabel was referring to herself, the girl's parents, or Penelope's name.

"Come on, Myles. We should let them get to bed," Isabel said abruptly, as if they were a married couple. Turning, she headed toward the front door of the loft. Hayden felt Penelope bristle next to her by the sink. It took everything in her not to smile. Obviously, Penelope didn't like that Isabel had suddenly become the one running the show. Showing up unannounced on their doorstep was bad enough. Isabel's ordering around Myles, whom she'd only met the day before, her "we" implying a deeper connection, had rankled Penelope.

"So tomorrow? We really want to ask you a few questions, okay? About what happened," Isabel tossed over her shoulder. Without waiting for an answer, she opened the door and walked out, with Myles trailing her.

At her desk, Hayden is suddenly glad they've come. Overjoyed that Isabel is this tower of power. This shit-kicking, tat-sporting, conniving badass. *Now it begins*, Hayden thinks. *Now we'll find out everything. What Penelope is hiding. And we can all go home and stop this charade.*

Standing, she switches off her desk lamp and pads silently down the hall to her bedroom. Hayden can't see a thing, but she doesn't need to turn on any lights to find her way. An interior bedroom, there isn't a hint of light from a window. There's a bookcase filled with more art books, a bureau with her clothes as well as a few T-shirts and some pants she still had mixed in with her clothes from living with Sandy, a double bed that she crawls into, and the nighttime darkness that obliterates everything and brings her relief. Hayden sighs, relaxing, as she bunches up the feather pillow under her cheek and breathes in the leftover smell of her shower lingering on the cotton pillowcase. Herbal Essences, Sandy's shampoo, the only thing that gets Hayden into the shower every morning. Her breathing slows and gradually, surprisingly, she falls asleep.

Chapter Nine

For the first time since I left Boston, I miss home. I should be ecstatic that I'm really doing this. I'm going to find out what really happened. Even the accommodations have changed for the better, from sleeping in Myles's human-trafficking-like container to this house porn loft, which quite possibly was a center spread in *Architectural Digest*. I should be grateful. Instead, I feel I'm on one of those reality shows that mess with people by switching their homes. A pig farmer swaps with the owner of a Malibu beach house. A longtime Wall Streeter trades his Upper East Side townhouse with an Amish carpenter from Lancaster County, Pennsylvania. See how you like barn raisin', Mr. One-Percenter. That sort of thing. It never works out as expected. Will this?

I'm already well on my way in this travelogue of revenge. I should be happy, shouldn't I? I'm not. I miss Sandy. She's disappeared ever since we entered through the front door of Building C. *Poof.* Gone. She'd done that several times already, but before it was a "Later, gator" type of disappearance. Tonight, lying in this queen-sized bed with its soft linen sheets and smooshy duvet and its cushiony, tufted grey headboard, her absence has more of a solid "goodbye" feeling. *You're overtired*, I think. *Get some sleep and she'll be back.*

Sandy always did show up when I least expected it. There was the time I won the spelling bee award in sixth grade and somehow, miraculously, she skipped out of her eighth-grade class two blocks away at the middle school and was standing in the back of my auditorium clapping and yelling louder than anyone else as the principal called me up to the stage. Or that Saturday lunch when I was waitressing at The Homeport and a bunch of our high school's football players were harassing me, smack talking about how I was the only sixteen-year-old virgin they knew, and they'd be happy to help me out with what one of them called "my handicap." Sandy was supposed to be taking the day off from the restaurant to study for her final exams. I didn't even hear or see her come in.

"I think you're done," I heard her voice say. She stepped out from behind me with a busing bin resting on her hip as if she'd been working the whole shift. Then she started to throw into the bin their plates of barely eaten cheeseburgers and fries, their full dishes of macaroni and cheese, and glasses of still fizzing Coke. They were so surprised it took them a moment to recover. Sandy made use of the delay by sweeping through the rest of the table.

One of them stuck out his hand fast and grabbed her wrist. "But we're not finished," he whined in a five-year-old's voice, not a seventeen's.

My sister beamed her coldest smile around the table. She shook her hand free. They were all junior varsity players. Not that it would've made an ounce of difference to her if they were senior varsity stars or played for the New England Patriots.

"I'm doing you a favor," she told them.

"I don't think so, babe," said the ringleader,

Tom Foley. He was the JV quarterback, a junior and a year older than me. I called him Fuck-up Foley in my head, which always made me feel better. He was the most intercepted QB in the region, he couldn't hit the side of a barn for shit, but he kept his coveted position because he was the nephew of the JV coach.

Again, Sandy smiled, but this time she focused its iciness on him alone. "Well, I..." Here she shook her head a little. "Well, okay, have it your way." Then, she held up her cell phone, touched the screen, and played back what I realized was a recording of Fuck-up Foley bragging how they would each have their way with me to put me out of my "tight-assed misery." The rest of them could be heard urging him on. "I got dibs on second place," one of them had said.

"Hey!" Fuck-up Foley sputtered. "That's illegal. You can't do that."

Another boy jumped in, weakly explaining that they were only kidding around. That boy, the team's wimpy field goal kicker who'd actually fainted in the biology class we had together during the frog dissection unit, looked at me for confirmation. I stared back at him, saying nothing. The truth is I was trembling so wildly by then that I was afraid I'd either start crying or laughing hysterically, I was so nervous. One of the others screeched his seat back in a hurry and said, "I'm outta here." The boy next to him did the same.

"That's the first sensible thing any of you has said," my sister replied coolly. She slid the busing bin on the table next to Foley. For a second, I thought— and I think Foley did too—that she was going to finish clearing the table and that would be the end of it. Then she reached over and before Foley could stop her grabbed his chin and stuck her face up to his. To any of the other customers who were sitting at the counter it might've looked like they were a couple joking around, and she was about to kiss him goodbye. Foley might've even thought that too. But only for a moment. She squeezed harder. His lips were forced into a pucker. His eyes widened. She was, after all, a senior, and one of the most beautiful ones at that.

"You ever bother her anywhere again, you little twerp," she hissed in his face, "and I'll be playing this tape at the police station and for Houser." Houser was the high school principal. Then, she dropped her hand, quickly lifted the bin, and told me to help her in the kitchen and for the rest of them to get out. She strode away, with me trailing behind her.

"Come back," I whisper now in the loft's darkness. "Please. I can't do this without you."

I can hear Myles's soft snoring coming from the pullout couch in the living room that oddly reminded me of the Venus di Milo: expensive, Italian, and armless. There are also two deep chairs covered in green velvet out there, a bathroom of grey tile and a walk-in shower big enough for Fuck-up Foley and his mates, and a kitchen that, although smaller than Penelope and Hayden's upstairs, is nevertheless state of the art. The length of the floor-to-ceiling factory windows is covered with mechanized blinds that go down and up with a flick of a button, padding the entire loft in darkness.

To get here, we'd first had to walk through the largest part of Level 2, which, when we came out of the elevator and turned on the lights, we could see was basically the printing department. Penelope told us all about Pen & Hay as I, ravenous from not eating all day, ate pizza that was cold by the time it was delivered. I tried to catch Myles's eye when Penelope told us the company name, hoping to see some kind of sign that his infatuation with Penelope was alive and kicking. Something I could use against him, or against Penelope. Instead, there was nothing. He barely acknowledged what she was saying, concentrating instead on the leftover slices still in the flat box as if willing himself to stir up his drug-dead appetite.

Now, as I lie in a cushy queen bed, there's a wall of cloudy glass between me and Myles. On my side of the glass there's also a midcentury bureau that has nothing on top or inside—I silently scoped out the drawers as if I were a cop searching the apartment of an arrested felon. Two lamps made of intricately ruffled paper are on either side of the bed, like two ballerina sentries, on matching midcentury night tables. As the night slogs on and I toss from side to side, the lamps alternate between feeling like fairy godmothers and prison guards. Myles has it worse: he's on the pullout in the living room, which appears to be one of those Italian couches that looks good and has all the comfort of a cement sidewalk.

You'd think that being in a place devoted to publishing there'd be at least one discarded and dog-eared paperback floating around on the night tables or the bureau—one of Ann Patchett's novels, or Sylvia Plath's *The Bell Jar*...Christ, even a James Patterson— but there are none. I'd give anything to fall asleep. I'd hoped the beers combined with the cache of sleepless nights would do the trick. Instead, it seems the alcohol has increased my agitation tenfold.

"Too bad you didn't make a visit to the sleeping beauty stockpile." Sandy's voice comes through the darkness. I've no idea what she's talking about. I can barely make her out either. There's a dim night-light hanging around her neck that gets brighter the more I focus on her. She's sitting on top of the bureau, her feet bare and her legs crossed, in the clothes that I recognize as what Hayden had been wearing earlier in the evening: black peg-legged jeans and a black hoodie. I'd believe that Sandy's blond hair has almost an aura, if I believed in such things.

"Where've you been?" I whisper.

Before I can even finish saying it, she's talking over me. "The family in 2-C in Building B won't last a month. Their two brats are running up and down the outside hallway screaming bloody murder that they want to go home, like they're in a lunatic asylum. It was just starting to get good when you called me. The guy in 2-B showed up with the hose from a vacuum cleaner in his hands like he was going to strangle them with it." She laughs softly. She holds up an arm, plucks something invisible off the hoodie's sleeve, and lets whatever it is drop to the floor, watching it the whole way. "Don't worry. I always get them back before she wakes up."

"What?"

She gazes at me. "Her clothes, silly. I hear your thoughts."

"What!"

She laughs. "No, you're not crazy. And no, it's not all the time." She runs her hand through her blond hair, which looks thicker than when she was in the car with me. "It comes and goes," she says thoughtfully. "At first I thought I was in control of it. But, I think it might be up to you. I wanted to see those two brats get their comeuppance and yet...here I am. You can't be moving around either."

She motions toward the bed. Suddenly, she's on top of the comforter, curled on her side next to me like she used to do when we were kids and I was upset about something.

"I hated when you got upset," she says.

"Stop doing that."

"I told you, I can't help it. In one ear and out the other. Only it's out of your ear and into mine. I wonder who said that originally." She taps her front tooth. "Ah. Got it. 'Oon ere it herde, at tothir out it wente.' Chaucer. *Troilus and Criseyde.* Act three…" She taps her front tooth again. "No, four. "

"It's like you've turned into a *Jeopardy* game."

Sandy laughs. "There are some nice perks." She zippers up Hayden's sweatshirt and covers her head with its hood. "The cold not so much. I wish Hayden still wore that great wool coat. Do you remember it?" She sniffs the side of the hood. "I'd give anything to smell her again."

Closing my eyes, I hold up a hand. "Please, don't."

Sandy stabs her index finger into my shoulder. "This is the problem, you know."

I crack open my eyes. "What's—"

"You made your feelings clear the last time, trust me. Remember?"

She's referring to the last time we were together and both alive. The night she stayed with me in Boston before leaving for the boat trip. Of course I remember. We'd fought. Or, at least, I did. She tried to tell me how heartbroken she was that Hayden had slept with someone. That she'd told Hayden to move out but immediately regretted it and wanted her to move back in. That she'd forgiven her. She was hoping she could convince Hayden on the boat trip to do so.

"What are you, Saint Teresa or something?" I'd snapped at her. "Goodbye and good riddance is what I say."

I didn't want to hear anything more about Hayden, not because of what Hayden had done. I told myself it was because I didn't want my sister to be with a woman. But the truth was, I was jealous of what they'd had together. It was a far cry from my relationship with Mister X.

"You were envious, not jealous," Sandy says now, reading my mind again. "Envy is when you want what someone else has. Jealousy is when you're afraid something you have will be taken away by someone else."

"Now you're going to give me a language lesson?" I want to correct her that it was a bit of both: I wanted what they had, *and* I didn't want to lose my sister. Instead, I try to turn onto my side, facing away from her, but her hand makes a fast, slight motion over my body, which somehow stops me, forcing me to stay on my back.

"You'll never learn anything…never know anything, if you don't open this." She touches my forehead. "And this." She pokes at my chest. I feel a spark of electricity in both places where she touched me. A tremor that starts out as a hairline fracture, but I sense will end in a deeper, more permanent break.

"'There is no darkness but ignorance,'" my sister says. "Good old Willie Shakespeare."

Then, *poof*, she's gone, and real darkness settles in again all around me.

❧❧❧❧

The next thing I know I'm being awakened by someone—Myles?—buzzing up the blinds, which immediately lasers a blinding light from the windows through the glass wall my bed is facing. I don't remember how soon after Sandy left that I fell asleep. For a moment I think I simply dreamed the whole thing, but then I see that she left Hayden's hoodie on the foot of the bed.

You jerk, I think. *How the hell am I going to explain that?* I immediately jump up and stuff it into my rucksack, but not before I catch a whiff of my sister's shampoo. I shove the sweatshirt in farther. Better that Hayden thinks I'm a thief if I'm found out than confessing that my sister is alive and well as Casper the ghost.

I'm not ready yet to greet Myles or the day. I get back into bed and crawl farther under the covers. Lying on my back, I make a tent the way that Sandy and I used to when we were kids: knees and elbows up, our hands clasped behind our necks as if we were about to do an abs workout, the comforter held up by our knobby joints. It was our fallback position whenever one or both of us had had a bad day at school or at the restaurant. We'd nicknamed it Batsville after Sandy had seen a photograph in a National Geographic showing bats folded up and hanging from a rafter. One of us would say, "Let's go to Batsville," and before you know it, no matter how bad the day had been, we'd be laughing underneath the comforter. Except for once. When our mother had died in the car accident and the police had left, we'd done it for as long as we could without saying a word until falling asleep from exhaustion, our limbs relaxed, and we let the comforter slip down on us, a protective shield under which we could hide forever. There'd been no laughter that day.

Batsville doesn't seem so protective anymore. It feels weird and lonely. I wonder if Sandy ever told Hayden about it. The thought pierces me; maybe they actually *did* Batsville together. Immediately, I sit up in bed, chucking the comforter to the side. I can't parse out whether thinking Sandy shared one of our childhood games with Hayden embarrasses or irritates me, or whether, well, I like it.

I was sixteen and a high school sophomore when Sandy brought Hayden home from Bennington College for the first time one weekend. It was the spring, their second semester, and they'd been put together as suitemates from day one. The college, with its clapboard houses and single rooms grouped in suites, lush Vermontian green mountains, even a barn where lectures were held, had shouted *New England old money* wherever we looked when my mother and I dropped Sandy off the first time. Sandy and Hayden were two of the few students who were on full scholarship.

Even before Sandy brought Hayden home, I'd sensed that my sister had a secret. I mean, here was my sister, more beautiful by the day, brilliant, at least if her grades at school proved anything, and she had yet to have a boyfriend. In high school we were too busy. Completely understandable. I suspected that, like me, the number of friends that she had was limited by circumstances, to put it nicely. First, because our mother wanted us either home studying or at

The Homeport pitching in. I also knew that Sandy's potential high school circle was constrained even more than mine because she'd always been in the "advanced track" that included only twenty other students. Every class she had was with those select students. I, on the other hand, was immersed in the general student body, one out of hundreds, which allowed me to go through the three years of high school unnoticed, unremarkable, and untested. I asked Sandy once how it felt migrating from class to class, year to year with the same pod of students. I think I stressed what she had that I didn't: the allure of knowing other students so well they must be a tight-knit family, a buttress against the ultimate daily horror in high school—lunchtime in the cafeteria. I used to see her sitting at a table with two or three of them every day. I sat with an odd mixture of sophomore nobodies and kids who didn't fit into any of the pre-defined table groupings of jocks, druggies, or smart ones. At my table we all dressed in bland clothes, khakis and button-downs. We wanted to meld into the cafeteria's beige walls.

Sandy had scoffed at me. "It's a pool of sharks that need to be constantly fed," she said about her classmates, with a tinge of sadness.

Then, she went away to Bennington and didn't have to spend her extra hours waitressing, easily aced her humanities courses, and lived within a larger student population, freeing her up in ways that she'd surely never experienced before. What was she doing with all that free time? I knew she had a heavy reading load; she was selecting as many Brit Lit courses as she could. Dickens and Trollope were particular favorites. The storyteller in them appealed to her tastes. But, still. She wasn't working. How did she spend her free hours?

As soon as Francis would hand the phone over to me during Sandy's Sunday telephone calls home and leave the kitchen, I'd eagerly ask my sister for details. She'd be evasive. "Oh, you know, this and that…lots and lots of studying. It's *college*, Tibbie, not camp. Before you know it, the weekend's shot and I'm back in classes. Speaking of which, I should get back to *The Small House at Allington*."

Then, she brought Hayden home.

Because there was no direct bus route to our town, Bellport, they took a Greyhound bus on Friday from Bennington to Hanover, New Hampshire, about thirty miles away from where we lived. My mother and I were waiting for them inside the bus depot. It was a raw afternoon in late March. We'd had what we prayed was our last snowstorm for the winter two weeks before, followed by a week of near fifty-degree days. Most of the snow had melted or was left as a crusty icing on the sides of roads and at the bottoms of driveways. Still, it smelled like snow was in the air again. The temperatures had plunged some twenty degrees overnight, although the forecasters insisted the warm weather would reappear by Sunday morning. Hanover is nothing to put on your bucket list of sights to see before you die; the dank greyness of this day made it seem even worse. The cold hadn't added a ruddiness to the cheeks of the people in the bus depot's waiting room, it simply made us look ashen or like flu survivors. Several of them stomped their boots, whether they were sitting in the room's plastic cold chairs or standing, and they periodically clapped their gloved hands together as if their extremities had fallen asleep. You could see our collective foggy breaths puffing from our mouths like we were a bunch of smokers outside an office.

Finally, a crowd of arriving bus riders funneled from the docking area, through the grimy glass doors and into the waiting area. In the midst of the crowd came my sister holding a suitcase handle in one hand and Hayden's arm in the other. Hayden was carrying what looked like a hatbox that you'd see in a 1920s flapper movie. Even in the hubbub of the arriving travelers being greeted by families and friends, they stood out. My sister had always been a modest dresser. Someone who wanted to blend in, as did I. From the day she'd turned thirteen her daily wardrobe was also a buttoned-down pale blue or white oxford shirt—always perfectly ironed—and depending on the season, khaki capris or full-length jeans paired with clean white Keds sneakers or L.L.Bean knock-off duck boots along with either a windbreaker or a puffy jacket that was a hand-me-down from our mother. Sometimes, she'd throw on one of the two crew neck sweaters she owned or, when she really wanted to be avant-garde, tie it around her neck and shoulders as a shawl.

That had changed. As she walked toward my mother and me, for a moment we almost didn't recognize her.

"Oh," Francis exhaled next to me.

"Wow," I said.

Neither of us made a move to her, we were so stunned. My sister, seemingly overnight, had changed from a preppy model to someone I'd now describe as East Village thrift store. Back then, however, she simply looked to my teenage eyes the same as Homeless Hattie, a fixture on the steps of our Catholic church on Main Street. Hattie's crayon-drawn cardboard sign always called for alms for the poor, only she'd spelled it, on purpose, a-r-m-s.

Sandy strode our way in a plaid mustard-and-green wool jacket, orange T-shirt, a wool checkerboard miniskirt, black tights that had white skulls running up and down her legs, and worn reddish cowboy boots. Hayden's outfit seemed milquetoast in comparison: a Confederate soldier, grey wool overcoat with a scalloped cape attached around her shoulders, grey wool stovepipe pants that ended too short above ankle boots with eyelets that I remember struck me as Victorian or hobo-ish. All she was missing was a top hat and she would've been a shoo-in as an extra in an *Oliver Twist* remake.

My first thought was that my sister had been chucked out of college. That somehow her financial aid had been terminated and she'd been living on the street, too ashamed to tell us, with the Artful Dodger in tow. *But that can't be right*, I thought. Sandy and Hayden lived together. Were they both tossed out then?

Sandy hugged my mother first. Taking a step back, she introduced Hayden to her. Then, my sister beamed her best Sandy Dyer smile as Hayden clasped Francis's hand and said some totally bullshit thing about how excited she was to finally meet her, how she'd been waiting for this day, blah blah blah.

"And you too, Isabel," Hayden said, fixing her eyes on me for the first time. I hated her as soon as she called me that. No one called me that except Francis when she was reprimanding me. At the same time, I felt a sharp pain in my stomach. There had been something alluring to me when she did it also.

Her eyes were an astonishing pale blue, almost white. To someone else, maybe my sister, they could look warm...calm...trustworthy. That day, I felt them as two ice picks.

Maybe that's not true. Maybe that's only now in hindsight. Even that first time, I was certainly stunned by how arresting Hayden was. Equally as beautiful as my sister, only her beauty was more unique. Next to her, my sister was suddenly your everyday high school beauty queen. A dime a dozen. Sandy's face seemed almost chubby next to Hayden's, which it wasn't, and her blond hair seemed ordinary as it fell in a straight line to her shoulders. In contrast, Hayden's chestnut hair with its red highlights was swept up into a messy, soft bun on top of her head, strands falling out willy-nilly and framing her angular face and small nose. Her mouth wasn't big except when it broadened into a warm smile, which it was doing now as she clasped my mother's hand.

I was jolted out of all this by my mother, who, recovering from her shock also, said, "Is it Dios de Muertos?" She laughed, pointing to Sandy's tights. Sandy smiled and, quickly scooping me into a hug, whispered into my ear, "Be nice." It was a combination of an order and a plea.

"Shall we go? It's cold in here," our mother said, and clapped her gloved hands as so many of our fellow waiting neighbors had been doing.

"Where's the car?" Sandy asked. I could tell right away she was nervous. There was only one parking lot, right outside the doors, which she knew.

Somehow, we made it to that parking lot, my mother and me sliding into the front seat of the Rambler, which we called The Gambler because you never knew if it would break down somewhere and if we were taking a chance with our lives especially late at night on dark, wooded roads where we might be left at the murderous hands of a serial killer. My sister and Hayden claimed the back seat. At first, Sandy asked questions that she wouldn't have normally asked. I was sure she was doing it out of continued nervousness rather than politeness. How's the house? How's school, Tibbie? When that petered out, Hayden jumped in by telling me that Sandy had told her I wanted to be a writer, what was I reading?

"Books," I answered. When Sandy jabbed my shoulder from behind, I added, "Flannery O'Connor. Southern Gothic."

"Oh?" said Hayden. "Is that the kind of writer you want to be?"

Before I could stop myself, I said, "We live in New Hampshire."

Unfazed, Hayden said, "Shirley Jackson grew up in sunny California."

I turned around and faced her and my sister. Sandy shot me a warning look. Hayden was smiling at me. You could tell her teeth were naturally close to perfect. One incisor was out of alignment the tiniest bit, which meant she hadn't been a braces type of girl.

"Who's she?" I asked Hayden, knowing fully well that Jackson wrote the pre-eminent gothic horror story, "The Lottery," and that my sister and my mother both knew that I knew this. It was my childish way of forming a wall around us, separating us from this intruder, ending this façade that we were supposed to welcome with open arms anyone Sandy brought home whom we knew nothing about.

Sandy slipped her hand through Hayden's arm.

"Don't mind my little sister. Sometimes her meds don't work," she said, surprising me. She squeezed Hayden's arm. It was the first time I was ever the brunt of a joke of hers. Hayden quietly said something about that not being funny and to spite her more than my sister, I barked out a fake, harsh laugh, as if it was the funniest thing I'd ever heard in my life, and turned back around to stare out the front windshield.

My mother cleared her throat and glanced in the rearview mirror. "Sandy told me you're studying photography, Hayden?" This threw me. When had my sister told her that, or even about Hayden's existence? Had my mother also known Hayden was coming and had kept that from me as well? Suddenly, I felt I was the odd man out, not Hayden.

"Yes, Mrs. Dyer," Hayden said. "Mostly portraits."

"You mean *weddings*?" I cut in. I didn't turn around this time. For a second, the word lingered in the air, like a bad smell.

"Tibbie," my sister said, warning me.

I'll say this for Hayden. Somehow, she didn't ask my mother to turn the car around and demand to be taken back to the bus depot. "It's okay, Sandy," she said good-naturedly. "More Dorothea Lange. Do you know her?"

She'd been asking me, but before I could snipe at her with something along the lines that I'd thought I recognized her lace-up boots from a Lange dustbowl photo, my mother spoke up. She had a small smile on her face as she drove our ancient car down I-89.

"I saw a fabulous exhibit of those photos in 1966 at MOMA," Francis said, glancing up at the rearview mirror.

"You did?" my sister and Hayden said at the same time and Hayden laughed. I hated her even more then.

"Mom, watch the road," I said.

My mother looked over at me, shook her head, and then, making a show of pointedly grabbing the ten and two positions on the steering wheel, she said, "Okay, Tibbie?" Not wanting an answer, she glanced at the mirror again. "I was fifteen. My mother took me."

"Mom grew up in New York City," Sandy added.

Francis shook her head. "I grew up in Queens, Sandy. You know that."

"It's the city, isn't it?" I said, hoping to show my sister I was on her side.

Francis sighed. "Yes, but when you say New York City, people get the wrong impression. Anyway, my mother loved art. We didn't have a pot to piss in, but she made sure we'd go into the city…Manhattan… to the museums and we'd see exhibitions of her favorites. She was a cleaner at offices in Queens, not even at a fancy one in Manhattan. If some artist she respected had a show that was up, she made sure to call in sick that day. It was always a Friday as the museums generally were free on Fridays, and we'd take the subway in. The whole time she'd be worried that we'd run into someone she worked with. As if they'd taken the same exact day off too. She'd hunch over on the train seat and keep her head down, like she was asleep or was on an FBI poster somewhere." My mother laughed wistfully at the memory. "But, as soon as we walked through the museum's doors, you could see her relax. She'd straighten her spine. She might've been living incognito before that, but now she could be herself. I think that was the best part of it for me. That and seeing that Lange exhibit that time."

"You never told us that," I said peevishly, smarting from what else she hadn't been telling me, from keeping Hayden a secret from me. Added to that, I was ticked off that Hayden, a stranger, had, in turn, stirred something up in my mother that my sister and I'd never been able to. Had never even known to.

"You never asked," our mother said offhandedly. "Anyway, we were talking about you, Hayden. Your work." The Gambler turned onto our road.

As if sensing that we shouldn't interfere further with the memory, none of us—even I knew to keep my mouth shut—said anything. However, when Francis made a left into our driveway, Hayden leaned forward so that her face was between my mother and me.

"If you don't mind my asking, why that exhibit more than others?" she asked quietly.

Francis glanced at her and then back at the garage door. She put the car in Park. She smiled. "I saw a lot of beautiful art growing up, but it was the only time I felt that I was seeing something I could understand in here." My mother touched her parka by her chest.

"Lange said photography was an act of love, Mrs. Dyer," Hayden said. "That was the deepest thing behind it, and the audience feeling it, gives that back."

My mother nodded her head. "Yes…I can see that." Turning around to face her, she shot Hayden another quick smile. "Please. Call me Francis." Then, she shut The Gambler off.

I'll say this for our Hayden. She's a charmer. Or a people pleaser.

Chapter Ten

Now that they've arrived in Skyville, Myles wishes he knew when they'd be leaving. He hasn't slept at all on the hard pullout. By six o'clock every morning he's stripped and folded his bedding and re-positioned the couch back. The problem is his stash is running low. It's the start of the third day they've been in Skyville. He's been cutting back over the last couple of days, weaning himself reluctantly but doggedly. During the one-day trip here he'd plowed through almost half of the small white pile he has. Consequently, he only has had one line in the last twenty-four hours. Such rationing unnerves him. Is he ready for a forced detox? He wants to believe he's strong enough, but is he? In the bathroom, after his shower, he slips his tin box out of his bathrobe pocket and gingerly uncovers it. Should he have his one allotted line now for the day—*my one-a-day*, he thinks and would laugh if it wasn't so scary—or try to hold on for a few more hours until at least he gets through the morning? The bathroom is still so steamy from his shower that his decision is made for him. At once, afraid that the little he has left will somehow turn into a papier-mâché-like paste when the humid air attacks it, he snaps the lid back on without taking any and shoves the tin into his pocket.

The bathrobe is ratty flannel. He doesn't know

why he packed that of all the clothes he could've brought. He'd packed in such a hurry that the first night he opened his duffel bag to get ready for bed, he was completely flummoxed. In addition to the bathrobe, the two T-shirts and boxer shorts, one sweatshirt, and long underwear aren't enough for a trip that doesn't have an expiration date. Luckily, the loft is overly hot. Old-fashioned, spitting and clanking radiators that belong on Captain Nemo's *Nautilus* keep the temperature around greenhouse level. For the first time in a long time, Myles is actually warm. The last two nights he slept in boxers and a T-shirt that he wore on the car trip and hadn't taken off.

In the living room he slips on a clean pair of boxers and T-shirt. Then, his jeans. He leaves off his Carhartt suit and his dirty thermal shirt, sweatshirt, and socks for now. Maybe he should ask Penelope about a washing machine.

Tibbie is still asleep, or at least pretending to be. She's stayed in bed the last two mornings until he buzzed up the blinds and let the sunshine pour in through the windows. Only then did she make her way to the bathroom. Yesterday it was without a "good morning" or even a "hey." Any civility on her part will be gone by this morning. The day before, Myles could feel her increasing frustration bordering on anger as both Penelope and Hayden dodged her questions with the slippery expertise of criminals with long rap sheets. He almost thought they were going to ask for a lawyer to be present. Except they didn't need to. They always seem to be on the way out somewhere or about to follow-up on some urgent business with someone connected to Pen & Hay.

As Myles walks softly into the kitchen to make

himself tea, he recognizes that it's actually Penelope who's been giving most of the excuses. "Can't right now, sorry. Too busy," seems to have become Penelope's mantra. The day after they arrived, Penelope and Hayden abandoned Myles and Tibbie to two choices: stay on Level 2 in their loft or drive into town to explore. What wasn't said was they could leave and go home.

"We don't have time to be tour guides. Too much to do here," Penelope explained. "But please feel free to go about *your* business. Town is, well, not much. Shoot, we're late. Come on." This last directive was aimed at Hayden. Myles wanted to shout at her that their *business* was interrogating them about the accident, but neither he nor Tibbie said anything before the door shut and he was left alone with her again.

Myles has noticed that Hayden is mostly silent, following Penelope's lead, which is weird in itself. Hayden never struck him as the meek and mild type, although he doesn't know her very well. They'd only met a few times at *Freedom*'s book launches or at office parties. And on the boat, of course. There had been that somewhat intimate moment when Hayden had almost fallen off the dock and had awkwardly grabbed his arm. It was really only, what…five seconds before they separated and didn't really speak again? After that they'd all been together a few hours when it had all gone to hell. It's not that he avoided Hayden on the boat. It was really Sandy whom he took pains to sidestep after they left the dock. Sandy was his boss. She had Luke's ear. And there had been that weird thing going on with Penelope and her to boot.

He fills the electric kettle with tap water and

turns it on. Despite his laying off the coke, his appetite is still off. He wishes he'd have the desire to fry up a few eggs from the refrigerator or even eat a plain piece of toast, but the mere thought of food continues to nauseate him. Cutting back on his drug intake has had the opposite effect of what his drug counselor had insisted would happen.

"Dump the coke and you'll be eating right as rain again," Ronnie had said.

If he ate something, maybe he'd be able to focus better. Leaning against the kitchen counter, waiting for the water to boil, he tries to remember what he'd just been thinking about. Yesterday, he'd started to say something to Tibbie and mid-sentence had forgotten what exactly he'd started to tell her. And it never came back to him. Yet another reason not to detox.

The kettle switches automatically off as soon as steam rises from its spout. Myles pours himself a mug of Earl Grey and wonders, not for the first time, if he should switch to coffee or even use the espresso machine and its pods that sit on the granite counter. Maybe that would help him concentrate more. What the hell was he thinking about when he came into the kitchen? It's stupid, considering the only thing he does think about these days is Sandy. *Or wanting to do a line,* he thinks. It's not rocket science.

That's right. He remembers what it was. Despite what Sandy told him that day, he is positive Penelope had been putting the moves on her on the boat, and he still can't believe that Sandy actually rejected her. That much he was certain of. Later, after dinner on deck, he watched Sandy and Hayden stack some of the dirty plates and begin to carry them downstairs to the galley.

"Who needs hired help?" Myles remembers Luke saying and then grinning like the asshole he was. "Bring up another bottle, will you, Sandy? That's a good girl." Taking out a penknife from his pants pocket, Luke began to cut around the end of a fat cigar like he was peeling an orange. The knife was the kind that you'd gut a fish with. Luke expertly flipped it closed again. It disappeared into his pants pocket. He lit the cigar.

Myles tried to convince him and Penelope that a storm was coming, but neither one would hear of it. And then, Penelope suddenly excused herself from the table. "Just gonna help out," she said. But she didn't carry down her plate or anything else as she went below.

Myles was left with Luke, who leaned back against his banquette seat, closed his eyes, and blew out an ugly-smelling cloud of smoke. Myles was just thinking he could escape by clearing Penelope's plate with its half-eaten lobster and gnawed corn cob, when Penelope, who had only been gone a couple of minutes—too short a time to either help the others or go to the head, as Luke would've called it—came bounding up the stairs, pink-cheeked, which might've passed for embarrassment had Myles not noticed her hands were curled into tight fists and were beating against her thighs like they were cold. Or she was getting herself pumped up for a fight. That's the image that haunts him. Not the rejected kiss. Not Penelope's scornful laugh filtering back from earlier that day from the boat's prow. Just those fists. That and Luke and his fishing knife.

Penelope and Hayden...Myles can't wrap his head around it. He wishes he could do one lousy line. To think straight. Did they end up together because they couldn't deal with what happened? Or because of it? Why move up here to Nowheresville? Why would Penelope leave her job at *Freedom*, leave her father, whom she'd always been joined to at the hip? He could understand it if the two of them had been friends before, but he remembers them almost avoiding each other at those parties. Unless that was a planned subterfuge and Hayden was in on it too. What *it* is, Myles can't pin down. The boat's hitting the whale? Sandy's death? *Stop!* he thinks. *You're getting paranoid.* He so desperately wants a line that his hand shakes as he lifts his tea mug.

"If you can't get out of your head, get out of your environment," Ronnie used to tell him. So, while sipping his tea, Myles walks back to the couch. He can hear Tibbie softly snoring on the other side of the glass wall. He sits down. He flashes back to a book party at a Tribeca restaurant a year ago when he'd gone up to the bar for another drink—what was he drinking? Gin and tonics? Rum and cokes? Shit, does it matter? A vague memory of him snorting in the men's bathroom. Focus. He remembers when he came out of the restaurant bathroom, Hayden and Sandy were standing off by themselves in a nearby corner.

"Look, you know I can't leave now," Sandy was saying. "I'll be home in an hour."

"Promise me you won't be alone with either of them," Hayden told her. "Especially CPD."

Sandy snorted. "Not going to happen. Stop worrying. I'm fine."

When Hayden passed Myles on her way out, however, she looked troubled.

At first, Myles sensed Hayden was warning Sandy

about Luke and maybe Penelope. But who was CPD, then? There was no one who worked at *Freedom* or who was at the launch with those initials. He wonders if he should ask Hayden now. Whether knowing that is important? Is it somehow connected to Sandy's death? That's the hard part about someone dying. The smallest details have taken on a looming presence in his mind as he remembers everything that happened right before the accident and right after. His memory of "the during" is nonexistent. Ronnie told him that it was a usual side effect of trauma, of PTSD.

"Maybe it'll come to you, and maybe it won't," Ronnie said, raising his hands up and down, weighing the prospects. "Trauma is fickle."

He was so smug that Myles almost lunged across the five feet separating their chairs to punch him. Instead, he walked out, never to return.

I'm gonna ask her, Myles thinks as his brain jumps a rail from the past into the future. *Who the hell was CPD?*

He'll have to wait until he can get Hayden alone. As if to get the plan in motion, he stands and walks over to the windows. He starts to buzz the blinds up. Tibbie groans from behind the glass. Myles decides he'll fry some eggs for the both of them, pop slices of the seven-grain bread into the toaster, and propel them both into the land of the living with a double espresso. He's going to force himself to get down every bit of it. He needs to get his act together.

☙ ❧ ☙ ❧

After breakfast, during which he did at least manage a few bites of toast and his egg along with the double espresso before feeling bile in the back of his throat, he and Tibbie drive four miles to ShopRite, the nearest grocery store.

"Just how long do you think we're staying?" he asks her as they pull into the parking lot.

"I didn't want you here, remember?" says Tibbie. She parks the car between a van that says *Finn's Electricians: Let us brighten your day*, and a rusted-out truck that sits four extra feet off the ground on supersized, heavily treaded tires. Myles remembers seeing similar trucks in TV ads for a Monster Jam stadium show when he was twelve. The trucks had names such as "Big Kahuna," "Gravedigger," and "Bad News Travels Fast." The next day, after school, he walked into Harvard Square and at a toy and game store bought his first of many Hot Wheels Monster Jam Truck replicas. How happy he'd been. He hasn't thought of those trucks in years.

"Earth to Myles," Tibbie is saying, snapping her fingers in front of his face. "Jesus. Get it together, will you?" As she opens her car door and steps out into icy mush in the store's parking lot, Myles is thinking about whether those trucks are somewhere packed away in his mother's attic. He doubts it. He remembers he still had a box of them when he was at college and living in Ithaca, New York. Like so much else in his life since the accident, somewhere along the line those trucks have been washed away and lost forever. *What are you doing?* he thinks. *Get out of the car.*

Within five minutes in the store, they run into Hayden as they're rolling their cart down the pasta aisle. Hayden is picking a box of spaghetti from a shelf. Penelope is nowhere to be seen.

"She's on the phone with Luke, in the car," Hayden tells them, as if they've already been chatting, assuming they'll know who *she* is. With her free hand, Hayden does a hand puppet talking into air, which surprises Tibbie and Myles. Then, regretting it, her face pinks. She tugs a black ski hat on her head. "So…" She draws the word out. "You're buying more groceries."

"Oh, is that what they sell here?" Tibbie says, looking around. "Myles and me, we couldn't figure it out."

For some reason, Hayden smiles. It's a genuinely warm smile. What Myles really can't figure out is *that*. Why didn't she say something smartass back to Tibbie? Then, Hayden does something even more surprising: she reaches out and briefly touches Tibbie's parka sleeve. "I'm glad some things haven't changed, Isabel."

To Myles's surprise, Tibbie barks out a laugh. Then, she looks down at her boots and shakes her head. "Yeah, well." She looks up. "You have."

Now it's Hayden's turn to glance away. At first, Myles thinks she's looking for Penelope, but when she faces them again he sees that her eyes are teary, like she's stifled a yawn. The wetness only magnifies their blueness. "It's not what it—" Hayden breaks off. She stares down at the spaghetti box, pretending to scan the nutritional information. "I should go. I only came in for this." She shakes the rectangular box like a maraca.

Watching all this unfold, Myles has almost completely forgotten his plan from this morning. Then, just as Hayden takes a first step away, he stops her. "Wait," he says, touching the sleeve of Hayden's black parka as she had Tibbie's.

Hayden looks at his hand, which he drops immediately. "S-s-sorry," he barely spits out. He could swear that a smile begins on her face, which she simultaneously shuts down. He pauses. *Get a grip*, he scolds himself. He knows he may never have a chance again. *Christ.*

Tibbie says, "Don't mind him, he can't help himself."

"Isabel," Hayden warns her, although her face is on the brink of falling apart into laughter at any moment.

Pissed, Myles gets the surge he needs to spit out, "Who's CPD?"

Immediately, Hayden's face blanches. "What?" she asks, but Myles knows she heard him.

"Who's CPD?" he repeats, more aggressively.

"Where..."

"It doesn't ma-ma..." Myles jerks his head to still his tongue. "Never mind. Just tell me."

"What are you talking about?" Tibbie asks.

Myles raises a hand to her in a stop motion. "CPD," he repeats, staring at Hayden.

Hayden lets out a breath of air. "Okay. But I wish you'd tell me why you want to know that."

Myles waves at the air. "It doesn't matter!" His voice sounds high and loud. He's tried to keep the excitement out of it, the sheer elevated pitch of anticipation, but he's failing miserably.

Hayden's ice-blue eyes seem to bore into him. "All right, all right." She sighs with weary resignation. Her eyes soften to a grey. "Controlling Personality Disorder. CPD."

This throws Myles. "I know CPD is a person," he says, frustrated. "Not s-s-some kind of-of-of m-med..." Here, he flags. To continue will only make him stutter more. His heart is racing. He's too angry. His tongue is the size of a shoe. Or at least that's the feeling whenever his stuttering takes off, his tongue expanding with each tripped up and tripped over word. Speech then becomes a wild horse: uncontrollable, capricious, bolting out of bad nerves and fear.

Hayden must take pity on him because she touches his sleeve. Myles almost laughs. They've become a support group of sleeve-touchers overnight.

Hayden tells him, "It's both," and looking past Tibbie and over his shoulder, calls out, "Hey, Penelope. Look who I ran into." Then, flitting her eyes from Myles to Penelope and back to Myles again, she says, only in a much lower voice, "A condition and a person."

☙☙☙☙

He could barely get through the food shopping after Hayden and Penelope headed toward the checkout. It's not that Hayden or Penelope held them up or pretended to want to chat. As soon as Penelope reached them in the aisle, she'd asked Hayden, "Where were you?" Then, she lifted the box of spaghetti out of Hayden's hands. "Is this all we need?" She tapped one of her Frye boots on the store's linoleum. Myles noticed that she didn't wait for an answer to either question before she added, "We need to get back to the office. Sorry." Then, she turned on her heels and strode away (those heels pointedly louder now), not saying goodbye or watching to make sure Hayden would follow her.

Hayden shrugged. "I guess I'll see you back at the doom and gloom," she told Myles and Tibbie. Then, she caught up to Penelope, the two of them disappearing around the corner display of on-sale baked beans.

"Did you hear that?" Tibbie said to Myles.

"Penelope is CPD. I knew it," Myles said.

Tibbie shook her head, not listening. "She called *The Loom*, doom and gloom. I knew they couldn't be so buddy-buddy. Sandy hated that bitch."

Myles was baffled. "Who? I thought they were lovers."

Now, Tibbie looked confused. Myles felt like they were caught in some vortex of mixed messages sparking off into deeper misunderstandings. The circuit board was shorting out.

Tibbie snorted. "Not on your life."

Myles frowned. "Of course, they were. You had to know that."

Finally, Tibbie understood. She snorted again. "I thought you were talking about Penelope and Sandy."

Myles shook his head. "Do you ever pay attention?"

"Look, we'll talk about it in the car." Taking out a handwritten list from her coat pocket, Tibbie tore it in half and shoved one half toward him. "You get this stuff and I'll meet you at the register. Go get your own cart." She started to throw in a couple boxes of ziti, two jars of pre-made tomato sauce. "Well, go on."

He'd practically raced to grab an empty cart from the front of the store and then zipped up and down the aisles, throwing in items that were on Tibbie's list and then adding six large jars of applesauce at the last minute—the kind heavy on corn fructose and double the amount of sugar he could get from a can of Coke. If he was going to beat this withdrawal thing he needed as much sugar as he could get. He met Tibbie up front and he bagged everything lickety-split as she emptied both carts onto the register conveyor belt.

"What's with the preschool snacks?" Tibbie asked, holding up one of the applesauce jars. Myles pretended he didn't hear her as he loaded the bags into a cart.

Later, they sit in the car in the parking lot, the engine running, the heater on full speed ahead.

"Doom and gloom, it doesn't matter," Myles impatiently tells Tibbie. One of his legs is jittery. He can't decide if it's from the past ten minutes or whether it's part and parcel of the involuntary drug detox he's suffering through. He's down to less than one packet in his tin. By now, back home, he'd have had four lines and several whiskeys. He wishes he had a soup spoon to start in on the applesauce. With his right hand he tries to discreetly hold his leg still. He has to calm down. He needs to tell her without stammering or making a jackass of himself.

"You're doing that weird thing again," Tibbie says, pointing to his hand. "What is that? Some kind of alien code?"

His fingers immediately cease. They'd fallen into their reflexive rubbing: the middle finger lightly brushing the index finger on top one, twice, followed by a heavier tap.

"CPD. It's what S-sandy and Hay-hay-*Hay*den..." He takes a deep breath. Starts over. Slows himself down, forms shorter sentences. "I heard them at a party. Hayden was begging your sister. Not to be alone with them. She definitely said 'them.' She said CPD."

Tibbie stares at him blankly.

"Don't you get it?" he says, his voice pitching up. He feels like he wants to flap his arms or grab her by her parka's zipper. Wake the hell up! Instead, he exhales loudly. "Hay-hay-Hay*den* was worried. She was scared f-f-f-*for* your sis-sis…Sandy. About Luke and Penelope. S-s-s-some*thing* happened. CPD is Penelope!"

"And Hayden knows what that is?" Tibbie asks him slowly.

Myles nods his head enthusiastically. He doesn't say a word for fear of continuing to sound like a psychotic fool. He can't afford any more roadblocks or slowing down the crash course they're on now.

"O-kay…" Tibbie says, doubt evident in her voice. "I'll tell you something else, though. This whole thing is a lie. Them living together all cozy. *The Loom*, my ass. Did you hear Hayden? She was telling us she's on our side. We need to talk to her again." She shifts the car's gears into Reverse and starts to back out of the parking lot.

"What do you think I just said?" Myles says defensively.

But how to get Hayden alone again? Myles for the life of him can't come up with the solution. As pumped up on adrenaline as he is, he thinks briefly, *kidnap her*, but immediately discounts that. They're in the middle of nowhere, a place they're easily lost in, GPS or not. Besides, Penelope would have the state police hunting them down in no time.

"CPD is a goddamn hawk," Tibbie says as they pull onto NY-32S. Despite being worried about the same thing, Myles laughs, giddy with their shared secret of CPD. He can't believe they're really going to do this. They're really going to crack it wide open. Together. How easily they've become conspirators. The problem is getting Hayden away from that hawk.

Chapter Eleven

In the car ride home from the supermarket over a rutty, icy street, Penelope springs it on Hayden that her father is coming to visit the next day.

"You invited him?" Hayden can't believe it. Why would Penelope add to the stress they're already dealing with? She immediately thinks of Isabel and Myles occupying Level 2 where Luke stayed the one time he visited after they first moved in. "Where's he going to sleep?" she asks, annoyed.

Penelope shoots her a hard look. "He'll stay in our guest room." She says it in a tone that warns Hayden not to argue, which irritates Hayden even more. She's already envisioning Luke on the prowl through their loft as soon as the lights are snapped off.

Hayden can't help but say, "You mean my bedroom? And where am I going to sleep? On the couch?"

Penelope shrugs. "That, or with me. It's your choice. Look, it's no big deal. He's only going to stay one night."

"Why would you invite him now, with them here?" Hayden says it even though she knows why: reinforcements.

"We should've picked up more food, with Luke coming," Penelope says, ignoring her. "Why were you in the store so long anyway?"

Hayden doesn't take the bait. "I guess you'll

have to go out to eat."

Penelope clenches her jaw but doesn't say anything else. Hayden shifts uncomfortably in the deep, cushioned passenger seat of Penelope's Range Rover. She dislikes riding in the SUV in the best of circumstances. It reminds her too much of the tourists who flocked in the summer months to the Hamptons and wanted to show off their wealth. She grew up in the next town over, Greenport, in a ramshackle, drafty house that her parents bought in the sixties for less than ten thousand dollars from an eighty-year-old fisherman with lung cancer. In the winter with the windows closed, the kitchen smelled of sea bass and fluke. Still, she'd take that house over her current living situation any day. She actually was very fond of that house.

Once the Rover is parked at *The Loom*, Hayden is relieved when Penelope says she needs to check on an order of packing boxes that arrived that morning. They take the elevator up together. Hayden feels foolish standing there holding the one box of spaghetti, so she tells Penelope she'll come down to help her with the boxes after she drops the spaghetti off in their kitchen.

"You know, it wouldn't kill you to pretend a bit harder that you care," Penelope says as she exits the elevator, alone, on Level 2.

Just before the doors close, Hayden, doubly provoked that Penelope is chastising her and that Luke will be visiting, pointedly tells her, "I won't be a tick." It's a British phrase that usually irritates Hayden because she knows Penelope's picked it up from her father. Luke repeatedly used it during the hours they were aboard *Stillwater*. Each time he said it, Hayden whispered in Sandy's ear, "Tick tock, what a crock. Let's bash him with a rock." They'd both gotten a kick out of that.

Hayden takes the elevator to the third floor. Inside their loft, she tosses the lone box of spaghetti on the granite kitchen counter, pours herself a bourbon, and settles into one of the beaten-up leather armchairs in her study. *She can wait. I need reinforcements too.* She takes a sip of the drink and then lowers it onto a coaster on the table in between the chairs. It's not like the table is something that should be safeguarded. It's a battered, English octagonal table, the kind that has wood legs that twine around like rope or snakes. One night, when she and Sandy were still living together, Hayden found it on the street in a neighbor's trash. They ate dinner on it that same night, their two plates and wineglasses and a single candle stuck onto a bread plate barely fitting across the tabletop. Luckily, Hayden took it when she moved into the studio. To her, it's priceless, especially given how little she has.

The thought of having to sleep in the same bed as Penelope—for even one night—leaves Hayden feeling queasy. She doesn't have much choice, does she? The loft, the building, is owned by Penelope. Hayden doesn't even pay rent. But the couch doesn't seem so safe either. Not with Luke able to roam around in the dead of night while Penelope enjoys the sleep of death under her Ambien cloud. In addition to the night, there will be the daytime to get through with Luke. Hayden tries to imagine it. In the morning, her usual coffee and a small yogurt will be replaced at Luke's insistence by cappuccinos and eggs and bacon, which he'll mistakenly call bangers and cook because "My own daughter can't boil an egg." Hayden envisions sitting across from him at the island as he yawns, his hair sleep-matted, his shirt—a new flannel that he's probably buying at this moment for his "trip upstate"—left unbuttoned and untucked because he wants to remind them that he's just gotten out of bed. Wrinkled, burnished corduroys and a pair of untied L.L.Bean duck boots will round out the outfit. No socks because he'll want the sound of those boots clomping and shuffling on the loft's wooden floors, announcing his presence.

At least that's how he was during his one prior visit when he showed up to inspect the printing presses that he'd practically stolen from the Albany print chain. He was supposed to stay one night and instead ended up there for most of the week. Except then, he was able to sleep downstairs in the loft that Isabel and Myles are in now. Even so, the long hours of each day during that visit dragged on as he talked incessantly to Penelope about *Freedom*'s latest numbers, questioned her about her business plan, and tried to instill doubt about the authors she was thinking of pursuing. It was obvious to Hayden that what he really wanted was for Penelope to stop this foolishness and come home. He'd paid for a couple of used presses, given her some start-up funding, but ultimately he didn't believe for a second Penelope would succeed. Nor did he appear to want her to.

The evenings were equally as painful. Over dinner, Hayden was forced to listen to the two of them, increasingly drunk, recounting what they thought were hilarious stories or experiences that they felt had enormous meaning, not just for them but the entire universe. By the second night it started to get on Hayden's nerves how Penelope, flushed and giddy

from the alcohol, would start every mundane anec-
dote with the phrase, "You won't believe this but…"
More times than not, there was never a need for any
suspension of disbelief.

Mostly, Luke ignored Hayden during that visit.
She was expendable: a gay woman whom he couldn't
flatter or finagle his way into bed. His daughter might
be living, albeit as a friend, with her, but only for now.
The degree to which he snubbed Hayden suggested
just how much he believed that this phase for his
daughter, whatever it was, call it a blip, an aberration,
would end soon and she'd come, preferably crawling,
back to Manhattan.

Yet, at least during that visit, Hayden was bliss-
fully ignorant of the real reason why she'd moved
with Penelope. To get through it, she kept reminding
herself that Penelope had been so kind to her before.
That reserve of good faith has been depleted, however. Now, Hayden worries that even if Luke will be with
them for only twenty-four hours, he'll figure out why
she continues to live with his daughter. Will detect
by looking in her eyes that she is there for only one
new purpose: to break his daughter into some sort of
confession about the accident. Some confession about
him.

How will I do it? Hayden thinks, sitting in her
study. *How can I possibly get through the next few
days?* She takes another drink, relishing the burn of
the bourbon down her throat as if it could indeed
toughen her up for what is to come. He might be able
to ignore her again, but seeing Myles and Isabel here,
how could he ignore them also? Will he simply do
what Penelope was unable to do for some reason and
throw them out? For the hundredth time, she wishes

Sandy were here. But if she were, none of this would
be happening, would it? Hayden can still imagine her
perfectly, but she's starting to wonder how long it will
be before she needs to have a photograph in her hands
to remember Sandy's face. She reminds herself that
this is what she's been waiting for...isn't it? Some kind
of resolution? She and, obviously, Isabel and Myles
are all in need of something. Part of her likes the idea
of getting them all in one room to see what shakes out.

She longs for Sandy. She knows most of the feeling comes from the not having, the can't have. Sandy
is gone. And what you can't have can suddenly be
transformed overnight into what you want more than
anything else. Hayden asks herself the same question
every time she feels herself slipping into that para-
lyzing ache for Sandy: If Sandy hadn't died, would
she have asked Hayden to move back in with her?
The truth is, Hayden doesn't know. Some days she
believes they would've gotten back together; others,
not. Would Sandy have forgiven her? Probably not. It
was Hayden who moved out. It was Hayden who got
her own studio in Park Slope to prove...what? That
she wasn't hurt when Sandy said that Hayden should
leave? By then, they'd been together twenty-five
years, ever since their college freshmen year. Maybe,
in hindsight, however, Sandy wasn't demanding that
Hayden actually leave. Maybe she only suggested it to
see what Hayden's reaction would be. Hayden thinks
about how often relationships suffer not because of
mistakes in judgement—those can be talked through,
apologized for, and forgiven—but because of mistakes
of missed opportunities when someone doesn't pick
up on the subtle inflections in what her partner says.
When you don't recognize supposed declarations

for what she really is saying: Not "Leave," but rather "*Stay.*"

Despite spending countless hours rehashing it, Hayden still hasn't totally figured out why she messed up their relationship by having the one-night stand with a tattooed bartender, a woman she wasn't even attracted to. The bartender had a stiff jaw for one thing, which, depending on the lighting in the bar, could look confident or mean. She worked at the bar right down the street from where Hayden lived with Sandy. The bar that they used to go to together every Friday right after Sandy's work ended for the week. Why had she done that? Gone to that bar on a Wednesday night, alone, when Sandy was tied up in some work meeting? Hayden hadn't been feeling suffocated, which is what she feels now with Penelope. To compare the two of them was ridiculous. She loved Sandy. She *was* drunk that night, but that doesn't explain why she went to the bar alone in the first place. Why the bartender's flirting with her on that night seemed to take on a bigger significance. Or was it some kind of test of whether Hayden had the courage to seize the opportunity to do something so different from her daily life with Sandy, so different from her own self. When it came down to it, it had been terrible. It wasn't a unique life-affirming opportunity. It was, in the end, a thoughtless, banal, spur-of-the-moment decision with predictable, long-term repercussions. It hadn't even been long enough to classify as a "one-night stand." The whole thing lasted, what? Fifteen minutes—the length of the bartender's shift break? No more than a frenzied grappling and rubbing through jeans and T-shirts in the bar's dirty back room where they shoved each other uncomfortably against stacked cases of beer. A lousy quarter of an hour ending a twenty-five-year-old relationship and starting Hayden's never-ending shame.

With her index finger, Hayden traces a gouge on the side table where her drink rests. As she moves her finger up and down the crevasse, she scrapes her nail a bit deeper. A tiny splinter sneaks under her nail and lodges.

"Shit," she says under her breath, worried that somehow the karma of her thoughts has led her to being punished. As she tugs the offending splinter out, she wonders again if, given time, Sandy would've forgiven her. It's a question that has hounded her since the accident.

"*We* might be done, but I can't lose you as a friend too," Sandy told her two weeks after Hayden had moved out. "It's too much. I lost a finger and now the doctor wants to unnecessarily amputate the whole arm."

And so, except for the nighttime, they began again to spend most of their free time together during the next month of separation.

"Come. Please," Sandy asked over the telephone a week before the boat trip.

"I can't. I have a grant deadline," Hayden told her.

"Please come," Sandy repeated. "I'll make it up to you. It's important. It's kind of a goodbye of sorts."

"What?" Hayden asked, suddenly worried that Sandy had decided to call it quits on their friendship also. But why would she do that in front of everyone at work?

"Not to you," Sandy said and laughed a little. "Jesus. To Luke. I'm handing in my notice." Then she added, "Please. I need you there for extra protection. Don't make me beg."

It was that note of desperation that convinced Hayden she had to go. They'd never had to beg each other for anything ever. They would freely give it. Now, Hayden questions whether Sandy had a premonition that the trip was going to end in such disaster for herself. She wonders if, all along, every day of those twenty-five years their two lives had been pointed to that one Friday night in the waters off Cape Cod, and that there had been no other path for either of them to follow except for the one in which one woman was destined to hold on to life and the other was destined to let go. Worst of all, Hayden wonders if the one was so willing to let go because there was no longer anything or anyone for her to live for. Whether Hayden's sleeping with the bartender had set all of the rest in motion. Whether she is somehow to blame for more than a simple infidelity. Why else would Sandy have given up in that cold water when everyone else clung on? She felt sick; she told Hayden so. But was that the only thing that weakened her so that she couldn't swim one more stroke? Or was it also despair over losing Hayden?

Hayden raises her drink again and then... click...she remembers. It's as if the tragedy, her grief, had been camouflaging the memory of a particular detail. A detail that had been biding its time until this moment to resurface and appear suddenly from under its bolt-hole of seaweed and boat debris, intact and threatening.

First, Hayden remembers the police officer. He came the morning after the accident to Cape Cod Hospital where the four survivors had spent the night.

Her nurse told her right before the cop showed up that Luke and Penelope had already left, insisting that they go back to Manhattan as soon as the sun rose. Myles was being air-transported to Massachusetts General Hospital at his mother's request. The nurse referred to them as "your friends" until Hayden said she hardly knew them.

Then the cop asked Hayden if she knew anything about her friends leaving.

"They're *not* my friends," Hayden snapped, gritting her teeth. Her head was killing her from the staples the surgeon had tacked into her forehead.

"No?"

"I barely knew them," she said and turned the side of her face that wasn't injured against her pillow so that her cheek could feel the coolness of the pillowcase.

"How about..." The cop looked down at his notepad. "Myles Small?"

Hayden shook her head once, then stopped because it only made the pain stabbing her head worse. Her hand touched the bandage on her forehead. The police officer stared at her, waiting for her to say something.

She finally was able to tell him, "Sandy worked with all of them." Saying Sandy's name made her falter. She felt a crease in the pillowcase. She adjusted her head again. "She invited me."

"Myles told us there was a bit of a celebration?" Before Hayden could correct him on that, the cop asked if she'd been drinking. Had they all been drinking? How much had, for example, the owner of the boat (here, he looked down at his notepad)—Lucas Blackmore—been drinking? He focused on Luke then, asking Hayden how many drinks she thought he'd had. What was he drinking? Had he seemed drunk? Hayden could barely answer him. He had so many questions. She was still in shock. Couldn't wrap her head around Sandy being dead, yet alone concern herself with how tipsy Luke was. She hadn't slept at all despite the nurse having given her a mild sedative on top of the sedatives they'd handed her when she'd arrived the night before. They were still swirling around in her system, making her numb and simultaneously on edge.

The thing is, Hayden can't remember now in her study if she told the cop that usually Sandy hardly drank. She did tell him that Sandy hadn't been feeling well. How she'd complained that it was the flu or something. It seemed important to tell him that.

"Huh," the cop said. "You're the first person to tell us that." She couldn't tell if he thought she was lying or not, but then he said, "That's good you told us." And he took out a pen from his inside coat pocket and, clicking it, wrote something down and circled it.

Hayden's mouth felt dry. The thought of pouring herself a glass of water from the sand-colored plastic pitcher on the swing table next to her hospital bed seemed reprehensible or inappropriate somehow, considering they were talking about Sandy's drowning.

She cleared her throat. Still, when she spoke her voice came out raspy. "Do you think that's why…" she began but couldn't finish because she'd started to cry. She really wanted to ask him where exactly they'd found her. Was she still locked up in that deathtrap of a room?

"What? Oh, no, well probably not. We don't know for sure," he corrected himself. "Either way. But we'll follow it up. It looks like she had a head injury. Probably when the boat capsized. Like you." He motioned to her bandage. "She was in the hallway, below deck. That probably didn't…well, it's more of a challenge."

"So, she wasn't trapped in the cabin?" Hayden asked, her voice cracking, irritated with herself that she was begging for such reconfirmation to assuage her guilt when he'd already said that was the case.

The cop shook his head, slightly grimacing. "No, the divers found her in the passageway. Her door was open. More likely, it was the blow to the head when you capsized."

Hayden imagined Sandy getting smacked on the head as everything was turned upside down around her and she tried to struggle out of that tiny room that was completely underwater. On deck, Hayden and the rest of them had had it relatively easier. Still, they hadn't been rescued for what? At least thirty minutes? An hour? When she surfaced, her forehead whacked the corner of the diving platform hard above her eyebrow. Stunned, she desperately pulled herself partially up onto the upside-down shelf. Nearby, Luke and Penelope were sprawled and clutching the tilting keel. *Sandy?* she thought, but then blacked out. Her memory is sketchy after that until she was being pulled up into the Coast Guard boat where there were so many people. She was wrapped in something metallic… one of those blankets that marathoners wear? There was so much going on, the boat's spotlight sweeping across the water, and she was wet and coughing and blue and numb and shivering as she'd never shivered before. Several Coast Guard guys ran from one end to the other. Noise, lots of noise. She kept wiping away what she thought was rain from her eyes. Later she'd find out it was blood from her forehead wound. Myles was huddled across from her half-covered in blankets. His right arm was in a sling that positioned his hand up by his throat. His other hand was pressing a bloody towel against his mouth. Wait, was his arm in the sling then, or later? More people were asking her questions, all the while the rescue boat moved in circles, the spotlight searching, searching, searching. Other boats nearby. Were those divers slipping into the choppy water? Rain was coming down in sheets. It was so difficult to see. She was in such a state of shock—it was the hypothermia, one of the doctors told her later—what the hell had happened? It had all happened so fast that she didn't realize Sandy wasn't there until she understood that they were headed toward the harbor, and even then, it didn't fully compute in her brain. She naturally assumed Sandy was somewhere else on board the rescue boat. She was a strong swimmer. Maybe the strongest of all of them. Over the years they'd been together, from the safety of a beach chair, Hayden had watched Sandy swim back and forth in the ocean along the shoreline on countless weekends they'd spent on Fire Island and in that same water off Provincetown. Sandy had never tired. Not once. Sandy had said it always invigorated her. Hayden didn't know how to swim, at least not the way someone learns from swim lessons at a town pool or at a YWCA. She didn't know how to rhythmically keep her face in the water and then swing it up for air. It was a source of embarrassment for her, given that she'd grown up in a Long Island beach town. She was fine body surfing, but had no endurance whatsoever propelling herself along without the helpful thrust of a wave bringing her to shore.

In the rescue boat, Hayden tried to stand, to find her, but someone stopped her, told her she had to sit down, they'd be there soon. "Where?" she remembers saying. "Where's Sandy?" Her body racked with shivering, her mind in a complete daze. It was all too much.

"Hold still, okay?" the person said, wrapping gauze around Hayden's forehead.

Now, in her study as she lifts her drink, she returns again to that police officer questioning her about how much they were drinking, and another memory slides in—for what are memories but one stepping-stone leading to the next in a never-ending bridge to the past? She sees Luke demanding that Penelope pass champagne around before dinner. Penelope was irritated about the whole thing.

"So, now I'm a waitress," Penelope sniped at her father in front of everyone on deck as he handed her some awful gold-plated tray with the filled crystal champagne glasses. Each of the glasses had one of those silly acrylic half-moon tags on swizzle sticks that you write names on so everyone knows whose glass is whose. Hayden removed hers as soon as she saw it was impossible to drink without poking out an eye.

"Poppycock. I'll help you, my darling," Luke murmured to Penelope, selecting a glass with a big S written in red on the swizzle and handing it to Sandy. Hayden was standing next to her. "Cheers," he said, winking at Sandy. "Cin-cin." When Sandy reluctantly took a sip, he added, "Good girl." He tapped the bottom of her glass once, saying, "Drink up. Cin-cin. To your next adventure." Then he handed out the rest of them.

In her study, Hayden suddenly leans forward in her leather chair. What does it mean? Does it mean anything? She wants it to mean something. Rather that than believing *she* was the cause. Her locking the cabin door wasn't to blame. Someone else must be at fault. Someone else must be punished. A rabid dog won't go after the culprit animal that originally infected it nor will it turn on itself either. It will hunt down something else to attack. Thus, the image of Sandy taking a sip from that glass is a needle pricking her. It's one of those cactuses that you brush past and you don't feel the tiny white hairs that have stuck into your hand until thirty minutes later. With each passing minute, the pain becomes more real, acute. Festering. Standing up from her chair, Hayden walks to the window and then paces back to the chair. And then... she understands. She hears Sandy telling her again in the galley, "Like father, like daughter," and envisions how she'd leaned against the counter complaining of feeling dizzy. Hears Luke saying, "Cin-cin." Hayden had been so wrong. It hadn't been the flu. It hadn't been a bop on her head. It hadn't been a locked door. She's wasted so much time thinking about herself and whether she's to blame, what she's lost, and then trying to get close to Penelope so she could get *her* to fess up. When all this time, she's had the answer. She fights the overwhelming urge to go to her bedroom, collapse on her bed, crawl under the covers, and never surface again. She has let Sandy down so much, then and now. But something shoves the urge to disappear aside. Something stronger. Her spine stiffens. *Isabel,* she thinks. *You have to tell her.*

She starts to walk rapidly through the loft. Just as she reaches for the handle on the loft's front door, the door swings open, almost knocking her down.

Standing in the doorway, Penelope says, "I was right! The box order is all messed up. Where are you going?"

"To take care of it for you," Hayden coolly says, immediately shifting into the familiar gears of restraint and conciliation. "Light on the peddle, light on the peddle," her mother used to tell her when she'd allow Hayden, sixteen years old with her new driver's permit, to practice driving with her in Greenport. "No one wants a heavy foot for a dance partner," she'd add.

"I'll take care of everything," Hayden assures Penelope and heads by herself for the elevator.

Chapter Twelve

W e'll have to split up," I say thoughtfully to
Myles in the car after our grocery trip as
we pull into *The Loom*'s parking lot.

Suddenly, my sister is in the back seat, stretched
out with her head resting on one window and her feet
crossed on the opposite window ledge. "Bravo, bravo,
little sister," she says, clapping as if she's just watched
an incredible finale on Broadway. "What an idea!"

"You're back," I say, filled with joy, and I realize
how much I've missed her not being around for two
days. Glancing up to the rearview mirror, I can see that
she's found the Confederate Army-looking coat she
was longing for the other day. In fact, she's wearing
the entire outfit that Hayden wore when I met her that
weekend they came home from Bennington, all grey
wool and those memorable lace-up shoes, the toes of
which are tapping against the window. I wonder if
Hayden will show up one day in my sister's clothes. Is
that what happens when you die? You raid your loved
one's wardrobe?

"What? Who's back?" says Myles.

I shake my head. "Nobody."

Sandy clicks her teeth. "She had them packed
all the way in the back of her closet, can you believe
it? Like some naked photographs she was ashamed
of. It took me all night to find them." Sandy hugs

herself and sighs. "Someone needs to tell her enough already with the funeral black every day. Did you see her beautiful hair? Gone!" She snaps her fingers. "My lovely girl is now…" She snaps her fingers again. "Joan of Arc. I hate seeing that scar too." She shivers, then shakes her head vehemently. "No, it's *not* mysterious, Tibbie," she says, reading my mind again. "Well, go on," she demands. Out of the corner of my eye I see her impatiently motioning with her hand. "You were saying?"

I speak slowly, pausing every so often, tentative. "So…we split up…and…"

"Do get on with it," Sandy says and takes a drag from a cigarette.

"Since when did you start smoking?" I ask.

"I don't smoke," Myles says and gives me a look that says I'm crazy. "What does that have to do with splitting up?"

Sandy sings, "Splitting up is so hard to do…re-member that?"

"*Breaking* up is hard to do," I correct her despite the fact that I really want to stop talking to her and instead focus on Myles. I shake my head again, trying to get back on track. "We split up," I repeat more forcefully to Myles.

Sandy starts to clap slowly.

"We split up—"

"Third time's the charm," Sandy cuts me off, continuing to clap a very slow beat.

I raise my voice. "You take Penelope and I'll take Hayden."

"Ooh-la-la," says Sandy. "Tomato, toe-mate-to, let's call the whole thing off," she sings.

"Wait—" Myles says.

But I can't wait for Myles. My sister has upped the clapping speed. She's urging me on. The crowd is impatient for the star to come out onto the stage. They're sick of the warm-up act, the preamble. They want the main show.

"You have to take Penelope. You know her. I don't," I say in a hurry, to shut Sandy up. "You had a crush on her, remember? Don't look at me that way. Sandy told me."

My sister stops clapping, thank god. "Encore!" she shouts.

"Not anymore I don't," Myles says belligerently. He's become a kid again who suddenly insists he hates chocolate ice cream. What's more, he *never* liked chocolate ice cream. When everyone knows he lusted for chocolate ice cream.

"Whatever." I wave my hand, dismissing him. "You're the only one between the two of us who can keep her occupied long enough for me to get Hayden alone and find out everything she knows."

"*Occupied?*" Myles voice goes up about ten octaves.

"Calm down. You don't have to fuck her. Just fuck *with* her."

Sandy does the clucking noise from the back seat, warning me to settle down. "He doesn't like being told what to do," she says in a maddening singsong voice.

"Shut up," I say.

To which, of course, Myles says, "What?"

"Nothing. Listen—"

"And how do you think I can keep her occupied?" he asks, but I can tell he doesn't really want an answer.

Sandy claps loudly at that. "This is better than when we pretended we were sick and we skipped school and watched soap operas."

"So, let me get this straight." Myles's tone and sarcastic emphasis tells me he doesn't believe for one second that my plan will work. "We split up and somehow *I* get Penelope to withdraw her claws from Hayden's hip and get her in another room *all by herself* and you somehow get Hayden off somewhere else so that you can spend hours *interrogating* her, flushing out everything she knows?"

I nod my head enthusiastically and shut off the car. "Yes, it's called divide and conquer," I tell him in a voice that's a cross between a librarian's and my own when I was that kid in the front row with her hand up before the teacher had even finished her question.

From the back seat, my sister echoes in a theatrical voice, "'Divide et impera!' Philip II of Macedonia. Well done! Take the bull by the horns! Leap into the breach! Man up!"

ༀ ༀ ༀ ༀ

Strangely, that's exactly what happens. I don't believe in god, but something, maybe the Queen of Fate, maybe my sister, turns the tumblers and opens the heavenly gates to us. By the time Myles and I unload the groceries from the back of the Saab, zip up to the second floor, and stroll out when the elevator doors open, Hayden is waiting for us in the area devoted to printing and packing supplies. Actually, she's sitting on the floor with several gigantic boxes opened around her, their piles of DIY cardboard shells fanned around her. She glances up as soon as we walk out of the elevator and, audibly sighing, immediately stands and says, "Thank god. I was hoping it was you."

I almost tell her that usually I'd take that as a compliment, but since the bar is so low, namely Penelope, I instead say, "What's wrong?"

She shakes her head. "There's not enough time." Joining us, she grabs one of the grocery bags out of my arms like she's done that a hundred times. "We have to talk."

"You're telling me," I say, moving to our apartment door to unlock it.

"What's ha-ha-ha*ppened*," Myles says, following us into the kitchen.

Again, Hayden shakes her head. "Look," she says, lowering her voice, although we're alone. "Luke is coming tomorrow."

"What!" Myles says loudly.

Hayden shushes him, lowers her bag on the counter. "I don't have time to explain." She starts to take out bananas, a loaf of bread, until my hand stops her hand mid-air.

"Stop. What's going on?"

She drops the bread on the counter and faces us. Myles and I stand there, two goons still holding our grocery bags.

"She'll go and get him from the airport," Hayden tells us. "In Albany. She'll want to be alone with him. I'll come down as soon as she—"

"Hayden?" Penelope's voice comes from the printing press area.

Hayden's face immediately has the splotches of someone who's been caught naked in the parking lot. I make a note to remember that while voices may not carry between floors, they certainly carry within floors.

"We're in here," I call out before Hayden can

say anything. Myles looks ashen. "Hey!" I say when Penelope opens our door and finds us in the kitchen. "We were just telling Hayden how much we'd love to live here."

That immediately unsettles Penelope. "Did you see? The boxes?" she asks Hayden, not looking at me. At first, I think she's either ignoring what I said or didn't hear it, but then she lifts up one of the bags of groceries and turns as if to skedaddle with it back to Level 3.

"Whoa there," I say, stopping her with a hand on her arm. Penelope's jaw is clenched. Through her closed mouth, I can see the slightest movement of her lower lip; her molars are grinding. "The bag?"

"What?" She looks down at the bag in her hands. "Oh, sorry. I thought it was ours." She fumbles the bag into my hands. "We have a lot to do for tomorrow. Coming?" This she clearly directs at Hayden, who I notice has already regrouped; she's brought her face color back to its normal porcelain white. Her eyes are such a pale grey they seem lifeless. Nobody home.

"Yes. The boxes," Hayden says mechanically and moves toward our front door.

Thank god for the boxes.

As soon as they leave and the door closes behind them, Myles starts to say something but I immediately put my finger up to my lips. I begin to unpack the food and motion with my eyes for him to do the same. He slowly empties his bag onto the counter rather than directly into the cabinets. Next door, Penelope and Hayden also aren't saying anything. At least not anything I can hear, other than the scraping sounds of their scooping up all the DIY box pieces and repacking the boxes they came in. There's the sound of a tape roll

screeching as the boxes are sealed. Then, the elevator
doors opening and closing. I motion again for Myles
to be quiet. I tiptoe to our front door, listen, open the
door a crack, wider, then close it and click the dead
bolt.

"Coast is clear," I say as I come back into the
kitchen.

Myles is perched on a stool at the counter. His
unloaded cans of beans and pickles, jars of tomato
sauce and applesauce, boxes of pasta, a family-sized
Styrofoam boat cradling ground beef, and a jug
of iced tea are strewn on the granite. It's clear he's
pushed them all back a bit, away from him, creating a
small bubble of space. Directly in front of him is the
tin I know he stashes his coke in. The lid is slid open.
There's his teeny salt spoon resting in white.

"What are you doing?" I know what he's doing
but isn't that how we always show our disapproval
of something? By asking a question to which we
already know the answer? I stand right next to him.
I could simply pretend to sneeze and blow all of that
stuff to kingdom come. Oops, I'd say. Sorry. My bad.
Gesundheit.

"Luke?" Myles says, agitated. "I can't." He lifts
his hand with his itsy-bitsy spoon to commence the
snorting, but I stop him with a touch on the wrist. He
rests the spoon back in the tin out of sheer fear that
he might lose some if it's in the air too long before
it finds a nostril. I notice he keeps his fingers on the
spoon, though. At the ready.

"This won't help," I assure him. "He's coming
tomorrow. Not in the next hour."

Turning his head, he looks at me. "It doesn't
matter."

"Sure, it does. We have to get our plan together. Keep our heads on straight."

Myles laughs sharply. "You're a B movie."

I shrug. The longer I can keep him talking the more chance I have, I think, of delaying what may be the inevitable. The truth is, I do need him relatively sober. As each day has unveiled something else, I'm starting to realize that I can't do this on my own as I previously thought.

"You signed on, remember?" I say to Myles. "Now, you're an ad for the army."

I raise my hands. "Wait. You knew we were going to see him eventually—"

"Not so soon." His index and middle fingers do their insectile soft-shoe on top of the spoon handle. Slowly, delicately. I realize then that he does it when he's nervous *and* craving the drug. A lot. He's been detoxing.

Taking a chance—who knows if he'll lash out at me in defense of his stash—I lightly cover his hand. Just enough to show I care but not enough to lose my hand for it. Sandy is nowhere to be seen, but I could swear I hear her voice say, "Be nice, Tibbie." And so, I say and do what I think she'd do, given the circumstances. "Please, don't," I tell him. Then, I squeeze his hand and let it go.

Surprise of surprises, Myles's eyes get teary. "Okay," he says, limply, nodding his head. "O-kay." He takes a deep breath. Slides the cover back on its runners. The tin is slipped back into his breast pocket. Then, it's as if we suddenly can't look at each other, as if we're both thinking, *what the hell just happened?* Because we both turn back to the groceries, shoving them haphazardly into the empty kitchen cabinets, not in any order or by any logic. Only to give us something to do. Only to make sure everything's hidden safely away behind cabinet doors as quickly as possible. Later, I'll have trouble finding what I want in those cabinets. But each time I see those cans in disarray, I'll think of Sandy and how proud she would be of me, of how for once I took care of somebody else.

Myles and I cook and eat a simple dinner of ziti with the tomato sauce. We only talk when it's necessary: *Do you think we should cook the whole box? Where's the salt and pepper?* That sort of thing. He adds frozen lima beans thawed under the hot water tap and cut-up heated hot dogs to his bowl, calling it his special gruel recipe.

"What?" he asks when he sees my horrified face as he mixes it together in a soup bowl. "It has the four food groups."

"No fruit," I say.

He smiles, showing that endearing broken tooth. Every time I see it recently, I think of the tooth fairy and how Myles must have looked when he was five or six. He raises one of the applesauce jars.

When we finally sit down at the counter, I notice he can't shovel his gruel in fast enough and wonder if that's because he really is that hungry, or because he's trying to trick his detoxing stomach into believing that he is that hungry. I have the urge to get up and hug him.

As soon as he finishes his dinner, he eats half of the applesauce before he lays his spoon down and screws the lid back on.

Later, sitting on the living room couch, we actually do watch a B movie. An old, lackluster crime drama. I know the identity of the serial killer within five minutes and not because the script tells us.

"It's the antique store owner," I tell Myles. I can't help myself. When I was in sixth grade I'd call out the answer to any question the teacher would throw at us. This was before I realized what a popularity buzz kill that was for a kid. My first clue about that was when Cindy Ames nicknamed me "Horshack" after the obnoxious student on the classroom-based show *Welcome Back, Kotter.* It raced through the playground like wildfire. But, some habits die hard. Or don't die at all, I can hear my sister say.

"I wish Sherlock Holmes was here to solve the mystery of *Stillwater.*" Myles says it so wistfully that I think he's trying to be funny, but then I see his face is serious as he watches the television.

"Me too," I agree, reluctantly.

Next to me, his hands are resting on his knees. Actually, they're twitching.

"How bad is it?" I ask over one of the movie's scenes set in the antique store. The owner, soon to be named as the murderer, is dusting every single antique in the place. I'm guessing it's the scriptwriter's way of clueing us into some cockamamie idea that all murderers are OCD.

Myles shrugs.

"Being high never helps," I tell him, surprising myself. Even more, I do my best to keep any school-marmishness out of it, instead saying it quietly and what I hope he'll perceive as caring.

Myles turns his eyes from the television toward me. I notice for the first time that they're a soft brown. His twitching has stopped. "It *is* the antiques dealer," he says, eyes overly wide.

I fake laugh. "Very funny." I stand up. "Well, I'm going to bed. Who knows what time Luke will be here and I want to be ready for him."

Myles stands also and walks over to the TV set, switching it off. On the way back to the couch, he picks up the pile of linens to make up his couch bed again. He'd tidily stacked them on top of his duffel bag after he awoke this morning. *Maybe Myles is the murderer after all*, I half-joke to myself. His routines, the spartan order of his train car.

"He never had a meeting before noon," he tells me matter-of-factly, the sheets and comforter in his hands. He lets the pile drop onto the couch. For a moment, I don't realize he's still talking about Luke. He pauses, looking at me. "I doubt he'll be here before then. Probably closer to dinner if he's flying into Albany."

"Okay, well, anyway. Goodnight," I say in a hurry. Suddenly, my acting the part of a caring drug counselor has thrown me. *Sandy*, I'm thinking. *This is all your fault.* Maybe she's found a way to channel through me everything she wants to say to Myles. What else could it be?

In the bathroom, I brush my teeth and get dressed in my sweatpants and a T-shirt that I got for free at, of all things, a Libertarian conference in Boston five years before; I was on a panel entitled, "Free Speech: At What Cost?" My boss at the newspaper, who refused to believe punk had passed its heyday, thought it would be good for business by attracting a younger audience. The T-shirt, lazily washed with black clothes countless times resulting in a greyish hue, had an illustration of a fist with the words *Free Speech* trailing straight upward on the muscled forearm. Between that T-shirt and my neck tattoo, I can become whatever hardcore persona I want before I even open my mouth.

When I come out of the bathroom, the lights are strangely off.

"Hello? Myles?"

Then I see it. On one of the living room walls, there's a pink neon graphic of what looks to be a Japanese anime cat dancing. Myles is laughing softly as the cat bounces across the wall, chasing a make-believe mouse.

"What the hell is that?" I sit on one of the velvet chairs across from the couch that Myles has already made into a bed and is sitting on.

"Jibanyan," he says, laughing. "And this…" The cat disappears, I hear a soft *snick*, and then there's a pink ghost-looking cartoon on the wall. "This is Whisper! Woooooooo," he says, gleefully, a kid's rendition of ghost noises.

"Go on, Tibbie," my sister says next to me in the other velvet chair, startling me. "Laugh. You know you want to." One of her legs is hanging and swinging over the armrest.

Myles switches it up again to the cat and starts to meow with each pounce. Then, I do laugh. I realize I haven't laughed in months, not since Sandy died.

"When I was a kid, I collected every Happy Meal toy," he tells me, like it's some deep, dark secret. "How 'bout you?"

He's still staring at the wall, watching the cat jump around, making it do nosedives and then, with a sudden jerk, makes it climb the wall.

"We never ate there," I say. With my eyes adjusted in the dark, I see his face turn toward me.

"You never ate at Mickey Ds?"

I laugh again. "Not before I was an adult. I told you. We had a restaurant. We either ate there or home."

"Wow." Somehow the way he says it, it comes out sounding shocked and also sorry for me.

"It's not like I was abused," I say and snicker. The whisper projector seems to have opened up the windows in the room. A weight has been lifted. The air pressure normalized. For the first time in a very long time, I can breathe. "I survived, trust me."

"I wouldn't have."

I can't tell if he's being serious, and the moment has taken a U-turn back to where we'd been before: worrying about Luke, about everything. Before I can stop it, a distance thuds in again between us.

Myles clicks off the toy, leaving us in darkness. I hear him scrambling under his comforter. I wait for him to say something else. Minutes pass. I'm about to give up and go to bed when he says, "It was all about the toys. Not the food." His voice sounds slightly faraway; he's falling asleep. Then, he yawns noisily. "That was the first thing I collected."

Leaning over, Sandy prods my shoulder with her finger. "Go on, he's waiting for you to say something."

"Oh yeah?" I say.

"Jesus, act a little interested, can't you?" Sandy says.

"Yeah," Myles says. I can make him out across the room in the darkness as he angles his face to me. He's on his back, his hands clasped between his head and his pillow. It reminds me of Huck Finn on a riverbank.

Sandy's swinging foot kicks the side of my chair.

"What else?" I ask. On my chair, I curl up on my side, one hand propping up my head on the chair's arm farthest from Sandy. "What else did you collect?"

"You name it," Myles says, staring now at the ceiling. "Matchbox cars, but only red ones. For a while I was into these toy people made out of wood, but they had to be made in Denmark or Germany." He pauses, thinking. "Snow globes. Every book on birds."

"What happened?"

"What?"

"I mean, where you live now. It's not exactly cluttered."

Myles doesn't say anything for a few moments. The weight returns into the air. I almost can't breathe, it's so heavy and suffocating.

"Nice," Sandy says.

I sit up. "Sorry."

Taking his arms out from behind his head, Myles turns his face to look at me. "Your sister. Your sister is what happened."

Automatically, I look over to my right, but I know Sandy has already gone. I felt her going as soon as I made fun of the train car that Myles calls home sweet home.

When I don't say anything, Myles looks up at the ceiling again. After a beat, he speaks in a trance-like voice that's so quiet I almost can't hear him. "And killing that whale. It was horrible. You can't imagine. It was such a beautiful animal. I've never killed anything in my life. I still have nightmares about it. What it all means, you know? Like, was it an omen? I tried to research it, but I couldn't find anything."

That pisses me off. "Yeah, well, I still have night-mares about *Sandy*," I snap at him.

He faces me again. "You think I don't?" He pauses and then says despondently, "I'm tired. I'm going to sleep." He flops on his stomach, his face turned away from me toward the windows.

And do I go to bed as well? Do I realize I should just zip it and call it a day?

Nah.

I stare at the back of his head for a minute, letting the silence and darkness eat us alive. Then I blurt out, "So, what *exactly* happened?" I'm about to add, "On the boat," but there's no need. His body visibly stiffens, his arms pulling in next to his sides, his legs—which had been akimbo before, with one foot hanging off the edge of the couch—straighten, that foot moving right next to his other ankle under the comforter. His head slithers under also. He's gone from a soldier at ease to someone taking cover in a foxhole.

He doesn't answer me.

After a few deadly minutes have passed, I finally concede defeat to myself and get up to go to the bedroom. I'm almost at the glass wall that will further divide us when his breaking voice pierces the dark quiet: "I pushed her! I think she hit her head. Oh, god!"

Chapter Thirteen

Momentarily, a horrible silence falls over the loft. Then, the industrial fluorescent lights snap on overhead. Tibbie stalks back into the living room, straight up to Myles. She wrenches off his covers. Throws them on the floor. He's so startled he doesn't sit up.

"You hit her?" Tibbie's hands are clenched down by her sides.

For a moment, Myles really believes she's going to hit him. *Do it*, he thinks. Instead, he haltingly corrects her, "Of course not!" Then, full of stumbles and stutters, his words a go-cart that's missing a wheel, bumping down a rutted dirt road, bludgeoning any sense of rhythmic calm, he pushes through, telling her what actually happened between him and Sandy on the boat that day. Surprisingly, Tibbie doesn't interrupt him once. She lets him go on and on. Myles gets scared that she's trying to get him to incriminate himself further. To break him. To get him to falsely confess that he forced Sandy underneath the water and held her head down until there were no more bubbles on the water's surface. To wind him down to an exposed, blubbering blob.

"I'm sure she wasn't blee-blee-blee-*blee*ding when she went below," he says at the end of it, but even he thinks he sounds guilty. "I don't know—"

"Did she hit her head or not?" Tibbie is standing in front of him, with her balled fists and her tight jaw.

Myles shakes his head and, sitting up, pulls his knees into his chest. "I don't...I mean, yes." He takes a deep breath. "She hit her head. But it *wasn't* bleeding." He manages to get the words out without stuttering by the sheer force of his exhale, but the pitch of them is all wrong: too high, too adolescent. Not convincing at all.

"Like you'd tell me—"

Myles cuts her off. "She was rubbing her head. There was no blood."

"Then. There was no blood *then*."

He looks down at his bare feet. He's afraid that he might cry. Is he going to cry? Really? Still, he plunges on. "It wa-wa-*was* an accident. She fell against the thing...what's it called?" He's frantic now, grabbing on to anything. "The seat on the boat. I've gone over it a mill-mill-*mill*ion times in my head."

"You sound guilty about something. Why didn't you tell me this before?"

"I didn't know you," he says defensively. "You show up at my door..." He swings his feet onto the wood floor. Tibbie is so close to the couch that she's barely left him any room to move. He stands anyway, right in front of her. Awkwardly, he shifts to the side and begins to walk toward the kitchen. He needs more air.

She follows right behind him. "So, what? And why wasn't it in the police report then? Huh?"

Why has he said anything? Later on, he'll chalk up his sudden confession to his detoxing. Wasn't that one of the twelve steps that made you come clean? To make amends? But now, all he can think is that his defenses broke down somewhere between the time Tibbie showed up on his doorstep and this night.

Myles grabs a beer out of the refrigerator. Then, he puts it back. Alcohol will only make it worse. Closing the refrigerator door, he turns empty-handed to Tibbie. She's leaning against the kitchen island with her arms folded across her small chest. He somehow senses it's not a stance to keep her distance. The way her hands are gripping her biceps, she seems to be holding her body together. Any minute now, all of her organs, her muscles, her bones, will shatter. Will project through the air, unable to keep connected. Myles knows the feeling well.

"I was in s…s…*shock*," he says, his voice cracking.

"You could've said this later. After. You could've gotten in touch after."

She drops her hands. There's a shift in the air. Myles wonders if the worst of it is over. Maybe she wants to believe he did nothing wrong.

He looks toward the windows with their motorized blinds shutting out the world. It's him and Tibbie in this pod. Alone. Are they? Not really. Hayden and Penelope upstairs, Luke on his way soon. And yet, that's what Myles feels for the first time since they met; they're alone in this *together*. When he glances back to Tibbie, her hands are hanging loosely by her sides. Open.

"I could've. But then I was in…" He hesitates.

"The loony bin?" Tibbie says. She waves her hand dismissively. "After that. You could've told me in the car, even. Coming here. You don't know if she had a concussion. You don't—"

"She didn't." Hayden's voice comes from behind them then. Startled, the both of them turned around.

Hayden is standing by the apartment's entry door. They hadn't heard the elevator or her come in. She's wearing a thin, blue T-shirt that says *Bellport High '90* in faded lettering and lime-green tight jeans. It's the first time Myles has seen her in anything other than black. Along with her short reddish hair sticking up, she's transformed herself from dressing the part of a monk to a skinny rock star in a flash. He senses something is happening, wants to ask her what's going on, but can't decide quickly enough how to phrase the question without it only being about a style change.

Tibbie doesn't stop to ask what Hayden is doing there, or what's up with the clothes switch-up either. "How do you know?" she asks, as if the three of them have been discussing it the whole time.

"'Cause I was there, remember? Do you have anything to drink?" Hayden asks as she moves toward the refrigerator. Myles quickly takes out a beer and hands it to her. "I need to sit down." She slides onto one of the stools. "Sit," she says to Tibbie, patting the one next to her. Then, Hayden motions with her chin at Myles to the stool across the island from her.

She takes a long drink from her beer. "First, you have to let me just tell it. Don't interrupt me," she says, giving Tibbie a look. "It's hard enough to get through it. Promise?"

Tibbie nods her head, and although Myles knows that Hayden isn't talking to him, he nods too. Tibbie glances over Myles's shoulder toward the door. Hayden says, "Don't worry about her. She's out cold. Sleeping pills." She drinks from her beer again. When she lowers the almost empty bottle onto the granite, she eyes Myles first and then Tibbie. She bites her lip. Myles thinks, *She's having second thoughts.* Maybe she will get up and go back upstairs without telling them anything and that will be that. Then, Hayden opens her mouth.

"The thing is," she begins. "I think Luke slipped Sandy some kind of roofie. And Penelope knows that."

Myles and Tibbie simultaneously start talking at Hayden, firing questions at her one after another like a rabble of children. How does Hayden know that? Did she see him do it? Was Penelope there too? When? Why? Not just why would Luke do that, but why didn't Hayden stop it? Throughout the grilling, Hayden stares at the counter, avoiding looking at them.

Finally, she holds up her hands. "Enough." She looks at them both for a beat to make sure they're paying attention. "I didn't *see* him do it. But..." She drawls out the word when she sees Tibbie open her mouth again. "But he handed her a glass and each of the glasses were marked with our names and right after that Sandy complained about not feeling well. When I checked on her twenty minutes after she went to bed, she was sound asleep. I just think...oh, I don't know what I think. I just feel he must've given her something. I mean, why else would she be the only one..." Hayden lets the sentence trail off. Then, breathing in sharply, she says, "If he did, I'm sure Penelope knows about it. Nothing he ever did escaped her notice. That's what I've been trying to find out."

"But why would he do that on a boat full of people?" Tibbie asks her.

"Because he'd already tried it before."

"What?" Tibbie pushes her stool back and stands.

Hayden holds up her hand again. "Not the roofie part. Comments about what Sandy was wearing in the office. He'd stand behind her too close when she'd get some coffee in the lunchroom. Nothing that she could directly accuse him of. When no one else was around. He's a master at that."

"She could've told him to fuck off," Tibbie shouts. Automatically, Hayden and Myles both shush her.

"She did," Hayden goes on, more quietly. "Or at least, she did in her own way. Will you please sit down?"

"I can't believe she never told me this," Tibbie says.

"*You* were sleeping with *your* boss, remember?" Hayden says and tugs her lower lip with her upper tooth. "Sorry. I shouldn't've said that."

"She told you?" Tibbie says, her face coloring. Myles feels badly for her—who wants to find out they've been the butt of gossip?—and at the same time, he's bothered that there's so much about Tibbie that he doesn't know.

When Tibbie continues to loom next to her, Hayden says, "Do you want to know about it or not? Can you sit down? Please."

Grudgingly, Tibbie drops onto her stool.

"It was hard," Hayden says. "She loved her job. He was her boss. The office was small. Who was there to tell? Penelope? They didn't have a human resources department. One night after an author party, when Luke was drunk, he was a little more direct. Said something about his apartment being close by. Again, subject to interpretation. Sandy and I weren't living together by then. We were..." Hayden falters for a second. "It doesn't matter. What matters is, your sister had decided to look for a new job. I thought maybe she could report him to someone after she left P-Town. We have this old Bennington friend who works at *The New Yorker*. Or at least maybe she'd see an attorney. I was going to talk to her after we got back. And then…" She doesn't finish the sentence.

"He killed my sister," Tibbie says harshly.

⚔⚔🗡🗡

An hour later, after Hayden and Myles physically block Tibbie from rushing upstairs and beating Penelope to a pulp, the three of them talk over their options. Myles argues immediately for calling the police.

"That's the stupidest thing I've ever heard," Tibbie snaps. "In case you haven't noticed, we're in New York State. They committed the crime in—"

"We don't know for sure who did what," Hayden interrupts.

Tibbie grabs the top of her head with both hands. "I'm going to scream if you stand up for them now."

Hayden raises her hands in surrender. "I'm not. I'm just pointing out that first we need to get evidence."

"Exactly," Tibbie says, banging the island counter to reinforce the point. "Which is why I suggest that we get them to confess on tape." She folds her arms across her chest again, only this time Myles notices it's not a protective measure. It comes across as daring them to challenge her.

A sudden image of Luke and his daughter tied up and gagged in the basement of the warehouse building that they're in makes Myles queasy. "How d-d-do y'…y'…*you* plan—"

"Myles, I'm a reporter," Tibbie says, exasperated. "My phone can do it. They won't know I'm doing it."

"I meant, get them to con-con-f-f-*fess*."

"Calm down." Tibbie's evident irritation was growing. "Trust me, we won't ask you to do anything that might get those pretty hands dirty."

"All right, that's enough," Hayden says. She stands and faces Tibbie. "First of all, if you say 'we' again make sure you know who 'we' is. Myles is right. Wanting them to confess and getting them to do it are miles apart." She sweeps her hand through the air to prove the point.

"That's it!" Myles says, standing up also. His heart is racing. The current of energy pushes the words out before his tongue can stop them from marching straight through on the conveyor belt. And whether it's sheer momentum or the fact that he keeps his sentences short and to the point, he's able to practically demand, "We separate them. Put miles between them. Play them off against each other."

Hayden barks. "Yeah, right." Her words sting him.

But he grabs Hayden's arm. "No, we do exactly that. And this is how we're going to do it."

❧❧❧❧

It's so dark outside, no stars, no moon, that Myles can't make out his own hands. He can, however, feel them trembling. Is it the frigid cold or is he scared? *Both*, he thinks. All that has to happen is for Penelope to come out of her meds-induced sleep and go into the kitchen for a glass of water, glance out the windows down into the parking lot, and he'd be fucked. *Focus*, he tells himself. He clicks the remote, which blessedly opens the Range Rover with the softest of ticks. In the car he quickly unlatches the hood. If he gets caught, these next few minutes will be when that would happen. Leaving the car door open, he races to the front, yanks up the hood. He unfastens the plastic safeguard cover on the brake fluid reservoir. *Thank god for the Internet and Hayden*, he thinks as he gets down to business. He slips a penknife out of his Carhartt and pokes several tiny holes in the brake line running from the reservoir. Then, after stowing the knife again, he latches the safeguard on, closes the hood as quietly as possible, and finally, risking a bit more noise, shuts the driver door. Thankfully, the Pisser's waterfall sounds drown everything out.

"Don't worry about any noise locking the car again," Hayden told him and Tibbie earlier. "She has some special ringtone programmed into the fob. Buddhist chimes or something." Still, he's so programmed to expect one of those obnoxious BEEP BEEP BEEP alarms going off that he holds his breath as he touches the remote's locking icon. Hayden was right. A soft chime sounds, barely registering over the Pisser.

His nose is dripping. It feels like it will cleave from the cold and drop off onto the snowpack like an iceberg abruptly sheering off into the Antarctic. Maybe ten minutes has passed. Maybe less. A sudden urge to take out his tin box and snort a few spoonfuls overtakes him. Wouldn't it warm him up? Wouldn't it calm him down at least? *Don't be stupid. Someone will see.* He glances up to the second-floor windows again. This time, he sees the dim outline of Tibbie and Hayden watching him. They're in the mailroom area, staring down at him, backlit from a light somewhere in the recesses of the apartment that Tibbie and Myles are staying in. Together with the dark woods encircling the parking lot, the Pisser's crashing turbulent water, the foreboding factory building that looks empty at three in the morning, all of it reminds Myles of every ghost story he's ever read: *A Christmas Carol* in elementary school, *Turn of the Screw* when he was, what? Sixteen? *The Haunting of Hill House* in a freshman college course. What ghost story has ever ended well? His whole body shivers. He practically runs for the building's door, his work boots crunching the dirty ice. The second he's at the door, there's a brief low buzz, which shuts off as soon as he clicks open the door.

His body is still trembling when he's safely back in the loft. He can hear Tibbie and Hayden murmuring excitedly in the kitchen. Discarding his jacket on the couch, he blows his warm breath on his hands. He almost calls out as a joke, "Mom and Dad, I'm home!"

In the kitchen, he finds Hayden and Tibbie perched on stools, drinking beers. Myles slides his tin across the counter to Tibbie. She picks it up and stares at it in her hands. Then, she glances up quizzically at his face.

"Just take it," he says, without enthusiasm, before he can change his mind. Walking over to the refrigerator, he grabs out another beer.

"Well, what should I do with it?" Tibbie asks. The palms of her hands are stretched flat and hold the tin as if it's radioactive. She sounds put out. Myles almost snatches the tin back, but then Hayden is suddenly there next to them, lifting it away from Tibbie's hands, and it disappears somewhere in the lime-green pants she's wearing. It's done so quickly

Myles wonders if he imagined it, except his shivering has started up again. Before he'd chalked it up to the cold, but now he wonders if it's also a mix of craving and detoxing. What has he done? A strong urge to tackle Hayden and wrench the tin back comes over him.

"I'm taking a sh-sh-sh-*show*er," he says, not looking at either of them as he hurriedly walks away.

By the time he's done showering and returns to the kitchen, only the overhead stove light is on, its pale light enough for Myles to make his way to the couch. Hayden is gone. He assumes Tibbie has gone to bed. Someone has remade his couch bed. The top sheet and the comforter are turned down at a creased angle at the top by his pillow. So much has happened in the past few hours he forgot that he'd actually already gone to bed earlier in the evening. As he crawls under the covers, there's a scratchy sound. He feels something. A piece of paper. Afraid to turn on any light that Tibbie could see through the glass wall, he shimmies completely underneath the covers and clicks on his cell phone light. Holding up the paper, it reminds him of all the nights he'd stay up reading when he was a kid, a flashlight in his hand instead of his iPhone, and a book instead of a mysterious note. Maybe it's nothing. A scrap of paper inadvertently dropped when whoever it was made the bed again. He angles the light.

Beautiful handwriting, full of flowing loops. *It wasn't your fault*, he reads. He wonders if it's from Hayden or Tibbie. Or maybe both. He can't decide which he'd rather it be.

⊱⊰⊱⊰

Four hours later, Myles and Tibbie are back at the kitchen island, eating breakfast. It's eight o'clock. His appetite has suddenly returned with a roar. He eats two eggs over easy, stabbing rectangular cut-up strips of his toast into the egg yolk and washing it down with the tea as fast as he can. He wants to convince Tibbie that everything is fine, he's okay, he's up for the job ahead, even as he has the horrible urge to snort up the entire tin of remaining coke that now Hayden has. *If Hayden walked in here this minute, I'd kill her to get it back*, he thinks. With his fork, he violently scrapes up every bit of yolk residue from the plate. Picking up the last two toast strips and shoving them in his mouth, he realizes Tibbie has been gawking at him, her eggs barely eaten on her plate.

"What?" he says. He dumps two more spoons of sugar in his tea.

"You're going to be a diabetic by the time you're my age." She points to his mouth full of the toast strips. "What were those? Did Mummy always cut off your crusts?"

Myles sips his tea. The sugary taste feels exceptional on his tongue this morning. He's hoping the extra carbs will at least get him through this morning and what they'll be doing. All told, he probably only slept two hours. He tossed and turned, thinking about that note and worrying that maybe the plan they've made is crazy and doomed for failure. He'll have to keep an eye out for any birds.

"Soldiers," he says. When Tibbie's face registers confusion, Myles smiles slightly. "That's what they're called when you dip them into eggs."

"Yeah, right. You just made that up."

Myles laughs nervously. He's struck by how innocent their conversation is, especially considering what they're on the verge of doing. They could be a brother and sister having brunch at home. Does eight o'clock qualify as brunch?

"We had a British cook when I was growing up." He shrugs as if in apology.

"La-de-da." Tibbie lifts her tea mug and exaggerates holding out the pinky finger off the handle.

"Violet was awesome."

"Awesome." The way Tibbie says it Myles knows right away that she's making fun of him. He can tell she's nervous, but that's no excuse. He wants to slap her.

Instead, he slides his stool back and picks up his plate and cutlery. "Anyone ever t-t-*tell* you you're not very n...n...*nice*?" He doesn't say it meanly. He simply wants to put her on guard that he's not a fool. Although even he can tell it's come off more hurt than smart.

Something flashes across Tibbie's face then. It's so fast that if Myles had been glancing away for a second, he would've missed it. It's there and then gone. He caught it, though. Clear as can be. Someone had told her that. Someone she had loved.

࿊࿊࿊࿊

An hour later, they're in Tibbie's Saab on their way to the Albany airport. Although there's plenty of time to get there before Luke lands, Myles notices that Tibbie is speeding along at a ninety-mile-an-hour clip.

Rigging the brakes in the Range Rover the night before was the first step of the plan. The second step was Hayden convincing Penelope this morning that she should go with her to the airport to pick up Luke.

"I'd like to be a fly on the wall for that," Tibbie told Hayden the night before when they were at the island deciding what they needed to do next.

Hayden's index finger traced the rim of her beer bottle. "I'll figure something out. She's been hounding me to get in touch with that company we bought the presses from. They forgot to send one of the stackers when they originally sent them over. But it weighs about a hundred pounds and they don't want to pay for the shipping costs. They're bankrupt and they can't stand Luke. He wheedled the price down for the presses so much they feel he screwed them." Hayden paused to take a sip of beer. "Anyway, I can suggest we could drive over there before picking Luke up. She needs me to help lift the stacker into the car. I think it's in a storage place twenty minutes from the airport."

"Luke's the spawn of Ebenezer Scrooge and Cruella de Vil," Tibbie sniped.

A thin smile came on Hayden's face. "That's what Sandy used to say." She gazed intently at Tibbie, who didn't look away.

"So…" Myles said, suddenly feeling uncomfortable although he couldn't say why. "You'll tell her you want to pick up the stacker then?"

"What?" Hayden slowly shifted her glance from Tibbie over to Myles. "Oh, right. I'll tell her we need to leave by eleven so that we can pick it up and then head to the airport to get Luke when he flies in at one. She always makes me drive her places, so I'll be the one driving when the brakes give out. I'll be ready with the emergency brake if we need it. But don't worry.

I'll pull over as soon as the brake pressure starts to go lower."

Immediately after breakfast, Tibbie and Myles drive off from *The Loom*. They have to leave before Penelope and Hayden; they can't chance driving past them after the Rover's brakes fail. Otherwise, on NY-199 Penelope The Hawk would undoubtedly see and flag down their Saab. If all goes as planned, Tibbie and Myles will be the ones retrieving Luke from the airport. They'll simply tell Luke that an important conference call regarding a potential book order needed to be dealt with by Penelope and Hayden.

The next part of the plan will be difficult. Once they meet up with Luke, Tibbie and Myles will have to insist that he sit up front in the Saab. Convince him there's more legroom. Tibbie has to pretend she's happy to have the chance to talk to him. Flatter him. She has to lie. Tell him how much Sandy used to speak about him.

"Remember, his ego is boundless," Hayden told them the night before.

"He'll probably steal the front seat anyway," Myles said.

"Perfect," Hayden said. "Don't forget you have to sit directly behind him, Myles. You'll deal with this." She pointed at two bottles of champagne that she'd ferreted out from a crate that Penelope kept in the supply room. "And he can't see you."

"I know, I know," Myles said. "I'm not stupid."

"What if he doesn't drink it?" Tibbie asked.

Hayden opened her mouth to answer her, but Myles jumped in. "At two hundred bucks a pop? Pass up his *champas*?" he said derisively. "I don't think so." He hated how his nerves were suddenly so on edge. The longer they talked about the plan, the more he wanted to get on with it. As the night wore on, the good adrenaline that had propelled him through messing up the Rover had turned into a bad case of the jitters. He needed to do something. Jog in place. Jumping jacks. Anything. Instead, he stood and slid the champagne bottles onto a shelf in the fridge.

"It's the same stuff he passed out to everyone," Hayden went on. "On the boat."

The refrigerator door slammed. Myles swiveled around.

"That's poetic justice," Tibbie said. She pointed at Myles. "Don't you back out."

"I won't," Myles snapped at her, but immediately felt badly for doing so. He had to calm down. He went back to his stool and forced himself to sit down again.

Hayden handed him a bottle of Ambien. "You'll need two of these, ground up. Go get a baggy and a hammer. They're in those drawers over there," she said pointing underneath the counter.

"I wish we had a roofie to give him a dose of his own medicine," Tibbie grumbled.

"This is why you're only to drive the car," Hayden said. "He's going to jail. Not us, remember?"

The plan is for Myles to slip the drug into a glass of the champagne before passing it to Luke in the front seat to drink on the way.

"Within ten minutes he should be passed out." Hayden held the plastic sandwich bag open for Myles to drop in two pills. Then, surprising her, he dropped in a third, followed by a fourth. "Just in case," he said, his hand raising the hammer as if he intended to bring that along for good measure. Instead, he lightly tapped the pills in the baggie against the countertop into a powder.

"You'll have about six hours." Lifting the pill bottle off the counter, Hayden slipped it back into her pants pocket. For a second, Myles felt a pang. What he wouldn't give to sleep tonight.

"Wait...what if we need more time?" Tibbie asked.

"Think of something else," Hayden said.

Tibbie snorted. She did a sort of beckoning motion with her fingers. "Give me back those pills."

Now, in the car on the way to the airport, Myles tells her, "Slow down, we have plenty of time. He's not getting in for four hours."

He should've saved his breath.

☙☙☙☙

At the airport with hours to kill, it takes them five minutes to walk through the entire first floor where departures are.

"International? I don't think so," Tibbie grouses, pointing to the large sign saying *Albany International Airport Welcomes You.* There are maybe ten airline carriers that touch down in Albany.

They ride the escalator up to the second floor, where the waiting area is for arrivals. They're stopped short from going very far, however, by the TSA Security Checkpoint. They can see three terminal arms spread-eagled behind the checkpoint, a smattering of signs for food places that are off-limits to them. That's it.

"Come on," Tibbie growls and heads back to the down escalator.

"I told you to slow down," Myles chides her. "Now, what are we going to do for hours?"

Tibbie's way of answering him is to put distance between them by skipping down the escalator. There's something so childlike, so loose and easy in her physicality, that Myles is instantly attracted to it. If he could only learn to be that free in life.

Tibbie strides over to the only food and drink establishment on the first level: a Dunkin' Donuts. The last thing he needs, Myles thinks, is coffee or a jolt of sugar. Lack of sleep and his jangled nerves from what they're planning to do has him practically gnashing his teeth. His big breakfast, a bad idea that fooled no one, is roiling in his stomach. If anything, it's increased his fear he's going to throw up. He's starting to seriously regret he handed over his stash tin. Maybe they could suck down one of the champagne bottles and just sit in the car until seconds before Luke's plane lands.

He joins Tibbie in front of the Dunkin' registers and tugs on her sleeve. "Let's get out of here," he whispers. "Drive into town."

"What? No way." Shaking her head, Tibbie turns back to the young, pasty-faced girl behind the register. She's wearing a mud-brown DD apron. This coffee bar is open twenty-four seven and she looks to Myles like she's been there all night.

Tibbie tells the girl, "Two chocolate glazed, a cruller, and a box of Munchkins."

And she accused me of ending up a diabetic?

"Would you like to try our new Girl-Scout-inspired flavor drink?" the girl says in a monotone that reminds Myles of this documentary he once saw about zombies in Haitian folklore.

"Wow. Did you hear that, Myles?" Tibbie half-shifts to him. "Girl Scouts inspired!" Then, she turns back to the girl. "Sure. Which one do you recommend?"

she asks as if the girl is a sommelier. If Myles didn't know any better, he'd think Tibbie was serious.

The girl shrugs. "Mint."

"Mint it is," Tibbie says, winking at her, which is lost because the girl has already turned her back to them and is picking out the donuts.

"Can we please go into town?" Myles whispers.

Tibbie ratchets her head around. "I said no," she says, scolding him. "We go into town, I know we'll miss him when he arrives. We're staying put like we agreed. Now, do you want something to drink or not?"

Myles almost bursts out laughing, it's so absurd. His nerves are frayed; he's all jammed up anticipating seeing Luke again. Tibbie is acting as if they're picking up a good friend and are about to go on a picnic. His stomach is in knots. There's no chance he'll be able to drink anything, let alone coffee. He's on the cusp of losing it, about to burst out laughing maniacally. *Just like Fitzy*, he thinks. Fitzy, another philanthropic friend of his mother's that Myles couldn't stand, whose real name was the more adult-like Frederick but who preferred the bubbly sound of his childhood nickname, began to have what his doctor called gelastic seizures caused by epilepsy, itself a side effect of a brain tumor. The last year Fitzy was alive, he'd succumb without warning into outbursts of uncontrollable laughter at the monthly dinners his mother still threw.

"Sorry. Pardon me. It's the tumor," he'd say, pointing at his head, his hand mimicking a gun. "Puh...puh," he'd sound out, tightening his lips and expelling two gusts of air. His version, Myles guessed, of a gun going off, followed by another bout of hysterical laughter, with the rest of the dinner guests either avoiding his gaze or trying not to laugh as well out of sheer embarrassment for him. Then one Friday Fitzy didn't show, and when Myles asked his mother about it she calmly pointed to her head and mimicked the same gun sound.

Now, without waiting for Myles to order something, Tibbie tells the girl they want another Girl Scout mint coffee drink.

"Recall," the girl shouts, *unnecessarily*, Myles thinks, as the only other worker is parked a mere two feet away from zombie girl, by the frozen drink station. "Two Thin Mints frozen chocolate."

For a few moments there's confusion between the two workers; did she mean in addition to the one already ordered for a total of three, or to replace the first order for a total of two? the frozen-drinks-maker asks.

"Nobody said there'd be math," Tibbie says to be funny, but no one laughs.

"I said *recall*, didn't I?" says the zombie, who suddenly seems to Myles to have a bit of hutzpah beneath that walking wounded exterior. "Recall means…" Unable to come up with something suitable, the girl barks, "Just make two of them, aight?" Then, surprisingly, both workers break into a fit of joint laughter. After that, they both keep saying "Recall!" to each other, which starts them guffawing all over again.

Finally, they're handed their two vat-sized frozen drinks. He follows Tibbie toward a row of empty, avocado-colored, hard plastic seats. She's already sucking her drink through a straw as her other hand swings a gigantic DD paper bag that's more suitable to hold new king-sized pillows.

"Take these," she says, placing the bag on Myles's lap.

"You don't want them? Well, I don't want them."
He shifts the bag onto the empty seat next to him.

Tibbie shrugs. Bites her bottom lip. Shifts her
weight, agitated, in her chair. Sucks her drink. Then,
she nervously laughs and just as suddenly stops
laughing, and not for the last time that day Myles will
think of Fitzy and will have the urge to raise a finger
gun to his head and, expelling air, puff out, "Puh…
puh."

Chapter Fourteen

Hayden has barely pulled the Rover over, telling Penelope that clearly something is very wrong with the car, when Penelope is on her cellphone trying to reach AAA. Hayden prays that in this cold there'll be many callers ahead of them. She's depending on it to take a long time to send a tow truck, bring them back to a service station, and repair the brake leak. They all are.

"Won't that hold you up for hours?" Tibbie asked the night before.

Myles shook his head. "Replacing a brake line is easy. I did it on my truck."

"Let's just hope it takes a long time for them to send the tow truck then," Hayden said.

"Hello?" Penelope says now into her cell, and Hayden's stomach pinches. "How long?" Penelope asks after she tells the AAA operator where they are according to the GPS. "Well, we're freezing here so can you make it as fast as—" She looks at the phone. "Shit, the call dropped."

"What'd they say?"

Penelope lets out a frustrated yell. "God, I hate it here!" She stares out the passenger window. There's nothing to see but telephone poles surrounded by a snowy landscape that stretches on for miles. It's the first time Penelope has said something negative about upstate New York since they moved there. Hayden has always suspected, though, that Penelope had simply buried her distaste by immersing herself in setting up her little fiefdom at *The Loom*.

"How long?" Hayden asks.

Penelope sighs. "At least an hour. Apparently, they only have one truck in this area and he's out on another call. Assholes." She yanks her parka's hood over her ski hat. "Maybe we should try walking."

Hayden laughs nervously. None of them had considered that Penelope would suggest walking aimlessly through the frozen tundra.

"It's warmer in here than out there. Besides, there's nothing in sight." Hayden swivels around in the driver's seat. "I'm going to get the blanket that's in the back."

Penelope grabs her arm. "Don't open the door. It'll let cold air in. Crawl back there."

"I'm not crawling all the way to the back. I'll close the door, don't worry."

"This is your fault!" Penelope yells, still gripping Hayden's arm. Hayden's stomach pitches again.

"What?"

"You should've checked the gauge."

Hayden relaxes some. "What gauge? There is no gauge for the brakes. I told you something is wrong. Maybe the brake fluid leaks."

"Please just get the blanket," Penelope says wearily, and releasing her grip jerks a thumb toward the back. "I'm freezing."

Not wanting to make a bigger scene of it, Hayden begins to crawl through their bucket seats toward the back seat and then climbs over that to the far back of the SUV where there is one of *The Loom*'s Mexican-style wool blankets.

"Hey," she says. "There's a first aid kit back here."

"That was my father's going-away gift. He thinks I'm going to die up here in the wilderness. And you know what? He's probably right."

Inside the kit Hayden finds one of those shiny foil heat-containing blankets, which jars her for a second by bringing her instantly to the rescue boat, but then Penelope calls back, "Can you hurry?" and Hayden returns to rifling through the kit to see what else they could use. There's an air horn that can fit into the palm of your hand (*To warn off rapists?* Hayden thinks), bandages, a roll of gauze, adhesive tape, a tube of antibiotic cream, two heat packs, a flashlight, and what seems to be an orange plastic toy gun. The gun couldn't fool anyone, not even a child.

"Here," Hayden says when she's up front again. In her absence, Penelope has shifted into the seat behind the steering wheel. Hayden hands her the warmer foil blanket and the heat packs, keeping the Mexican wool blanket for herself. "Wrap this under your jacket."

For once, Penelope does as Hayden says, quickly removing her coat, wrapping the foil around her hoodie, then putting her coat back on. The entire time she huffs and puffs as if it's already freezing in the warm car. The engine is still on, although Hayden did suggest they'd need to turn it off at some point to conserve fuel.

"Don't snap those until you absolutely need it," Hayden says, pointing to the packs on Penelope's lap.

"Why are you being so nice?" Penelope eyes her from within the recesses of her hood and scarf that she has pulled up to her nose. She could be a terrorist on an FBI poster.

Hayden tenses again. Her stomach is a mess. *Calm down*, she tells herself. *She doesn't have a clue.* But Hayden wonders why Penelope slipped behind the driver's seat. *Okay, she thinks you somehow messed up the car. But does she think it's more than that? Is she putting it together?*

Hayden tries to hold her voice steady, tries to look straight at Penelope when she says, "I'm always nice. You just don't notice anymore."

To her immense relief, Penelope barks out a laugh. "Yeah right," she says. "Poor misunderstood you." She looks away, over the dashboard.

On any other day Hayden would've bristled at that, but now it reassures her. As long as Penelope is being sarcastic or criticizing her, everything is normal.

"God, it's bleak here," Penelope says as she starts to type into her cell.

"What are you doing?" Hayden asks.

"Texting Luke." Penelope continues to type. "We're probably going to be late. At least he'll see it when he gets off the plane."

"Maybe his plane will be late." Hayden's voice sounds weak as she says it, however, because she's simultaneously thought what a disaster that would be.

"Shit, there's still no signal."

Hayden looks at her watch. Only fifteen minutes has passed. This was her idea, but she hadn't realized how hard it would be to wait with Penelope. To not worry that something will go wrong, such as the truck rescuing them sooner than she wants it to. How stressful it would be to spend the time listening to Penelope, watching for any signs that she'd somehow caught on to their scheme.

"What's with the getup anyway?" Penelope suddenly asks her. She points at Hayden's coat. She's wearing her old Confederate-style overcoat that she hasn't worn since Sandy died. Underneath, she still has on Sandy's T-shirt from Bellport High School, a thermal sweatshirt, and her own lime-green pants from the night before when she'd met up with Isabel and Myles. Because of the snow, she chose her sensible L.L.Bean boots instead of her vintage lace-up ones. All of it was selected with care that morning. If she was going to do what she had to do today, she needed to feel like herself. Her *old* self.

Hayden shrugs nonchalantly. "It's how I used to dress." She doesn't have to say, "Before I met you." Penelope understands that to be the case. At once, Hayden feels badly that she's been so hurtful, has lowered herself to Penelope's mean level. So, she adds, "I just need to do laundry." Penelope doesn't belabor the issue by pointing out that surely her normal parka doesn't go in the laundry. Instead, Hayden is alarmed to see that Penelope's attention is fixated on her phone.

"Come on," Penelope coaxes, jiggling the phone the way she would if she were shaking a box of candy. "What about yours?" She glances up at Hayden.

"My what?"

"Honestly?" Penelope gives her an incredulous look. "Your phone. Does it have a signal?"

Hayden slips her phone out from her coat pocket. "No," she says, barely looking at it and shoving it back into her pocket before Penelope can ask to see it. They have different phone carriers, which could make all the difference between getting a connection or not.

"Come on," Penelope says, again jostling her

phone. Finally, she tosses it on the dashboard in disgust.

"Was there any food there?" she asks, motioning with a thumb again toward the back. Hayden feels like she can't keep up. It's like being stuck somewhere with a five-year-old who needs something to foist their attention on after I Spy gets too boring. Here, have some Goldfish, she wants to say.

She shakes her head. "Just first aid stuff and some kind of toy gun. Why did Luke pack that anyway? Was it yours when you were a kid?"

"The flare gun!" Penelope shouts. Immediately, she starts to launch herself between their seats.

"What are you doing?" Hayden twists around to watch her, but Penelope doesn't answer her right away. Instead, after she climbs over the back seat, she opens the first aid kit. She holds up the air horn in her gloved hands and with her thumb pushes down on the top button. A huge blast of noise startles Hayden so badly she thinks for a moment her heart actually stopped.

"Christ!" Hayden shouts. "That scared me."

Penelope just laughs as if it's the funniest thing in the world. She tosses the air horn back into the kit and then she's holding the flare gun in her hand. Her black leather gloves give her the appearance of a professional hitman determined to leave no fingerprints. "Ta da!" she cries giddily. Gripping the top of the back seat, she starts to flip sideways over it. Her chest pins her hands down as they grip the top of the seat with the flare. Her legs swing over. She's on a Black Ops mission scaling a fence.

Then, suddenly, there's an ear-shattering explosion. Penelope's parka bursts into flames. She falls onto the back seat screaming, her gloves flailing at a blaze that's sizzling the polyester of her coat along with the metallic blanket underneath, instantly filling the car with a horrible, chemical smell.

"Shit!" Hayden yells. She scrambles into the back seat. Throwing herself at Penelope, she straddles her and starts to pound at the flames, beating them out with her gloved hands. Underneath her, Penelope is writhing against the seat. There's an ungodly sound coming out of her mouth, a keening that's part moan, part screech, part sob. The flames are gone and still Penelope wails and thrashes side to side. One arm is braced across her chest.

"You're okay, you're okay," Hayden shouts. She tries to pull Penelope's arm away so she can undo what's left of the parka's zipper, but Penelope fights against her, struggling to cross her arms over her chest while yelling, "No, no, no!"

Hayden ends up straddling her, holding Penelope's arms down with her knees. She rips off her own gloves to get a better tug on Penelope's zipper, but the metal is white-hot. Instead, her fingers quickly start to tear the burnt jacket off Penelope's shoulders. The polyester looks like it's glued in spots to what's left of the foil blanket, and Penelope's sweatshirt, T-shirt and bra. *God, her skin.* Hayden tries as fast as she can to peel away whatever isn't directly on her skin. Blood is seeping from Penelope's left shoulder out of a blackened hole where a rubber stub of a burnt-orange cartridge pokes out from her clavicle. The skin on her shoulder is raw and spotted with glistening red stars, like something out of a comic book.

"Oh god," Hayden says, and now she's crying too. "Oh god. Shh. Shh. You're okay, you're okay."

She says this knowing Penelope is not okay. "Stay there. Don't touch anything." She leans over the seat, hauls up the metal first aid box, and flings it to the floor next to them. "No, no, you can't touch," she says because Penelope is grabbing her own shoulder again, yelling that she's going to be sick. Hayden pulls her hand away. She kneels on Penelope's wrists, just enough to hold them in place while she jerks open the first aid kit and takes out the gauze and the tape. She should probably use the antibiotic cream. There isn't time. Should she yank out the cartridge or leave it in? The blood is trickling more now around the plug. She decides on the spot it'll be better to leave it in, to staunch the blood. If she pulls the plug out, who knows what will happen?

"Sit up. Sit up," Hayden says, still straddling Penelope's stretched-out thighs. She pulls Penelope up to a sitting position so that they are nose-to-nose. She starts to wrench the rest of Penelope's clothes from her back.

"Cold," Penelope wails. Her head lolls, signaling she's going to pass out. Snot is running from her nose.

Hayden holds her fast. "Hang on." She wraps the gauze tightly around and around Penelope's shoulder, on top of the cartridge. Penelope lets out another scream as Hayden tugs the gauze even tighter. "Why the hell would your father put a loaded flare in there?" Hayden shouts as she winds the tape around the top of the bandage, which sends Penelope screeching again. "Fuck!"

Hayden feels her getting more limp in her grasp. Penelope's eyes are fluttering. "Flare fun," Penelope mutters, shaking her head. "Fun gun."

"No! No, don't pass out." Hayden tears at the

tape with her teeth, which makes Penelope yelp like a
wolf whose leg is caught in a trap. She props Penelope
against the car door and then reaches over the front
seat to grab the wool blanket. After covering Penelope
with the blanket, Hayden slips off her own coat, tucking it around Penelope as if that will solve everything.
Still, that doesn't stop Penelope from starting to shake
violently. Hayden's shaking also, and sweating. She
presses down on the bandage over the wound, almost
throwing up when she feels the butt of the hard cartridge through the gauze. Penelope cries out again.

"You have to stay awake," Hayden tells her,
smoothing Penelope's hair out of her face. "They'll be
here any moment." Who's "they"? The tow truck guy?
She hasn't called anyone for help. "Press down on
this," she tells her, placing Penelope's hand on top of
the cartridge. Penelope moans. Hayden pulls out her
cell from her coat wrapped around Penelope. "Stay
here. I'm going to see if I can get a signal."

"No," Penelope whispers. "Don't leave me."

"Just for a minute. Don't fall asleep. Keep pressure there." She pushes Penelope's hand back to her
shoulder.

Outside, the air is so frigid Hayden gasps. Yanking her sweatshirt's hood up, she runs away from the
car in the direction that they were driving. She has
no idea which direction would be better, but maybe
this direction is closer to civilization, to a cell tower.
Please god. She holds up the phone as if it is an anten-
na. Two bars. She starts to type in 911. No bars. She
has to stop herself from pitching the phone as far as
she can over the cruel landscape. She waves the cell in
the air. Three bars. With freezing fingers, she punches
in the number. "Hello! Hello!"

Chapter Fifteen

I have to hand it to Luke. When he comes down the ramp and he finds out that we're his escort service, he acts like he's happy that it's us doing the pickup and not his daughter. Of course, it could be that he's blotto despite it being only a bit past noon. So much for airlines limiting customers to Lilliputian Bloody Marys on morning flights.

Although I catch a slight wobble as he strolls toward us, he's immaculately dressed in a camel wool overcoat that's open, showing a three-piece grey suit complete with a striped tie held at the top by a fussy tie pin. The clothes and his blocky head of closely cropped grey hair give him, unexpectedly, an air of authority. He's so short and stout, he might've otherwise passed unnoticed without the wardrobe.

"Myles, old bean," he exclaims, one hand holding a leather overnight bag with large gold embossed initials *LBIII* on the side. His other hand is raised and clamping onto Myles's shoulder. "What's this I hear about you being the new Grizzly Adams? Love the hat and the onesie."

Strangely, in all the planning and everything else, I've forgotten that Myles worked with, actually *for*, Luke. Sandy's told me so many stories about Luke as her boss that it seems that he was exclusively her boss and no one else's.

Myles winces. I can't tell if it's because Luke's grip is hurting him or he can't stand the guy. Or maybe, with Luke in the flesh before us, our boy Myles is having second thoughts about what we're about to do. I pretend to reach over to shake Luke's hand, but what I'm really doing is stepping on top of Myles's foot and giving it a good grind.

"Tibbie," he says through gritted teeth.

"I'm so glad to finally meet you," I say to Luke, drowning out Myles. I give him the best monster grin I can muster. I hold out my hand. "My sister told me so much about you."

This visibly unsettles Luke. He drops his grip on Myles. Awkwardly bypassing my stretched-out hand, Luke hugs me close. "Your sister…your sister…" he mumbles into the side of my head. Not coming up with any way to end the sentence, he stands back. Astonishingly, he makes a show of wiping his eyes despite there not being a tear in sight.

"Shall we?" he says. He raises his overnight bag in the general direction of outside. "Crack on, oh intrepid guides."

If I didn't already hate him, I'd certainly detest him right about now.

I have to say that everything goes pretty smoothly after that. If Myles and I ever want a life on the lam, it's frightening how easily bad behavior comes to us. Myles was right. Luke doesn't even wait for us to suggest or convince him to sit up front. He casually hands Myles his bag as if he's a porter and, as soon as my car beeper goes off, opens the passenger door. Before Myles and I can close our own doors, Luke's sucking down something from a flask in the passenger seat next to me. He tucks it back inside his coat pocket, like a comb. Then, he rubs his hands.

"Drive on, James," he says, realizes that it's me behind the wheel, and gives me a smile that comes off as a quasi-leer. "Or Jane, as the case may be."

Murderer, I think. I wish that Sandy was along for the ride then. But then again, maybe not. She might try to talk me out of it.

It has begun. I'm rolling out our planned script, repeating that we're sorry that Penelope couldn't meet him, how she gave us strict instructions to open and drink his favorite bottle of champagne on the way.

"Oh-ho," Luke says, chuckling. "I'm not *that* easy."

We have no idea if he's referring to his not forgiving his daughter for not showing up, or if there's a deeper, more sinister meaning to what he says, such as he thinks we're going to have a three-way with him as recompense. We've been so on edge ever since Hayden told us about the roofie episode that it's everything we can do not to pull over the car and beat Luke to death here and now with the tire iron. I say *we* because I also can feel Myles's hatred of Luke infecting the air in the car like some bad burnt smell. As soon as I drive us onto I-90 E in the opposite direction from Skyville, Myles pops the cork, purposely pointing it so that it makes a beeline for Luke's left earlobe, nips it perfectly, and then bounces off the windshield.

"Jesus, what the fuck, dude?" Luke yells, dropping the snob act and slipping into what he really is: someone who grew up in Yonkers, outside of New York City. He grabs his injured ear and then checks his fingers. No blood. His ear is bright red.

"Sorry," Myles says, barely containing his glee.

"Are you okay?" I ask, unable to suppress my

smile, which is diametrically opposed, of course, to my question. *Diametrically opposed.* If Sandy were here reading my thoughts, she'd make fun of me for saying that. I used to trade such redundant phrases with my sister whenever we were bored at the restaurant. Bunny rabbit. Cash money. Rat fink. Taxi cab. Diametrically opposed. Thinking of Sandy sobers me, wiping the smile off my face.

In the meantime, Luke is wrenching his body against his seat belt and glaring at Myles. Then, he thinks better of it, swivels back around, and forces another fake chuckle.

"You better give me a hefty sample after that, old sod," he says, gingerly touching his inflamed ear again. "And take off that wretched hat. You look like the Unabomber."

"Of course, Mr. Blackmore." Myles says it so smoothly it disarms me. His tone is that of an obsequious underling who's about to shank the abusive company boss. I glance at him in the rearview. He's actually done what Luke asked and taken off his flap hat. He pokes his head through the gap between the front seats and says, "Coming right up."

Luke is so thrown by the nearness of Myles's face that he turns his face away, toward his side window, which I realize is exactly what Myles wants. Quickly, Myles leans back. With Luke diverted, Myles can easily do anything he wants to Luke's drink now. After slipping in some of the already ground-up sleeping tablets, he hands Luke a glass flute filled to the brim. The flute was Hayden's touch. "Trust me, he'll love that," she'd said the night before. We brought two of the flutes with us. One for Luke, of course, and one for Myles if he lost his nerve. My script is to beg off, saying that I have to drive and New York Stateys are no-nonsense when it comes to locking people up for DUI.

Luke quickly drains his glass.

"Thank you, old bean. May I have another? Tickety boo." He hands back his empty glass over his shoulder without a glance in Myles's direction.

Done.

He downs that one too.

"So, what are you two doing visiting my beautiful daughter?" Luke says as if he's asked where we're going for lunch. I suddenly feel there's ice water in my veins; I think I even raise my shoulders closer to my neck. Glancing in the rearview, I see Myles has closed his eyes. His jaw is rigid. Maybe he's gearing up so he won't stutter. We'd rehearsed last night what we'd say if Luke asked this question. "Of course, he's going to ask *that*," was what Hayden had said. It was the only time all night that she showed any impatience when we asked questions. Regardless of the dry run Hayden put us through—"Just tell him you're visiting *me*, that I asked you to come"—both Myles and I falter when the actual thing happens now.

"What?" I reply, pretending I didn't hear the question, and Myles stays mum. When Luke repeats the question, it comes out a bit garbled. Then, before I can begin to recite what Hayden told us to say, Luke's head suddenly dips and crashes against his side window. He mumbles something, his eyes fluttering shut. Then, silence.

"Jesus, how much did you put in them?" I look nervously at Luke and then at the rearview.

Myles stares back at me. "No going back now," he says and, surprising me further, flashes what seems to me to be a cold smile, showing off that severely chipped tooth that now makes him look rough and dangerous. His eyes are practically glittering. For the first time I realize that Myles has been carrying a secret this whole time: he hates Luke even more than I do. That perhaps that idea of his, the night before, of calling the police might've been only a ruse. Maybe he's been waiting for something like this to happen ever since the boat went down. Maybe he's been waiting for me. Waiting for me to set everything in motion.

But maybe I'm wrong. Maybe it's simply my own nerves that are skewing everything. There's nothing to do but drive on and find out. As the miles and hours tick past, that feeling of courage, however, disappears and another feeling starts to seep in. Dread.

Several hours later we're again bumping over the muddy driveway to Myles's train wreck in P-Town, also part of the plan. Luke is still passed out. The winter sun is almost down and darkness is settling in, which we were counting on. It was Myles's idea to come here. When he first mentioned it the night before, I thought it was his way of easily getting Luke to confess in the same town where everything had gone so wrong. Maybe by forcing Luke to be near the murder scene, Luke would immediately fall to his knees and beg for our mercy while he admitted everything and our job would be done. Tickety boo, as Luke would say. We could simply hand him over to the police along with his taped confession, our vengeance completed. No fuss, no muss. That's what I assumed. Now, as I shut off the car, I'm edging toward full-blown anxiety that there was more to it than that. Much more to our Myles.

He persuaded Hayden and me that it was the perfect place to bring Luke because only one of his neighbors would be home—the silver train car with the smoke now coming out of the metal exhaust tube on the roof. Myles told us the owners of the other two train cars go to Florida every winter. The neighbor that's here is a deaf eighty-five-year-old who hasn't said a word to Myles or acknowledged him when they've seen each other.

"It's creepy," Myles had said to Hayden and me. "No one else comes in or out either, except once a month some other old guy pulls up in a van and they must go shopping at the BJs in Barnstable because when they come back, they unload boxes of toilet tissue and canned goods. They're stockpiling for Armageddon."

"Perfect setting for a murder," I told him. "I'm kidding," I added because Hayden's face showed that she thought I was serious. Some part of me—the part that wanted so desperately to avenge my sister—possibly had convinced myself that I was serious. After Myles's heavily dosing Luke, however, I'm starting to wonder if he was the one that had that in mind all along.

Getting Luke into the house isn't as easy as we thought it would be. Or at least that I imagined it would be. I've never actually carried someone in my life. Luke is short, but he's what you might call a beefcake. It doesn't help that there's a foot of snow, which his feet drag through like an anchor catching on weeds as we walk a few steps, holding him up on either side under his arms.

"Here," Myles says and stops, his breath puffing out little clouds into the cold air. He passes me his keys. "Go open the door. I got this." As soon as I grab the keys, Myles is flipping Luke over his shoulder as easily as if he were a longshoreman used to grabbing up fifty-pound sacks of potatoes. I watch, astonished. He's so skinny. How in the hell did he do that?

"What?" he says, not breathing any heavier from the exertion. "I've been moving bodies for the past three months. Go open the door."

I've been moving bodies… The way he says it makes me forget that he's an EMT. Instead, a chill washes over me with a ridiculous thought: *He's done this before.*

"Go. Open. The. Door," he says again.

Once inside, Myles dumps Luke onto a kitchen chair. Luke immediately begins to slump over to the floor. "Come here and hold him up," Myles orders me.

"No," I say. It's all moving too fast. I don't know what story I'd previously concocted as to how this would turn out, but now that we're here I admit that there's no way I can actually touch Luke again, knocked out or otherwise. The anger and adrenaline that originally propelled me from Boston to here and then to Skyville and back again has suddenly dissipated into a shitstorm of regret and a desire to be anywhere but here. Against my wanting to be otherwise, I realize that I may not be as badass as I thought. I want to go home. My real home. The one we grew up in. I miss Sandy fiercely. Only she isn't here to defend us against whatever evil has been brewing.

So, it's up to me to tell Myles, "No. I don't want to."

"You don't want to?" Myles mimics me, laying a whiney voice on thick. "Bullshit," he hisses. "Get over here."

Something in his voice compels me to do it.

"Listen, let's just sit down and think this through," I say as I hold Luke in place with the barest touch of my fingertips.

Myles, meanwhile, is rummaging underneath the sink. He pulls out a toolbox and a red case with an illustrated heart with a lightning bolt and the word "HeartStart" on it.

"What the hell is that?" I say, knowing perfectly well that it is a defibrillator.

"Too late for that now." Myles's statement confuses me until I realize that's his delayed response to my asking for a powwow to rethink the plan.

"No, it's not."

He drops the toolbox and the HeartStart on the Formica table. Flips open the toolbox. Pulls out a roll of electrical tape and a scissor. He begins to wind the tape under my fingers steadying Luke against the chair, then around Luke's chest, his biceps, and the back of the chair. It's shocking how quickly and efficiently he does it. I want to walk away, but I'm rooted to the spot.

He shrugs, glancing at me through his sweaty bangs, all the while the tape is screeching as it's yanked away from the roll. Myles isn't stopping for a second. "You'd be surprised how many people we have to tape down in the ambulance. You can step away now." He saws through the tape's end with the scissors.

That done, he strides over to his bureau and opens the top drawer. He takes out a sock. Flexes it like an elastic band. Walks back over and, even as some part of me knows for damn sure what he's going to do with that sock, I'm paralyzed to stop him from opening Luke's already gaping mouth even wider and stuffing the sock inside. Luke's head lolls back under the pressure.

The shock of that somehow surges me into action. I grab Myles's hand. "Are you crazy? He'll suffocate. He's out cold."

Myles throws my hand off. "He won't. And what do you think he'll do as soon as he wakes up and finds he's not in Kansas anymore? He'll start screaming, that's what."

"Myles, please, just wait a minute." I hate how frantic I sound, but I've started to panic. Everything is spiraling out of control. He's not even fucking stuttering anymore. Who is he? "Wait. Please."

He doesn't. The tape expertly starts again on its merry-go-round, locking the sock in Luke's mouth.

An overwhelming rush of nausea hits me then. I race for the bathroom.

"Where are you going?" I hear Myles calling.

I slam the door closed behind me. My hands brace the tiny sink, my head hanging low, almost touching the thin porcelain ledge, and I stay that way, slowly counting to ten until the feeling subsides to the point where I know I'm not going to throw up right this instant, although honestly, anything could change that. Tentatively, I raise my head and look at my reflection in the glass shard that poses as a mirror. It's a jagged triangle that's been glued up on its side, rather than straight up. I can only see half of my face in it as the triangular shape is widest on the right side but slopes to nothing on the left. *Who has a mirror like that?* I'm thinking. And more importantly, *Why didn't I see how weird that was the first time I came here?* My cyclops eye looks crazed. No, scared. *Sandy, please* is my next thought, although I'm not sure what exactly I mean. Please what? Please come and get me out of here? Please tell me what to do so I can get myself out of this? Please help? I realize Sandy has been nowhere to be seen ever since Myles did his little Japanese lightshow the night before. Did she think I no longer needed her? *Please Sandy, I need you*, I think, only this time closing my eyes, which I hope she'll see as a sign of sincerity, like when someone shuts their eyes in prayer. Or, is it really the sign of defeat of someone before a firing squad? Either way, when I open them, she still isn't there. Only my one unhappy eye stares back.

When I return to the kitchen, Myles is busy filling his empty canning jar with the champagne from the second bottle we brought. *When did he go out to the car for that?* I'm disturbed that he would see this as something to celebrate. From across the room, he holds up the bottle in my direction, but I shake my head.

"It'll steady your nerves," he offers. Shrugging, he takes a long drink from the jar.

I sit at the Formica table across from Luke, his head still slumped on his chest and unaware that he has a sock taped in his mouth. "If we put him back in the car right now, we can probably make it halfway before he wakes up again," I say.

Myles places the jar on the counter. Then, he leans against the sink, folding his arms across his chest. "Halfway where?"

"Back. To Skyville. We'll tell him he passed out. We were so worried about him, we missed the exit ramp. Got lost."

Myles laughs. "And ended up three hours away?" He shakes his head. "No, we go through with the plan.

We're here. We do what we said we would."

"We never said anything about taping him to a chair with a dirty sock in his mouth."

Myles smiles coldly. "It's clean. I washed it myself." He shrugs. "Either you help me and we get this over faster, or…" He lets the sentence trail, implying that without my help this could go on for days, weeks.

Now, I'm really rattled. I look around nervously. *Goddamn it, Sandy, where are you?*

"What's happened to you?" I say to Myles, hoping to stall for more time.

"Me?" Lifting the champagne bottle, he pours his Tweety mug full.

"This isn't you."

"You don't really know me," he says, quietly, with his back to me.

"I know what Sandy—"

Here he scoffs and looks at me.

I forge on before he can say anything. "Sandy told me you were sweet." Another snort. "And you were serious about being an artist." Shaking his head, dismissing me, he looks away. Grabbing at anything to make him stay in the conversation, I tell him, "She told me about that great book you're doing about birds and superstitions. How she was going to talk to Luke about it for you." That last bit isn't exactly true. It was Myles who mentioned it to me when he confessed about shoving her on the boat. I'm so anxious I don't know who told me what anymore. Some journalist I am.

"You don't know what you're talking about," he says, practically spitting at me. "That book…" He pauses. It's obvious he's trying to get a grip on whatever he's feeling right now. To shove it—whatever *it*

is—back down. "I don't want to talk about it," he finally says.

Then, he walks over, slides the mug in front of
me, and sits down next to me so that he's also across
from Luke. The setup mimics how a TV crime drama
would envision a police interrogation scene taking
place: two detectives across from the perp. Only we
don't have photographs of the murder scene to shove
in front of Luke's face to make him crack. For all I
know, though, Myles might have such photos of my
sister being hauled up by the team of state police
divers.

"I'm. Fine." Myles enunciates each word, which
shows he's anything but. "The only thing that's happened is you getting cold feet." He swallows too much
of the champagne too fast and grimaces. For an instant, he's the "old" Myles. Hurt. Struggling. He lowers the jar. On his other hand, his middle finger rests
on his index finger on the table. I'm praying he's going to fall into his insectile dance, the one I know
soothes him, the one that screams insecurity and fear,
but instead he drums the table with those same fingers
and pushes back from the table, forcefully becoming
a chairman of the board about to make an important
point. "Look, he'll be okay. I'm—we're—not going to
hurt him."

"You planned this. Before I showed up."

This startles him. "What? No…it was your idea,
remember? I wanted to call the police. But, we're
here now, so we might as well get what we said we
would. We—I—need to hear him say it. I need him
to tell me exactly what happened. And you do too.
And Hayden. If we bring him back now, all of this
will be for n-n-n-nothing." Here he sweeps his hand

around the room as if he's talking about the way he's been living for three months, implying it's all Luke's fault that he lives in an abandoned train car. I remember reading one of the posted Gorey quotes at the museum: "Crime tells us in detail about the way people really live." I almost tell Myles this to divert him, but I notice it's the first time he's stuttered since we got here so maybe he's being honest, vulnerable. Maybe he *is* holding Luke responsible not only for my sister's death, but also everything else that has sucker punched all of us since. Maybe I've been letting my dark imagination run away too much. Maybe all he wants are some answers. Just as I do.

"So, we get him to confess and then we turn him over to the cops, like you suggested, right?"

"Ye-yes," he says, and then repeats it with more confidence. "Yes."

It's then that Luke starts to come to. He moans, his head lifts a bit, only to drop again, his chin on his chest. Myles scrapes his chair back farther, and after standing reaches out and begins to unzipper the red HeartStart case.

"What are you doing?" I stand too. *My* heart has started to race. "You said—"

"Only a precaution," he says, cutting me off. He walks around to where Luke is sitting, pushing the defibrillator across the table, closer to Luke. The lid flips open. Inside, on top of a blue plastic machine, there's an illustration of a human body torso on a large white label. A red arrow points to a red dotted circle around a drawn electrical pad on the illustrated man's left shoulder. There's a lever saying: "PULL." Myles does. Immediately, a mechanical voice instructs, "Begin by removing all clothing from the patient's chest. Cut clothing if needed." Myles, meanwhile, is already tugging Luke's camel wool coat off his shoulders above the tape across his chest and then, flinging Luke's tie pin onto the tabletop, he undoes his tie. It's clear he doesn't need a machine or some wimp-ass reporter to tell him what to do. He's been in training for the past three months for this day.

"Yes, yes," he murmurs as the mechanical voice barks out: "Look carefully at the pictures on the white adhesives pads. Peel one pad from the yellow plastic liner. Place the pad exactly as is shown on the picture."

Myles is already done placing the two pads on Luke's torso before the voice finishes its instruction. That's when I really do throw up.

Chapter Sixteen

I'll ask you one more time."

"Whaa…" Luke's head tilts to the side, his eyes closed. His slurred words are impossible to decipher anyway behind the sock in his mouth.

"No, you can sleep later. Hey!" Myles yanks the tape away, freeing the sock, shocking a drowsy Luke awake. He pats Luke's cheek sharply three times. "Answer the question and we'll let you go to sleep."

"I don't…know—"

This time, Myles slaps him.

"What the fuck?" Luke's head jerks away automatically in response.

"You said you wouldn't," Tibbie says. She's leaning against the kitchen counter. She starts to walk closer to them, but Myles holds up his hand, which halts her two feet away.

Myles grips Luke's head and puts his face directly in front of Luke's as if he's going to kiss him.

"Steady on," Luke slurs out.

Myles shakes Luke's head a little. "What did you do to Sandy?" He enunciates each word as if Luke doesn't know English.

Luke's eyes open a little wider. "What?"

Myles slaps him harder.

"Hey!" Tibbie yells, but Myles isn't having it.

"Last time," he tells Luke, who's now more alert

and looking around, with Myles's hands still cupping his jaw, slowly realizing what is going on. "What did you do to Sandy?"

"Sandy?"

Myles watches as Luke becomes aware and then confused by the tape around his chest. He knows Luke is thinking, *Why am I in this chair? Where am I?* It's only a matter of seconds before he will start thrashing and screaming for help.

"Okay," Myles says calmly. He reaches over to the defibrillator and yells, "Clear!" and stabs the orange button with the thunderbolt. Immediately, Luke's eyes enlarge and his feet on the floor involuntarily thrust his chair backward.

"Stop it!" Tibbie shouts. She grabs Myles's arm, but he throws her off. How many times has he listened to people telling him to stop? How many times can you be disappointed? Not gotten the answers you wanted? His mother, not allowing him to go home with her after his time in the hospital? Barely slowing her car down when she deposited him at the airport? His own mother. Giving away his birds. *His* birds. He cared for them, and what? She gets to decide what is best for them? His book? No one would ever give him a chance with his birds and the bad things they bring. Penelope laughed at him for it. Penelope laughing at him, period. And Luke, barely noticing him for ten years. Ten years! Only stopping that once to ridicule him in the men's room. All the times someone cut him off mid-sentence because they were too impatient to wait for him to stumble his way through the nouns and the verbs and the adjectives and adverbs. How many times can you be shut down, stopped at every streetlight that's been programmed to mess with you so that you can only drive a measly block before you get another red? Well, he won't be stopped now. It's green all the way!

"What did you do to Sandy?" he shouts, his finger poised, trembling with mad energy, over the orange button.

"What the fu—" Luke gasps the *ck* out as another jolt hits him, this one throwing his head back.

"Just tell us!" Tibbie pleads as she hugs herself, twisting her waist from side to side, agitated. Myles can see she's scared and something about that makes him drop his hand to his side. He squats down in front of Luke.

"What did you do to Sandy?" Myles repeats, quieter.

Tears begin to slide down Luke's face. "She had it coming," he says and spits in Myles's face.

That's when Tibbie runs over and punches the hell out of the orange button.

Chapter Seventeen

Before twenty minutes had gone by, the ambulance, the fire truck, the State Troopers arrive in a swirl of sirens and lights. By then, Penelope has passed out despite Hayden's repeatedly encouraging, then begging her to stay awake. Just as the first emergency vehicle shows up, Hayden is seriously considering whether she should try slapping Penelope's face like they do in the movies whenever they want someone to come to.

"Hayden?" a State Trooper says when he opens the back door. Hayden's facing away from him in the back seat with her hands on either side of the mound of blanket and her coat covering Penelope. Her face is inches away from Penelope's as she cajoles and compels and pleads with her to wake up. And then, suddenly, she's no longer in the car and men are pushing past her to also get into the back seat. It's a mob of clowns clambering over each other into a tiny car at the circus. There's a riot of activity and the sense that what you're seeing is the unimaginable. Later on, she'll think she remembers the trooper saying, "We'll take it from here, Hayden." Or maybe he asked, "You all right, Hayden?" Tacking on her first name made it seem that they were old friends. But probably she imagined it all and he actually said nothing before leading her to a nearby snowbank where she sat shivering until one of the firemen came over and put blankets around her.

Then, she's riding to the hospital in the back of that trooper's car. The siren blasts during the entire trip as if they're in pursuit of a criminal. Hayden becomes irrationally anxious that they're not actually going to the hospital. That somehow the trooper knows what really happened, about the plan to kidnap Luke and separate Luke and Penelope to get confessions out of them. She starts to wonder if the trooper means to try to get a confession out of *her*. That *she's* the criminal. She's in the back of his car after all, breathing the ghost air of how many arrestees over the years? *He's taking me to the station*, she thinks absurdly.

They're only following the ambulance, however, which also has its siren on. Hayden tried to ride in the ambulance with Penelope, but they wouldn't allow it. On the gurney as they loaded her into the back of the ambulance, Penelope had come to, thrashing in pain and screaming gibberish.

"We need to keep the risk of infection down," said one of the EMTs, refusing to let Hayden join them in the ambulance. Hayden noticed, as you do in such catastrophes, the small details, which are the only things you can control in such events; he wasn't wearing a mask. She was about to yell at him about Penelope's risk of infection from *him* when the trooper steered her away by her elbow toward his squad car.

She has no idea how long the hospital ride took. Suddenly, she is in the waiting room and an ER doctor, a woman who has the face of someone who religiously adheres to a morning and night moisturizing routine, her skin is so luminous, is asking a steady stream of questions about what happened. How long had her friend been unconscious? What's her name? What's Hayden's name? Was she a family member? Questions Hayden has already answered multiple times before arriving. Hayden is thankful for two things. That no one asks her where they were going when the brakes failed. And for some reason she had it together enough to lie about her name from the get-go when she made the 911 call. "Hayden…Hayden Prince," she told the emergency operator and stuck to it. It's close enough to Pierce that if someone asks to see her ID, she can pass it off as their mishearing her. Each time she hesitates a beat too long, though, before telling them she's Penelope's "partner." She leaves it at that. Ambiguous. Let them figure out if she means it's business related or something more intimate. She realizes she does that out of some kind of loyalty vestige to Sandy. She can't believe she's thinking of that now. Then, the ER doctor pauses. "Are *you* injured?"

It's the first time anyone had thought to ask, but Hayden feels absurdly guilty about it anyway. "No, no," she murmurs. She starts to cry.

"What about her parents?" the doctor asks.

Hayden faints then, slumping to the floor before the trooper can catch her.

When she wakes up, she's on the floor. There's a nurse waving a vial of something awful smelling under her nose. Hayden coughs. She tries to sit up.

"Lie there for a minute," the ER doctor tells her, pressing Hayden's shoulder down. "You fainted. You're all right."

Black shiny lace-up boots are by her elbow. "You okay there, Hayden?" she hears the trooper ask her. She nods.

"Did you hurt anything? Hit your head?" the

doctor asks. A surge of guilt washes over Hayden
again. They should be with Penelope, not her. When
Hayden says no, the doctor tells her she needs to get
back to Penelope, and leaves. A nurse helps her up
slowly and guides her over to a row of chairs that were
probably once a beautiful turquoise knobby wool but
now have rough black streaks and splotches. There's
an unexpected heavy odor of cigarette smoke. At
first, it seems to be coming from the chairs, but then
Hayden senses it's emanating from the sixty-some-
thing man who sits across from her, overweight and
stuffed into very worn motorcycle gear, except for the
helmet, which is on a chair next to him. One mitt-
sized hand is draped on top of the helmet. Intermittently, his thick fingers drum the top of it. *He's either
bored or nervous*, Hayden thinks.

"I'll be right back. Wait here," the nurse says and
speeds away down the hallway to the left, her rubber
clogs squeaking on the linoleum.

Many of the chairs, Hayden sees now, are filled
with people. Some gingerly hold an arm or a forehead.
Others have their eyes closed and might be mistaken
for being asleep were it not for the uncomfortable
positions their bodies are in, curled to the side in pain
and sickness. They might've just rolled out of bed
with their unkempt hair, T-shirts, and dirty jeans. A
few are still wearing their pajamas. One elderly couple
is dressed in their Sunday best: a grey flannel suit for
the man, a light blue sweater set with a pearl necklace
over a soft grey wool skirt for his wife. Their overcoats
are neatly folded on their laps. The woman also holds
a black patent leather purse from which she takes out
a small tin of mints. For a second, Hayden thinks of
Myles. She wonders if he and Isabel are with Luke

now. Where they are.

That thought is disrupted by a woman's husky voice announcing over the loudspeakers that a Ford Taurus is blocking the ambulance entrance and must be removed immediately. Everyone looks at each other trying to suss out the owner. Hayden feels so guilty about what's happened to Penelope that she almost raises her hand to claim the Taurus. It's not that she feels like she pulled the trigger. But none of this would've happened if they hadn't messed with the brakes.

The nurse is back. For the first time, Hayden notices that the nurse's grey scrubs have llamas with striped scarves all over them. They strike Hayden as better suited for a veterinarian's office, not an ER. The nurse hands her a paper cup filled with water. "Sit here. We'll keep you updated," she says and then walks briskly away again, through two doors that swoosh shut behind her.

Before Hayden can swallow a sip of the water, the trooper is slipping into the chair next to her. Where he took off to after she fainted, she doesn't know. She watches motorcycle man get up and steal away to the other side of the room, choosing a seat located partially behind a fake potted ficus plant. *I'm not the only one with something to hide.*

The trooper takes out a small notepad from his breast pocket and lays it on his lap. There's a stubby pencil in his hand, the kind golfers use to keep their tally. He clears his throat. "Are you up for a few questions?"

Hayden finally considers him for the first time as if she's been hired to photograph his portrait. Before, there had been so much chaos and the shock of everything and her fainting that she hadn't noticed what he actually looked like. He simply wore a grey wool coat with a thick belt around the middle, ending in those black shit-kicker boots. But his face? For all Hayden knew, he could've been a head with only a mouth that opened and closed, a childhood nightmare figure. Something out of one of Francis Bacon's paintings. Maybe the triptych where amorphous beings writhe in agony, their mouths vised open by their silent screams.

Hayden sees he has the obligatory brush cut of every trooper. But there ends any perfunctory resemblance of a fit and trustworthy public servant. His cheeks have the ruddy puffiness of a drinker or a recently recovered alcoholic. He's maybe forty years old, although it's hard to tell with those cheeks. His nose is slightly crooked, with a bump where glasses—if he wore glasses—would rest. Was it broken previously? And then there's the thin scar that starts on the bottom of one of those inflamed cheeks and rivers its way past the corner of his mouth to his cleft chin. Ever since she's had her own attention-grabbing scar on her forehead, Hayden notices everyone else's disfigurements with revulsion and interest. Every scar tells a story. None of them good. In a prior life the trooper could've been a boxer or a heavy at a speakeasy. Except the tough-guy image is marred by an angry-looking pimple on his cheek. She notes all of it now in a flash with her photographer's eye.

"So, your friend's parents? Know how we can reach them?"

Hayden forces herself to stare down at his notepad for ballast when she says, "Her mother died years ago." She watches as he flips the pad open and

writes under other scribbled notes: *Mother—deceased.*
He turns to her. "And her father?"

She hesitates, then shrugs. "I'm not sure," she tells
him, which is actually true. Luke could be anywhere
on the way to Cape Cod. Wherever he is, Hayden is
pretty sure his phone is turned off. It might've already
been thrown into a garbage can somewhere, or maybe
into the ocean. But she wonders if those words will
come back to haunt her. What if Penelope wakes up
and tells some orderly that they were on the way to
actually pick Luke up at the airport? They'd know
Hayden had been lying then. They wouldn't know
why, but they'd sense something was wrong. That the
accident wasn't a simple case of a flare gun going off
mistakenly. Should she tell him now they were on the
way to the airport? She remembers hearing once that
the criminals who get away with it, whatever *it* is, are
the ones who stick closely to the truth when they're
hauled in by the police. Or is that just folklore? All of
it is so absurd. She can't believe that she's here, being
questioned by a trooper, when just four days ago
Isabel and Myles had yet to ring the bell at *The Loom.*
Tell him, she thinks. *Just say that Luke was flying in.
No, don't. He'll send another trooper to collect him
at the gate. When Luke isn't there, who knows what
they'll do? They'll have a missing person on their hands
to boot.*

"No idea?" the trooper prods her.

Hayden stands. "Sorry. I need a bathroom."
Without waiting for him to say something, she walks
away, scanning for signs of a bathroom where she
hopes she'll figure out what the hell she's going to do.

In the bathroom, on her way to a stall, she catches her reflection in the mirror. She's wearing her coat

again. She hadn't realized that when one of the emergency personnel gave it back to her, after they'd lifted Penelope out of the Rover onto a gurney, that it was stained with blood across the chest. When Hayden wets a paper towel she sees that her hands are blood-stained also. Worse, there's a small melted remnant of Penelope's parka stuck on her thumbnail. She scrubs and scrubs at her trembling fingers and part of a palm. Then, she violently rubs at the spots on her coat, feeling overwhelmingly nauseous and dizzy again. *Think*, she says to herself. She dries her dripping hands under the heated air blower. It sounds incredibly loud. If she can just stall the trooper, she can make the excuse that she needs to lie down and ask him if there is a hotel nearby that she can go to. She can even ask him for a ride. No, not a ride. She'll tell him she'll get a taxi. *Shit. Think. That won't work. Stick as close to the truth as you can. It's the only thing to do. If Penelope wakes up...what do you mean, if? When she wakes up, you can tell her she isn't remembering correctly. That she's in shock.*

Fifteen minutes later, Hayden is walking back toward the trooper, who's staring at the news on a TV hanging from the ceiling with the sound turned off. His head swivels in her direction. He stands, like he's a gentleman with manners.

She says, as if their conversation hadn't been interrupted, "Sorry about that. I thought I might be sick." When she sits down, he does also, right next to her again. Their knees practically touch. She tells him, "Her father is flying in. Or flew in by now. We were on our way to get him. At the airport. It's okay, though," she says. Her fingers are trembling on her knees. She immediately rubs her forehead over the ridge of her scar, which she knows will settle her nerves. At first, in the weeks after the accident, the scar appalled her and brought her back to that horrible night every time she saw it in a mirror. Touching it chilled her, as if she were plunged back into the cold ocean again. By the time she was living in Skyville that changed, however. Suddenly, the scar became her talisman, her touchstone. Never forget, it said. Never stop until you know everything.

"We called our friends to pick him up," she continues. "I mean, when we were waiting." She pauses because she's seen the trooper eyeing her as she traces the scar. She clasps her hands on her lap. "For the tow truck. Before the gun went off. The flare, I mean." *Christ, shut up. You even sound guilty.*

"Where was he flying in from and who are these friends? What are their names?" He's flipped open his pad again.

Even as Hayden changes their names, she senses she's digging a bigger hole for herself and for them. For one thing, she should've changed both names. Not just the last name. If someone does a search on Penelope's name alone, the publishing company—not just Pen & Hay, but also *Freedom Press*—will show up on the screen. She instantly remembers, however, that Penelope hadn't posted any content with her name on the Pen & Hay website yet... But her father's name. That will pop up on the *Freedom Press* site. It'd only be a matter of clicks to find links reporting the boat accident. The newspapers weren't alone in picking up the story. It also had been broadcasted on TV and radio news programs, including NPR. It's big news when someone drowns, but even bigger when a whale is killed.

"What's Michael's phone number?" the trooper is asking her. She's so mired in her own thoughts she doesn't know if it's the first time he's asked her or if he's repeating the question. Michael was the name she gave him in place of Myles. *Not Myles,* she thought. *Don't let him call stuttering, broken-down, detoxing Myles. Not Myles the hot mess. He'll confess everything.*

She shakes her head. "He doesn't have a phone." The trooper's thick eyebrows raise. "He's a bit of a Luddite," she explains, but as soon as she says it she wonders if he'll have the foggiest idea what a Luddite is. He'll probably think it's some branch of a religious cult.

"O-kay," the trooper says slowly and blows out a gust of air. He glances at his notepad. "What about... Izzy?" *God, he wrote down all their names already?* "Is she a...Luddite...too?"

She's so thrown that he's asking about Isabel, a/k/a Izzy, that she's about to automatically lie and say, "Yes" when she remembers she told him already that she and Penelope *called* them to pick up Luke while they were waiting for the tow truck. One of them had to have had a cell. Hayden worries for a second that he's trying to trap her, then dismisses the idea just as quickly, and before he can ask something else, she abruptly stands, saying, "Good idea. I'm going to call her and see if Luke...that's Penelope's dad, has landed yet. I'll be right back." Immediately, she heads for the entry doors, happy that she's put him off but mad at herself that she blabbed out Luke's real name.

The trooper doesn't try to stop her. Maybe it's because he thinks she's simply searching for the best cell phone reception. Or that she'll need privacy to break the news to the father. Outside, Hayden makes sure she stays in view so he can see her. She starts to automatically call Isabel's number. Simultaneously, an alarm goes off in her head: *Don't.* By now they'd definitely have Luke in the car, drugged and passed out. It's too late. They can't exactly change their part of the plan and bring Luke here now. And to tell them what has happened will only add to what they're dealing with. Better to keep them in the dark about this for the time being. Her index finger stops before hitting the Call button. She pretends to be talking to someone. She speaks aloud, telling the air and a nearby gaunt patient in a hospital gown—who's hooked up to an IV and smoking—what happened in a rush of words as if Isabel really is on the other end. Hayden gesticulates with her free hand and then holds her forehead, pretending she's the bearer of bad news. Her shoulders hunch. Every now and then she glances over to the trooper, realizing she doesn't even know his name. She'll ask him as soon as she goes back in. She needs to take control of the situation. Ask *him* the questions. Play the role of the shell-shocked witness of a horrible accident. She knows how to do that. It's in her bones. It took up residence that beautiful fall evening she lost Sandy, that feeling that the bottom had dropped out, the horizon had tilted, and the ensuing clawing instinct to survive. The lie. All of it moved in and never left.

Hayden had been at the front of the boat when the *ship strike* happened. That's what the Coast Guard calls it when a boat hits a whale. Hayden remembers one ensign in particular who kept asking, "Tell me again where everyone was when the ship strike occurred?" It sounded then as if the boat had torpedoed the whale instead of the other way around. Which was the truth, when it came down to it.

It was nine o'clock. The sun had set in a fiery burst the hour before. Luke had turned on the boat's lights around the deck. He was casting a huge searchlight out over the water around them. He was drunk. They all were. Except for Hayden and Sandy. Sandy, not feeling well, had gone below deck after dinner to their cramped "bedroom." She'd shown Hayden the tiny room as soon as they'd boarded. It was more like what you'd call a "berth," where crew members might sleep. Worse than that, it'd been near the staterooms where Luke and Penelope were to sleep. Myles was to sleep on the upper deck on a makeshift bed transformed from the dinette table and banquettes in the salon.

"I don't like this," Hayden had whispered. "It's too close to them."

"We'll be fine," Sandy said. "He knows I'll scream bloody murder if he tries anything. Besides, the door has a lock."

Later, at around eight thirty, Hayden decided to say goodnight to the others. She wanted to check on Sandy. But as she was walking toward the stairs leading down to where their cabin was, Luke suddenly cried out, "Look! A whale! Straight ahead." Then, he turned on the motor and headed for it.

Hayden knew she should check on Sandy. Although, when Hayden had tucked her into the twin bed, Sandy had fallen deeply asleep even before Hayden had turned out the light. Maybe it *was* the flu. Maybe she just needed sleep.

So, as soon as Hayden heard that there might be whales, she pivoted from the steps and joined Penelope and Myles at the front of the boat. She didn't think twice about it. Not until later. Nor did any of them try to stop Luke from going toward the whale. What Hayden did think was: *I'm so glad I brought my flash.* There they were, picking up speed fast, ten miles an hour, twenty. Still, in such a large boat, the largest Hayden had ever been in, they didn't seem to be traveling that fast. Later, after she returned home from the hospital, she'd research and find out that there's over a ninety percent chance that you'll kill a whale if you hit one speeding at even twenty miles per hour. It doesn't matter if the whale you hit is a growing forty-ton young whale named, she found out later, Woodrow. Your boat *has* become a torpedo. For a minute or two, she consoled herself when she read that at least in ship strikes that kill, they do so quickly. As opposed to whales that die from entanglement. That can take years of the whale dying a slow, horrible death. The consolation was short-lived. She couldn't get past the idea that she had contributed to the death of a whale. Nor could she get past the thought that she, Hayden Pierce, had possibly caused the death of the love of her life by stripping Sandy of anything to live for.

"Ten o'clock!" Luke yelled from the bridge deck, one hand on the steering wheel, the other on the searchlight, which, along with the full moon, illuminated what seemed to be a tremendous lone whale smacking its tail against the water and then disappearing entirely, only to surface again two minutes, then, five minutes later. *It's right out of Moby Dick*, Hayden thought. It was breathtaking. They were full-on in pursuit as it swam mere yards in front of them, all of them propelled by the game of it, the novelty of it, the once-in-a-lifetime adventure of it.

"There! There," Penelope or Myles cried out, jabbing and pointing and holding on to the front railing, leaning over it as if they would reach out and touch Woodrow. Hayden was shooting photograph after photograph, the camera's flash sparking repeatedly, her heart racing. *God, I wish Sandy was here*, she thought. But by the time she woke her up, surely the whale would be gone. Hayden stayed where she was.

Then, suddenly, it disappeared. They waited. It didn't surface. The boat kept moving ahead. The searchlight roved the surface like there'd been a jailbreak.

"You've lost him, Dad!" Penelope shouted from the bow, turning toward Luke.

"It was quiet," Luke told the Coast Guard later. And therein was the queen of all lies.

"So, you weren't moving or going toward where the whale was? The motor wasn't on? You weren't following it?"

The guard asked them that when they were all together in the rescue boat, headed back to the distant shore, shivering under blankets, in shock. No one said anything. Myles was lying down on the floor of the boat, writhing in pain. His shoulder had gotten dislocated when he'd foolishly tried to hold on to the railing during the impact and was thrown into the water. An EMT, with his foot braced on Myles's chest, yanked hard on Myles's outstretched hand while a Coast Guarder held his legs down. Penelope was huddled with Luke on a nearby bench. Where was Sandy? Hayden felt dizzy. Her head was pounding. An EMT stood in front of her, blocking her view of the others while she mopped up Hayden's blood with a clotting sponge and then applied Steri-Strips to temporarily seal the wound closed.

"So, you'd anchored?" the Coast Guard officer asked.

Still, no one answered him. Not until Luke spoke up in a booming voice that bad liars use when they're about to lose it or feverishly deny their part in anything. "We were getting ready for bed. One of us drowned, for god's sakes, man!" He paused—a beat too long—and then, suddenly belligerent, fumed, "The engine was off. End of story."

For days afterward, Hayden obsessively thought, *Why did we keep silent? Why didn't one of them speak up and correct Luke? Why didn't I?* It could've been the shock that they were all experiencing. Mostly, though, Hayden thought it was something more insidious. They'd been innately scared of what the legal repercussions were for killing a whale, let alone the consequences of killing a human being. Sealing them together, their guilt made them mute, making them complicit.

None of them corrected Luke. None of them had clean hands. The EMT stepped away. It was then that it hit Hayden that there was no below deck on this rescue boat. They weren't all together. Sandy was not with them. Sandy was the "one of us."

Chapter Eighteen

I lied when I said I'm the one you want to be with in a foxfire, or a terrorist attack, or when a tornado rips through your town. Whenever you want to take cover. Here's the truth. I'm the one who panics. Who usually can't witness anything more aggressive than a cat being shoved from a kitchen table to the floor. I'm the one who fights her way through life with words. And not because I think the pen is mightier than the sword. If you're in a knife fight, I'd suggest you bring a gun, not your smart mouth. Everything I've done, however, since Sandy died has been unexpected, surprising, and since I'm confessing here, at times downright scary because somewhere along the line I've lost sight not only of my sister, but of me as well. I've chalked it all up to Sandy or Sandy's spirit. Her mojo. I'm not the girl who jumps in feet first. Who grabs the bull by the horns. Who seizes the day. Who remains clearheaded no matter what horrible craziness is threatening to bring down civilization around her. I want to be that girl. I do. But, really, I'm the girl who believed my sister hung the moon every night until the moon disappeared. What does that tell you? I'm not your savior. I'm the one who needs saving.

But when Luke says that awful lie about Sandy—"She begged me for it"—on top of what I suspected he had *wanted* to do to her before Woodrow crashed the party, something snaps in me, and in one final shocking move, I'm the one who instantly becomes a push-comes-to-shove kind of woman. I'm the one who stabs that button as hard as I can, pressing my index finger there for far too long as if I'm gouging out Luke's very heart until it finally stops beating.

In hindsight, I'd like to think I did it to put him out of his misery, like when you shoot a lame horse. I didn't.

The truth is I've never been accused of being too pragmatic or equable or compassionate. "But *why* did you do it?" my sister would resignedly ask me whenever I'd commit yet another impulsive act. In my teens, when I thought of myself as smarter than anyone, I'd shrug and recite back a quote of the writer E.M. Forster: "The only evidence of life is change."

"Thoughtful change is good," Sandy used to tell me. "Blind recklessness is not."

"Why did you do it?" she asked again four years into my relationship with Mister X when one night I'd stolen his wedding ring. It happened during one of our twice weekly rendezvouses at the Midtown Hotel on Huntington Ave in Boston. Mister X was taking a shower as he always did after sex and before leaving around eleven at night for his home and his wife. He'd also ritually remove his wedding ring before we had sex, placing it on the hotel's end table on his side of the bed. He definitely didn't want it touching my body at any time. After the shower, he'd slip it back on his finger. But, this night, he hurried me through perfunctory sex, claiming his wife had explicitly asked him to be home by nine o'clock to watch *The Sopranos* with her. We'd only been in the room a half hour when he was already lathering up in the steamy bathroom. I was so pissed, I started to hurriedly dress so I could be gone before he finished showering. Just as I was about to leave, however, there was the ring, staring me down, gold and shining under the lamp. I slipped it into my pocket and left before I could stop what I was doing.

"But *why* did you do it?" Sandy repeated, sighing, on the phone, and for once I couldn't answer her with a glib remark.

Neither did I tell her that when I'd gotten home to my own apartment, I wished I hadn't. I tossed the ring on my kitchen counter only to feel as if it were again watching me, like one of those creepy Jesus paintings, when I moved around the kitchen. As I poured myself a glass of Scotch. As I got out a can of peanuts. So, then, I threw it into the trash, thinking if it was out of sight I'd feel better. I didn't. It became even more firmly fixed in my mind's eye. Finally, I retrieved it and drove back to the Midtown where I found Mister X still frantically tossing the room.

"Here," I said, handing the ring to him. It felt gritty now, probably from the coffee grounds I'd deposited in the trash that morning. He stared at me as if he'd discovered I was a serial killer. There was nothing else for me to say—I certainly wasn't going to apologize—so I went back to my car and wasn't a block away before I called Sandy.

In high school English, we read a short story by Edgar Allan Poe called the "Imp of the Perverse," which espouses the philosophy that we are driven to do wrong in spite of ourselves. Maybe that's what had happened. Or maybe it had been the journalist in me wanting to propel the story's end along. Any good journalist knows to use the inverted pyramid structure: you tell the ending in the first line, then fill in the details, like the why, afterward. Maybe I wanted to know where all this would end with Mister X. Maybe I wanted to just end it.

Mister X didn't speak to me for two weeks. After that we resumed our Midtown visits, but he never took the ring off again. When I returned from P-Town after I'd collected Sandy's ashes, I broke it off altogether.

It's Myles who comes to the rescue. First, he shoves me so hard that I'm thrown several feet away onto the floor. Then he quickly lowers Luke, still taped in the chair, onto the floor. By the time I scramble up, he's already giving Luke CPR, one hand pressing down on the other on top of Luke's chest in quick compressions, followed by his blowing into Luke's mouth while holding Luke's nostrils closed.

"Cut the damn tape off!" he yells in between pumping Luke's chest.

I run for the scissor on the table. Snipping and tearing away at the tape around Luke's chest, my head is almost touching Myles's forehead as he continues to fight to revive Luke. My hands are shaking. What have I done? I've killed someone. I've killed Luke.

"Stand back!" Myles shouts. Quickly moving to the table, he yells, "Clear!" I'm not even sure if he checks to see if I've backed away before he zaps Luke. At this point, I'd only be collateral damage. Luke's body shudders and then, nothing. Later, I'll realize how ironic it is that Myles is applying the very same method to bring Luke back to life that I'd used to kill him. But in that moment, all I can think is we're— *I'm*—fucked.

"You're not going to die, you idiot!" Myles screams. "Clear!" He hits the button again. Immediately, he's leaning back over Luke's body, holding his nostrils closed, breathing into Luke's upturned mouth, followed by pushing with all of his strength down on his chest. Myles leaps back to the table. "Clear!" This time Luke's chest lifts off the floor.

I almost hear my sister's voice saying, "'Third time's the charm!' Anonymous!" because this time Luke coughs, groans, coughs, and starts to breathe again.

"That's right. Breathe," Myles says, cradling Luke's head, lifting it gently from the back of the chair. "Cut the tape on his ankles, Tibbie."

Stunned, I stand where I am, a foot away, not moving. Suddenly, I'm so cold that I'm shivering. My skin is clammy. The hairs on my neck are limp with sweat. I stare down at the two of them and for a moment I can't make sense of what Myles is saying, his face turned up to me. What's happening? One night, when I was in high school, I went to an out of control party and while looking for the bathroom mistakenly opened a bedroom door to find the high school quarterback mounting the team's center lineman. For a confused moment, I thought they were practicing their hikes, snapping the ball or something. Shock will turn any scene into a Rorschach test. One minute it's two human faces. The next, a torture collar for your neck. So, almost simultaneously with my thinking that they're running through their football moves, I realized what they were actually doing. By the time I came to my senses and slammed the door closed again, I'd started to sweat and shiver at the same time and almost threw up from sheer shock. That's exactly how I feel now, staring at Myles and Luke.

Luke coughs again. A saliva dribble dips on his chin. His eyes are still closed.

"Tibbie!" Myles yells. "Cut the tape! We need to get his feet down. He needs to lie flat!"

That jolts me back into action. As soon as I cut and rip away the tape, Myles gently pulls Luke from the chair, laying him on his back on the floor. He cradles Luke's head against his thighs. Myles is murmuring something that I can't hear. I think he's saying, "I got you, safely," but then I hear it more clearly.

"I got you, Sandy," Myles whispers over and over. Then, he starts to cry.

❧ ❧ ❧ ❧

Reviving Luke was one thing. Figuring out what to do afterward is actually harder. There is Myles the EMT, who, once his patient has been restored, falls apart, weeping to the point where I almost slap *him*. And then, of course, there is Luke. What should—*can*—we do with him now? How did we—*I*—ever think we could pull this off without consequences?

What have I done?

"I'll make you some tea," Myles says to a semi-conscious Luke, as if we're in one of those British whodunits that my sister and I had dreamed up on our trip to London with our mother. Myles snuffles back his tears and wipes his cheeks with the backs of his hands. He stands.

"Tea? He's going to go straight to the cops!" My voice is bordering on hysterical, high-pitched and out of control as I point down at the prone Luke whose eyes flutter open and then close again. I know this is all my fault. I'm scared shitless now that the two of them will turn me in.

Luke is still out of it, what with the drugs, the zapping, and the near-death experience. Or would this qualify as one of those after-death experiences where people report being in rooms of the most beautiful white light, of going on picnics in buses that have wings and fly, with friends and family members that they've lost years before, everyone dressed in white robes and flower garlands, talking gobbledygook languages that only they understand?

Myles shakes his head. "He won't," he says in an elementary school teacher's low and stern voice. He starts to fill up the kettle with tap water.

I fast-walk to the counter and, standing right next to him, bump his elbow on purpose. I'm not usually this physical. I'd be the one to give someone who's crowding me on the PO line a cold fish-eye. But it's as if that surge of energy that propelled me to almost electrocute Luke to death is still circulating within my veins.

"Why wouldn't he?" I demand.

Myles places the kettle on the hot plate. Turning to me, he says loudly, "Be-be-*cause* he admitted everything to us, re-re-re-re*mem*ber?" He pauses, catches his breath, closing his eyes in concentration. *Good god, he's stuttering again.* I start to be really worried then that on top of his crying jag, his confidence is plummeting. It's bad enough that my short stint as executioner has landed us here. I need Myles to get us out of this. That we see this thing through together. As if he's hearing my thoughts, he opens his eyes. Then, he speaks out even louder than before, in a flurry of words: "If he go-goes to the cops, we will too. He has more to lose. He *practically* mur-mur-*murdered* your sister. If we hadn't hit that whale, he would've raped her." He snorts back some leftover mucus from his tears. Despite the stuttering, the snort comes across as a kind of take-that-you-asshole gesture. The whole speech and act are so over the top, so drag-queen dramatic, I would've burst out laughing had the circumstances been different.

We both look over at Luke to see if any of this has registered. It has. On the floor, Luke's head is turned to us, unhappy eyes wide open, his bottom lip visibly trembling. His hand swipes agitatedly at the air to make us disappear. Wipe the nightmare away.

"No," he croaks out. "Please." He tries to sit up, but whether from dizziness or something more abstract such as fear, he thinks better of it, and, groaning, drops back down again. "Okay, okay. I might have." Here, he pauses. He waves his hand in the air again.

"What?" I say, my heart racing. My fists are clenched by my sides.

"I'm responsible for her passing out," he says flatly, like it's nothing. But before I can run over there and strangle him, he says quickly, "But I wouldn't have."

"Wouldn't have what?" I demand. I want him to say it. I want him to say what he was going to do.

He's shaking his head. "No! No. Not that. I just didn't want her to tell Penelope anything. I saw Penelope all over her."

"What are you talking about?" I yell at him.

"No, he's right," Myles says. "I saw it too."

Before I can tell them they're both crazy, Luke shouts over me. "I saw my daughter kiss her." He struggles up to lean on an elbow. "But your sister pushed her away." When he sees me take another step toward him, his words start to rush out in a hurry. "Sandy gave me her notice before she left for Boston that Thursday. In the office. She told me she'd still go on the trip to end things right. She still needed a reference from me. We'd worked together for ten years and that had to count for something, but if I tried anything else, she might tell some friend of hers at *The New Yorker* that I'd been harassing her for years. Jesus. I mean, did you see what came out about *The Paris Review* and Stein last year? Your sister. It was all a mistake. I thought it'd all blow over on the boat. I'd tell her she was mistaken. I hadn't meant anything by any of it."

"Yeah, right." My fists are still clenched.

Luke raises his hands in front of his face, apparently afraid I was going to punch him. "Okay, okay! I might've stepped over a line or—" He stops when he sees me come closer. "I was going to apologize," he says quickly to prevent me from coming any nearer. "But then when I saw that she didn't like Penelope kissing her, I panicked. I mean, was she going to tell her *New Yorker* friend about that too? Some story about us being some creepy father-daughter." He hesitated. Raked his fingers through his hair. "Christ. I thought I'd just shut her up until the next morning and I could reason with her. I panicked. I didn't give her a roofie. Just sleeping pills. I had no idea that whale…" Luke coughs, rolls onto his side and, curling up into a fetal position, cries, "Please don't tell the cops. I won't. I promise. If you promise also." He curls tighter as if he's afraid he's demanded too much and we're going to stomp him to death.

In that moment, I'm ashamed to say, Myles and I seal a pact with the devil. I realize immediately that I stand no chance now of ever seeing my sister again. No chance of more ghostly appearances. No more riding shotgun in the Saab. No more joking or quoting funny one-liners by writers I might or might not know. No more speaking in antiquated languages. Who could blame her? Why would she ever want to see me again, knowing that I'm agreeing to never bring her murderer to justice? Knowing that even if Luke was as innocent as he professed about the harassment, that it was all a misunderstanding—which I didn't believe for a minute—he'd still slipped her those pills. Knowing that within an hour Myles and I will be back on the road. That we'll be driving that despicable man, whom I wasn't strong enough to actually kill because adrenaline and impulse can only take you so far, back to the airport and tucking him into a plane to go safely home. Who could blame my sister for never reaching across the great divide to connect with me again?

I'm pissed too, I want to tell her. I wish I'd killed him. I'll regret that for a long, long time. But let me just say this one thing in my defense, Sandy, all right? This one thing. What choice do I have? I tried to kill him, but Myles saved him, and frankly, I was glad in that moment that he had. What I didn't realize then was how screwed we would be now. What choice do we have but to keep our end of the bargain and deliver him to the airport? Otherwise, it's possible Myles and I will end up in jail for attempted murder while Luke might not even be charged with anything. He'd slipped her pills and killed a whale. As far as I know, there is no jail time for either of those. On the other hand, we'd kidnapped and tortured him, and I'd tried to kill him. We'd be the ones to end up arrested. There is no other choice but to let him go.

For a brief moment there in Myles's crappy kitchen, I swear I hear Sandy repeating what she told me almost twenty-five years ago, after the weekend ended when she brought Hayden home from college to meet Francis and me for the first time. She'd been packing her suitcase in her old bedroom. Hayden was in the bathroom blow-drying her perfect hair into what glamour magazines would call "romantic tresses."

I had to pass the bathroom on the way to check on Sandy. The door was open, the dryer making such a racket that I automatically glanced to my left and was stunned to see Hayden naked. The reflection of her face, with her eyes closed, was framed in the mirror as she finger-combed her hair under the heat. She must've sensed me, or I stood there a beat too long, because she lowered her hand holding the dryer and before I could move, those pale blue eyes opened and locked on mine. My heart began to race. Neither of us said a word. I felt a frisson, the delicious spark of static electricity you get when you pull on a sweater directly out of a dryer.

Down by the side of her thigh, she clicked the dryer off and placed it in the sink in front of her. Finally, she smiled, lifted a red silk-like robe off a wall hook, turned to me, and slipped it on. But not before she'd seen me take her entire body in. Not before I noticed that she was lean and muscular, except for her breasts, which were full and with what seemed to be hardening nipples. Not before I spotted a small bird tattoo, a canary, resting atop her thatch of auburn pubic hair.

Her putting on the robe released me from whatever spell I'd been under and I quickly made my way to Sandy's bedroom. *What was that?* I thought, my heart still beating to beat the band. The whole thing made me so uncomfortable I practically threw myself into Sandy's room.

"Why her?" I asked Sandy abruptly. "You could have anyone. Why her?" I repeated to indicate just how absurd I thought *her* and the whole thing was.

Sandy's back was to me. She was folding an identical shimmery red Chinese robe that I'd seen Hayden slipping on. There was a huge green dragon across its back. Sandy stopped what she was doing, the silk belt slipping sensually between her fingers, and faced me.

"Life is full of alternatives but no choice, Tibbie. One day you'll see that," was all she said before resuming her packing.

After they left, I looked up what she'd said on the high school library computer. I'd been stung by her dismissal of me as naïve, not as worldly as her or, worse, Hayden. I had a feeling she hadn't made it up herself. I found out it was a quote from a Patrick White novel, *The Aunt's Story*. I didn't know him or any of his novels. I remember wondering how my sister did. Something about that made me feel a great chasm opening between us. Ultimately, I scoffed first at him and then my sister. The line was what my sister would've once said was "a load of malarkey."

So, now, faced with the prospect that I'm letting Luke off the hook, I'll rely on that old sawhorse—*I had no choice*—that wonderous excuse that we all fall back on. The ultimate it's-out-of-my-hands excuse of all time. With it, Sandy's words, or rather Patrick

White's, come full circle back to haunt me. And then, a deep-seated ache almost bowls me over there in Myles's boxcar of a home. How I long to tell my sister, "I understand now. I understand all about choice. How there never is a choice. Not really."

How I wish she could see that I've changed.

But she is unequivocally gone.

❧❧❧❧

Within an hour, the three of us are back in the Saab and driving to Logan Airport in Boston. Thankfully, there are hourly flights to New York City. Luke has agreed the best plan for moving ahead is for him to fly home as soon as possible. Once he's safely in his own high-rise condo, he'll text Penelope with some cockamamie excuse for not being able to visit. It turns out he has as much desire to see his daughter as we do. In fact, we realize he hasn't mentioned Penelope once after we initially picked him up at the airport.

"She thinks I messed up her life," he tells us morosely. He's sitting in the back seat. Whether he chose it to be polite or because he still didn't trust us and didn't want one of us sitting behind him, is anyone's guess. I, myself, breathed a sigh of relief when he automatically opened the back door. I didn't want to have to give him side-eye the entire two hours it will take us to get to the airport. I didn't want to spend the trip in regret and wondering if I could kill only him by side swiping his side of the car on one of the many trees bordering Route 6.

"Everyone thinks I messed up their lives," Luke goes on. He sounds baffled by this.

Myles twists around in the passenger bucket

seat to face him. "Did Penelope know what you did?" He asks it so matter-of-factly. It strikes me that the three of us have been through so much together today that, strangely, any censoring barriers between Myles and me have been lifted. It's how I used to feel around my sister. They have seen you at your worst. Might as well get everything out into the open. I'd never felt that for one moment during whatever it was I'd been doing with Mister X. Maybe Sandy was right about him, as she was about so many things. Maybe Mister X was a handy replacement for the father we never had: someone who exuded confidence with a firm grip on life, no matter what the crisis was. Someone who had the hutzpah to keep his enemies close.

In the back seat, Luke clears his throat. "Let's just say Penelope suspected something was...untoward." It's obvious that Luke is starting to recover from his ordeal; he's parsing his words again and is sounding more in keeping with his old priggish, fake self.

"But you denied it," says Myles. It's not a question. For a second, I wonder if he might get all worked up again, jump into the back seat, and pummel Luke senseless. But he only stares at Luke for a beat and then, turning back around, switches on the radio to a news program.

"Like I made my daughter a lesbian or something," Luke complains over the radio's emotional interview with a survivor of yet another high school classroom rampage. What he says is such a non sequitur that neither Myles nor I respond right away. I glance sideways at Myles, who, unsurprisingly, is smiling. A spark of a connection fires up between us. We know exactly what the other is thinking. Suddenly, I start to laugh, and Myles does also. It's a way to let out all the nervousness, the frustration, the anger, and lastly, the disappointment of this day. But it's more than that too. We might've failed in what we set out to do, but along the way, well, we formed what might be a more lasting bond between the two of us and that was something, wasn't it? It's the closest I've felt to someone since my sister died.

"What's so funny?" Luke says, irritated.

"Well, after today...I'm not sure she and Hayden will still..." I sputter out, still laughing.

"You won't have to worry about *that* anymore," Myles says, which makes us laugh, inappropriately, even harder.

Chapter Nineteen

In the end, it's the ER doctor who saves the day. She propels through the doors that suction close with a whoosh, making a beeline for Hayden and Trooper Bob Hawkins—by then, Hayden has found out his name.

Oh God, she's dead, is Hayden's first thought as the weary doctor approaches them. The doctor's skin is no longer luminous. It's slightly flushed. Simultaneously, Hayden realizes she is more scared than sad at the loss of Penelope. What would happen now? Without Penelope telling them the truth, will Hawkins arrest her? Penelope's fingerprints, though. Won't they be found on the flare gun? The flare gun. Where is it? Is it still in the Rover? Does Hawkins have it? Or has it already been bagged as evidence?

With the doctor approaching them, Trooper Hawkins stands as does Hayden, as if they are family members steeling themselves for bad news.

But Penelope hasn't died. On the contrary, she had two or three lucid minutes before the morphine kicked in, before the team had started to work on her burns. Penelope had talked. Hayden briefly imagines Penelope turning to the medical team around her and saying, "You won't believe this, but…"

"She wanted to make sure that you knew how sorry she was," the doctor explains to Hayden, making her feel guilty once again that she may have been unfair to Penelope. The thought strikes her that Penelope probably knew nothing about what Luke did or didn't do. That she hadn't been part of a conspiracy against Sandy. Penelope was simply a tease who liked to mess with people's lives for her benefit. No one else's.

Then, the doctor faces Trooper Hawkins. "She said she shot herself. She was climbing over the back seat and the flare went off." The doctor shrugs. "Just another freak accident on a Friday night. You should go home." This is directed at Hayden. "She'll be sedated for some time now. You might as well get some rest." She touches Hayden's arm briefly. Then, she turns on her heels and strides back through the hissing doors that speak of lives of misfortune, lives that can sometimes be saved and other times, not. Lives that ultimately end up in the hands of this woman on a freaky Friday.

As if the good news had somehow been communicated telepathically, both Hayden's cell phone and Trooper Hawkins's walkie talkie squawk simultaneously.

"Okay, then," Hawkins says, even as he's accepting his next assignment and walking toward the exit, not saying goodbye or good luck to Hayden. She's no longer his responsibility.

When Hayden looks at her phone screen, she suddenly sways with the dizziness that you feel during an earthquake. She leans against the dirty turquoise chair she'd been sitting in. The digital letters on the screen spell out S-a-n-d-y. The phone continues to ring. Hayden's hand is shaking. Has someone stolen Sandy's phone and had it all this time? For three months? Another two rings. Now, her entire body is trembling with the crazy thought that it *is* Sandy. Her stomach churns. She never died at all. It was a mistake. She washed up on some remote island. Hayden feels a gut-wrenching longing for Sandy. For the loss of *us*. A small moan comes out of her mouth. Four more rings. Finally, reluctantly, Hayden slides her finger across the screen.

"Hello?" she whispers, her heart racing. Her other fingers grip the back of the chair for ballast.

"Hayden? It's Tibbie. *Isabel*. Is the car fixed?"

For a moment, Hayden feels relieved, but also deeply saddened. *Did you really think it was Sandy?* She chastises herself while the vicious depression that she's felt since right after the boat accident resurrects in her bones.

"Hayden?"

"What? No...no," she tells Isabel. She watches as a couple enter fast through the sliding doors, looking startled and ill at ease, their faces ashen. Hayden wonders if they've just received the death call. Your [son] [daughter] has been in an accident. I'm sorry we did everything we could. And bam, their lives will never be the same.

Hayden starts to race through the waiting area, picking up speed past the reception desk, toward those doors. She needs to get out of this hospital. To get away as fast as she can. The doors can't swoosh aside fast enough for her. Her coat sleeve grazes one side as the doors open.

Isabel is rattling on and on. "You're still waiting for the tow? Jesus, so much has happened...I can't believe you're still sitting there...you won't believe what's—"

Hayden cuts her off. "I'm at the hospital." It's freezing cold outside. The day looks gloomier than when she and Penelope left that morning. The air is practically heaving with icy moisture. It's the kind of day where a blizzard seems to be right over the hill, in the next county over. But it never comes. The anticipation of it, though, paralyzes everyone. Stores are ransacked for staples of bottled water, canned soups, bread. Anything that isn't perishable. People call in sick to their jobs. Take personal days. Schools close. Life stops, everyone waiting for something that never comes. The next day, everyone faults the weather people because they can't stand the thought that they were the true fools. Before the accident, Hayden was such a person. Worried about a big nothing that never comes. Now, she despises them. They should be glad the storm missed them. They should be glad they got off scot-free. They should be glad they're alive.

Hayden looks around, frantically scanning the parking lot for a taxi stand. There is none. Family and friends, not cabs or Uber, bring patients to and from such community hospitals in upstate New York. Public transportation is something available in cities, not here. For the thousandth time since she's moved from Brooklyn, Hayden curses the day she did.

"What? You're at a hospital?" Isabel is yelling in surprise. Then, Hayden hears her muffled voice repeating that to someone else.

"Is that Myles?" Hayden asks. "Where are you?" Her breath ends in puffy clouds. She pulls up her sweatshirt hood to cover her cold head. She always forgets her thick, long hair is gone. She misses that too. They should be interrogating Luke by now. How in the midst of that are they calling her?

"What's happened?" Isabel asks, her voice more urgent. "Why are you in the hospital? Oh god, did you have an accident?"

Hayden shakes her head, then realizes that Isabel can't see her. She tells her quickly what has happened as she watches a rusted old station wagon pull up and creak to a stop. A mid-aged woman in a housedress splodged with faded flowers jumps out of the driver's seat. She leaves the car running and rushes around to the passenger door, opening it to lift out another woman in a matching housedress; she must be the woman's mother, she's so frail and elderly. The mother is holding up a bloody wad of paper towels to a gash bleeding on her cheek. Hayden briefly worries that the town's only ambulance must've been tied up with transporting Penelope so that this woman was forced to drive at breakneck speed to get her mother to the hospital. They'd gone in such a rush that they left without their winter coats.

"Jesus!" Isabel says, bringing Hayden back to the conversation. Hayden's having trouble keeping focused. To stop her mind from following one tragic path after another for the people she sees around her. How will she get away from the hospital? Maybe she can slip into their car and drive away? She hears Myles asking repeatedly in the background, "What? What's ha-ha-*ppened*? What's *happened*?" She can almost envision him hopping up and down in frustration.

Isabel shushes him. She tells Hayden, "Look. You don't have to stay there, right?" She doesn't wait for an answer. "Can you get to an airport? Can you fly here? To Boston? We'll wait for you."

"Boston? Is Luke with you in Boston? I thought—" She stops. She sees a yellow car coming

slowly over the icy hill, then sliding down the lone
road that feeds into the hospital.

"Luke's gone home. Look, can you get to the
nearest airport? Just call me back when you're on your
way…I'm sorry I called you on Sandy's phone. It's just
easier. She had your number on speed dial."

"How do you have…" Hayden's voice drops off.
"Oh my god! There's a taxi," she shouts as she sees it
is a yellow cab in the distance coming closer to her.

"Good. Grab it. Just jump in the back seat and
lie. Tell him there's an emergency and you have to
get to the airport. We'll wait for you. Call me when
you get your ticket. We'll wait for you. Just get in that
cab."

❧❧❧❧❧

Safely in the back seat of the taxi, Hayden wonders if the cab had been sent somehow by Sandy.
How else to explain its appearance in the middle of
nowhere? Not really nowhere, though. I was at a *hospital*. That taxi company may make repeated runs to
the hospital throughout the week. Maybe her driver is
even assigned to that one route.

Hayden slumps against the window, her eyes
closed. Her body feels as if she has been doing sprints
for the past two hours: exhausted and aching, coupled
with an unexpected feeling of letdown. It doesn't
matter if you win the race or not. Whether she
escaped free from the hospital or not. The letdown
courses through your limbs, your heart, undeterred.
Her body has cycled through so many emotions in the
past two hours it doesn't know how to deal with any
of them anymore. Triage isn't a possibility. More than

anything, right now she just feels numb.

She hadn't had to lie. When she'd started to tell the driver that she had to get to an airport, he'd cut her off. "It's your dime," he'd said, shrugging. "I got nowhere else to be." He twisted around so he could see her. There was no scratched plexiglass between them. Ordinarily, Hayden might've felt threatened by the intimacy of there not being a barrier between them. Awkward at the very least. She's too tired for that. Besides, he was so overweight Hayden could see the strain that his parka was putting on his craning neck. She'd be a mile from the car before he'd even be able to remove his seat belt.

"Closest is Albany. Seventy will do it." He stretched out a big paw of a hand, resting it on top of the front seat like it was too heavy for him to even hold up.

Hayden took out thirty-five dollars from her wallet. "Half now," she told him. "Half when I get there."

For a minute he stared at her. Then he shrugged again, crumpled up the bills in his huge paw, and, facing forward, slipped the car into Drive. "Visiting family?" he asked good-naturedly. He glanced at her in his rearview. When Hayden looked out the window, her eyes teary, he told her gently, "You just relax now. I'll get you there."

Hayden lets out her breath. It's the first time in months that she feels her body relax, the knots in her stomach gradually coming undone. She stares out her window at the stark-naked trees, the winter daylight weakening in the late afternoon. She remembers watching a documentary about the abstract artist Joan Mitchell with Sandy. Looking at the barren landscape,

she can hear Sandy's voice repeating something
Mitchell recited from a poem that Mitchell wrote
when she was in elementary school: "Bleakness comes
through the trees in silence."

"What kid would think that, much less put that
in a poem?" Sandy had asked later at dinner, her fork,
twirled with pasta, hanging in mid-air. Sandy laughed.
"I mean, was she a genius or not?"

As Hayden thinks of that now in the cab, the
trees with their bleakness fly by. She wants to tell
Sandy that wasn't her favorite line from the film. Her
favorite was when Mitchell was asked if a specific
analysis of one of her paintings was accurate and
Mitchell replied, "The moment you put the blah blah
blah on it, you destroy the thing."

The taxi skids onto NY-199, but Hayden doesn't
notice because she's so deep in thought now. She worries whether that's what she did so wrong when she
questioned her life with Sandy, leading her to sleep
with the bartender. Maybe she had simply put the
blah, blah, blah on it and because of that, she'd destroyed everything they had. Yes, it had only technically been fifteen minutes, but the consequences had
been without end. She had changed the course of the
rest of their lives that one night. Had she not done
it—*think of it*—she'd have had sixty more nights with
Sandy. Before she'd drowned, sixty would've seemed
paltry. Nothing to hinge a relationship on. Now, it
seems an eternity. Well, it's deeply ingrained in her
now, isn't it, how life can change in just twenty-four
hours? Twenty-four seconds. And not just for her.
For Myles and Isabel too. In the back of that taxi that
smells of fast food and the ubiquitous undertone of
chemical pine trees, Hayden makes a promise to her-

self. She knows it's one of those sayings that she and Sandy used to make fun of, to banter back and forth. The kind that appear on coffee mugs or on posters, Kahlil Gibran or something similar. She doesn't care. From now on, she will live each day as if it were her last. She can at least do that for Sandy.

Chapter Twenty

Myles and Tibbie walk Luke inside to the ticket counter, taking no chances. For one thing, he's still woozy-weak. It's not every day that you're drugged, zapped, die, and then brought back to life. The last thing they want is for him to fall down or draw any other attention their way. Myles also has the small thought that Luke might give them the slip and call Penelope.

"No way he'll do that," Tibbie whispers as they follow Luke inside Logan Airport's terminal. "He's going nowhere but home. He won't want this getting out." She holds up her cell.

"Don't be stupid," Myles says. He hasn't forgotten that they recorded Luke's confession. How could he forget that? He's just so tired that doubt has taken up residence in his mind and heart. Who knows what will happen next? Maybe Luke will get a surge of adrenalized energy and make a break for it. Nothing about this day has run true to the original plan.

They're in luck. The next plane leaves in twenty minutes. There are seats left. Boarding has just begun. After Luke hands over his credit card to the ticket agent, Tibbie and Myles stand on either side of him, each lightly cupping his elbows. Bounty hunters bringing their escapee home. There's a clumsy moment when they steer him to the weaving security line. How do you say goodbye to someone you tried to kill but then brought back to life? Myles doesn't know if he should bash in Luke's teeth or hug him. He realizes he's Luke's worst enemy and ultimate savior all rolled into one.

Right before Luke is about to get in line, Tibbie drags him off to the side. Myles notices that somewhere during the drive she's regained her bravado. Her face is tight again. Not with worry. With determination. It reminds him of when she originally showed up at his boxcar. Except then she had the past to propel her through to the future, and now, that's changed. She's put everything that happened today behind her, left it behind in the dust. Her compass has righted itself, the needle is pointing true north again. There was so much passing of the control baton that Myles doesn't know anymore if he's handing it off or expected to let his hand drift trustingly into the air behind him until Tibbie slips it back into his grasp. Does it really matter anyway? Isn't what matters the fact that they've gotten to the proverbial bottom of the whole thing? Luke confessed. So, in the end they've won. Or at least achieved what they'd set out to do, haven't they? It isn't lost on him either that he's spent every minute of the last six days virtually with one person, something he's never been able to do before. Not only that, but he feels, well, alive. Accepted for who he is for the first time in his life.

"Listen," Myles hears Tibbie say to Luke in a low, don't-mess-with-me voice as Myles walks up to them. She grips Luke's arm tighter. "You get on that plane and go home. If you tell Penelope or anyone else anything, we'll go straight to *The New Yorker*. Understand?" She squeezes his arm. Once again,

Myles is struck by how comical everything they say sounds. Then Tibbie surprises him and Luke also by grabbing Luke's chin and moving it up and down. Luke's become her marionette. "Say yes, like a nice boy."

"Yeth," Luke is able to murmur, although Myles can see that Tibbie's grip is so tight it hurts for Luke to open his mouth.

"Let's go," Myles says in her ear. He tugs on Tibbie's arm.

They don't leave, however, until they see Luke shuffle through security and then disappear around the bend toward the gates. Even then, they stay. In silent agreement, they move to the glass wall where you can watch family members and friends board their planes for back home or their vacation weeks in Puerto Rico and Hawaii. This gate requires that travelers walk onto the tarmac for a few yards to a metal staircase leading up to the plane's open door. The tarmac is lit up in the night as much as an outdoor theater. The spotlighted passengers file out like actors appearing on stage for an ensemble work. Stooping over slightly, Luke climbs the steps in the line, his head hanging down, his eyes on each metal stair, his hand gripping the railing, seemingly aged twenty years or like he is taking his last walk on death row. On the fifth step, he stumbles but catches himself. As if he can sense Myles and Tibbie there, he looks over his shoulder. Myles knows by the way that Luke hand-visors his eyes that the spotlights are too bright for him to see anything. Still, they watch as Luke hesitates and then, almost as an afterthought, salutes in the direction where Myles and Tibbie are standing. Tibbie audibly gasps. Then, Luke disappears through the airplane's open door.

"It'll be okay," Myles says, thinking that Tibbie has flipped back to worrying what Luke will do. He slips his arm around her shoulders as if it's the most natural thing in the world. Surprisingly, he feels it is, like he's done it all his life.

Tibbie shakes her head. "The last time Sandy..." She begins but leaves off finishing it. She shakes her head again. "Forget it."

Without saying it out loud, they both know that they will stay in that same spot until they see Luke's plane taxi. Until the plane races down the runway in front of them. Until it lifts off. Until there's not a chance that Luke is not going home, not absolutely out of their lives.

Someone's cell phone rings loudly. It takes a minute for Tibbie to realize it's Sandy's phone, which is in her parka's inside pocket. Shifting away, she retrieves the phone.

"Answer it," Myles says, looking over her shoulder. "Hurry." Tibbie's fingers tremble as she holds up the phone. It's not *her*. They both read Hayden's name on the screen.

Tibbie positions the phone so that she and Myles can both listen, head against head, like siblings will do when they call home.

"I'm about to board," Hayden's voice comes through, tired and cracking. She's been crying. "United Airlines. There's a connection in Newark or something ridiculous. We land in three hours. Will you be there?" Before they can answer, there's a loud announcement telling passengers in rows twenty through twenty-five that their number is up. "That's me," Hayden says. "Please. Just be there." Then, the phone goes dead.

≈≈≈≈

With three hours to wait, they find the nearest bar to United's arrivals. The bartender is a young woman with enormous brown eyes and breasts. Her tattooed arm sleeves have so many swirling, brightly colored female icons from *Games of Thrones*—Daenerys Targaryen the mother of dragons, Arya Stark, Brienne of Tarth—along with the show's three dragons, their mouths shooting orange and red flames, that Myles feels dizzy looking at them.

"You need to eat something," Tibbie says, her sisterly tone surprising him again. "Sit," she commands, pulling him onto a bar stool. They've switched the older sibling role so many times by now that Myles doesn't know who is taking care of whom. Tibbie slides onto the stool next to him. When the bartender slaps down two menus, Tibbie shakes her head. "We know what we want. Two fish and chips. Two Scotches. Two Heinekens." She hands the menus back to the bartender.

"Two salt and batteries." The bartender writes on her notepad. "Two shiver me timbers. Two walk the planks." She looks up and shrugs. "The manager gets all pissy if we don't write down what's listed on the menu." She smiles at Tibbie. "Love your tat. Someone local?"

"Ernest Hemingway," Tibbie says, beaming the smile that Myles can tell is completely fake, although a few days ago he would've seen it exactly the way the bartender does now: an invitation to join in the fun. The bartender gives a short laugh as she walks away to get their drinks.

Myles stares at Tibbie.

"What?" Tibbie says to him. "Sandy used to say that stories are better than the truth."

"But they have to sound like the truth in order to be believable," he tells her in a kidding voice. He rotates the bar's cardboard coaster around in his hands. For the first time in a long time, Myles feels happy. Free. The bar's name is The Stowaway. *What a stupid name for an airport bar,* he thinks. There's a drawing of a pirate's chest with a businessman—suit, fedora, briefcase hanging over the side—hiding amid the tangle of booty: jewelry, chalices, and coins. As Myles turns the coaster clockwise it looks like he's dumping the man out of his treasure.

Tibbie laughs. It's her real laugh. Myles smiles. Looks over at her.

"People believe what they want to believe," Tibbie says, shrugging.

His smile vanishes. He hesitates. Sifts the coaster around again, this time nervously. He wants her to know that he sees her. The real Tibbie. The flawed, reckless Tibbie. He likes her more now because of that. They've shown each other their worst. Maybe he needs a little more of that recklessness himself. Obviously, trying to control everything wasn't working. They could balance each other out. But only if they're absolutely truthful with each other. Not afraid to say anything. He realizes that the most truthful they've been, that *he* has been in months, was when they were in his wretched home with Luke. Not that he wanted to do that again, but he'd at least felt alive, hadn't he? Turning to look at her, he says, "You know, we almost did terrible things to them."

Tibbie squints her eyes and bird-tilts her head,

appearing to not understand what he's talking about.

"Luke and Penelope," he says, coaxing her along.

Tibbie barks out a scornful half-laugh. "Electrocuting him or having her immolated by a flare gun isn't terrible?"

Myles turns away. He stares at their reflection in the humongous mirror behind the rows of liquor bottles. Why are there always those large mirrors in that exact place? So that you can watch as you drink yourself into oblivion? Or to remind you that you cannot escape from your demons?

"You know what I mean."

"They weren't exactly innocent," Tibbie says. "Especially him." She takes a long drink from her beer, finishing it.

Myles faces her again. "No, he wasn't. But, all we know for certain is that he gave her some kind of sedative. That doesn't make him a murderer."

"But you think I am."

"You could've been."

Tibbie starts to pick the label off her beer bottle. She can only scrape off the teeniest of pieces with her nail. She ends up with a disappointing dusting of damp confetti on the bar.

Myles wants to assure her that they all were guilty, not just her. He wants to talk it through. Ask her what it was all for. When it came down to it, didn't they—she and he and Hayden— only do what they did to make themselves feel better? To give their lives back some kind of meaning? He's sure now that it wasn't for Sandy, despite that being what the three of them agreed at first. It wasn't. Really it was because ever since Sandy had died, their lives had become stagnant. Or stuck. It was the only way they could live again. It wasn't revenge. It was a rebirth.

Finally, Tibbie says quietly, "Everyone could murder someone, given the right circumstances."

The bartender has somehow snuck up on them. She plunks down beer bottles along with Scotch chasers. "Well, that sounds interesting," she says. She folds her arms across her chest, waiting to hear more.

Myles manages to give her a weak smile. He says the first thing that pops into his head. "She wouldn't hurt a fly." It sounds so lame that Tibbie jumps in to save him.

"I even tried to kill a fly this morning and ended up missing it and busting a window."

"Ouch," the bartender says, automatically glancing at Tibbie's hands. Myles doesn't know if she's being sarcastic because she knows Tibbie's lying or that she really believes that Tibbie possibly got cut from the shattered glass.

When neither Tibbie or Myles says anything else, the bartender moves on to another customer.

❧ ❧ ❧ ❧

By the time Hayden's plane arrives at half past midnight, they've each consumed two more drinks and beers, and four slices of Ahab's Key Lime Pie. Myles is so worn out from the day's events that he feels swimmy as they walk to the waiting area for Hayden's gate. Tibbie sways a bit too.

"Guess we don't have our sea legs," Tibbie tells Myles, nervously giggling. Myles wonders if she's lost her nerve to meet up with Hayden again, waiting for the last three hours. Whether she's worried what Hayden will say when she hears what happened with Luke. How they let Luke leave the premises.

They're to the side of the welcoming ramp, away from the security guard who makes sure no one will get overly stimulated and charge the ramp to clasp their loved ones in their arms. Tibbie's mumbling, giving herself some kind of instruction.

"Are you okay?" Myles asks her.

"I'm fine," she says, irritated.

"Well, you're kind of jabbering about being nice or something. People are looking."

"I am not. You're paranoid." She starts to walk away.

"Where are you going now?" he asks.

Before Tibbie can answer him, they both see Hayden, a lone wolf to the side of the pack of passengers who are eagerly racing down the slope to join their families or to secure a spot on the taxi line. Hayden is bedraggled, thin and pale-looking, her Confederate coat held loosely bunched in her arms, a sleeve of which is dragging on the linoleum floor. Even her shorn hair looks limp.

"You're here." Her voice is weak, almost indecipherable in the jubilant crowd around them. Her eyes red-rimmed. It's clear she's been crying. Probably since they'd talked to her on the phone at the hospital, hours ago. She holds one hand up as if to touch Tibbie's cheek, thinks better of it, and instead pats her shoulder.

"Of course, we're here," Tibbie says in a clipped tone. She's drunk and exhausted and Myles can tell she's thrown by what it looked like Hayden was actually going to do. Was she really going to stroke her cheek? Hug her? He's briefly envious. "What about me?" he wants to tell Hayden. "You coming here was my idea too."

It hadn't been. Deep down he knows that it had only been Tibbie's suggestion. More of a demand, really. Still, he wishes just once in his life, someone would choose him. He was the one who fixed everything. If it had been left to Tibbie, they'd still be chiseling away at the snow mounds outside his home with an ice pick and a shovel to bury Luke's body. Hayden would've been stuck at that hospital. It's not even that he wanted Hayden to touch him. When it came down to it, he knows that he sensed there was something more in Hayden reaching for Tibbie's cheek. He remembers back to when Tibbie and Hayden had locked eyes in the loft's kitchen. How awkward and out of place he'd felt.

As he's standing there thinking this, something shifts in the air between the three of them. Later, when they talk about it, they won't agree on what happened. Myles will say he felt that without warning an air conditioner turned on, blowing icy air on them, and it instinctively made them take a step toward each other. Tibbie will insist it was the crowd shoving them closer together. Hayden will be the only one who'll confess that she felt as if Sandy was right behind them, stretching her arms around the three of them, enclosing them in a warm huddle. Whatever the cause, the three will agree on one thing: once they grabbed hold of each other, they didn't let go, not for a long time. Not until the security guard told them they'd have to "move it along." Afterward, they walked through the terminal, Tibbie in the middle, between Myles and Hayden, their arms firmly locked around each other's waists.

༄ ༄ ༄ ༄

They don't have to talk about it. Outside, there's a bitterly cold wind that lashes at their faces as they find their way through the parking lot. Once they're in the car, Tibbie simply says they can stay the night at her apartment in Boston, leave first thing in the morning for P-Town. They'll pick up some clothes at the apartment. Hayden can borrow some of Tibbie's clothes. They're the same size. They can all get some sleep.

"Good, because I'm freezing," Hayden says, her face almost hidden, wrapped in a scarf and within her sweatshirt's hood.

Tibbie reaches into her rucksack and pulls out a black sweatshirt, the one that Sandy left on her bed in the loft, and hands it to Hayden.

"What...where did you find this?" Hayden asks. "I looked all—"

Myles playfully accuses Tibbie of stealing it when they were staying at the loft.

Tibbie shakes her head, smiling. "You wouldn't believe me if I told you. Just put it on."

They decide that Hayden should drive the Saab because she's the only sober one. On the way home, Tibbie stays in the passenger seat, laughing and barking directions at the last minute in a giddy, boozy-slow reaction time. Every once in a while she playfully taps Hayden's shoulder.

"A little warning would be good, *Tibbie*," Hayden says, laughing good-naturedly as she turns the wheel sharply, narrowly almost missing the turnoff for the Sumner tunnel into Boston. Cars honk behind them.

"Whoa!" Myles shouts, the suddenness of the turn throwing him sideways in the back seat. Before the turn, he'd been perched on the edge of the seat, his head stuck between their bucket seats up front, an excited kid telling his parents about his field trip to the zoo.

They're all goofy with the adrenaline born from relief that they are free and headed toward safety. They don't talk about what has happened, about Penelope or Luke. In silent agreement, they're simply grateful to be together for these twenty minutes that it will take to get to Tibbie's apartment. There will be time enough later to tell everything. In the night's darkness, the car has hermetically sealed them off from everything that has come before. Now, there are only the three of them, alive, the prospect of staying together a glimmer, then electrifying the air as they drive.

☙ ❧

Tibbie shows them around her apartment, pointing out where the coffee cups and silverware are kept in the kitchen, the location of the bathroom, how to work the television remote in case anyone can't sleep in the middle of the night. Old-fashioned radiators, big as tractors, clang with the heat of a greenhouse. They shed their coats and scarves and hats and move in a daisy chain, holding hands as they weave through the rooms. Hayden and Myles ooh and ah as they go along as if they are a married couple at a real estate open house. Myles senses by the way that Hayden lightly touches a lamp here, a book there, the soft blanket thrown over the back of the couch, that she is feeling, while she's never been here before, it's soothingly familiar.

"Is that?" Hayden asks Tibbie, pointing to the plaid couch with her free hand.

Tibbie nods. "I can't believe you remembered that," she says. Then, turning to Myles, she explains. "The couch. It was in my mom's house. Where we grew up."

"I remember all of it," Hayden says softly as Tibbie leads them on. They pause reverently at Sandy's white orchids lined up on a table by a window. They've been kept alive during Tibbie's absence by one of her neighbors who'd followed her detailed instructions taped to the wall. ONLY WATER ONCE A WEEK. DON'T OVERWATER! DON'T PUT IN DIRECT SUN! DON'T TOUCH THE PETALS!

Despite the instructions, Hayden reaches out and gently traces the edge of one of the white flowers.

"She always insisted that they grow better if you talk to them and every so often touch them," Hayden tells Tibbie.

Tibbie shrugs, half-laughs. "Well, you know my sister. She had some crazy-assed—"

She stops mid-sentence. Myles has begun feeling one of the other petals.

"They're more substantial than you think," he says. He glances at Tibbie. "Go on."

With her thumb and index finger, Tibbie tugs gently, once, twice, on another petal, then lowers her hand. She clears her throat. "It's funny, isn't it? How we're the only three people in the world who know about these orchids? I mean, anyone else would—"

"Think they were—" Hayden says.

"Nothing special," Myles finishes the sentence.

When they get to the one bedroom, the covers on the queen-sized bed are in disarray and Myles wonders if Tibbie actually had raced out of the apartment when she left for Provincetown.

Tibbie finally releases their hands, turns to Hayden, and says, "You must be starving. We ate at the airport."

Hayden shakes her head. She glances at the bed. "Oh!" she says. Myles sees what has startled her. A Chinese robe folded at the bottom of the bed. He immediately understands that it must've been Sandy's.

"I think I want to lie down," Hayden tells Tibbie quietly. When Tibbie steps forward to remove the robe, Hayden's hand stops her. She moves her head from side to side: no.

"Aren't you going to tell us what ha-*happ*ened?" Myles asks, disconcerted. He's confused what the robe means. Obviously, it's something important, something that only the two of them know about. His hand still feels the loss of warmth from when Tibbie took her hand away. He wonders if Hayden feels the same.

Hayden shakes her head again. "Later." She takes up their hands and leads them toward the bed. Fully clothed, they lie down on top of the comforter, with Tibbie in the middle, Hayden behind her, Myles in the front, spooning each other in a line. Out of the corner of his eye, Myles notices when Hayden's foot slips under the robe. Maybe tomorrow he'll find out more.

"Just so you know," Hayden says sleepily. "I snore."

Myles listens to her and Tibbie sync their way into slower breathing. He hears a clock somewhere ticking in the dark. The hum of the refrigerator. Tibbie's stomach gurgling. Hayden's soft snores. Smiling, he falls asleep.

Chapter Twenty-one

I lied. Again. Okay, I promise that will be the last time. Honest.

The last time I saw my sister wasn't when she was waving at me through a glass wall at Logan Airport. The last time was the night that Hayden, Myles, and I slept together when we got back to my apartment. That was months ago. I've since sold that apartment and we live in Provincetown now. Not in Myles's train wreck of a place. God help us, no. Gratefully, out of guilt and then joy seeing that her son had ended up with not just one woman but two, Myles's mother bought him—*us*—a stunning, rambling three-bedroom house on Commercial Street, right on the water. Needless to say, none of us have corrected her about how we feel that Myles is the younger brother neither Hayden nor I had.

In the mornings, while Myles sleeps in or pretends to, Hayden and I have our coffee together on the back deck. We gaze out over the sand and water toward the place where Sandy died, savoring the quiet of our memories before everything went so wrong. Savoring my sister. The woman we both loved more than anything. Sometimes we tell each other a story about her that only one of us knows. We offer glimpses of how funny Sandy was, or how consistently, unconsciously she loved us, like breathing in air. The best of Sandy.

A week after we moved here, one morning, Hayden took a sip of her coffee and said, "I was so in love with your sister. Then, I messed it up." She had no idea that Sandy already had told me why they'd broken up before the accident.

"I know," I told her to spare her the agony of reliving it all. I touched her hand that was resting on the armrest of the Adirondack chair she was sitting in next to me. But it was obvious from her face that she was surprised that Sandy would've actually admitted the details to me: the bartender, how Sandy had asked her to leave.

"But you two were hardly speaking then," Hayden murmured, half in thought, half in shock that not only had Sandy told me but also that I'd kept it a secret.

"We weren't speaking but we were talking, if that makes any sense," I said. "Whenever we did call each other, she always was honest. Sandy didn't do chitchat, remember?" Hayden nodded her head in agreement. Then, I stunned her even more by telling her what my sister had confided in me the night before the accident. How Sandy admitted that she was hoping to convince Hayden to move back in during that weekend. I told Hayden this hoping that it would make her happy, would give her some kind of closure. But she let out a kicked dog's yelp and, lowering her coffee on the other armrest, covered her face with her hands. I jumped up, pulled her hands away from her face, and lifted her out of the chair, holding her by the elbows.

"I'm so sorry. I shouldn't have said that. I'm so stupid."

"No, I was," Hayden said. Picking up her coffee

cup, she went back inside the house.

Neither of us said anything more about it. Later, she left for a solo, long walk along the ribbon of beach below. She didn't return until it was almost time for dinner.

In the mornings that followed, she and I mostly sat in silence, each in our own thoughts yet still connected by the common yet unique thread called Sandy Dyer. It took weeks before we could venture back to sharing any stories again.

Usually, the three of us spend our afternoons off in our own worlds, with Hayden off photographing cormorants and plovers—sometimes with Myles, mostly not—and me plugging away on a freelance magazine article in my bedroom upstairs, while Myles, his fingers smudged with charcoal, draws his birds in the bedroom down the hall from mine. Most evenings, we meet on the deck to watch the sunset over the water and talk about what we're working on. Sometimes one of us will toast my sister, the reason for us going on together in this cruel but beautiful life.

"To Sandy," we'll say as we raise our glasses toward Long Point, the spot in the distance marking the end of my sister but also the beginning of us, I suppose.

The three of us did actually try to walk, twice, to the Point to dispose of Sandy's ashes. The first time was on a cold, blustery day in March. Scattered clouds alternated between hiding the sun from us and then allowing it to warmly tease our faces before disappearing again. When we came over the final sand dune before hitting the ocean, we were shocked and stopped in our tracks. Below us lay Woodrow's whale carcass, or what was left of it on the sand. It had been swept there after the accident. Much of the skeleton was still intact, although half of its jaw was missing. It was obvious that some of the ribs had been sawed off by someone who had wanted a souvenir. One of its fins lay broken at an abnormal angle. Several areas of bruised blubber and a gash in its side had been further destroyed by the gulls, insects, and the tides, which must have shifted Woodrow up and down the shoreline like a bobbling ball. Next to what remained of his head—one large sightless eye still in its socket staring into nothingness—someone else had thoughtfully laid a prayer circle of large grey beach stones and white shells. It must've been recently because high tide hadn't swept that out to sea yet.

Stunned, we stood speechless on top of the dune. It was so horrible to see that I had to look away, toward the ocean which was shrouded in darkness because at that moment the clouds covered the sun. For the first time, I imagined how doubly worse it must be for Myles and Hayden, who'd actually been there when the boat struck Woodrow. Briefly, I even thought of those two rather sweet whale huggers who had tried to connect with me at the bar during that night which seemed so long ago. I glanced again at Woodrow, and before I knew it, I was crying quietly. He was still so unspeakably magnificent. To see him was to see my sister. To remember how my sister had similarly looked on the morgue gurney: battered and so alone. My sister whose remains were in the urn that I was hugging tightly, my shoulders touching Hayden's. Myles was on the other side of her. I couldn't look at either of them.

Hayden gasped, which made me finally turn to her. Her head was leaning on Myles's shoulder, her face burrowed into his red scarf wound around his neck. Shifting away from me, she wrapped both arms around his shoulders, pulling him in tighter. They both began to sob, although Myles also was trying to talk simultaneously. Agony words. Something about it being unbearable. How sorry he was. How awful. He made a loud snorting sound, mucousy and wet, and the words shifted to more soothing ones. It was good they'd seen him. Good they could say goodbye. Poor Woodrow. At some point, I'd edged two steps away, letting them have this, whatever *this* was, for themselves. I'd stopped crying by then, concentrating on staring at Woodrow while cradling the urn in my arms like a baby. Finally, Hayden pulled away from Myles, wiped at her eyes, and took a step back toward me. Reaching out, she caressed my cheek. "I'm sorry. I don't think I can do the rest today, okay?" she said. I didn't have to ask her what she meant. Neither did Myles. None of us could've said goodbye to Sandy in that moment. I nodded because I was afraid if I began to talk, I'd start crying all over again. Without another word, the three of us walked the long way back home, our fingertips occasionally grazing each other's arms or backs, checking that we were still there.

Two weeks later, we decided to try again. Myles had found out from an acquaintance he knew at the Coastal Studies Center that the Center staff had finally been able to haul Woodrow back to the Center for research purposes. The beach would be clear.

We set out on a brilliantly sunny day. As we reached the top of the last dune, a snowy owl swooped in the sky above us. We'd seen other owls in the last few months; barn and screech owls were frequently seen on Cape Cod, but never a snowy owl. Sightings were somewhat uncommon, I'd already learned from Myles.

"Look!" he said, pointing although he didn't have to. Its gorgeous white, four-foot wingspan was hard to miss. Even from a distance we could see it scanning the dunes for voles and other food.

"She's beautiful," Hayden said.

"It's a he," Myles corrected her. "Males are whiter. Females have more black flecks."

"Well, he's beautiful then," Hayden said.

We stood there, our hands visoring our eyes as we watched the owl circle in the air. My other arm was holding the familiar urn against my hip.

"What does it mean?" I said, for once taking Myles's knowledge of omens seriously. Who was I to judge? I believed I'd seen and had conversations with my sister's ghost.

He smiled slightly, still observing the owl. We watched as it suddenly dove toward the beach grass, and then we lost sight of him.

"They're symbols of endurance," Myles said. "New beginnings."

I laughed, relieved. I was certain it would foretell some kind of tragic death. "Well, thank god for that."

"But you don't believe in all that, right?" Myles teased me. He smiled, this time more broadly, showing me his chipped tooth that I was so fond of and had nicknamed in my head his "badge of courage."

Hayden held out her hand to me. We started to make our way down the dune toward the sea's edge.

From the safety of the shoreline, we emptied the urn holding Sandy's ashes into the ocean, our arms looped around each other, our fingers laced as we jointly raised the urn. Myles stood off to the side, staring at us with a strange smile on his face. The off-white ashes were caught by a winter breeze and drifted down like dust to waves that brought those fragments of my sister back to us and then, away.

Back to us, then away.

And then…endlessly away.

When we returned home from Long Point, Myles unexpectedly told us he needed to drive to an art store in Hyannis, fifty minutes away. Snatching up my Saab keys and before either Hayden or I could offer to go with him, he said in a hurry, "I'll grab dinner out, so I won't be back until later tonight." Then, he rushed out the door.

"Well, that was weird," I said. We stood in the kitchen, still dressed in our parkas from the beach trip.

Hayden shrugged. "Maybe he has a hot date."

"I doubt it," I said. "He would've told me."

Hayden laughed, which surprised me.

"What?"

"He's too afraid of disappointing you."

Now it was my turn to laugh. "You're crazy. He's like a little brother to me."

"Exactly." Hayden gave me a meaningful look. "He doesn't want to be the one to tell you our happy family might not be forever for him. He's going to want more one day, Isabel. He's going to want to bring someone home sometime."

"Do you?" I asked, suddenly nervous. It was the second time I'd asked her that. A week before, I'd asked her rather awkwardly during one of our morning coffee-times on the deck if she thought she'd ever go out with someone again.

She smiled. "Sandy would be proud of you right now for asking me that." She hesitated and looked away, down the shell-strewn beach we loved to walk on. "Maybe someday," she continued on. "I'm still in love with her. I still miss us." When she looked back at me, her eyes were wet. "But when I'm with you, like this, I miss 'us' less."

"Good," I said, although I couldn't decide if I was saying it in response to her still missing her life with my sister or because her life with me made her happier these days.

Now, asking her again, I realized I wanted her to say no with conviction, that she didn't want to see anyone else. That she wanted to go on living with me, but in a different way.

Instead, she turned and opening the French door on the deck, and said, "Come join me. Bring some beers."

Despite it being March, the sun was still strong. Dressed in our parkas and hats in the Adirondack chairs, we drank our beers, taking in the expanse of the bay, which was unseasonably tranquil and lovely. A family of ducks was trailing slowly over the glassy water. I glanced at Hayden. She was smiling at me.

"What?"

She laughed and shook her head. "Nothing. You just…"

"What?" I said, laughing also, although I didn't exactly know why. I felt a sort of happiness and at the same time, unaccountably, a bit nervous. Happy because I'd—we'd—done it: finally, what was left of Sandy was where it should be. Back where she'd left us. And nervous, because Hayden still hadn't answered my question.

Hayden was grinning. She shifted in her chair next to me so that she could face me better. Reaching over, she tucked a blue strand of my bangs away from my eyes behind my ear. Her fingers lingered there before moving away.

"You...we just...belong here," she said.

My heart began to race. Ever since that first night together in Boston we were comfortable touching each other, a hand on a back as we passed each other in the kitchen, say, or piled against each other on the couch, watching television. Or even holding hands as we'd done on the beach earlier. But this felt different. It felt more deliberate. More weighted with meaning. More similar to that moment in my mother's house when she caught me looking at her with what, I realized now, was gut-wrenching desire, a moment of unexpected connection.

"We belong here? In these chairs?" I said, stubbornly making fun rather than acknowledging what really was going on. For a minute I hesitated. Was I really ready for this? A memory of the last thing my sister ever said to me flashed into my mind, but before I could follow that down a rabbit hole, Hayden was cupping my neck. She pulled me toward her and tenderly kissed me on the lips. I felt my mouth start to tremble, and for a second I was afraid I was going to start crying because I wanted her so much.

"Come on," she said, standing. Reaching for my hand, she pulled me up and led me upstairs.

And by the way, her tattoo? It wasn't a canary at all. It was a beautiful goldfinch. You just had to get close to tell.

≈ ≈ ≈ ≈

So, the last thing my sister ever said to me. It was that night Hayden, Myles and I spent together in my Boston apartment. I was falling asleep to Hayden's steady breathing on the back of my neck, when some slight movement in the doorway caught my eyes as they closed. For a second, I thought a bird had survived the bitter cold winter night, somehow finding its way into my warm apartment despite the windows being shut and locked and the lack of a chimney. The blurry motion happened so fast. It had to be a bird.

It wasn't. Of course, it wasn't. It was my sister. I smelled her shampoo before my eyes adjusted to the dark.

"I'm so happy, Tibbie," Sandy whispered. She was leaning against the doorjamb, a bit wearily. "You've found your way finally. 'Wander no more, I say; this is the end.'" She paused. "Virginia Woolf."

"What?" I tried to sit up, to lean on my elbow, but it was impossible, what with being scrunched between Hayden and Myles. Myles grunted in his sleep.

"Where have you been?" I asked her.

She held up her index finger to her lips. "Don't wake them," she said. "It's better this way. Just you and me. Like it always was, right? From day one, when you were born and Dad brought me to the hospital to see you and Mom? I claimed you right then and there." Her eyes welled up. She pretended to brush a strand of hair off them. "You were so beautiful. So innocent. I had to protect you." She paused again. Wiped at her eyes. "But, you'll be fine now. You did good, Tibbie." She looked over her shoulder as if someone had called her, or she was scanning the apartment for an item she'd forgotten. Either way, I started to panic. I hadn't seen her in days. I sensed with a sinking feeling that this may be the last time that I would. It was too soon. What she said was so scattered that I couldn't keep up.

"Wait," I told her. "What do you mean 'this is the end'?"

She pointed first to Hayden, then to Myles.

"No. You can't mean that," I said, my voice growing louder. Sandy quickly shushed me. "You can't mean that," I insisted more quietly. "The only reason we're here is you. Because we're grieving you—"

She hushed me again. "There's no greater bond than tragedy," she said. She looked so sad when she said it.

"Who said *that*?" I didn't really care. I just wanted her to stay.

"I did." She gazed down at Hayden. Then, her right hand began to float slowly, caressing the air as if she were gently conducting a beautiful aria. Hayden mewed something indecipherable behind me as she slept. Although the room was dark, I could see that my sister's eyes were glistening. From crying? From happiness? From longing? To this day I couldn't tell you.

"Let them love you, Isabel," Sandy said in a low voice with great tenderness. "Let her love you." It was the only time I ever remembered her calling me by my real name out of love. It made me think of Hayden calling me Isabel the weekend my sister brought her home. How irritated, yet how special it made me feel.

"I know," Sandy said, reading my mind for the last time. "To tell you the truth, I was a bit jealous when she did that...*Isabel*. Why didn't Mom or I ever call you Belle or Bella?" she mused. "I should have seen the handwriting on the wall then." She paused again, this time to rub the bridge of her nose as if she were suddenly overwhelmingly tired. "I have to go now. But will you do something for me? Love her, like you loved me. As I loved you from the first. Unconditionally."

And then, she was gone. I thought she would pop back up. "Ta da!" she'd say, holding her arms out, expecting applause for this incredible act she'd just performed, spouting some funny quote or talking in another language she wouldn't have known when she was alive, Mandarin or Urdu. Minutes passed. The doorway stood empty, forlorn, as if it had lost its use. Its reason for being. A portal of connection. More minutes passed. Then, I started to convince myself that I'd been dreaming. That I'd only awakened from the shock of a dream. Its realness. I was still drunk from the airport bar, for Pete's sake. I told myself that I'd been passing out when she'd appeared. I'd just nodded off. I'd imagined the whole thing. That was all there was to it. After all that had happened that day, of course I'd dream of her. My wacky sister, my best friend, the first but not the last love of my life.

Then, Hayden's arm tightened around my waist. "Bella," she murmured, sleepily, her body tucking in closer. "I like it."

If you liked this book?

Share a review with your friends or post a review on your favorite site like Amazon, Goodreads, Barnes and Noble, or anywhere you purchased the book. Or perhaps share a posting on your social media sites and help spread the word.

Join the Sapphire Newsletter and keep up with all your favorite authors.

Did we mention you get a free book for joining our team?

sign-up at - www.sapphirebooks.com

About The Author

Randi Triant's debut novel, *The Treehouse*, was selected as an ultimate summer read by *AfterEllen* in 2018. Her short fiction and nonfiction have appeared in literary journals and magazines, including an anthology of writing about HIV/AIDS, *Art & Understanding: Literature from the First Twenty Years of A & U* and the anthology *Fingernails Across the Blackboard: Poetry and Prose on HIV/AIDS from the Black Diaspora*. She received her MFA in writing and literature from Bennington College. She has taught writing at Emerson College and Boston College.

Check out Randi's other book

The Treehouse – ISBN – 978-1-948232-00-5

Camilla Thompson, a Humanities college professor who never did write that Great American Novel, hasn't seen her son Nico for two years.

One morning she drives to the house where her ex, Allison, is still raising Nico. Knowing that they are away for a week's vacation, Camilla begins to build a treehouse as a surprise for the son she's not allowed to see.

But Camilla's regrets, grief, and lack of construction skills aren't the only challenges she'll face. Old friends and unexpected visitors show up to help—and complicate matters. Free-spirited Taylor, Camilla's best friend, arrives with her lover, Audrey, whom Camilla finds herself falling for. Then Wallace, Camilla's Department Chair, disrupts everything with startling news that threatens to end Camilla's career.

At first an impulsive idea, the treehouse soon promises to be an oasis for Camilla's redemption that could free her for another chance at love and family. Then again, it might simply be just a bad decision.

Other books by Sapphire Authors

The Dragonfly House: An Erotic Romance - ISBN- 978-1-952270-14-7

On the outskirts of a small, picturesque Midwestern town, sits a large, lovely old Victorian house with many occupants. This residence, known simply as The Dragonfly House, is home to Ma'am, the proprietor, along with several young women in her employ. One such woman, Jame, is very popular among the female clientele. One such client, Sarah, fresh from a divorce and looking for a little adventure, as well as some gentle handling, becomes one of Jame's repeat clients. Once Sarah enters the picture, Jame and Ma'am, as well as the brothel, will be forever changed.

The Coffield Chronicles – Hearts Under Siege: Book One – ISBN – 978-1-952270-12-3

The year is 1862. The war between the states has been raging intensely for a year now. The country is in complete and utter turmoil, and brother is fighting brother to the death, dying for what each believed. It seems it's all the townsfolk of New Albany, Indiana can speak of, and Melody Coffield is paying attention. Through a series of heartbreaks and sorrow, she settles on the decision to cut her hair and don men's attire. Going under the alias of Melvin A. Coffield, she leaves her childhood home, the only home she had ever known, and enlists in the United States Army. Chewing tobacco and drinking liquor were ways of men, and she learns quickly how to behave like one. She would soon know the horrors of battle, and what was called the glory of war, through roads that led straight to Vicksburg, Mississippi. However, her biggest concern was making sure she was not detected by the others. Keeping her secret would not only be challenging, but trying as well. Will she remain in this solitude the rest of her life, never allowing anyone into her heart again? Or will she find love, once more, in a world that was intolerant and unaccepting of who she truly was?

Keeping Secrets – ISBN – 978-1-952270-04-8

What would you do if, after finally finding the woman of your dreams, she suddenly leaves to fight in the Civil War? It's 1863, and Elizabeth Hepscott has resigned herself to a life of monotonous boredom far from the battlefields as the wife of a Missouri rancher. Her fate changes when she travels with her brother to Kentucky to help him join the Union Army. On a whim, she poses as his little brother and is bullied into enlisting, as well. Reluctantly pulled into a new destiny, a lark decision quickly cascades into mortal danger. While Elizabeth's life has made a drastic U-turn, Charlie Schweicher, heiress to a glass-making fortune, is still searching for the only thing money can't buy. A chance encounter drastically changes everything for both of them. Will Charlie find the love she's longed for, or will the war take it?

Diva – ISBN – 978-1-952270-10-9

What if...you were offered a part-time job as the personal assistant to someone you have idolized for years? Meg Ellis has just completed the school year as a nurse in the Santa Fe school system. It isn't her first choice of profession, but a medical problem derailed her musical career years ago. The breakup of a bad relationship is still painful. The loving support from her close-knit family and good friends has buoyed her spirits, but longing still lurks below the surface. She can't forget the intoxicating allure of the beautiful diva who haunts her dreams.

Nicole Bernard is a rising star in the world of opera, adored by fans around the globe. When Meg learns that Nicole is headlining a new production at the renowned New Mexico outdoor pavilion—and then is asked to accept a job offer to be her personal assistant—she is beside herself. After a short time learning the routine and reining in her hormones, Meg discovers that Nicole's family will be visiting for the opening. Her responsibility to the charismatic singer immediately becomes more difficult when Nicole's young husband Mario shows up and threatens the comfortable rapport between Meg and the prima donna.

The two women brace for a roller-coaster interlude composed by fate. Will the warm days and cool nights, the breathtaking scenery, and the romance of the music create summer love? A heartbreaking game? Or something very special?

Made in the USA
Middletown, DE
30 May 2021

40705359R00203